Sweet Saint Bridget, he was more god than man.

From broad shoulders glimmering with rain, his chest tapered lean and well muscled to a line of dark hair dipping beneath linen drawers slung low on his hipbones. After years on her father's ship, Viola had seen plenty of men undressed. Sailors were either wiry from life on the sea or bulky from the work. Jinan Seton was neither. His height rendered his corded arms, chest, and tight belly perfectly aesthetically pleasing.

Her breaths shortened.

"Enjoying the view?" His lips barely moved but his voice was remarkably strong and hard.

Arrogant son of a humpback whale. Well justified, though.

He grinned. "Overly warm for spring, wouldn't you say?"

Yes. But not on the outside of her skin. She should move closer to see if his smooth skin was covered with gooseflesh too. The ship dipped against a swell; he steadied his stance and his muscles flexed— chest, arms, neck, calves.

She nearly choked on the shock of heat that went through her.

His grin widened . . .

Romances by Katharine Ashe

How to Be a Proper Lady

Katharine Ashe

AVON

An Imprint of HarperCollinsPublishers

AVON BOOKS
An Imprint of HarperCollins*Publishers*
10 East 53rd Street
New York, New York 10022–5299

Copyright © 2012 by Katharine Brophy Dubois
ISBN 978–0–06–203176–1
www.avonromance.com

First Avon Books mass market printing: July 2012

Avon Trademark Reg. U.S. Pat. Off. and in Other Countries, Marca Registrada, Hecho en U.S.A.
HarperCollins® is a registered trademark of HarperCollins Publishers.

Printed in the U.S.A.

10 9 8 7 6 5 4 3 2 1

Conscience, the torturer of the soul, unseen,
Does fiercely brandish a sharp scourge within.

JUVENAL, *Satires* XIII, 1ST CENTURY
(QUOTED IN *The Pirates Own Book*, 19TH CENTURY)

Carlyle-Lucas Family

Fionn Daly - m. - Maria Harrell - m. - Charles Carlyle, Baron - m. - Lady Davina Lucas - m. - Sir Reginald Lucas
1787-1816   1772-1803   1760-1808

Viola Carlyle
1793-
How to Be a Proper Lady
(Falcon Club #2)
featuring Captain Jin Seton

Serena Carlyle
1791-
- m. -
Alex Savege
Captured by a Rogue Lord
(Rogues of the Sea #2)

Faith Carlyle
1812-

Tracy Lucas
1790-

Charity Lucas
1799-
- m. -
Aaron Savege

Diantha Lucas
1801-

Savege Family

6th Earl of Savege - m. - Ellen Clemens - m. - Douglas Westcott, Lord Chamberlayne

Alex, 7th Earl of Savege, a.k.a. "Redstone"
1785-
- m. -
Serena Carlyle
Captured by a Rogue Lord
(Rogues of the Sea #2)

Aaron
1785-
- m. -
Charity Lucas

Kitty
1791-
- m. -
Leam, Earl of Blackwood
When a Scot Loves a Lady
(Falcon Club #1)

How to Be a
Proper Lady

Prologue

Devonshire, 1803

The girls played as though nothing could harm them. For nothing could on the crest of the scrubby green Devonshire hill overlooking the ocean where they had played their whole lives. Their father was a baron, and they wore white quilted muslin to their calves and pinafores embroidered with silk.

The wind was mild, blowing their skirts about slender legs and whipping up their hair, dislodging bonnets again and again. The elder, twelve, tall and long-limbed like a boy, picked the most delicate bluebells, fashioning them into a bouquet. The younger, petite and laughing, swung her arms wide, scattering wild violets in a circle about her. She ran, dark ringlets streaming behind, toward the edge of the cliff. Her sister followed, a dreaming glimmer in her eyes, golden locks swishing about her shoulders.

A sail appeared upon the horizon leagues away where azure sky met glittering ocean.

"If I were a sailor, Ser," the younger sister called across the hillock, "I would become captain of a great tall ship and sail to the ends of the earth and back again simply to say that I had."

Serena shook her head fondly. "They do not allow girls to become sailors, Vi."

"Who gives a rotten fig for what they allow?" Viola's laughter caught in the breeze curling about her.

"If any girl could be a sea captain, it would be you." Serena's eyes shone warm with affection.

Viola rushed to swing her arms about her sister's waist. "You are a princess, Serena."

"And you are an imp, for which I admire you greatly."

"Mama admires sailors." Viola skipped along the edge of the sheer drop. "I saw her speaking with one when we were in Clovelly for the ribbons."

"Mama is kind to everyone." Serena smiled. "She must have been giving the man an alms."

But it had not looked like Mama was giving him alms. She had spoken with the sailor for many minutes, and when she returned to Viola, tears teetered in her eyes.

"Perhaps he wished for more alms than Mama could give him."

The ship came closer and lowered a longboat, twelve men at oars. The sisters watched. They were accustomed enough to the sight, living so close to a harbor as they did, yet ever curious as the young are.

"Do you think they are smugglers, Ser?"

"I suppose they could be. Cook said smugglers were about when she went to market Wednesday. Papa says smugglers are to be welcomed because of the war now."

"I don't recognize the ship."

"How would you know to recognize any ship?"

Viola rolled her dark eyes. "Its banner, silly."

The boat came toward the beach fifty feet below, knocking against the surf, its bow jutting up and down like a butter churn. Men jumped out, soaking their trousers in the waves. They pulled the craft onto the pebbly sand. Four of them moved toward the narrow path that wound its way up the cliff side.

"It looks as though they mean to climb straight up," Serena said, taking her lower lip between her teeth. "Onto Papa's land?"

Viola grasped her sister's fingers. To be so close to real smugglers was something she had only dreamed. She might ask them about their travels, or their cargo. They could have something truly precious aboard, priceless treasure from afar. They would surely have stories to tell of those far-off places.

"Hold my hand, Ser," she said on an excited quaver. "We shall greet them and ask their business."

The sailor in the lead was a stocky man and well-looking in a dark fashion, not in the least scabrous or filthy as one might expect. He and his companions came along the crest of their father's land directly toward Viola and Serena.

"Why," Viola exclaimed, "that is the same sailor Mama gave alms to the other day."

But nothing concerned the girls in this, or in the sailor's greeting, broad and smiling as he glanced at their locked hands. For they had the love of sisters, fierce and tender, and nothing could harm them.

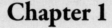

Chapter 1

London, 1818

Fellow Britons,

    The people of our great kingdom must not suffer another farthing of their livelihoods to be squandered on the idle rich. Thus, my quest continues! In rooting out information concerning that mysterious gentlemen's establishment at 14½ Dover Street, the so-called Falcon Club, I have learned an intriguing morsel of information. One of its members is a sailor and they call him Sea Hawk.

    Birds, birds, and more birds! Who will it be next, Mother Goose?

    Unfortunately I have not learned the name of his vessel. But would it not be unsurprising to discover him to be a member of our navy or a commissioned privateer? Yet another expenditure of public funds on the personal interests of those whose privilege is already mammoth.

I will not rest until all members of the Falcon Club are revealed or, due to my investigating, the Club itself disbands in fear of thorough detection.

—Lady Justice

Lady Justice
In Care of Brittle & Sons, Printers
London

Madam,

Your persistence in seeking the identities of the members of our humble club cannot but gratify. How splendid for us to claim the marked attentions of a lady of such enterprise.

You have hit the mark. One of us is indeed a sailor. I wish you the best of good fortune in determining which of the legion of Englishmen upon the seas he is. But wait! May I assist? I am in possession of a modest skiff. I shall happily lend it to you so that you may put to sea in search of your quarry. Better yet, I shall work the oars. Perhaps sitting opposite as you peer over the foamy swells, I will find myself as enamored of your beauty as I am of your tenacious intelligence—for only a beauty would hide behind such a daunting name and project.

I confess myself curious beyond endurance, on the verge of seeking your identity as assiduously as you

*seek ours. Say the word, madam, and I shall have my
boat at your dock this instant.*

Yours,
Peregrine

Secretary, The Falcon Club

Dear Sir,

*I planted the missive bearing the code name so that
LJ might find it and busy herself chasing shadows.
The old girl's pockets are no doubt as empty as her
boasts, and she must keep her publishers happy.*

*In fact, the code name Sea Hawk may well be de-
funct. I have had no direct communication from him
in fifteen months. The Admiralty reports that he yet
holds a privateer's commission, but has had no news
from him since the conclusion of the Scottish affair
more than a year ago. Even in his work for the Club
he has rarely followed any lead but his own. I suspect
he has resigned as we previously imagined. We must
count England fortunate that he is now at least nominally loyal to the crown, rather than its enemy.*

In service,
Peregrine

Chapter 2

Jinan Seton stared at his true love, and the blood ran cold in his veins. Rain-splattered wind whipped about him as he watched her, beauty incarnate, sink in a mass of flames and black smoke into the Atlantic Ocean.

The most graceful little schooner ever upon the seas. Gone.

His chest heaved in a silent groan as the final remnants of burning wood, canvas, and hemp disappeared beneath foamy green swells. A scattering of parts bobbed to the surface, slices of planking, snapped spars, empty barrels, shreds of sail. Her lovely corpse rent asunder.

The American brig's deck rocked beneath his braced feet, rain slashing thicker now, obscuring the wreckage of his ship fifty yards away. He clamped his eyes shut against the pain.

"She was a good 'un, Master Jin." The hulking beast standing beside him shook his chestnut head mournfully. "Weren't your fault she's gone into the drink."

Jin scowled. *Not his fault.* Damn and blast American privateers shooting at anything with a sail.

"They acted like pirates," he said through gritted teeth, his voice rough. "They lowered a longboat. They shot without warning."

"Snuck up on us right good." The massive head bobbed.

Jin sucked a breath through quivering nostrils and clenched his jaw, arms straining against the ropes trapping him to the brig's mast. Someone would pay for this. In the most uncomfortable manner possible.

"Treated her like a queen, you did," Mattie mumbled above the increasing roar of anger in Jin's ears that obscured the shouts around him and the moans of wounded men. Jin swung his head about, craning to see past his helmsman's bulk, searching, counting. There was Matouba strapped to a rail, Juan tied to rigging, Little Billy struggling in the hands of a sailor twice his breadth. Big Mattie blocked his view of the rest of the deck, but thirty more—

"Th' others scrambled for the boats when she caught afire," Mattie grunted. "Boys are well enough, seeing as these fellas ain't pirates after all. Nothing to worry about."

"Nothing to worry about." Jin cracked a hard laugh. "I am trussed like a roast pig and the *Cavalier* is hundreds of feet below. No, I haven't a care in the world."

"Don't you try fooling me. I knows you care more about our boys than your lady, no matter how much you doted on her."

"Wrong, as usual, Matt." He glanced up and saw clearly now the flag of the state of Massachusetts hanging limp in the rain that pattered his face. He'd lost his hat. No doubt it happened at some point during the scuffle from longboat to enemy deck when he'd abruptly realized he had ordered his men to board an American privateer, *not* a pirate vessel. Rain dripped from the tip of his nose into his mouth. He spit it out and slued his gaze around.

Shrouded in silvery gray, the deck of the brig was littered with human and nautical debris. Men from both crews lay prone, sailors seeing to wounds with hasty triage. Square sails hung loose from masts, several torn, a yardarm broken, sections of rail splintered and cut through with cannon shot, black powder marks everywhere. Even taken unaware, the *Cavalier* had given good fight. But the Yank vessel was still afloat. While Jin's ship was at the bottom of the sea.

He closed his eyes again. His men were alive, and he could afford another ship. He could afford a dozen more. Of course, he had promised the *Cavalier*'s former owner he would take care of her. But he had promised himself even more. This setback would not cow him.

"We seen worse." Mattie lifted bushy brows.

Jin cut him a sharp look.

"What I means to say is, you seen worse," his helmsman amended.

Considerably worse. But nothing quite so painfully humiliating. No one bested him. *No one.*

"Who did this?" he growled, narrowing his eyes into the rain. "Who in hell could have crept up on us like that so swiftly?"

"That'd be Her Highness, sir." The piping voice came from about waist-high. The lad, skinny and freckled, with a shock of carrot hair, stretched a gap-toothed grin, swept a hand to his waist, and bowed. "Welcomes aboard the *April Storm*, Master Pharaoh."

Every muscle in Jin's body stilled.

April Storm.

"Who is the master of this vessel, boy?"

The lad flinched at his hard tone. He flashed a glance at the ropes binding Jin and his helmsman about waists, chests, and hands to the mizzenmast, and the scrawny shoulders relaxed.

"Violet Laveel, sir," he chirped.

"Quit smirking, whelp, and call your mistress over," Mattie barked.

The boy's eyes widened and he scampered off.

"Violet *la Vile*?" Mattie mumbled, then pursed his thick lips. "Hnh."

Jin drew in a slow, steadying breath, but his heart hammered unaccustomedly quick. "The men are prepared?"

"Been pr'pared for months. Won't do a lick o' good now they're all tied up."

"I will do the talking."

Mattie screwed up his cauliflower nose.

"Keep your mouth shut with her, Mattie, or so help me, I will find a way to keep it shut despite these ropes."

"Yessir, Cap'n, sir."

"Damn it, Mattie, if after all this time you so much as think of throwing a wrench in—"

"Well, well, well. What do we have here, boys?" The voice came before the woman, smooth, rich, and sweet, like the caress of brushed silk against skin. Unlike any female sailor Jin had ever heard.

But as she sauntered into view from around the other side of Jin's helmsman, she looked common enough. Through the thinning rain, he had his first view of the notoriously successful Massachusetts female privateer, Violet la Vile.

The woman he had been searching out for two years.

Sailors flanked her protectively, casting soft, liquid glances at her and scowls at Jin and his mate. She stood a head shorter than her guard, coming to about Jin's chin. Garbed in loose trousers and a long, shapeless coat of worn canvas, a thick bundle of black neck cloth stuffed beneath her chin, a sash with no fewer than three mismatched pistols hanging from it, and a wide-brimmed hat obscuring her face, she didn't particularly resemble her sister. But Jin had spent countless nights in ports from Cape Cod to Vera Cruz drinking sailors and merchants under the table and bribing men with everything he had at hand in search of information about the girl who had gone missing a decade and a half ago. That she looked less like a fine English lady than any woman he'd ever seen did not mean a damned thing.

Violet la Vile was Viola Carlyle, the girl he had set out from Devonshire twenty-two months earlier to find. The girl who, at the age of ten, had been abducted from a gentleman's home by an American smuggler. The girl all except her sister believed dead.

The brim of her hat rose slowly through the rain. A narrow chin came into view, then a scowling mouth, a slight, sun-touched nose, and finally a pair of squinting eyes, crinkled at the corners. They assessed Jin from toe to crown. A single brow lifted and her lips curved up at one side in a mocking salute.

"So this is the famed Jinan Seton I've heard so many stories of? The Pharaoh." Her voice drawled like a sheet sliding through a well-oiled block. Thick lashes fanned down, then back up again, taking him in this time with a swift perusal. She wagged her head back and forth and her lower lip protruded. "Disappointing."

Mattie made a choking sound.

Jin's eyes narrowed. "How do you know who I am?"

"Your crewmen. Boasting of you even as they were losing the fight." A full-throated chortle came forth and she plunked her fists onto her hips and pivoted around to the sailors gathering about. "Lookee here, boys! The British navy sent its dirtiest pirate scum to haul me in."

A cheer went up, huzzahs and whistles across deck. Seamen crowded closer with toothless grins and crackling guffaws, brandishing muskets and cutlasses high. She raised her hand and silence descended but for the whoosh of waves against the brig's hull and the patter of rain on canvas and wood. Her gaze slued back to Jin, sharp as a dirk.

"Guess I should be flattered, shouldn't I?" Her voice was like velvet. For a moment—a wholly unprecedented moment—Jin's throat thickened. No woman should have a voice like that. Except in bed.

"Why did you sink my ship?" The steely edge he had learned as a lad came to his own voice without effort. "She was the fastest vessel on the Atlantic. What kind of privateer are you, putting a prize like that under water? You could have kept her, or sold her. She would have taken a fine price."

She screwed up her brows.

"It's true, I could've kept her, Master Brit. Or sold her. But I'd a feeling the master of the *Cavalier* wouldn't allow his ship into another's hands. Was I right?" She grinned. "Of course I was. Then when you found your freedom you'd be pestering to get her back until I'd have had to sink another of your ships until you left my coast alone. No thank you kindly." Her eyes glinted.

"Our countries are no longer at war. You should have released us when you realized who we were."

"You didn't give me much choice, swarming aboard my vessel without invitation."

He shook his head in astonishment. "You were making to board us. What are you doing sneaking around like pirates in the rain?"

"Looking for fools bent on glory," she said with infuriating ease. "What kind of idiot attacks a pirate vessel?"

The sort that had seen firsthand a man's feet nailed to planking and other unique freebooter tortures. The sort that had once been as merciless, and now spent his days trying to atone for those sins. He would never again allow a pirate ship to sail free.

"Anyway"—she shrugged—"it was such fun seeing the mighty *Cavalier* go down, I couldn't resist."

Red washed across Jin's vision. He tried to blink it away. His gut hurt. Damn and blast, he wanted a cutlass and pistol more than life at this moment. Or perhaps just a bottle of rum.

She smirked.

Two bottles. They said she was a fine sailor for a woman, but no one said she was mad.

"What will you do with my crew?" His voice sounded uneven now. *Damn and blast.*

A single brow arched high again. "What do you think I'll do with them? Trade them for profit?"

Jin's spine stiffened. "You would not. You couldn't sell more than half, if you did." The half with brown skin.

"Of course I won't, you heathen." Her tone did not alter from the satin.

"What then?"

A gust of breeze blew the misty rain sideways. The ship leaned and the woman widened her stance. She pursed her lips.

"I'll put you off tonight when we come into port. They'll take you into the jail there and the constable will decide what to do with you."

"Constable?" Mattie grunted.

"What, big fellow? Afraid of the law? Do you want to stay aboard?" She cast him a crooked grin. "I could use a brute like you around here. You're welcome to remain if you wish, and leave Lord Pharaoh here to rot behind bars with the others."

Mattie's cheeks went beet red. Jin's fist ached to slam right into his helmsman's meaty jaw. Mattie was a fool about women.

But he took a measured breath instead. With that speech

she had given away all he needed. She had given away proof of her origins.

In his twenty-nine years Jin had sailed from Madagascar to Barbados. He had drunk with men from Canton to Mexico City, and he had heard nearly every language on earth. No single utterance had ever sounded so sweet to him as Violet la Vile's West Country long A. The woman was Devonshire born and bred or Jin wasn't a sailor. It did not matter that he had lost the *Cavalier*. He had found his quarry.

His crew believed she was yet another bounty to be collected, a quarry assigned to him through his work for the government. She was not, rather his own private mission. With Viola Carlyle's return to England, his debt to the man who had saved his life would be repaid at last.

"Thank you, mum." Mattie ducked a jerky bow against his bonds. "I'll be staying with me mates."

"Suit yourself." She eyed Jin. "I suppose you expect me to have you untied, pirate."

"I do. Quickly."

"Not a pirate no more, miss," Mattie grunted. "Not for two years now."

Her eyes glinted. "It gives me pleasure to call him one." She lifted a brow. "He doesn't like it, obviously. He is as arrogant as they say." She sauntered toward him, halting inches away. She tilted her head back, her hat brim hovering just above his nose as she scanned his face slowly with her squinting eyes. Unusual color. So dark blue they could be called violet. Thus her false name, no doubt.

Up close her skin shone warm from sun even under the canopy of rainclouds, nothing like an English lady's delicate pallor. Her mouth was fuller than he had first thought, lips chapped at the bow, a small, flat mole on one side riding the curve of her lower lip. Freckles dusted her pug nose.

Not pug. Delicate. Almost ladylike.

He gave her stare for stare.

She wrinkled the almost ladylike appendage.

"Arrogant." She sighed on a rough whorl of air. "And still disappointing. I'll admit I expected more of the legend."

"I can give you more, if you wish." And he would. As soon as he got free of these bonds he would give Viola Carlyle exactly what she should have had fifteen years ago.

He would give her family back again.

Viola chuckled. "Oh can you?"

"I can do you damage even with my hands tied behind my back." His voice was gravelly, ice blue eyes intense.

In all the stories Viola had heard of the infamous pirate-turned-British privateer, no one ever mentioned those eyes. But sailors were a pack of fool men and never noticed details like that. Every member of her crew could tell her the exact direction the wind blew across Nantucket Sound in December, or the difference between a rolling hitch and a double sheet bend. But she wagered none of them could state the color of her hair if she stood hatless before them, and she'd captained them for almost two years and known them fifteen. Most sailors weren't observant in that fashion.

Pity she wasn't most sailors. Jinan Seton was a fine specimen of masculinity.

She grinned. "I'd like to see you try." Taunting a man bound to a mast with ropes wasn't gracious. But it was fun, especially when the man was too handsome for his own scoundrel good.

"Would you like that?" The ice glittered.

"Talk bluster-cock all you want, pirate." Viola ignored her abruptly dry throat, gesturing to the ropes strapped about him. "My boys know how to tie a fine knot."

"I have no doubt they do." His voice was deep. Relaxed. Far too confident. "Are you daring me?"

"Surrounded by sixty of my men, with yours all tied up just like you?" She waggled her brows. "Why not?"

His teeth snapped. Her nose exploded in pain.

She wrenched free and leaped back, slapping a hand to her face.

The hulk roared with laughter. "Guessing you haven't heard all the stories about Cap'n Jin after all. Aye, miss?"

She glared, dropped her hand, and pushed her face up to Seton's again. Whiskers shadowed his jaw, nearly black, all of him wet just like everything aboard her ship. It had been raining for three days, the downpour thick as fog, and she hadn't meant to sneak up on the *Cavalier* at all. It had just been good luck.

Seton's eyes looked hard as crystal.

Or perhaps not such good luck.

She gritted her teeth. "Don't you dare do anything like that again." She poked her finger into his soaked waistcoat. Muscle beneath. Hard muscle. But that was typical enough for a sailor. "Or I'll have you strapped to the hull in less than an instant."

"You dared, in point of fact. Faulty judgment." The cool blue glimmered now. He was enjoying himself. His gaze, so close, slipped to her throbbing nose, then returned to her eyes. His voice rumbled like a summer storm, low and mildly threatening. "I could have taken off the tip."

"Done it before," the hulk grunted cheerfully. "Earlobes too. A bloke's finger one time."

Viola couldn't drag her attention from the icy eyes. "I retract the Pharaoh sobriquet. You are an animal."

"And you are standing far too close for your own good." With his dark hair plastered to the bridge of his nose and high cheekbones, his eyes looked preternatural and uncannily knowing. A long nose and a strong jaw lent him an aristocratic air. And he spoke with the accents of an educated man, but with a foreign timbre. He was not fully English. In ports from Boston to Havana, they called him the Pharaoh for good reason.

A gleam of white showed at the crease of his mouth. Teeth. Deceptively sharp teeth. She should move away from them.

She did not—not only because she had never backed down from an opponent in front of her crew. She was, quite frankly, rapt. His lips were perfect, the most decadent dusky shade curving in wonderfully sensuous dips and rises. Flawless masculinity. Viola tried to conjure Aidan's lips in her memory. She couldn't. It'd been months since she last saw him, true, but she was in love with Aidan Castle. Ten years in love. She should surely remember his mouth.

Seton's perfect lips curved into a slow smile. His breath tickled her face, mingling with the rain. Her gaze crept up. He leaned slightly forward and murmured as intimately as though they were lovers sharing a bed, "I will do it again if you do not move away."

"I suspect you will." Her insides shivered, the betrayal of a grown woman too long in command of a bunch of scabrous salties. But her father had always told her she was hot-blooded. "But then I would have to kill you, and neither of us want that, do we?"

"Move away, or we will find out."

"Don't tempt me. The dirk at my hip likes the taste of pirate blood."

"Not a pirate no more, miss," the hulk mumbled.

"It seems to me, madam"—Seton bent his head, tilting it so that those perfect lips hovered a mere sliver of damp air above hers—"that you are ignoring an important message here."

He smelled of salt, rain, and wind. And something else. Musky and male, but not filthy, sweaty male sailor. Rather, male *man*. A scent that ran right through her like a little flame.

Viola willfully shut off her nostrils.

"Perhaps I'm hard of hearing. Or perhaps I just sank your ship and you are my prisoner."

A brow lifted. "Kill me then, if you wish."

"I may."

"You will not." He sounded certain.

"How can you know that?"

His voice dipped to a whisper, his gaze slipping to her mouth so close. "You have never killed a soul. You will not begin with me."

She didn't respond. How could she? The blackguard was right.

Slowly, he drew his head back. Viola allowed herself a sip of fresh air. His face remained perfectly passive. Her right foot slipped back several inches. Then her left. If he smiled, she would stick him with her dirk and damn him and her vow never to be the kind of sailor her father had been.

As though he knew exactly what she was thinking, his eyes seemed to light again. A wicked glimmer.

She narrowed hers. "You really don't believe you'll be behind bars tonight, do you?"

He did not respond.

"Master Jin's not one for telling fibs, miss," the hulk offered gruffly, "but I don't think he wants to be insultin' you in front of all your men like, you sees."

"What's your name, sailor?"

"Matthew, miss."

"Matthew, keep your lip buttoned or I will button it for you."

Seton's perfect mouth slanted into a half smile. Viola's breathing halted.

She snapped her gaze away and shouted toward the helm. "Becoua, make our course for port."

"Yes'm, Cap'n!"

"Mr. Crazy," she called across deck to her lieutenant, "we'll take everything off these sailors for prize before we give them over to the constable."

Her lieutenant scuttled up like a crab, all bones and white whiskers beneath leathery skin. "Everything, Cap'n?"

Viola smiled, breathing deep again, and crossed her arms. "Everything." She tilted her gaze back toward the Pharaoh. "And, Crazy, start with Mr. Seton."

She realized her mistake immediately. After a long cruise, her crewmen valued good clothing more than firearms and coin, and the sailors from the *Cavalier* were better clad than most. But she should have let Seton be. He'd been the master of his own ship for years, after all, her equal on the sea. It was common courtesy to treat other captains respectfully.

More to the point, his perfection continued below the mouth.

She could not look away. He held her gaze as a pair of deckhands loosened the ropes and stripped him first of coat, neck cloth, and waistcoat, then shirt and trousers. Through the disrobing, his stare challenged. But after a point, she gave up looking at his face.

Sweet Saint Bridget, he was more god than man.

From broad shoulders glimmering with rain, his chest tapered lean and well muscled to a line of dark hair dipping beneath linen drawers slung low on his hipbones. After years on her father's ship, Viola had seen plenty of men undressed. Sailors were either wiry from life on the sea or bulky from the work. Jinan Seton was neither. His height rendered his corded arms, chest, and tight belly perfectly aesthetically pleasing.

Her breaths shortened. It had clearly been far too long since she'd seen Aidan.

"Enjoying the view, Captain?" His lips barely moved but his voice was remarkably strong and hard.

Arrogant son of a humpback whale. Well justified, though.

"Enjoying the weather, Seton?" He had to be cold as a Nova Scotian iceberg. His crew too. She'd better get them to shore before they froze to death.

He grinned. "Overly warm for spring, wouldn't you say?"

Yes. But not on the outside of her skin. Beside him, Matthew shivered, but the Pharaoh remained perfectly still. She should move closer to see if his smooth skin was covered with gooseflesh too. The ship dipped against a swell; he steadied his stance and his muscles flexed—chest, arms, neck, calves. She nearly choked on the shock of heat that went through her.

His grin widened.

Ever so nonchalantly she strolled toward the companionway, putting her back to him, and descended below deck.

In her cabin she unlocked the medicine chest and pulled out powdered root, salve, and a few other bottles, and dropped them into her wide coat pockets along with a pair of shears and a thick roll of linen bandaging. She would be busy until sunset seeing to nicks and gouges, but she hadn't seen any serious wounds among her men or the sailors from the *Cavalier*. She added a needle and thread and headed back up top.

She set to tending wounds as she found them, accustomed to the occupation. From the time she was ten and she'd first crossed the ocean in her father's smuggling brig, he let her take care of this part of his captain's responsibilities. He had claimed it would make the men appreciate her so they would not mind her aboard.

Most never had, growing accustomed to her quick enough. She made certain of it. The one consolation to losing her family in England, after all, had been the adventure of life at sea. In those days Viola had done everything she could to convince her father to keep her aboard rather than leave her on land with his widowed sister and her three squalling infants. He had rewarded her all spring and summer, each fall setting her ashore to remain in his little house in Boston the rest of the year, to learn her lessons and wait impatiently for his return in April.

Later, when she'd grown up a little, she realized he kept her with him on the ship because she reminded him of her mother. His only love. After she met Aidan Castle, she had finally understood her father's singular devotion.

The rain let up just as Viola tied off the final bandage and sent the sailor back to work. Her crewmen industriously scrubbed and hammered, tying and splicing and patching. All in all, her ship hadn't come out too badly. Given her opponent, Viola was astounded they'd come out of the fight at all.

She forced herself to look aft. Still strapped to the mizzen, Seton stood with his eyes closed, his head resting back against the mast. But she wasn't fooled. A sailor like him wouldn't sleep while prisoner aboard another's vessel. He was probably calculating his escape.

He opened his eyes and looked straight at her. This time he didn't grin.

Viola knew that over the past decade the swift and clever *Cavalier* had spent most of her time harrying British yachts, and during the struggle with Napoleon she had bested a handful of French men-o'-war. Here and there she had taken American merchant ships selling weapons and supplies to the French colonies, but never a U.S. naval ship. Not many months ago, however, rumor had it the *Cavalier* sank a Spanish pirate sloop round about Havana. Shortly after, she turned over another buccaneer—a Mexican schooner—to an American naval captain off Trinidad. Good work. Decent work.

Still, with the vessel's colorful past and the Pharaoh's reputation, if Viola turned its crew in to the port authorities in Boston, Seton and his men might very well hang.

She glanced over her shoulder at her quartermaster making fast a halyard to the mainmast.

"Crazy, how dishonest would a pirate have to be to keep his identity secret so he wouldn't be hung?"

"Not dishonest at all, Cap'n." The old man's eyes were knowing. Since she was ten, Crazy had taught her half of what she knew about sailing and life. "Wise, I'd say," he added, casting a quick look at the *Cavalier*'s master.

"Can our boys keep it quiet, do you think?" She hushed her voice. "Or will they want to brag? It's not any ship they've sunk, after all. They've every right to be proud."

He scoffed. "These boys'd do anything for you." He said it without sentimentality. Sailors didn't get teary, no matter how much affection they held for one another. Viola had learned that early on. She had learned to hold her tears like a man.

"Then make it so." She paused. "But don't tell Seton or his crew."

Crazy nodded his white head and went off to see to her orders. Viola's shoulders relaxed. When they came into port in an hour or so, she would tell a tall tale to the constable of a stranded ship that fired on her accidentally. Of how she had taken the crew aboard and tied them up in case they intended trouble. Of how, still and all, she was convinced they weren't any harm. Hell, they couldn't even keep their own vessel afloat. How much of a threat could they be?

The *Cavalier*'s papers had gone down with her. Without proof of identity her crew would be held overnight. But with Viola's story they wouldn't be held any longer than that unless Seton opened up his arrogant mouth and proclaimed his identity and the identity of his ship.

Viola wouldn't be at fault in his hanging. She would allow the Pharaoh to take care of that all by himself.

Chapter 3

The port constable, an old friend, bought her story hook, line, and sinker. Or pretended he did. The sack of gold she'd taken off a Spanish brigantine two months earlier and slipped into his pocket probably didn't hurt matters any.

She saw the crew of the *Cavalier* off her vessel and into the harbor jail, and wiped her hands of them.

"You done the right thing, Miss Violet." Crazy walked with her along the lantern-lit quay toward the street bustling with sailors, dockworkers, merchants, and the bawdy women who gave them all pleasure. Laughter and raucous amusement tumbled from pub doors, and mist still hung in the night air. "Had myself a chat with some of them boys from the *Cavalier*. They weren't none of them a bad lot."

"Except their captain."

"Rumor is as rumor does. Some men's bound to change."

Viola slanted her quartermaster a narrow look, unwinding her thick cravat and scratching her neck, her legs steadying to land slowly. The ten-week cruise had not wearied her. She would appreciate a hot bath and clothes washed in fresh water, but she was anxious to get back aboard her ship and head south.

To Aidan.

She was nearly five-and-twenty, and she had decided to tell him she was willing to live on land for at least six months every year. This time, he would marry her. He would.

"Think your wife will take you in this time, Crazy?"

He rubbed his hand across scruffy white whiskers. "Said she would when I left last time, but she's none too consistent, you see."

"Good luck to you. We'll pick you up when we return in August."

"Heading on to Port of Spain, then?"

Viola passed her hand across her brow, shoving back matted hair. Everything was damp, from her coat to—oddly—her anticipation.

"Mm hm." She stared at the torchlight illuminating the doorways along the street. But she would not find answers there, only in the bright Caribbean sun.

"Haven't heard from Mr. Castle lately, now, have you?"

"Not since December."

He cleared his throat. "Them planters gets busy sometimes. And he's still learnin' the ropes, mind you. 'Taint every day a sailor sets onto land to farm."

"It's hardly a farm, Crazy." With the money Aidan had saved from six years as lieutenant aboard her father's ship, he had purchased fifty acres of sugarcane.

His brow frazzled. "You go on down there and see what's what."

"Will you check up on my house on your way home? The renters are good folk, but I should see if they've need of anything."

"You won't be pushing off for another fortnight. Why don't you take a stop by yourself?"

"Too much work to do here unloading the cargo we took on, and refitting. I won't have the time." Or the will.

"Got no fond feelings for that old house, have you?"

"You know about that jail we just sent those boys off to?" She gestured. Crazy nodded. She lifted a brow.

He chuckled. "Never did like to be left there, did you, Miss Violet?"

"No, sir." But her father had left her there nonetheless, for months on end with her aunt and three baby cousins while he'd gone off smuggling, then in 1812 when the war began, privateering for Massachusetts. Viola had never cared for cooking or washing or sewing. She'd only liked to read the newsprints and, when she could get her hands on them, stories of adventure.

Every spring when he'd taken her back aboard, he swore she was born to it. He couldn't keep her ashore.

Serena had always said she would take to sea life like a natural. Serena . . . her beautiful, sweet elder sister who long since believed her dead, just like their mother. Who probably never thought of her at all now. Who would be shocked to see how her little sister had turned out, tanned and uncouth and leading a scruffy band of seamen working for Americans.

For years after her father stole her out from under her sister's eyes, right off the property of the man she'd always thought was her father, Viola had hoped to return to England. She had written letter after letter, sending them off when her real father wasn't ashore so he wouldn't know and be hurt by it. For a hardened sailor, Fionn Daly had a heart of jelly when it came to the females he loved—his widowed sister, Viola, and Viola's mother, whom he never gave up on despite the fact that she married another man. Right up to the day his extravagant devotion killed her.

Serena never replied to Viola's letters, not one in six years. So at sixteen Viola ceased writing. But sometimes she still wondered, and wished she had a spyglass that reached all the way to Devonshire. Serena would surely be wed now, with a handful of babies of her own . . .

But Viola might never find out. She was going to marry Aidan. Since he refused to go back to England until he made his fortune, she wouldn't be going there anytime soon either. Her life was here. In America. With Aidan.

"Good luck with the missus, Crazy. Hope she takes you back this time."

"God willin', miss." He chuckled. "Could use the extra prayers if you got the time."

"Oh," she laughed, "God doesn't listen to me about that sort of thing any longer. Hasn't for years." She waved and continued on to the boardinghouse. On a quiet, narrow street removed from the bustle of the docks, it boasted the peace and quiet she never got on board her ship. She couldn't stand it for more than a fortnight or so at a time.

A withered old lady answered the door.

"Mrs. Digby, your apple cobbler has beckoned me back once again."

"Miss Violet." The woman's eyes crinkled. "Welcome home."

Hardly home. But the linens were always dry and hadn't any bugs.

"For your trouble." Viola pressed a dozen coins into the proprietress's shaky palm and climbed the stairs to her room. She couldn't afford extravagance, but Mrs. Digby kept her in reasonable comfort.

In her chamber she stripped off wool and linen thick with rain and salt and sweat. The serving girl came to make up the fire and Viola gave her a penny, then stood in a tin basin with a pot of hot water to wash. Before the hearth she dried her hair, finger combing out the knots, then fell into bed. She would sleep till Sunday if she didn't have to rise early the following morning to see to the *April*'s cargo.

Before her eyelids fluttered closed, her gaze rested on a tiny statuette on the table beside her bed. Her most prized possession except for her ship.

Her father had traded a whole set of silver plate he'd taken off a Dutch merchantman for this treasure, her thirteenth birthday present. About the length of her forefinger, it was intricately carved and painted with graceful precision. Gold, red, blue, green, yellow. A tiny figure of an Egyptian king.

A pharaoh.

Years later, when she first heard of a pirate with that name—a sailor so brutally successful even Spanish buccaneers feared to cross him—she wanted to meet him, to see with her own eyes the man who was bigger than life. A real legend. Recently, when talk at dockside taverns said the Pharaoh had turned to wrecking pirate vessels *exclusively*, she wanted to meet him even more.

Now she had.

And because of her, a mere woman, the mighty Pharaoh was sleeping in a jail cell tonight. Also because of her, come the morning, he would be free. If he kept that gorgeous mouth shut.

She fell asleep smiling.

Jin awoke shivering.

He clamped down on his body's reflexive reaction. Not to the cold. To the iron bars hovering before his eyes.

He shrugged up straighter against the wall, pulling in long, chest-deep breaths, willing away the crawling damp of his flesh and the throb of panic weakening his limbs. Dawn light filtered through the tiny square of a window just above a man's head in the ten-by-ten cell. About him and in the adjoining cage his crew slept or slumped on the musty floor. The lot of them rested soundly anywhere. So could Jin. Usually.

He hadn't been behind bars in twelve years, since he was seventeen. On that occasion, two men had paid for his liberty. At his hands. With their lives.

Eight years before that, with wrists in irons, he'd been dragged fighting onto an auctioneer's block in the blaze of the Barbadian sun. That time a boy had paid for Jin's freedom. With gold. A twelve-year-old boy to whom Jin owed his life. Each day of freedom since then still seemed like a stolen gift.

A steady, muted click turned his head. In a corner of the cell across the way, Little Billy knocked a battered wooden die against the wall. His neck craned up and he flashed a quick grin.

"Mornin', Cap'n." At sixteen, Billy had not yet outgrown his name; short, skinny, gangly, and grinning like a lad. "Ready for the judge?"

"There will be no judge, Bill." Jin ran his gaze along the walls and bars of the port jail cell, searching for weakness in the structure. Out of habit. He needn't. They would be released within hours. He had already heard it from the harbor officer the night before when the fellow delivered the rags Jin and his crew now wore in lieu of their own clothes. The *April Storm*'s master had lied to the port master about him and his ship.

She was mad. He would be taking a madwoman back to her respectable family in England.

Beside him Mattie expelled a great cavernous yawn. Lifting hands as big as hams, he rubbed them up and down his face and shook his heavy head, then set a glowering look on Jin.

"What's the plan, Cap'n?"

"I am working on it."

"Why don't you just pays these fellas for her, Cap'n?" Little Billy scuttled toward them and gestured to the ceiling, apparently intending to indicate the coastal officials. "Take her off their hands, like?"

"You ain't thinking straight." Mattie slugged the lad on a bony shoulder. "That mort ain't nobody's property."

"Didn't matter with that gal he took up with back in Coruna." Billy's pale brow wrinkled.

"What'd you know 'bout that?" Matouba's bass sounded from his barrel chest. Across the narrow cell, his round eyes were two spots of white in his ebony face. "You weren't but a mite at the time."

"He didn't take up with that one," Mattie grunted. "And she weren't free. Master Jin bought her off that bloke as was beating her." He turned his head to Jin. "Whatever happened to that little Spanish girl?"

Jin shrugged. But he remembered. He remembered every one of the people he freed, their faces, their names. He had found that girl a post as a domestic servant in an old spinster's house. The woman was ancient but respectable. It was the best he could do in a foreign city. In ports he knew better, he had an easier time of it.

It didn't matter. Every time he bought someone's freedom, another chip of the hard, cold stone of rage and old despair inside him fell away. But they were, each one of them, tiny chips indeed, and the stone still quite large. He had a thousand more to go before the rock finally disappeared.

"I sez you buy yourself 'bout four ships, Cap'n, maybe five or six, and stock 'em with crews," Matouba intoned. "Then you sneak up on that *April Storm* in open water, close her in, and 'scort her to England like that."

"No." Jin shook his head. "She must come willingly." A

woman like Violet la Vile would not come any other way, unless he tied her up and stuffed her in the bilge for the month's journey. But Jin did not treat other human beings like that. Not any longer. "No," he repeated. "I have another plan."

When he first started searching for Viola Carlyle, he had harbored hope he would find her holed up in some little house ashore, anxious to return to England, merely lacking the resources or even the gumption. But after months of searching, when clues finally led him to the privateer captain Violet the Vile, he had been forced to reevaluate. Her real father, Fionn Daly, had been first a barely successful smuggler then an even less successful privateer. He probably only allowed her aboard for practical purposes—to see to the domestic tasks so he would not have to pay a sailor for it. No doubt she'd be glad to return to England and society, Jin guessed.

He'd guessed wrong. The captain of the *April Storm*—confident, brash, and nothing like a lady—quite obviously would not come easily. Jin must convince her. But he had spent a lifetime alternately lying and knifing his way to victory after victory. In the end, Miss Viola Carlyle would sail to England with him of her own accord and take up again the life she was born to live. He had no doubt of it whatsoever.

Neither did he have a choice.

Twenty years earlier Alex Savege had bought his freedom and saved his life. Nearly a decade after that, when Jin had been nothing but a thieving, scrapping ball of anger directed against the whole world, Alex again offered him another option. He had taken him aboard the *Cavalier* and shown him how to be a man. Alex's new wife still believed her half sister to be alive. A lord now, Alex did not need Jin's money or even his assistance with his ship any longer. All Alex cared about now was his wife's happiness.

And so, unbeknownst to either Lord or Lady Savege, Jin had set out to find Viola Carlyle. To repay his debt. He would return her safely to the bosom of her family, or he would finally die trying.

The harbor constable pursed his lips, looked Jin up and down for the third time, and demanded gold.

Jin produced a vowel. The port master's lips curved upward. He locked the office and went to the bank himself. Jin waited without concern. The Massachusetts Bank account of Mr. Julius Smythe, merchant, boasted a hefty balance.

In short order the port master returned, all smiles.

"Congratulations, Mr. Smythe." He bowed as though Jin were actually the gentleman he pretended to be when he did business at the bank. "You and three of your men may go free."

Back on the docks with the late-spring morning sun shining through masts and rigging onto worn planks, he told Matouba, Mattie, and Billy to take themselves off until he needed them. The boy and Matouba went off bickering as usual. Mattie cast Jin a dark look, then lumbered away as well.

He walked down the quay, scanning the scene already busy with the traffic of carts, sailors, and merchants, and found what he sought: a sparkling new vessel, the railings not yet even affixed. The sounds of hammers smacking at wood echoed from atop. A pair of boys sanded the main deck, still fresh wood without varnish or tar.

She was not the *Cavalier*. Nothing would ever be the *Cavalier*. But she was a beauty, small and fast, just as he'd heard she would be when he passed through Boston six months earlier and saw the plans for her. She would suit his needs perfectly.

But a man could not purchase a ship appearing as though he'd spent the night in jail. He turned and made his way toward his bank.

Two hours later, freshly shaved and clothed, Jin folded the letter that had awaited him at his bank these four months, and tucked it into his waistcoat. He nearly smiled. The Admiralty occasionally managed to send him correspondence via commanders in the field. This letter, however, had not come from the navy.

Viscount Colin Gray was still looking for him.

For years Jin had labored on behalf of another servant of the crown than the Admiralty, a secret organization buried deep in the Home Office, known to only those who required its assistance. The Falcon Club.

The Club had disbanded the previous year—rather, nominally so. Only five of them to begin with, four yet lingered. Jin's fellow agent and sole contact with the Club's shadowy director, Colin Gray, had not given up on the organization's mission, a mission dedicated to seeking out lost souls and bringing them home. Not any lost souls, though; the Falcon Club's quarries were those whose disappearance, even existence, threatened the peace of the kingdom's most elite and whose absence and recovery must not become public knowledge. For the safety of England.

Jin had not quit—not in so many words. But for the present, he hadn't the time or inclination to humor either Gray or the Admiralty. He had finally found the quarry he had chosen for himself two years earlier. Another lost soul. A woman gone for so long that she no longer knew she was lost.

Moving along the quay, he came to the ship that had

brought him into port. Resting in her berth like a sway-backed carriage horse in the traces, the *April Storm* had to be twenty years old if she was a day, a mid-sized brig, square rigged for speed but too heavy in the hull for true maneuverability.

His gut ached. Having been taken by such a ship after outrunning nearly every other vessel on the Atlantic was nothing short of travesty.

His gaze alighted on a girl working at a pile of rope on the dock beside the ship, and his jaw relaxed. She bent to her work, her back to him, revealing a backside perfectly rounded for a man's hands. Snug breeches encased thighs that stretched sweetly to shapely calves. A white linen shirt pulled at her shoulders as she worked, defining delicate bones and slender arms.

His boot steps sounded on the planking and she glanced over her shoulder. She paused. Then, straightening, she drew off her hat and passed the back of her hand across her damp brow.

Jin's blood warmed with the appreciation of a fine woman, all too infrequently enjoyed these days since he had bent to his current mission. Her brow was high and clear, dark eyes large and shaded with long lashes, nose pert, and her mouth a full, rosy invitation to pleasure. Strands of richly brown hair curled upon her brow, the rest of the long, satiny mass pulled back in a leather thong. She looked vaguely familiar. And pretty. Far too pretty to be laboring dockside.

"Is the master of this vessel about?" He gestured to the *April Storm*.

She nodded. Her eyes seemed to sparkle in the spring sunlight. Jin smiled slightly. It was an age since he'd had a woman beneath him, and the way this one stared him straight in the eye looked promising.

"Fetch her then." He allowed his grin more rein. "And be quick about it."

"I can be quicker than you imagine, sailor. She's already standing in front of you." Her voice was as smooth as her satiny hair. She set her fists upon her curved hips and Jin's gaze dropped to the dark spot just beneath her lower lip.

His grin faded.

A smile like Christmas cake curved across Viola Carlyle's alluring lips.

"So they let you go free, did they? More the fools they." She laughed, then turned back to her work. "I see you found some clothes."

"I did indeed." And hers still clung to her damnably feminine body the same as a moment ago when he did not know she was a madwoman and a lady. "I bought my way free." Along with Mattie, Billy, and Matouba. The rest of his crew would have to wait. He could not be seen to be throwing about gold too freely. But they were accustomed to tight quarters, and without charges to hold them the harbor master would release them soon enough.

She shook her head. "Port officials will do anything for a sack of coins."

"And a good word from a trusted privateer. Thank you for your assistance."

She straightened up again and gave him a slow, assessing stare from boots to brow. She did not move, but her very stance shouted swagger, sun-gold hand resting upon the long knife at her hip as though born to be there.

But it was not. That hand had been born to wear kidskin gloves. To have a dance card ribbon wrapped about the wrist. To find its place upon a gentleman's arm.

"I don't like to see sailors trapped on land," she said. "Even pirates."

An honest response. He had to admire that.

"I have not pirated on American ships for years." Only during the war, and only those ships carrying supplies to England's enemy, France. The *Cavalier*'s first master, Alex Savege, had preyed upon wealthy English noblemen's vessels. "But you know that, don't you?"

"Perhaps." Her mouth twitched up at one edge.

"This does not bring us even." He held her gaze steadily. "You sank my ship."

"What do you think I owe you, sailor? Mine?" She laughed, a rich, throaty release of pure pleasure. "Think again."

She liked to laugh, and that silken laughter acted like a caress right down Jin's chest, straight beneath the front fall of his trousers.

"Your ship isn't worth it." His voice sounded unnecessarily hard even to his own ears. "You owe me the opportunity to regain some of what I have lost, and I haven't a ship now with which to do that."

Her brows tilted up. "Don't tell me you expect me to hire you on."

"I do. And three of my men."

"I said don't tell me. I don't believe it. The Pharaoh wants to join the crew of a privateer in the pay of the state of Massachusetts? Tell me another tall tale, sailor."

No easy riposte came to his tongue. Damn but that golden voice could distract a man.

"You had the funds to buy your freedom and clothes," she added.

"I have spent all the credit I have in these parts." Not even a quarter of it. "I put a down payment on that vessel by the slipway yonder."

She sucked in a whistle through her teeth and wagged her

head. Clearly she had lost every last vestige of ten years of upbringing in a nobleman's household.

"She's a beauty." She peered into the bright day toward the dry dock. "She'll be fast too. Possibly faster than the *Cavalier*."

"I will need to settle the balance once she is finished. I hear you are heading south when you put to sea in a fortnight."

"I am. But I'll not be picking up prizes along the way, unless I come across one I can't turn down. I'm carting a cargo on this trip."

"I have assets in Tobago I intend to collect to purchase that ship. I could use the ride in that direction, and you could use me aboard."

She seemed to mull, a wary glint in her dark eyes. Then she pivoted around back to her work.

"I will consider it."

Jin's shoulders got hot and prickly. He moved forward, his boots halting within the fall of her scant noonday shadow.

"You will consider it now."

She looked up at him, eyes narrowed, but the pulse at her tender throat leaped. "Come any closer, sailor, and you'll be eating my long knife for lunch."

"Deny me my due, madam, and you will regret it for longer than it would take to make this dilapidated old barge into a seaworthy vessel."

Her cheeks reddened. "This dilapidated old barge sank your ship. And didn't your mother and father ever teach you manners, Seton?"

His mother had not taught him anything that had been of use once he had been sold into slavery. And his father, the Englishman whose name he had never known . . . Well, that was another stop he would be making in Tobago.

"I guess not." He kept his tone even. "Will you hire me and my men?"

"Move off my back and I'll let you know."

He obliged by a pace, withholding his satisfaction. Already she was bending. This might not take as long as he had thought.

She pushed her hat back on her brow again and stood.

"My quartermaster has gone on furlough," she finally said. "And this morning my mate and cook signed on with a naval frigate. Can any of your men wield a pot?"

They would now. He nodded.

"Truth be told, I could use an experienced first lieutenant." Her eyes narrowed again, squinting as he had first seen in the rain. "But how would you like it after commanding your own vessel?"

"I will not give you trouble."

She frowned. "I doubt that."

Jin allowed himself a grin. This woman had not won her own command by making mistakes.

Now she scowled. "This isn't a pirate ship, Seton. My men are loyal to me. You won't steal my vessel out from under me if that's what you're imagining."

"I do not want the *April Storm*." He wanted Miss Viola Carlyle upon his ship come July, sailing east toward England. "Will you take me on?"

She seemed to study his face, her eyes keen. "I will come to regret this, I suspect." But she moved forward and extended her hand.

He grasped it. Her palm was rough, fingers slender, grip tight. Sailor and lady both. And up close prettier still. The spring sun showed her features to be finely shaped. By accounts she was nearly five-and-twenty, but despite the sun-tinted tone of her skin, she still looked like a girl. It could be the twinkle in her rich eyes that shouted confidence to the world in the face of the constant uncertainty of a sailor's existence. That confidence had been engendered in her during the first decade of her life in which she hadn't a care in the world.

"You will not regret it." How could she? A lady belonged in a gentleman's house. Jin would make certain she got there.

Chapter 4

Viola allowed her crew a fortnight's furlough stirring up trouble in alehouses about town while she fitted out her ship, did noisome paperwork, and argued with the clerk who worked for the merchant whose goods she would carry to Trinidad. Once she unloaded the cargo and enjoyed a few weeks of Aidan's company, she would return to northern waters and scouting out enemies of her adopted country, as the state of Massachusetts had commissioned her to do nearly two years ago when her father died. She had been de facto captain since his illness grew debilitating two years before his death. But he had never wanted to leave the ship, and aboard she had been able to look after him.

Finally the cargo was loaded—barrels of flour, beans, hams, apples, and a vast quantity of furniture that filled the hull but provided little ballast. The *April* sat so light in the draft now, they would make the journey quickly, in less than a month if she was clever and they didn't run afoul of brigands along the route.

But that's why she had hired on the Pharaoh. Her own personal assurance. If trouble came looking for her, she would have the right man at her back.

When finally she climbed aboard, a single traveling case in hand, he was already amidships handing out orders to her men. Everything atop was industrious preparation.

"Cozening up to the crew already in hopes of a mutinous promotion, Seton?"

"No, sir." His very fine mouth barely tilted up at one corner. "Merely doing my job."

She forced herself to look away from that mouth to the decks and rigging and dozen sailors heaving the capstan round, weighing anchor, getting under way just as she would have it. Her crewmen took to Seton's leadership naturally. She couldn't blame them. His very stance suggested command—confident yet easy—the sort of mien she'd struggled for years to perfect so that when her father's long illness finally took him, she was able to be an effective master over five dozen men.

The sky sparkled bright blue, the bay water inviting, the breeze fresh and promising. But a frisson of unease tickled her neck swaddled in thick fabric.

"Everything in order?"

"Yes, sir."

"All hands aboard?"

"Yes, sir."

"You've never sailed under a woman before, have you, Seton?"

"No, sir."

Of course he hadn't. She could count on one finger the female shipmasters she had met in her life.

"You may call me captain."

"I will call you whatever you wish." His tone was unremarkable enough, but a glint lit his light eyes.

She didn't trust him. He'd said she would not regret taking him on. But pirates lied as a habit. She doubted he intended revenge. He seemed more the sort to demand what he wanted—as he had demanded she hire him on.

He had not yet called her captain.

She met his stare as she had in the rain when, nearly naked and strapped to the mizzenmast, he'd been her prisoner. Now he wore neat trousers, a pristine white shirt that complemented his tan skin, a simple linen waistcoat and cravat, and an expression of ever-so-mild challenge on his handsome face, as if he needn't even bother with a more threatening air.

She broadened her stance, the comforting weight of the pistol on her sash bumping against her breast.

"What are you staring at, sailor?"

His ice eyes did not flicker. "My captain, ma'am."

"Get back to work, Seton."

He bowed.

Bowed?

Then he did as she ordered. Viola drew in a long breath and headed toward her cabin. They hadn't left port and already he was mocking her. She had made a foolish mistake taking him aboard. But she certainly would not admit it now, even sitting at dock while she could still send him packing. Perhaps once they were seaboard she could throw over some of the cargo, make her load lighter, and run down to Trinidad that much quicker. Or she could throw Seton over.

* * *

He had never seen anything like it. And the more he observed, the more astounded he became.

They worshipped her. From her bit-sized cabin boy to the mountain manning the helm who made Big Mattie look like a child's doll, every one of her crewmen treated her like a queen. Like a queen they could not get enough of. When she was out of hearing they spoke of her in reverent terms. Complimentary terms. Affectionate terms. When she was atop they alternately fawned on her or snapped to her orders without a grumble. Mattie and Billy were already head over ears, the two-faced idiots. But even stolid Matouba seemed to be coming under her spell.

Jin was not a man to be befuddled. But he was.

To a certain extent, he did understand their besotment. Most sailors saw few women in the course of things, and even fewer women without rouge, brass-tinted hair, and sickly white skin from days spent sleeping off the night's work. When she removed the hat that gave her the look of a witch crossed with a sandbag, Viola Carlyle's cheeks glowed with life. The hair she bound in a braid or knot was richly dark and curling in satin twirls everywhere it escaped its bonds. And her skin was smooth and fine despite her years at sea. She was a taking woman, even if she never showed a glimpse of the sweet, curved figure he'd seen dockside. Her crewmen were bound to admire her.

But there was more to their devotion. It required no more than several days in the men's company to understand that.

"Cap'n says as she'll read to us tonight like she done last cruise." A narrow, salty fellow going into his sixth decade mounted a yardarm, making ready to strike a tattered sail.

"I likes that one 'bout the fellow what's got nicked in the heel with the arrow," his partner, a dark youth, replied as he climbed the rigging. "His mum better've dipped him in that river up to her elbow instead."

They chuckled.

"Did ye know, Master Jin, Cap'n can read?" The youth's eyes gleamed down at Jin with unmistakable pride.

"Can she?" Naturally. She had been schooled in a gentleman's nursery.

"Yessir. Read to us all 'bout that there horse made of wood and them dolts what didn't see the trick till it was too late."

Jin had never heard of a lady reading about the Trojan War. The heel of Achilles—and the rest of that bloodthirsty warrior—were not typically considered suitable fare for gently bred females. But a man who kidnapped his daughter and set her to work on a smuggling ship at ten years of age would not fret over niceties.

"Though usually it's them preachers' sermons." The older fellow nodded with a smile.

"Captain's a God-fear'n woman."

God, perhaps. But she did not yet fear Jin. When she spoke to him she held her chin high and gaze direct. On the other hand, she spoke to him infrequently, and never when she needn't. She took her meals alone in her cabin. Likewise, she did not linger about deck in the fair weather when the sea was clear of company and the men were relaxed enough to pipe a tune or sing. Whether it was due to his presence he could not know yet.

But when she passed him on deck or the companionway, she did not pause to converse. That was as good a sign as he could wish for so early in their journey. She was uncomfortable with him. If she feared him, eventually she would do his bidding. They always did—both women and men.

"What are you standing around for, Seton? Waiting for someone to come along and carve a statue of you?" Violet la Vile's smooth tones came from the quarterdeck above. "Oh, I mistake it. You're already still as stone. A statue would be redundant."

Definitely no fear yet.

He tilted his gaze up to the rail. The afternoon sun slanted behind her, casting her in silhouette. Clothed in canvas bags and a ridiculous hat as usual, she looked like a sack of potatoes.

He knew better. He had seen her curves. He had imagined them at his service.

He nodded. "Seeing to this torn sail, ma'am."

In the shadow he could barely see her eyes narrow to their usual squint. Ladies did not squint. That habit would have to be broken once she resided in her father's house again. But amid the piles of neck cloth stacked high around her cheeks, the squint did not render her features less attractive. Only more provoking.

"It's not torn sufficiently to risk losing the wind by switching it out now." She gestured. "Wait until dark."

The sailors halted their work, casting uncertain glances back and forth between them.

"Respectfully, ma'am," Jin replied evenly, "the wind at present is negligible. When it picks up at dusk you'll want her full ready."

"Are you questioning my orders, sailor?"

Jin drew in a slow breath. For two years he had been his own master. Before that he was independent most of the year when Alex was on land and he captained the *Cavalier* in its master's stead. For over a decade he had never had an argument with his superior.

But before he had signed on with Alex, the last commander Jin sailed under taunted him aplenty, questioning his authority with the men, and his decisions. That particular pirate captain's disrespectful attitude had come to an abrupt halt when, after he attempted to take a stick to Jin, instead he bled to death from a wound inflicted by his own knife.

Jin had been borrowing the knife at the time.

But Viola Carlyle was not a pirate. She should not even be a sailor. However much she behaved and looked like a high-handed ruffian, she was a lady, and his current project was to rescue her from this existence. Even if she got under his skin in a way no other sailor quite had. Or woman. Then again, he'd never known a woman sailor with a voice like brandy and a penchant for saying precisely what he did not wish to hear.

He swallowed back the response that rose to his tongue. "No, ma'am."

"No . . . *Captain*."

It was a damned good thing the sun was setting swiftly. In the slanting shadow he could not discern her eyes now. Big, dark eyes with thick lashes even her foolish costume could not hide.

He slid his gaze to the sailors balancing on the spar. "Mr. French, Mr. Obuay, unfurl that sail and come on down."

The men hoisted the torn canvas back into place, the light breeze snapping through the fissure in it. Without glancing at her again, Jin turned and crossed the deck to the forecastle.

"Keepin' it real friendly like with the captain, hm?"

"Cork it, Mattie." Jin waved a pair of sailors loitering nearby toward the foremast. They hopped to it, lowering the colors for night.

"So, this be your plan?"

"It is." He unsnapped the spyglass from the cradle on the rail in which he had set it earlier. A sail had breached the far horizon just after dawn, and Jin assigned Mattie the watch all day, with sharp-eyed Matouba in the crow's nest. She might be the most contrary female on the seven seas, but Jin would not let anyone near her. Until he had her safely aboard his ship, no vessel would come within range of Viola Carlyle—friend or foe.

He peered out over the darkening horizon, the current

lifting the bow in easy dips and rises beneath his feet. The ocean in all directions was perfectly clear.

"Seen anything today?"

Mattie leaned his bulk against the rail and picked at his teeth with a stick. "Fish. Swells. Clouds."

"Clouds?" The sky was wide open, clean blue darkening to pink and lavender.

"Just testing. You seem over distracted lately. Didn't know if you'd notice."

"Mattie," he said quietly, "I have killed men for offering me less grievous insults."

Mattie glowered then pursed his fleshy lips. "Ain't ever kilt no lady, though, have you?"

Jin turned about and strode toward the stair, then down into the brig's belly. The air was close below, the low-ceilinged deck lined with sixteen heavy iron cannons tail to tail. Hammocks hung between their hulks, the lumpy shapes of sailors resting in preparation for the night watch. The *April Storm* was much larger and considerably less graceful than the *Cavalier*, an inelegant, aged brig. Its boards creaked beneath his footsteps as he moved forward toward the officers' closetlike quarters, the shipmaster's cabin dead ahead. She liked to spend dusk atop the quarterdeck. Now he could return the spyglass to her quarters without confrontation.

He moved into the narrow corridor between the officers' bunks and almost collided with her.

Without hat and cravat obscuring it, the shape of her face was nearly a heart. Dark curls swept back from the peak of her brow, revealing quite clearly her delicate chin, soft mouth, and big eyes staring up at him as though he were some sort of monster. A swift flutter of black lashes dipped over violet pools, and slowly, like a rising tide, a pink flush stole over her cheeks.

As though in choreographed response, heat funneled into Jin's groin.

Inconvenient. He should have seen to that particular necessity while in Boston. He didn't need a woman aboard turning him into a randy lad, a sailor after a long cruise confronted with an unreasonably pretty face.

Not merely a pretty face. She wore only a plain white cotton shirt now. No coat or waistcoat disguised the edges of the useless undergarment beneath it—an undergarment that did nothing to hide the round beauty of her breasts pressing at the laces of the shirt. Breasts the perfect size to fit into a man's hand.

A lady should wear more than that. If this lady wore more than that she would not be quite so . . . distracting.

Mesmerizing.

But he didn't need her breasts at such close quarters to remain stalled in the corridor. The curve of her lush lower lip to her chin decorated with the small dark mole fixed him in place. It seemed as though a master artist had lovingly painted a portrait of a pretty girl, only to find her too perfect, and added that spot to mar his work, but it produced the opposite effect.

"Can't help yourself, can you?" Her voice came between them beautifully smooth.

Jin blinked. Lifted his head he had not realized he lowered.

"They never can." Her tone did not alter.

He stepped back. Straightened his thoughts.

"I was returning this." He proffered the spyglass. His voice was rough.

"Stole it while I wasn't looking, and now you hope to return it before you're caught?" She arched a single, slightly unkempt brow. "Take care, Seton. You're acting like an anxious pirate."

He drew in a tight breath through his nostrils. "A sail breached the horizon this morning. I put a watch on it."

The dark eyes narrowed. "And you didn't see fit to inform me?"

"It failed to show again."

"You're accustomed to doing things your own way, I think."

"I like to spare my captain unnecessary concerns when she no doubt has more important matters to see to." Like taking the damned telescope from his outstretched hand so that he could return atop where he belonged and where she and her underclad, soft-lipped, sharp-tongued provocation were not. His collar felt hot. And other regions of his body. But he had never been a man ruled by lust. He would not become one now.

But something more than lust drew him. He knew this even as he sought to deny it to himself. Her brazen confidence, her unafraid tongue, her successes in the face of the setback of her entire life, even her crew's idiotic devotion marked her as an exceptional woman. A woman quite unlike any he had known.

He had known many women.

"Your responsibilities are not modest," he murmured.

Her brow crept higher. "Doing it a bit too brown, don't you think, sailor?"

"I am endeavoring to serve my captain, as promised." And he was. Not as she expected. But a vow was a vow, and no peculiar confusion of desire or little woman's taunts could undo what he had labored twenty-two months preparing.

"By setting her crew against her?"

He screwed up his brow in question.

"Frenchie and Sam," she supplied. "The torn sail."

"I did what you told me to do."

She set her hands on sweetly curved hips. "And they knew you disagreed with me."

"I shouldn't think it would matter if they did. A captain is bound to overrule his lieutenant when he sees fit."

"*His* lieutenant?"

Would that she were not a woman. "*Her.*"

Her eyes narrowed to a squint. But it did not detract from her loveliness. Goddamn it, he wished she were a snot-nosed lad he could take down with a well-aimed fist.

"You really can't say it, can you?" Her voice rose slightly. "You can't bear to *call* me captain. It kills you to even imagine it, you arrogant son of an Egyptian."

Jin's temper, well tied for days, slipped free of its moorings. He moved so that the space between them nearly disappeared and he was looking down at her upturned face.

"See here, you spoiled minx, I may be under your command but I am not required to accept—"

"Spoiled minx? *Minx?*" she exclaimed. "I don't think a man has ever dared call me that."

"Maybe if one had, you wouldn't be so damned—"

"How could you possibly know whether I am spoiled or not?"

"I can see it well enough in your men's behavior."

"I warned you, you wouldn't like it."

"Would not like what?" Her flashing eyes? Her full lips? The wavy lock of hair tumbling over her brow, obscuring the perfection and rendering her yet more enticing?

"Serving under me."

Under. Atop. Any way she liked it. And with a fiery temper like hers, he suspected he would like it quite a bit. Given all, the notion appealed more than it ought. The sparkle of challenge in her eyes went straight to his cock.

"You can't bear it, you conceited excuse for a respectable privateer." Her mouth curved into a satisfied grin. "Aha. That's got a rise out of you."

In a manner of speaking.

He sucked in breath slowly, battening down on his temper and arousal at once. "I am not an excuse for a respectable privateer. I *am* one."

"You think that simply because you have a commission from your British government you no longer have the instincts of pirate scum?"

The rise abruptly fell, a bucket of ice dashed on his unwelcome ardor.

"I do."

"Prove it."

He grasped her hand, found it clenched, and peeled her fingers apart. He placed the telescope in her palm and closed her hand around it.

"I do not take that which is not mine by right." He released her.

Her big eyes were in a tumult, her breaths fast. The reaction seemed excessive, but it suited Jin. It was closer to fear than her earlier attitude.

"It's because I am a woman." A quaver threaded through her satin voice. "Some men cannot accept orders from a woman."

"It is because you are a harpy. And I am not *some men*."

He left. If he remained in that damned corridor for another minute he might be tempted to tell her the truth.

It was not because she was a woman, a remarkably pretty one with ripe lips he could imagine performing all sorts of tasks other than spewing insults. It was not because he had been a pirate for much of his life. It was not even because he had promised himself to see her to England come hell or high water. It was because sometime over the past two years searching for a girl stolen from her home at a tender age, Jin had realized something profoundly disturbing. Something he rarely allowed himself to ponder.

She had a home to return to. She had a family. That she denied that now, even after so many years, living her life as though the family who cherished her did not exist, infuriated him.

He felt fury. Toward a woman he barely knew.

In his youth, anger had consumed him. For over a decade now, however, he had trained himself to turn that anger toward useful occupation. But this time it stared him in the face in the form of a willful woman who did not understand that the gift she threw away was everything some people—*he*—ever dreamed of possessing.

Chapter 5

Glum today, mum? On account of the weather, I wager."

Viola slanted her cabin boy a scowl, then regretted it when his freckled face fell. He wasn't but seven, full of good cheer and excitement about everything, much as she'd been when her father first brought her aboard his ship. Her ship for nearly two years now. The ship she called home, currently on its way to a man she hoped to also call home someday.

She ruffled Gui's carroty hair and his grin resurfaced, making him look a great deal like his grandfather, Frenchie. He jumped off the quarterdeck rail onto the planks and slapped his little thigh, the wind ruffling his disordered locks further.

"I know what'll pick up your spirits, Cap'n. A bite of Little Billy's grub." He scampered down the narrow quarterdeck stair and disappeared below.

Little Billy's grub couldn't pick up anyone's spirits. If that lad had cooked a day in his life before setting foot aboard the *April Storm*, Viola would sell him the whole ship for a dollar.

But she was indeed ill-tempered. Already today she'd snapped at Sam, burned her arm on a sliding line, and tripped over a bucket, and it wasn't even noon yet under the canopy of low gray clouds. Like the early summer sky, her mind wasn't clear, and it made her tetchy.

She knew perfectly well what caused it. Who. He stood at the forecastle, his back to her as always, broad shoulders and long legs cut against the bright ocean. He seemed to like spending his leisure time at the fore of the ship. Probably because it was as far away from her as he could get.

He hadn't liked her insults three days earlier. No man would. She didn't even know where they'd come from. Her mouth simply opened and out poured nasty word after nasty word. He probably deserved most of them, but that didn't mean she should give her tongue free rein. Especially when he'd been looking at her like . . .

No. She must have imagined it.

In the early days, Aidan had gotten that look in his eyes just before he kissed her. That hot, focused look like he was thinking something very different than what they were talking about. But she didn't know a thing about Jinan Seton. He probably looked at everybody that way when they were insulting him.

He'd kept his temper fairly well. If he truly lost it she could accuse him of mutiny. But a man who lived the life he had did not lose control often. When he did, though, it was a little alarming.

Rather, *thrilling.* He'd grabbed her hand and the controlled strength in his firm, deliberate touch rocked her.

As he often did when she was staring at him from afar, now he turned and met her gaze. Without hesitation he descended from the forecastle and came aft across the deck and up the companionway to the quarterdeck. It was as though with simply her gaze she beckoned, and as her willing servant, he responded. As though he wished to please her.

Idle dreams. Serena had been the dreamer, Viola the adventurer.

Jinan Seton was certainly an adventure of sorts.

From along her nose, she looked him up and down. She'd learned that commanding men looked other men up and down, honest men looked other men in the eye, and dishonest men looked everywhere else.

"The men have been talking about making port at St. George's Island." He met her gaze directly, all business since the interlude below deck when he touched her perfunctorily and made her tremble. "They say you did so once before on this route."

She furrowed her brow. "They have a spot they'd like to return to there." A brothel where the girls wore nothing but net stockings and lace undergarments. Or so a seaman, drunk as a sow, had told her that night long ago. Only seventeen at the time, and longing to know what would encourage Aidan's interest, Viola had nearly bribed the sailor to return to the brothel and purchase a set of the girls' garments for her. She hadn't the courage to do it, though. When she told Aidan about it later, he chucked her on the chin and said she was too good a girl for that sort of thing.

"Why not allow them?" Seton glanced at the horizon, then the water running fast along the port side. The breeze was fair, and she had noticed he didn't miss a thing. He was always watching, calculating, planning the ship's next move. "A day in port will not put us off schedule."

But it would give the men a chance to introduce him to that brothel.

"No." They could afford a few days in port. Stopping at Bermuda wouldn't hurt a thing. "No. We should continue on. With storms unpredictable as they are, I don't want to lose time while I have the advantage."

"Unpredictable?" His handsome face remained passive.

"Early summer storms. You must have sailed these waters a hundred times." She set a suspicious glare upon him.

"Not recently. I have spent a great deal of my time during the past several years on the other side of this ocean. Along the coast of England, principally."

He spoke with such ease, as he did everything. She'd never met a sailor so competent and purely confident, perfectly settled in who he was and what he intended. It stirred a frisson of memory in her, of a time when the men of her world walked with a sense of entitlement. In her child's recollection those men treated women not only with deference—as her crew did now—but with consideration. Men who not only did as one told them, but anticipated a girl's wishes.

On her seventh birthday, the baron had walked her to the old oak and showed her the swing he'd installed there. Without even asking, he knew she'd wished it above all things. He'd held her hand, her tiny one in his warm palm, and she'd looked up into the smiling face of the man she loved like a father, because he'd been that to her, even though all along he knew he was no such thing.

Strange how a former pirate should seem familiar to her in the same manner as her former father. But there was something uncannily gentlemanly about Jinan Seton, a manner that bespoke cultivation despite his ungentlemanly profession. Perhaps that was how he'd gotten his royal nickname. And his arrogance.

He seemed to be studying her, almost as though he were waiting for her reaction. As he did so, his gaze grew oddly intent, and warm, as in the corridor the day before.

"Whatever the case," she said, ignoring her tripping pulse,

"you know how common sailors can seek to inveigle their captains into doing what they wish despite the negative consequences."

His brow creased. "What sort of negative consequences—"

"Cap'n!" A shout came from the lookout. "Spar's loose off the foremast."

"Again," she muttered. "It'll have to be refitted when we dock at Trinidad." She began to make for the stair.

Seton put out a hand to stay her. "I'll see to it." His clear eyes did not question but looked once again carefully at her.

She nodded him on.

He saw to the dislodged yardarm. She watched as best she could between the full sails, impressed as always with his calm command of her men, their ready acceptance of his orders. Difficult task completed, he returned to her post at the helm as though she had called him back. Which she had not, although a demon in her had been wishing it for no apparent reason other than she liked to be goaded. Or simply merely to see him up close. At certain angles, the sight of him made her a little breathless.

At all angles. She couldn't ignore his lean physique she'd seen unclothed, his gorgeous mouth. If she were a regular woman, she would probably be falling all over him.

Her tetchiness redoubled.

"What do you want, Seton?"

"Further orders."

"No you don't. You want to annoy me."

"Seems like you are taking care of that well enough on your own." He folded his arms over his chest, and his perfect mouth tilted up at one corner. He wore only a waistcoat over his shirt, and the beauty of pure male muscle stretching the linen tight muddled her wits.

"It's the men." She admitted a partial truth. "Little more than a sennight out and they're eager to be back on shore."

"They have only recently returned from your last cruise. Perhaps you are a bit hard on them?"

"Well, I may be that after all." Not much of a retort. But it made his grin broaden slightly. Viola found herself seeking for more not-so-clever ripostes that might stretch that grin into an actual smile.

"You needn't deal with any of this." He seemed to speak slowly. "Ever again. You could cash in the *April Storm* and say good-bye to grumbling sailors and broken yardarms forever. If you wish."

She released a tight chuckle, struggling not to stare at his arms. But his crystalline eyes were compelling enough, a fall of dark hair shadowing them.

"Why would I wish a thing like that?" She made an effort at a scoff. "Sun getting to you, Seton?"

"Perhaps only your men's vain wishes."

Again with the brothel.

"The men don't need a stopover in Bermuda this week." She rushed the words because the sudden notion of his clear blue gaze fixed on her while she was wearing nothing but net stockings and lace wiped her mind clean of all else. "They need a golden beach under swaying palm trees three weeks from now."

For a moment he said nothing. Then, "And what do you need, Viola Carlyle?"

Her every muscle went still as stone.

"Your sister still believes you are alive, Miss Carlyle." His steady gaze did not waver. "I have searched you out and come here to bring you home."

Chapter 6

Viola's throat seized up entirely.

"I don't have a sister."

"You do, and she has been waiting for you to return for fifteen years."

"You're mistaking me for someone else."

His brow lowered. "Why haven't you?"

She twisted her lips to control her sudden quivers. "Mistaken—?"

"Returned home."

She had no response that she could share with this man. She'd barely even told her father as he lay dying, when finally after thirteen years he had asked her that same question.

"You could have returned to England at any time these past years. You have a ship of your own, and sufficient funds." Seton's regard remained constant. He had a way of doing that, holding her gaze as though he could wait an hour, a day, a fortnight for a reply.

Except in the corridor below three days earlier, when for a moment he had looked—strangely—impatient.

"I don't have sufficient funds for anything. Why do you think I work for rich American merchants?"

His gaze seemed to sharpen. "So you admit to being English."

"I admit to being born in England. But that doesn't make me who you say I am."

"You cannot deny it."

"I can. Do you have any proof?"

"I need no proof. You give yourself away every time you open your mouth."

She opened her mouth then snapped it shut. He leaned back against the rail, as though he had all day to pursue this conversation. Which he did. He had trapped her on her own ship in the middle of the Atlantic Ocean. Criminally clever, the Pharaoh.

"Your accent is nearly as flat as an American's," he said, "but inflections, certain vowels bespeak your origins." He ducked his head. "And you speak words no lowborn sailor would know."

"I don't."

"The first time I came aboard your ship you used the word *sobriquet*. A few moments ago you said *inveigle*."

"I read quite a bit."

"Why is that?"

"Why shouldn't I?"

"You should. You are the daughter of a gentleman. A nobleman—"

"Everyone knows my father was a smuggler."

"—and a lady."

That, she could not deny. Her mother had been born into a gentleman's family, well situated with a fine house and good lands. When Maria Harrell's father gave her to wed to the quiet, book-loving Baron of Carlyle in order to improve the social fortunes of the family, she'd been but seventeen, suitably dowered, very pretty, and already in love with Fionn Daly—a common sailor she should never have even met let alone given her heart to.

They had never fallen out of love. Four years later, in a blooming spring when Lord Carlyle was in town for the session and Lady Carlyle at home tending to her firstborn, the Irishman had sailed into port and . . . made Viola. Ten years after that, Fionn returned again to finally claim his love and his child. With disastrous consequences.

Viola held her tongue. Nothing she could say now would suffice, and her heart beat too swiftly to allow for measured speech. She slipped her gaze across the deck, at the sailors about. All loyal to her, most she'd known nearly her whole life. Her life. Her reality. *Not* that world she'd been born into that now seemed a million miles away plus an ocean.

But not all the men aboard belonged to her life. Big Mattie stood at the base of the mainmast, glowering over a young sailor at the lines. An intruder in her home. Like the other two sailors from the *Cavalier*. And Seton.

She pivoted to him. He was watching her carefully. She tried to brush off the sensation of being known by him. He did not know her. He knew only a name from another time.

"Do your men know?" she demanded.

"Your true identity?"

"My past."

"Only the three aboard this ship." His expression remained sober.

"And my men? Have you told them?"

"No."

"Why not?"

"Why should I have?" His brow was firm, his look honest. Unnervingly so.

She moved toward him swiftly, pulse racing, until she was as close as they'd stood belowdecks the day before. The gray sky framed his handsome face.

"Who are you?"

His clear gaze did not waver. "My identity has never been in question here."

"Why have you sought me out? What business is it of yours whether I return to England or not?"

"Your sister is lately wed. Her husband wishes you found."

Amid the tattering of thoughts and emotions, something sharp twisted inside her. He had come aboard her ship with gain in sight. But she had known that all along; it should not bother her now.

"You imagine that some stranger's wish is sufficient to drag me back to England against my will?"

"I do. But I prefer you to come willingly." He said it simply enough, but a glint of fierceness entered his eyes. Instinct told Viola to retreat. She did not. She could not show weakness. A man like this would use vulnerability to his advantage.

"Why can you not simply tell him—both of them—that you found me happy and hale, and leave it there? After all these years she must be satisfied with that." If she cared at all. Serena had not returned any of Viola's letters in those early years. Perhaps Serena had still loved her, but with Viola's parentage known, her elder sister must have been ashamed. And her poor father . . . Rather, the baron.

A hint of hardness flashed at the edges of Seton's beautiful mouth.

"Say her name."

Viola blinked. "Whose name?"

"Your sister's."

There was a fastness about his gaze now, a swift, assessing penetration that sought her insides and made them quiver.

At the fringes of her consciousness clung the remnants of memory again—of sunlit parlors scented with lavender and roses, of eyelet and lace and silks of pale pastels and ribbons of jewel tones threaded through hems and hair. Of the scent of dry, old wood and damp mossy cliffs, the dust of books in the library and polish on the banister, sweet polish, lemon and thyme. Of emerald fields dotted with fluffy white sheep and meadows of wildflowers. She saw a kind, wide-lipped smile and a pair of mismatched eyes surrounded by dark golden hair. Her sister, her fondest companion, her best friend, the girl with whom she had lived every single day of ten years of life and whom she still loved.

All this came to her with the mere thought of her sister's name and the unrelenting gaze of an Egyptian pirate.

Not only Egyptian. And no longer a pirate. A British privateer. Sent to seek *her* out? The illegitimate daughter of a smuggler and an adulterous woman now deceased?

"Who is my sister's husband?"

"The Earl of Savege, Lord Carlyle's close neighbor in Devonshire."

Viola's stomach twisted. It just got worse and worse. A nobleman? A *lord*? She must be glad for Serena, and wish for her happiness, and that it was a match her half sister liked. But there was no place there for her now, and she did not want it.

"He will be disappointed when you return without me, no doubt. But he has no authority over me, even if he is an earl."

"You will return with me."

"I will not." She broadened her stance and set her fists on her hips. The pose cut the edge from her agitation and made her feel nearly at home again. In her own place. A place that suited her.

"You belong there." He spoke as though certain.

She laughed, but it sounded forced. "I belong here aboard

my ship with my men. Accustom yourself to the idea, Seton."
She pivoted and strode to the stair and down, snapping commands as she went. But she felt his gaze on her, and inside
she was a welter of confusion.

If she belonged here on her ship with her men, why was
she so determined to settle down to life with Aidan Castle
on his farm in the tropics, even for part of the year? She
loved him, of course. She had loved him since he clerked
in that Boston merchant's office and her father brought him
home to dinner one night. The night Viola discovered her
woman's heart.

She'd been but fifteen, still hoping someday to return to
England but not knowing if it could be done. Her mother
was dead; without that tie, Viola was nothing to Charles
Carlyle. And Fionn always insisted she meant everything to
him. His only child. His best little sailor. And someday, he
hinted, Mrs. Aidan Castle.

He'd often left them alone. He loaned Aidan the funds
to help him purchase the farm, even when his ship barely
had sufficient canvas for sails. Clearly he regretted what
he'd taken from Viola, a life of stable respectability, and he
wanted better for her someday. He had seen better in Aidan
Castle, self-made man, born in England like Viola, cousin
to British gentry but now as American as Fionn. Like Viola.
Her father had provided her at a tender age with the perfect
match. And she had not disobliged him in falling in love.

Then why did the notion of meeting Aidan in mere weeks
no longer fill her with anticipation? She was no fool. He
hadn't written to her in ages. But when he saw her again
they would be as they were before, and he would ask her to
marry him, as he had hinted for so many years. She should
be happy.

Images of Seton standing so close in her cabin doorway
steered her away from that refuge. She descended instead

into the hold. Every crack in the wood, every sagging beam
and worn plank loomed in her vision as her feet met the
lowest deck. Stacked with barrels and crates and cloth-
wrapped furniture, it looked like a merchant ship. The sailor
guarding the powder magazine and his companion tipped
their caps. She nodded, scanning the cargo.

Why was she carrying mercantile goods to Trinidad? She
was a privateer, for pity's sake. She ought to be searching out
ne'er-do-wells, not carting flour across the Atlantic.

She breathed in the thick, close air and hated her unsettled
thoughts. Seton was to blame. Everything had been perfectly fine until he boarded her ship. She could make a stop
on Bermuda as the men wished, and put him ashore there.
She didn't need him to sail her ship for her.

She didn't need him for anything.

"Sam!"

The sailor chatting with the guard at the powder magazine
jumped to attention. "Cap'n?"

"Go tell Mr. Seton we will double our pace to Trinidad. I
want to make port in sixteen days."

"Aye aye, Cap'n." He leaped to the stair. Viola stared
blankly at the floor of her ship covered with another man's
property, and for the first time in her life felt trapped upon
the sea.

"Cap'n Jin?" Little Billy slopped a ladle of a runny stew into
a bowl and proffered it. "I been thinking."

Jin settled with the bowl at the tiny table at the edge of
the mess. The cabin that passed for a kitchen wasn't five feet
square, but it was one place he had never seen Viola Carlyle
on her ship.

He needn't make an effort to avoid her; she was seeing
to that well enough. For four days she had passed every
order to him through her sailors. His revelation had made an

impression on her. Now he only needed time to determine how to make that impression serve him. And to control his temper. Her foolish defiance still burned as though she had insulted him personally. He must dampen that anger before approaching her again.

He lifted a spoonful of stew. "Thinking about what, Bill?"

" 'Bout them rebel Scots we chased in the North Sea. And that boy we brung home afore that, from Spain."

Jin swallowed the flavorless goo and took another bite. Best to get it over with swiftly, as he should be dealing with Miss Viola Carlyle. But he had not counted on her outright refusal.

He should have. He realized that now.

"Have you?" he murmured.

"That's right, sir." Billy dropped a whole unpeeled potato into the pot and stirred. "Didn't see a lick of swag from them, though the gover'ment paid us all nice like. But I been wondering what we done them missions for."

For justice. To help those in desperate straits. To serve the crown. In service to the Falcon Club.

Nearly two years ago he had set aside the work of that exclusive club and set out to find a missing person whose family had long since presumed her dead. All but her sister. But Serena Savege did not know of his mission, nor did Alex. He had not told them.

"We did those missions because His Majesty asked it of us, Bill." The partial truth was better than none. Perhaps he should have given Viola Carlyle only the partial truth. Perhaps he still had leeway to invent another story, one that would convince her of the wisdom of his intention.

No. He had spent far too many years of his life embedded in lies. He would not begin that again now, especially not with a lady, no matter how hardheaded.

He swallowed the remainder of his stew and set the bowl on the counter.

"Enjoy the grub, sir?"

"No. But you are doing a fine job of pretending to cook." He patted him on the shoulder. "Thank you, Bill."

The lad's face broke into a toothy grin. "Welcome to it, Cap'n."

"Billy."

"Welcome to it, *Master* Jin." The lad winked.

Jin scanned the cannons and nodded to the sailors on the gun deck, then climbed the sagging companionway to the main deck. Atop, he halted. Beneath sails filled to capacity, Viola Carlyle sat at the forecastle surrounded by sailors and backed by a vibrantly blue sky and foam-tipped sea. Before her, a quartet of men stood in a perfect line, singing.

In the middle of the day. Flying at ten knots on a following sea.

Singing.

To her.

The song was unremarkable, a well-used chantey, though this time in impressive harmony. She obviously approved. She had pushed her hat back on her brow, revealing most of her face. She smiled, resting her gaze upon each singer in turn with appreciation, sun sparkling in her dark eyes.

For a moment, Jin could not move, restive heat tugging at him. In four days of barely glimpsing her he had simply not allowed himself to think about how pretty she was.

Clearly her men were thinking about it now. The gaze of each singer, and that of every other sailor sitting about her, was pinned to her. Nearly forty men sat rapt by their captain as the ship cut across low swells, bobbing forcefully yet nevertheless speeding on, apparently manned by ghosts.

The song came to an end, she lifted her hands to clap, and the sweetest, richest laughter came to him upon the wind.

Beautiful laughter, full of fresh delight and incautious pleasure. Sailors stomped their approval on the boards. But Jin
could hear only her.

Then her gaze shifted aft and came to him, and all sign of
her enjoyment died.

Jin's lungs tightened, his breaths thin. Even scowling, she
enticed. She allured as she threw out spikes and he wanted
to take her down beneath him and strip the displeasure from
her eyes and replace it with eager compliance.

Which he could not do. Not in the manner he wished.

She broke the gaze. He strode forward, the dispersing
sailors making way for him. The singers clouted each other
on the backs, offering congratulations and looking smug.
With sweet smiles and dulcet tones she doled out praise and
thanks, rousing blushes on swarthy cheeks. As they passed
Jin, he set them to tasks they should have already been
doing, and continued toward their captain.

"Jonah, do you recall that little problem I mentioned last
night that requires tending?" she said as he neared. The
sailor before her pulled off his cap like a lackey addressing
a lord and nodded eagerly.

"Sure do, Cap'n mum. The head's needin' unstopperin'."

"Yes." She offered a sympathetic tilt of her lips. "Things
are bound to get uncomfortable if we leave it plugged up for
long, aren't they?"

"Yes, mum! I'll set right to it in a jiffy." His head bobbed
on his skinny neck and he scampered away.

Jin stared at his back for a moment, then turned to the
woman who sent a man off to clean the refuse hole with a
happy grin. He gestured toward the forecastle.

"What was that about?"

Her brow lowered and she pushed her hat lower on it.
"Good day to you too," she muttered. "What's got your goat?
Or perhaps you're always this ill-tempered."

"Ill-tempered? This from a woman who insults me every occasion she can manage, then avoids me on all others?"

"I am not ill-tempered." Her gaze flickered. "At least I wasn't before you stepped on deck."

"What were those men doing? The wind is full in the sails. They ought to have been at the sheets holding her to a steady course, not singing like fools for your pleasure."

"The ship is running perfectly well," she snapped. "As you can see."

"And if the wind had changed abruptly, we would be capsized by now."

"But it didn't change and we are afloat," Viola snapped. He was correct. But for a moment enjoying the simple company of her men and a relief from her too constant thoughts of *this* man, she'd been perfectly happy. And thoroughly irresponsible. "Are you questioning my knowledge of my ship?"

"Only your handling of its crew. What sort of captain countenances a concert at full sail on a following sea?"

"A captain who knows much more about her sailors than apparently you do. No surprise." She moved to go around him and he stepped into her path. "Get out of my way, Seton, or I'll take the butt of my pistol to your head."

His voice lowered. "Do not threaten a man with beating who knows well how to give as good as he has gotten, Miss Carlyle."

Something had changed, and for the first time since this man with a reputation for unbridled violence had come aboard her ship, she was frightened. Not by threat of violence to her. She didn't believe he would harm her, not when he was calling her Miss Carlyle and intending to carry her back to her brother-in-law *the earl* in England. But the acute clarity had disappeared from his eyes, replaced by something quite different. Something heated and unsteady. On any other man she would think it uncertainty. Perhaps even confusion. On Jinan Seton—arrogant as the day was bright—it alarmed her.

Her hands went damp and cold, her belly contrarily hot.

She tried to shake it off. "If you call me that aboard my ship one more time, I will have you thrown over."

"If you continue to sail this ship as you are doing, we are all likely to take a swim together."

She eyed him narrowly, but it only increased the heat in her twisted belly. She crossed her arms.

"If you must know, it is my birthday. The singing was a gift."

He appeared nonplussed. "Your birthday."

"Yes. I am five-and-twenty. As of today I have achieved my majority. Even in England, no man has authority over me now."

"Is that what this is about?" He gestured toward the sailors. "Asserting your authority over men?"

"This is about sailing my vessel in the manner I see fit. Do you have a problem with that, sailor?"

"I do when you put all aboard in danger." He scanned her face, his enigmatic gaze by far the most dangerous thing aboard to Viola's unsettled senses. "You treat them like suitors."

"I treat them like family. For that they are to me." Her only family after her father stole her away from the one she had known.

"You flirt with them."

"I make difficult work seem appealing."

"And Jonah's fawning when you assigned him to clean the head just now? What was that, his sheer idiocy?"

"He is very loyal. He gladly does what his captain wishes, unlike some sailors who shall remain nameless although we both know exactly who I'm talking about."

He shook his head, his look incredulous. "And I suppose if you told Jonah to jump into the belly of a whale he would do it without hesitation."

"Very clever. I am really astoundingly impressed."

"What? Would you prefer classical references from the stories you read to them at bedtime like a nursemaid reads to her infant charges? No wonder they all make dog's eyes at you."

She was getting to him. She could see it in the tight sinews of his neck, the taut line of his jaw. She was making the cool, confident Pharaoh agitated, and the success swirled inside her like a dram of gin. Beneath his crystal gaze she did feel a bit drunk. A bit reckless. Like the girl she had once been.

"Jealous of their devotion, Seton? Perhaps if you read to them they would make dog eyes at you too." She waggled her brows.

"This is no way to captain a ship. These men are all half in love with you."

Her heart did an odd little jump, but she forced a shrug.

"If it works, who's to complain?" She allowed herself a taunting smile. "Is that why you're distressed that I've been avoiding you? Are you half in love with me too, then?"

"Good God." He scowled. "What do you take me for, a complete fool?"

"A man must be foolish to fall in love with me?"

"That, and nearsighted and bereft of the capacity for rational thought, not to mention in possession of a death wish."

That stung, and she didn't like that it stung. She struggled for a retort and words tumbled through her lips.

"I'll wager I can make you fall in love with me." Oh, *God*.

He cracked a hard laugh. "I dare you to try."

"Do you?" Her cursed tongue! "All right. What shall we wager?" The unbidden words just kept popping out. But there was something exciting about the idea, something dangerous and tempting that she should not feel.

His mouth actually hung open. But holy Magdalene, what a mouth. She could nearly taste him with her imagination, male heat and smooth command. Pity he was looking at her like an escapee from McLean Hospital. And of course, pity she couldn't stand him.

"You are mad," he said in wondering tones. "Aren't you?"

"I never back down from a dare. How do you think I got here? A mere woman?" She gestured aft to the quarterdeck.

"You are serious." His eyes narrowed. "You cannot be serious."

"Afraid I'll win?"

"Patently, no."

"Then let's agree to terms. If I win, I get your new ship."

"*No.*"

"And if you win, I will return to England with you."

He went perfectly still. Viola struggled to breathe evenly. She didn't know where her words had come from. She did not wish to return to England.

On the other hand, it might be worth it to watch him squirm while she hung all over him in an effort to seduce him. She would not meet with success. He had a heart of stone and a will of iron and he would win. But she could always turn right around and come home afterward. After seeing Serena. Her half sister. The countess.

Oh, good God, *what had she done?*

"The duration of the wager?" he finally asked.

"A fortnight."

"A *fortnight*?"

She lifted a brow. "Men have fallen in love with me in minutes before." Aidan always claimed he had.

He looked at her with clear disbelief. "I have no doubt that some men are equally as mad as you."

That was rather lowering. And more than a sting. It actually hurt.

Her ire flared. "Perhaps you are as well, pirate scum."

"Again with the insults. You are losing your moral high ground."

"My high ground is well enough. Will you take the wager?"

He studied her for a silent moment, his ice eyes enigmatic now. "Yes."

She found it a bit difficult to breathe. But she'd gotten herself into this. And she now would have to touch him, and feel the heat simmering beneath his skin again, as she had in the corridor. A touch that had left her sleeping fitfully every night since.

His eyes glimmered. "Regretting your impetuosity already, Miss Carlyle?"

Her pulse stumbled. "I said *do not call me that aboard my ship.*"

His perfect mouth slid up at one edge, and this time the grin was purely confident. "Name your terms."

Terms? He must speak to her with deference and allow her all sorts of liberties with his person.

Her cheeks flamed. His gaze shifted across them and the slightest crease appeared in his cheek.

"You must remain aboard at all times," she said in a rush, "even when we come into port, until the end of the fortnight, unless I disembark as well, and then you go with me where I go." Goddamn him for doing this to her, for making her tongue say things it should not and for being so arrogantly gorgeous she was quivering with anticipation.

"All right."

Beneath his steady gaze, her thoughts tangled. But she must see this through. Her pride was at stake. "If you disembark for any other reason, you forfeit the wager and I win automatically."

"And the corollary terms? If you throw me off, you forfeit the wager and I win?"

"Exactly." She would not. She had borne his unnerving presence for a fortnight already. But in his light eyes now was calculation. This was a foolish mistake. Her gaze dropped to his lips. A colossally foolish mistake.

"And at the end of the fortnight you must tell the truth," she added. "No lying about it just so you will win."

"Of course."

She thrust out her hand. "Agreed?"

He encompassed it, and her entire body got hot. His grip was strong and she wanted to feel that strength elsewhere. To feel his hands on her. She was a disloyal tart, daring a man to touch her while her heart belonged to another.

"At the end of the fortnight, Viola Carlyle, you will board my ship and sail to England with me." He spoke quietly and steadily, entirely unlike her shaking insides.

"At the end of the fortnight, Seton, you will regret that you ever came within a league of Violet Daly."

He released her and walked away, completely at ease, unaware of the shimmering air about him. She stood immobile, staring at his back until he descended belowdecks, cursing herself and him. She would make his life unendurable. With her attentions she would force him off her ship and he would leave her alone. Then she would take up with Aidan exactly where they'd left off last when he held her and told her she was the best thing that had ever happened to him.

But the notion of embracing Aidan again didn't speed her heartbeat now. Not Aidan at all.

Chapter 7

My lady,

My father, brother, and I are delighted with your latest pamphlet on the Despicable Conditions that Manchester textile workers are forced to endure. Your prose exhortations continue to inspire the people of Britain to seek justice.

With the most sincere apologies, however, I must beg you to remove The Mermaid from the office. Her size and State of Undress have caused discomfort to our clients and not an insubstantial Lack of Focus among the press operators. If you prefer, I will be most happy to arrange for her disposal.

Josiah Brittle

Brittle & Sons, Printers

Dear Mr. Brittle,

    I am terribly sorry for the inconvenience the statue has caused. Pray arrange for her Return to Sender to the following address: Mr. Peregrine, The Falcon Club, 14½ Dover Street, London.

    A siren belongs where she will wreak destruction most effectively—not on poor laborers but on the indolent rich who best deserve it.

Sincerely,
Lady Justice

Chapter 8

Viola Carlyle was shameless.

Overnight her prickly combativeness transformed into sloe-eyed glances and lowered lashes. Jin might be amused if she weren't so good at it. Convincing. As though she truly wished for his attentions. She enacted the role of a demure female throwing out lures like an actress trained for the stage, but with a great deal more finesse and the advantage of a pretty face and perfectly shaped body.

The body he was now able to fully appreciate again.

She discarded the sacklike coat, donning instead a fitted waistcoat that hugged her breasts and narrow waist and emphasized the delicacy of her form. The sash slung from shoulder to hip bore a single small pistol, the hilt of a short dagger pointing at an angle designed to draw a man's attention where it should not linger. The ungainly hat went too, replaced by a brimmed cap when she was atop and nothing when she was belowdecks. Her thick tresses, bound only in a queue as he had first seen on the dock weeks earlier, shone like satin in the sunshine and tangled in the wind, brushing across her lips.

She did not make the mistake of giving up her command to him. She maintained firm control over her ship and her crewmen's activities to a reasonable degree, leaving to Jin his regular duties. But now she proffered her commands without taunting or insults, instead with modulated tones that suggested she had every faith in him to carry out his responsibilities.

She was beguiling, gracious, and not in the least bit obsequious or overly retiring. She was damnably alluring, like a gently bred female withholding favors she would eagerly relinquish to a man worthy of her—but only that man.

She was a conniving, manipulative she-devil.

More than anything as yet, all of it went further toward convincing him that she belonged in English high society. Beauty and subtle flirtation combined with a quiet, confident mastery of her realm marked her as the aristocrat she was meant to be—her mother's daughter if not her father's.

But for two decades Jin had played games far more perilous. He knew how to handle this. He kept his distance.

She made it difficult. She began taking her meals with the men. When he was atop, she made it her business to be there as well. She clearly believed proximity was the key to her success. He found himself walking away from her more often than he liked. No man dictated his actions, and certainly no woman. Not for twenty years. But her nearness distracted him. Too much.

Following the clouds and high winds, then the single sunny day on which he had agreed to the wager, rain finally came. He was settling into his cabin preparing for bed when Becoua appeared.

"Clouds parted a bit, sir. There's a few stars showin'. Thought you'd like to know, seein' as the captain's asleep already."

"Thank you, Mr. Maalouf."

Becoua turned, then paused. "Master Jin, Captain's smelling of flowers lately, ain't she? Perfumey like?"

"I had not noticed."

Becoua met his gaze with a bemused question in his own.

Jin shook his head. "Back to work, sailor."

The boatswain grunted and shuffled off. Jin passed a hand across his face, then gripped the back of his neck. He must assess the ship's direction by the stars. It might not clear again for days.

She stored the sextant in her cabin.

She was there now. He had known it since she walked past his door earlier, trailing the scent of flowers mingled with rich herbs. She had indeed taken to wearing perfume, an East Indian attar of roses and golden champa. A heady, lush fragrance that mingled with her woman's scent and even at a few paces away seemed to reach out and touch a man precisely where he most needed it.

Blatant.

Shameless.

And it was having its effect. The rest of the ship smelled like sweat and unwashed men and its master smelled like a lady's boudoir. Jin now fully regretted eschewing the Boston brothels before embarking upon this journey. With her soft, dark-eyed glances and beguiling scent she had him hard, and hard put not to teach her a lesson in what it meant to tease a man who had gone too long without a woman.

If he was frustrated, her crew members must be as well. Becoua's confusion proved it.

Irresponsible she-devil. Or perhaps merely insane as he had first thought.

He went the few steps to her cabin door and knocked. It opened on a woman as unlike a shipmaster as could be. Her unbound hair fell about her face in waves like costly Russian mink. She wore only a thin white shirt, its laces untied and parted over the cleft of her breasts, and breeches. An open book rested in her palm.

Slowly, her wide, hazy eyes seemed to focus. Her lashes flickered, a rose veil suffused her cheeks, and for a moment she looked flustered. Then she lowered the book and offered him a feminine smile with a mile of calculation behind it.

"Calling so late, Mr. Seton. What a pleasure."

"Do you always answer the door to your sailors dressed like that?" He gestured to the creamy expanse of soft womanhood visible at her parted shirt, perfect swells of temptation.

He was.

Tempted.

One corner of her smile lifted. "Not at all. I was expecting you."

"You're more likely to drive me to jump ship with further insults and transparent bravado than with this."

"There are two ways I can win this wager."

"There are two ways I can as well." He leaned his shoulder against the doorjamb. "You will not endure my indifference for long. Your pride will get the better of you. You will throw me off the ship out of sheer vexation."

"That might be the case if you were actually indifferent." Her gaze slipped to his mouth where it lingered momentarily, then down his chest. Slowly, like a caress. And his body felt it. Like a caress.

She met his regard again. "But you aren't."

He crossed his arms with careful nonchalance and allowed himself to grin, but he knew why he was trapping his arms. His hands. "You would like to imagine so."

"The other day, standing in this corridor," she said softly, a seduction of sweet, rich femininity, "you wanted to kiss me."

"If I had wanted to kiss you, Viola Carlyle," he replied just as quietly, "I would have."

"You're lying."

He did not respond, merely regarded her as though she hadn't insulted him, a glint of pure confidence in his eyes. Viola's mouth was unbearably dry. She wanted a cup of wine in her hand and Jinan Seton out of her sight. This charade was unendurable. The more she was obliged to bat her lashes and stand close beside him on deck wearing considerably less than she usually wore to bed, the more difficult it was to convince herself it was all an act. She had answered the door in her present state of undress because she'd been attempting to read a book she loved as a girl, and instead spent the time imagining how it would feel if he were to put his lips on hers.

"What are you reading?" He asked it as though it were the most natural thing in the world.

"A book," she snapped, his perfect, breathtaking mouth and arms and everything far too close. "Is this conversation you're attempting to make?"

"Ah. The return of the shrew." He grinned, sending her belly into tingling somersaults. "I may leap overboard yet."

"I can only hope."

He had the audacity to chuckle. "Come to think of it, I prefer this attitude to the other. I appreciate honesty in a sailor."

"Don't you mean in a woman?"

His eyes seemed to shadow. "In anyone."

But those words were not his thoughts; she saw it in his face and knew beyond doubt that this man had been betrayed by a woman and it had wounded him.

Abruptly beset by a most pressing urge, then Viola did a very foolish thing. She reached forward and placed her hand on his chest and heard herself murmur, "I am always honest." She was in this. Despite herself she wished to be near him, and to touch him.

Beneath her palm his chest rose and fell sharply, but his voice remained even.

"You are playacting a role that neither of us is enjoying. Put an end to this wager. It is childish and you know you will lose."

But she didn't feel like a child. The way he looked at her with such crystal intensity even as he remained aloof made her feel very much like a woman. She should remove her hand from his body. Beneath fine linen—far too fine for a common sailor—he was all contoured muscle.

"What if I don't care to lose?" Her fingers spread and she felt him, his heartbeat and heat, and a soft tension gathered in her. She traced a fingertip to the laces of his shirt and with the smallest movement stroked the linen open.

Skin. Male skin beneath her touch, firm and hot. She pushed the fabric aside, baring hard collarbone and sun-darkened man. Her breaths stuttered. "And if I'm enjoying the wager itself?"

He caught her wrist in a strong grip and slid her hand fully beneath his shirt.

The air sank from her lungs. For a moment he simply held her there, her palm pressed to his skin over his flat nipple. Then he leaned forward, bent his head, and spoke low.

"You needn't strap me to a mast in order to undress me, Miss Carlyle. I am more than happy to oblige you at any time."

"Are you?" Dear Mother Mary, he must feel her trembling. She wanted to sink her fingers into him, to order him to oblige immediately. Oh, God, she really wanted to feel him—*more*. And to feel more of this strange, delicious quickening inside her. She'd never felt it before. Not for any man. Except Aidan, of course. Possibly. Or perhaps not.

What was happening to her?

He whispered at her brow, "Say the word, Captain."

She stilled. In the close space she could draw into her senses his man's scent. He smelled so good, intoxicating and familiar and warm. "You do realize you just called me captain?"

The pad of his thumb slipped over the tender center of her wrist.

"I did." There was a rumble of laughter in his voice. "Fancy that. Must be because I am awaiting an order."

If she turned her head, their lips would meet. She wanted it more than pride and reason. More than Aidan.

"Why don't you tell me first what brought you to my cabin door tonight."

His hand loosened, slipped along her arm, and with a gentleness she never imagined he possessed, he disengaged her from his body.

"The sextant."

She blinked, knowing her cheeks were flushed, and knowing from the clear certainty in his eyes that he knew he had affected her.

"Well, you might have said that before." She turned into her cabin, hiding her burning cheeks, and set down her book to take up the navigation instrument.

"It amused me to tease you," he said as she came to him again.

"I'm certain it did." She lifted a brow, pretending she wasn't perfectly aware that he was perfectly aware of the truth, and pretending the truth simply was not the truth— that for a moment in his hold she'd been a puddle and might still be if he hadn't released her. "The clouds have cleared?"

"Some." He accepted the sextant and glanced at the table she'd set the book on. "You are reading Herodotus."

It was not a question. A statement, rather, without inflection, but there was some hint of surprise in it. He brought his gaze to hers, and the hot, throbbing tingles started all over again.

"A history based on his." She wished her shirt were laced to the throat. She wished she had on her canvas coat buttoned to her chin. She wished she were anywhere but beneath this man's clear eyes. She wasn't made for this sort of confusion, wanting to touch him though she loved another. "Do you know Herodotus's history?"

He nodded, his brow still taut.

"Well," she said as evenly as she could manage, "then there's something we have in common other than this wager. How remarkable." She forced what she hoped was a demure smile onto her lips.

He lifted the sextant in a gesture. "Thank you." He turned and moved away. Viola stared at his back until he disappeared into the dark of the gun deck.

Fionn always told her she was too headstrong. With a twinkle in his eyes and a smile, the baron had called her reckless. In this, both of her fathers had been right.

"What d'you think?" Mattie leaned his thick elbows on the rail and scratched his whiskered jaw. The sea stretching beyond was dark and tipped with whitecaps, the sky leaden, the wind briny and damp.

Jin lifted the telescope and studied the vessel on the gray horizon. From its movement, erratic and slow, it was surely adrift. Its sails were furled, one mast split to the deck, and an unfamiliar banner of red and white flapped in the wind. A square-rigged brig not unlike the *April Storm*, but much larger and heavy in the draft. A stranded merchant ship not entirely stripped of her cargo. Pirate prey, or not?

"We cannot take the chance," he said quietly.

"Becoua!" The master of the *April Storm* shouted from

the quarterdeck, her voice beguiling even at full volume. "Make a course for her, slow and steady."

Beguiling, like her half-bared breasts and wide, questioning eyes, and slender hand exploring his skin.

He turned and from midship met her gaze. He must convince her to leave the alien vessel alone. But that would require private conversation. After the incident at her cabin door, he was honest enough with himself to admit that getting close to her again would not be wise. For three days he had avoided it.

She had kept her distance as well. Which suggested to him that it might be useful to alter course in his pursuit of Viola Carlyle's return to England. He might achieve his goal through another method.

She was not immune to him. In the lamp-lit doorway as she touched him, he had watched her body respond. If she had known it, seen the taut linen over the risen peaks of her breasts, she might not have recovered her bravado so swiftly.

But perhaps she had known it.

She captained a ship like a man, read books university-educated gentlemen read, yet was the most damnably enticing woman Jin had known. In that doorway, with her eyes sparkling in the golden light and her soft lips smiling, he had nearly done what he knew he should not. But perhaps that would be a quicker route to getting her home. A woman under the influence of desire often did whatever the man she desired wished. He had learned this early in life, from his mother's behavior with his father. Later he had occasionally used that lesson to his advantage.

He did not wish to lie to Viola Carlyle. She was not what she appeared on the surface, not what she wished others to see. For a moment in that doorway, he had seen something quite different in her dark eyes. Vulnerability. And confusion about her desire.

If he were so inclined, he could take advantage of that. But he was no longer that man. He would rather she came without lies.

"You ain't gonna convince her."

Jin's head swung around.

Mattie screwed up his lips. "She ain't gonna listen if you tell her not to sidle up to that boat."

"Then perhaps you should tell her. She likes you, I have noticed."

Mattie guffawed, his cheeks shading crimson. Jin shook his head and returned his gaze to the horizon.

By the time they were within a half league of the vessel he could no longer delay. Setting his shoulders, he went to her post at the quarterdeck.

"This is unwise." He scanned the sea anew.

"I didn't ask for your opinion."

"It is my duty to offer it when I see the necessity."

"What necessity? She's obviously abandoned. We have nothing to fear."

"It could be deception. To lure you."

She cast him a glance, tilting her brows high. "Oh? A tactic you know? Practiced in your pirating days, no doubt." Her tone remained perfectly sweet and her thick lashes dipped over wide dark eyes. He had to grin. The combination of insulting harpy and demure temptress suited her.

Her lashes flickered again, then she snapped her gaze away. He followed her averted face, unable not to. Here was innocence and allure wrapped in sailor's swagger, and he was a fool not to have seen this danger the moment he encountered her on the dock in Boston. In twenty years he had not stood on a ship's deck and felt his heartbeat quicken. Now it did.

"If you wish to make Trinidad within a sennight," he said, a roughness to his voice he did not intend, "you will be well served to sail on. It is the safer course."

She set her fists on her hips. "What is it? I can't believe the Pharaoh is concerned over the possibility of a little skirmish, so it must be something else." She held her attention to the horizon. She lowered her voice. "Afraid I'll die and you'll lose your prize to carry back to the earl?"

"Yes."

The wind whipped her hair about her cheeks and she brushed it away.

"Well, that is a possibility you will simply be obliged to live with."

"I cannot."

Her hands slipped from her hips and her slender shoulders dipped. Without a word she walked away.

The strange vessel's crew had clearly tried to give fight. Canvas hung torn from the spars and shredded on the deck, black powder marks and cannon shot wounds gaping in the main deck and rails. Most telling, the foremast was snapped, leaning out over the bow at a sickening tilt. Four crumpled bodies littered the deck, too few men to mark it as anything but a merchant vessel, sailors sufficient only to keep her on course. If there were no others below, the rest of the crew might have been pressed into service. Better living the life of a pirate until the next port than dying on the spot. Jin had seen plenty of sailors make that choice.

"Rum business," Mattie grunted as he came alongside him at the rail. "What's she gonna do?" He gestured with a jerk of his meaty jowl toward Viola standing amidships below, calling out orders to her crewmen to maneuver their approach.

"Go over there and invite them to tea, no doubt." Jin took a deep breath and descended to the main deck. He went to her side. "Don't do it."

"Be silent, Seton, or I will relieve you of duty."

"You hired me for this purpose."

"I hired you under false pretenses. Gui, fetch my sword! Sam, Frenchie, lower the boat. Then both of you and Stew, Gabe, and Ayo come with me."

Sailors were gathering at the rail, peering onto the other ship's deck.

"Then allow me," Jin said quietly.

"I said be silent."

"A captain should remain with her ship."

"And leave all the fun to others?"

"Fun? There are dead men on that deck."

She glanced down at the boy. He proffered her a thick-bladed cutlass and she strapped it to her belt. "You stay here, Gui."

The cabin boy scowled and glowered nearly as convincingly as Mattie. She ruffled his hair, then loosened the strap of the pistol on her sash. "Men, secure the sheets and lower the boat."

Jin kept his voice low amid the bustle. "What sort of sailor puts her life at risk simply to amuse herself?"

"You're starting to sound like my old nurse."

"Perhaps because you are behaving like a rash child who knows not what is best for her."

She turned to him fully then, pure determination in her eyes.

"I got along well enough on the sea for fifteen years without you, Jinan Seton. I've no doubt I will get along for at least another fifteen in the same manner." She pushed through her crewmen toward the gangway.

He followed, cursing under his breath. She made it to the ladder first and swung down it to the boat below, perfectly agile. The boat rocked on the striated swells, sailors set oars to water, and they headed toward the immobile ship. They neared and Sam tossed up a hooked rope. Jin grabbed it first, secured it and went up, then threw the ladder down.

She climbed aboard and stopped middeck, surveying the scene.

"Damned pirates," she muttered.

Jin moved to a prone figure and knelt. Dried blood matted the man's hair and stained his shirtfront burned with pistol fire, and blood caked the blade of the sword trapped in his waxy grip. He straightened. "Three days at most. No carrion birds as yet."

"Too far from land." She crossed herself, her lips moving in a silent prayer, then said aloud, "No one is looking for them."

"Don't be a fool." Prickling heat stroked at his shoulders. "Someone is always looking."

"Why didn't they scuttle her or take her for parts?"

"Because they are hiding below until the ideal moment when they will spring forth and kill us all and seize your ship? Just a guess."

"Coward."

He simply stared at her.

She grinned. Unremarkably, and despite circumstances, it went straight to his groin. She was, apparently, quite fearless. And quite beautiful when she smiled with impish challenge.

"Boys," her rich alto cajoled her men, "who wants to go below with me and see what these poor souls were cooking for dinner before the good Lord took them to fairer fields?"

Jin moved toward the companionway, the others remaining motionless—wisely. She came behind him.

"Not too skittish to take a peek now, hm, Seton?" She was right at his back, their footsteps echoing into the deck below.

"Call me a coward again, Miss Carlyle, and I will shoot you myself and endure the earl's chastisements."

She laughed, a full-throated, musical chortle. She was brazen, he must give her that. And entirely unafraid.

Ducking their heads, they came onto the gun deck. The air in the narrow space was oppressively close, the gunwales shut tight, and no sign of the cannons having been fired. No bodies were anywhere in sight here, but a stack of empty cages gaped open at the base of the bowsprit.

"They took the live animals but not all the cargo, and none of the rigging or canvas. Not even the water."

He nodded. "In a hurry. Moving on to another goal, perhaps."

"Then you don't believe any longer that they're waiting to jump out at us like ghouls? I am so sorry for your disappointment."

A grin tugged at his lips. "Perhaps I will have to kill you myself after all."

"You try it." She swung around the rail and continued down into the hold. Jin found himself following again.

"Not interested in checking the master's cabin?"

"Don't need to. He was on deck."

"How do you know that?"

"I knew him."

Forcing his gaze away from the fall of satin hair down her back, he scanned the broad space only half-filled with barrels and canvas sacks, some broken open and their contents scattered. No humans here, either. "Who was he?"

"Jason Pettigrew. A friend of my father." She set her fists on her hips. "Fionn captained a brig for him—not this one— right before the war. Jason always said—" She broke off and lines appeared between her eyes.

"Were you aboard that ship?" he said to encourage her to continue.

"Fionn nearly always took me along."

"From the beginning?"

"Yes. Is this an interview, Seton? Should I sit and narrate my life for you here? Or perhaps you could simply read my diaries, although you would no doubt find them too tame for your tastes."

"I suspect they would be as fascinating as their author."

Her gaze snapped to him. But there was no scowl on her face, only a bright-eyed wariness. She pivoted and sprang up the steps.

He climbed up behind her, tracing the curve of her hips with his gaze. "Shall I have the men transfer the cargo?"

"Only the fresh water. We've sufficient supplies."

"And the bodies?"

She cast him a quick glance, surprise in the violet. He held her gaze evenly. If she wished to believe him inhumane, at one time she would not have been far off the mark.

"Tell the boys to cut the canvas and line from this ship to wrap them. We'll bury them at dusk."

"Aye aye."

She unstrapped her pistol and cutlass and handed them to Sam. Then she unbuttoned her waistcoat and kicked off her shoes. She went to the rail, testing the draw of the dagger in her sash.

Jin frowned. "What are you doing?"

With a half grin that sent heat straight to his groin, she dove into the sea below.

Chapter 9

J in lunged forward to grab her, but too late, clutching the rail as she disappeared beneath the gray water.

"*What in the blazes—*"

"Cap'n's got a bee in her bonnet, sir, no doubt 'bout that," Sam said.

"A *bee*?" His head spun, heart racing. Panic sluiced over him like the waves that had swallowed Viola Carlyle. His gaze pinned the ocean. "What is she doing?"

"Dunno, sir. Must be somethin' she's lookin' for. But she's got powerful big lungs."

"To the boat." He grabbed the ladder.

They were the longest moments he ever lived, including those he had spent bound in iron manacles to the floor of a slaving ship as it crossed the deep Atlantic twenty-two years ago. Two minutes passed. More. He dragged off his coat, readying to dive. Viola's head bobbed above the sea's frothy surface, and he pulled in hard breaths.

She swam to the boat, arms cutting above the shifting foam, hair plastered about her head. Not only hair—a rope, caked with blackish sea vegetation that clung to her cheeks, held between her teeth like a bit.

He leaned over the side of the boat and grabbed her, Mr. French on the other side, and in a splashing rush they hauled her aboard. She shed water, gaining her bearings, but Jin did not release his grasp. Pulling the rope from her mouth she swung the object tied to its end around from her back, leaving trails of green slime across her face, neck and the white shirt plastered to her body. Her visibly cold body.

He wrapped her in his coat.

"What ya got thar, Cap'n?"

"A treasure, of course, Ayo."

Viola grinned at the sailor, waiting for the storm to break at her side. Seton's hand gripped her arm like a vise. He dragged her to a bench, released her, and her sailors set oars to water. She was glad for their haste, and for his coat. The sea was unforgiving today. She was accustomed to lengthy dives, but she'd been under this time longer than she should. Her teeth made little clicking sounds in her muzzled head.

He didn't speak or look at her. Settling the small box she'd retrieved from the bottom of the merchant ship on her lap, she flickered a glance at him. A muscle worked in his jaw. She closed her eyes.

In a moment, it seemed, they were at her ship and she was climbing, sodden and cold, to the deck. Behind her Seton gave orders for the men to transfer the merchantman's stores of water to the *April Storm*. She moved toward the stairway. He followed but said nothing until they'd moved beyond the sailors clustered about the main deck. She put her foot on the first step and finally he spoke, but in an even, steady voice.

"Pettigrew once told you of that box, I presume."

She swung down the steps, clutching her hard-won prize

tighter. She'd lost her dagger when the final nail binding the box to the hull popped abruptly and the hilt slipped out of her numb hand.

"Obviously."

"Its contents must be very valuable." He followed her aft toward her cabin, but his calm tone did not deceive her. "I know something of such prizes. Innocuous containers with valuable contents. I know how one might take foolish chances in order to retrieve such an object." An edge cut his voice now.

"It was not so foolish. I have stayed below for longer."

"Sam mentioned that." He was right behind her. He reached forward and pushed the door of her cabin open, surrounding her for an instant. She ducked out from beneath his arm and moved to the washstand. He entered behind her. "Nevertheless, it was unwise, taking that chance."

"Not much of a chance." She swiped a cloth across her cheeks and brow, smelling the thick brine of the sea. "I knew what I was looking for and retrieved it quickly. My men know—"

He grabbed her shoulder and spun her around.

"I am not one of your men and I did not know that you are likely to hurl yourself into a rough sea." His crystal eyes glittered in the pale light, fingertips digging into her flesh.

She shrugged out of his hold, her skin hot where he'd touched her.

"You sound like a hen-wife, Seton. Go nag someone else."

His gaze, intense and hard, scanned her face. But there was something else in the blue, something seeking. Quite abruptly her knees weakened.

Her knees weakened?

She clutched the washstand. "Go away."

"Goddamn it." His voice was low. "You behave as though possessed sometimes."

"Possessed by the rapidly increasing regret that I signed you on?"

"What is in the box, Viola?"

Viola. Only *Viola*. Not Miss Carlyle. Not Captain.

The air petered out of her lungs. Perhaps she was insane. At the very least, a fool. The mere sound of only her given name upon his lips, that simple familiarity, turned the remainder of her joints liquid. No man had called her by her real name in fifteen years. Not even her father.

"A letter."

"What letter?"

"If I knew that, would I have swum under the belly of a ship in a freezing ocean to get it?"

"*Viola.*"

"A letter to his wife and children." She shrugged. "Nothing, really. He'd told me he always nailed a box to the underside of his ship whenever he was making ready to set off on a journey. That way if brigands took his boat and threw him overboard someone might someday find the letter and send it to his family. As a final good-bye of sorts."

His chest jerked in a sharp inhalation but he said nothing.

"I told him that was the most ridiculous thing I'd ever heard." She waved it off, but her motion was unnatural. "What pirates would send a letter to the wife of the man they killed? And there was every chance it might end up at the bottom of the sea, in any case, or just rot away no matter how finely soldered the box. But he said that if there was even one small chance it might reach . . ." Her voice faltered beneath his regard and she was shaking now, soaked to the bone. "I mean to say, it didn't seem very logical for him to . . ."

His lips parted as though he might speak, but still he did not.

"Why are you looking at me like that?" she snapped.

"You risked your life to retrieve a dead man's last letter to his family?"

"I already told you there was no risk in—"

He grabbed her shoulders and pulled her close, knocking a gasp from her. He bent his head, his breath filtering over her chilled skin. She fought not to close her eyes, not to wish for what she was wishing.

"Going to bite my nose again like a ten-year-old, Seton?" Her voice quavered.

"No."

At that moment Viola discovered that the perfect mouth felt even more perfect than it looked. He kissed her, and quite abruptly the question of whether she would allow it became instead how long she could make it last.

It was not a short or simple kiss. Not from the moment it began. They met, fully, and they held, immobile. Far too long. Far too close. Far too intimate. Far too much like he might have been wanting to kiss her as much as she had been wanting to kiss him and now if they were to move or part even slightly the reality of it might scamper away. As though he were imprinting the feel of her upon him. Aidan had never kissed her like this. Aidan kissed her like he could step away at any moment, like kissing her was something he bestowed upon her as a favor and he might cease easily enough.

This was different. This was possession. It was relief and certainty at once. It was a need to be close and remain so for as long as possible without breathing. To underscore the impossible intimacy of it, his hand scooped behind her head and held her still, attached to his mouth, where she was quite willing to remain in any case and he needn't bother trapping her. But so help her God she liked being trapped. He was heat and strength and she needn't ever breathe again if he would not release her.

He did finally, but only to drag in air as she did, then cover her mouth again with his.

Now it became clear that this was not only a man who could dazzle a girl into suffocation. He was also a man with an impressive knowledge of what sort of kiss turned a woman to pure desire. In an instant, unsettling intimacy gave way to drugging sensuality.

He tasted her, it seemed, his attention first on her lower lip and the tender inside edge of it, then the upper edge, and she got hot everywhere. She opened her lips and let him have her. Tilting her head back, he played with her hunger, unbearably, caressing slowly until she was leaning up into him for more. She pressed onto her tiptoes. With the tip of his tongue he traced her lips, urging them apart with the lightest caress. Her body flushed with pleasure.

Like some sort of desperate cat, she whimpered.

His fingers sank into her hair and his tongue slid alongside hers, testing. The ache spread, throbbing as he kissed her with this intimacy beyond intimacy, dipping into her so she could feel him inside her and making her tremble. She grabbed his wrist, the taut sinews of a man, his strength holding her and she wanted to feel him holding her all over. Her skin sought it. His hand slid down her neck, and Viola's blood turned to fire.

He lifted his mouth. For a moment he hovered there, both of them breathing fast.

"There." His voice was low. "That shut up that mouth for a minute."

"More than a minute." She swallowed around the anchor apparently lodged in her throat. "Surely." His hand was hot heaven on her neck. He seemed very large. She had always been short, but for the first time in her life she felt delicate too. Like a lady.

But a lady would not ache to dart her tongue out and lick

his lips, even if she could summon the courage, which Viola could not despite the perfection of that damp mouth so close to hers.

It curved up at one side. His hands fell away from her, he lifted his head, and Viola stood wet and warmed only by his coat as he crossed the small cabin and went out, shutting the door behind him.

She leaned back, her knees gave way against a chair, and she sank onto her behind. She ought to be furious. She ought to have scratched out his eyes. Instead she had allowed him to kiss her without the slightest bit of resistance.

But she had not kissed a man in a very long time. Of course she hadn't resisted.

The next time, she would.

There would not be another kiss. It had been a mistake. Jin's brain knew it even if his perpetually aroused body did not. She tasted sweet and hot and like a woman who needed kissing. Like a woman who needed a great deal more than kissing.

But he should not have done it. The plan of winning her agreement to return to England through seduction was not realistic. He could not control her desire if he could not first control his own—which he now knew he could not do while touching her hair and face and body. Wet and bedraggled from her swim, and rushing to justify her foolish behavior in stuttering fits, she had set her dark liquid gaze upon him and he felt her desire in his gut. In his *chest*. He'd had to kiss her. He only managed to leave it at a kiss by reminding himself that despite all appearances to the contrary she was a lady.

He was not a gentleman. He was the bastard son of a woman who had cared for him so little that she allowed him to be sold into slavery. He was a man who had done evil deeds in cold blood that had nothing of honor about them.

He was not a man to be enjoying the touch of a woman of aristocratic blood, no matter how she denied her birthright or how eagerly she responded to him. And he was the man who was taking her home to England whether she wished it or not.

But neither was he a man of regret. He simply would not allow himself to make the mistake of coming too close to her again.

To that end, he steered clear of her. She obliged. It was remarkable how on a modest-sized ship they managed to successfully avoid each other. It would not be possible on his own considerably smaller vessel when they sailed east. But he would deal with that when the time came.

They skirted Barbados, catching sight only of an American naval frigate, then losing it in the rain that began falling heavily, and Jin counted each day closer to port. The downpour lasted twenty hours, soaking the sheets and canvas and all aboard while the wind remained high, driving them west. The men barely grumbled, trained to constant good humor by their mistress. Like dogs. Even Matouba climbed down from the crow's nest drenched yet with a smile for his captain as he lumbered below.

But rain was not storm, and Jin must be content with their progress.

The night before they were to make port, the rain let up entirely, clearing on a swift northerly wind. He took the chart to the bow and settled on the forecastle to study it at his leisure. But he knew these islands already, their inlets and beaches and mountains. He had spent most of his youth sailing between them, picking up work where he could, stealing it where he could not.

Sixteen hours and they would be in port. Two days after that the fortnight would be over, and he would return Viola Carlyle to the home in which she belonged. To her family.

Her footsteps sounded on the deck behind him, approaching. She moved with a confidence her men did not possess, and he knew her by her tread and the scent of spiced flowers coming before her on the wind. He knew her satin voice and the flavor of her mouth and the texture of her skin at the delicate curve of her throat. He knew her stubborn determination and the reluctant flicker of uncertainty in her violet eyes. He knew her more than he wished to.

He turned his head, met her unshrinking gaze, and feared that two days and sixteen hours might prove an eternity.

Chapter 10

Avoiding him had not served the purpose she hoped. He was as gorgeous as he had been four days earlier when in her cabin he kissed her into a rag doll. The slant of the setting sun rendered his face and hands dark and set him before a curtain of cobalt fading to lavender. It was not a sight conducive to steady nerves.

She sucked in a breath and poked her fists into her hips. "I don't want you to kiss me again."

His brow tilted up, a look of tolerant endurance settling on his handsome features.

"Don't look at me like you don't know what I am talking about."

"I have no intention of kissing you again."

"I don't think you had any intention of kissing me the other day either, but you did it anyway."

He chuckled, shaking his head. "You cannot refrain from quarreling—about anything—can you?"

She had intended a more seductive approach, along the lines of flirtatiously refusing him her favors so he would grow desperate for them and declare himself in order to have her, and thus she would win the wager. Her quartermaster, Crazy, had once told her that it drove a man wild when a woman he desired would not kiss him or cuddle with him. He'd said at those times he would have promised anything, *said* anything to his wife, even things he didn't mean, merely to encourage her to touch him.

But Seton didn't look desperate. At best, he seemed mildly amused. This was not going as she'd planned. Neither of them was following the script.

She pursed her lips. "I don't argue when I agree with someone, which I never do with you, so you are unlikely to witness my compliance."

The golden light of the fading sun glimmered in his eyes. Viola's throat dried to the texture of a ship's biscuit. He had witnessed her compliance quite well. He had taken part in it.

"Have you business you wish to discuss?" he asked with maddening calm. "Ship's business, that is?"

"After we drop anchor in the harbor and unload, you and I will head along the coast to a farm not far away."

"For what purpose?"

"To pay a call on a man my father used to do business with. An old friend."

"I can remain with the ship." Until the fortnight of the wager was out, he meant. But she wasn't about to lose, and she had an ace up her sleeve: Aidan Castle. That, Crazy had told her, was another certain method for making a man mad with desire. Present him with competition.

"You'll come with me," she said. "Bring Mattie along, if you like. For protection." She grinned and lifted a single brow. But she did not receive the reaction she expected. Instead of denial or cool indifference, his gaze remained steady upon her and rather warm.

"I do not need protection from you, Viola Carlyle."

"Our first three weeks out I didn't see you atop for one sunset," she replied, "and yet here you have been five evenings running now, since you kissed me. It can only be because you like to see me." She cocked her head. "Certain you don't need protection from me, after all?"

"Why aren't you at the helm? That is where you like to be at dusk, is it not?"

"Trying too hard to get rid of me now. That's interesting."

"If you say so." His mouth tilted up at one edge and for a moment the sinking sun seemed to flare upon the horizon, shooting sparks into the darkening sky above.

This was strange, knowing one another's habits as sailors on the same vessel always did, yet not really knowing anything of him in truth. Most of her crewmen confided in her, seeing in her a sister or daughter, even a mother. But this man kept his own counsel. The Pharaoh, she suspected, needed no confidant. The cut of his jaw and cast of his features, the manner in which he held himself, square-shouldered and in command—these bespoke a man of thorough independence.

She knew nothing of Jinan Seton except that his rare smile . . . made her see stars.

She saw stars when he smiled.

Stars.

She blinked it away.

"My first few years aboard ship, it was the only time of day Fionn allowed me up there." She lowered herself to the bowsprit, her behind settling onto the beam's curve. He watched without expression. But it was her ship and she could sit where she wished. And she wished to sit with him in the sunset.

It seemed natural.

And perhaps if she sat here long enough, he would smile again.

"I have very fond memories of that time," she added.

"They are not your only fond memories." It was not a question.

She shook her head. "No. I have plenty. But . . ."

He waited, as he always did. He was good at being silent and listening. She had never been, not from her girlhood. The quiet, dreaming daughter had been Serena, a perfect complement to Viola's madcap energy.

She looked off to the glistening horizon.

"Dusk is special." She liked to be atop at dusk, for then the sunset shivered through her and made her feel weak with lonely longing. It was the time of day that seemed least safe, when no matter which direction the *April*'s bow pointed there seemed no secure port in the sightings, no home ahead. At dusk Viola could stand upon her quarterdeck and feel weightless and directionless beneath the changing sky, as though she might fly away at any moment, or simply disappear into the colors above, swept away with the winds. She imagined at those moments that only her grip on the helm bound her to the deck. To reality.

It was nonsensical. And it was the way Jinan Seton made her feel.

She could admit this to herself now looking into his eyes glimmering with the twilight. Since the moment she'd met him weeks earlier, a sliver of that lonely longing had threaded through her and remained. And she fed it because she loved the feeling. He made her feel like longing was something to be wished for, something to be enjoyed, as she always secretly had.

"What about you, Seton?" She leaned back onto her hands. "What are your fond memories of childhood?"

His gaze slipped over her body leisurely, laying tendrils of heat beneath the surface of her skin. Then he looked into her eyes.

"I suppose that standing beside the auctioneer's block while the boy who purchased me unlatched the irons from my wrists and gave me freedom must rank as my best childhood memory, Miss Carlyle."

For a long moment she could not draw air into her lungs properly.

"I suppose it would," she finally said. After another minute during which lines creaked in blocks and sailors' voices at the other end of the ship came along the breeze, she said, "Did you know your family?"

"My mother."

"Only your mother?"

"She watched her husband sell me to the traders. He had noticed that the boy who ran about the servants' quarters looked a bit too much like his wife and an Englishman who had lived in Alexandria seven years earlier. He beat the truth out of her, then he punished her for her infidelity. And me."

"Barbary pirates." Sea bandits who would sell anyone into slavery for a price. Even a boy with white skin. But then to be brought *west* to be sold at an English market—that was unheard of. Someone had paid the slaver richly to make it so.

He regarded her with unreadable eyes. "So you see, Miss Carlyle, our stories are somewhat similar. But given the principal difference, perhaps you understand now how I am less than sympathetic to your reticence to return to England."

Her heartbeats came thick in her chest. "One has nothing to do with the other." The wind snatched up her hair and whipped it between her lips but she felt frozen and could not lift a hand to dislodge it.

"You owe it to your family to tell them you are well."

Prickling heat swiped at her insides, driving her tongue. "Did you tell your mother when you were sailing around robbing other people's ships?"

"By the time I was able to return to Alexandria, she was dead."

She stood up. "They needn't hear it from me. You could tell them. Indeed, you will be obliged to because I am not going with you."

"Why not?" He remained still.

"I don't belong there," she blurted out. "I am going where I belong now, and no one can force me to do otherwise." But that was perhaps a lie, because looking into his crystalline eyes she feared greatly that she would do as he bid when the time came. She should not have asked him about his past. The longing rushed inside her now like a bow cutting through water at full sail, clogging her throat and making her feel filled up in a manner she did not like. He was not what she wanted—a man who did not need anyone. She wanted Aidan Castle, who always told her how good she was for him.

Seton said nothing now, as he always did precisely when she most needed him to say something that could derail her thoughts, something with which she could quarrel.

"Tomorrow when we come into port, you will go with me to the farm as I wish," she said.

"I will."

"Because if you do not, you will forfeit the wager and I will win."

"I will go with you because until you are in the home of your sister I do not plan on allowing you out of my sight."

Weakness swamped her, from her throat to her legs. He made her feel weak where she had felt strong her whole life. The strongest most adventuresome girl in England, the baron had always said. The most reckless.

Years after he took her, Fionn learned from an old smuggler friend who had passed through Devonshire the story of her English family's reaction to her disappearance. They had believed her reckless enough to climb the bluff by herself, without ropes, without an adult, and had died because of it, dashed upon the rocks in the water below.

Viola didn't blame them. As a child she had often behaved rashly, but not on that day when Fionn Daly grabbed her up, bundled her into his longboat, and stole her away, using her as bait for her mother, whom he thought would follow. Instead, she had died.

Now this man said Serena had never believed in her death. To learn the truth of it she could go to England easily enough with or even without her ship, then return and slide smoothly into her life again, with her crew and Aidan alike.

But panic swirled in her, insisting she must not go. For, if she did, she might never wish to return to this life, to the life she had made for herself upon the sea. To the people she cared for and the man she intended to marry. All of it might be lost, just as that other world had been lost so completely once. She had learned to live without it. She had *fought* to learn to live without it, pressing down her memories and bidding her heart do as she commanded as day after day the sea became her home.

"Damn you, Jinan Seton."

He laughed, but there was no pleasure in the sound now. "I am afraid you are far too late for that, Miss Carlyle. I signed that contract years ago."

She swallowed through her aching throat. "I cannot think of a worse curse at present."

"I will await your pleasure." He bowed.

She expelled a hard breath, jumped off the bowsprit and strode aft. Not to the quarterdeck. Night had fallen and there was no lonely longing there now to clean her head of confusion.

For that was why she loved that place the most of all aboard ship, why that time of day called to her most profoundly and made her ache so hard yet with such sharp pleasure. Because amid the pain of losing those she loved, then the everyday dangers of life on the sea that made the affection of rough and weathered sailors an uncertain gift as well, what she could count on most was loneliness.

Loneliness was not like love. Loneliness was pure. It was constant. It would never fail her.

And now it wore the face of a man.

Chapter 11

Odwall Blankton Fishery, Billingsgate Wharf
RECEIPT OF PURCHASE:
10 lbs Mackerel, smoked
20 lbs Sole
1 doz. Lobsters, live
2 lbs Sturgeon Roe
3 doz. Oysters
20 Lemons
TO BE DELIVERED TO: Lady Justice, Brittle & Sons,
Printers, London
ATTACHED: My lady, with my compliments. Peregrine

Chapter 12

M atthew?" Viola slid her hand around a thick peg of the helm, wind blowing her hair about her cheeks. Land ran close along the ship's port side, rising into the island in green slopes to the mountaintops, bending toward the cape. They would make the harbor of Port of Spain on Trinidad well within an hour.

"Cap'n ma'am?" Big Mattie tugged his cap and his leathery cheeks colored up. For a great hulking beast of a man, he was as shy as a girl.

"Are you boys bounty hunters? Is that what the *Cavalier* turned her canvas to when she quit pirating?"

He screwed up his cauliflower nose and scratched behind his ear. "Just simple sailors, ma'am."

"'Cept Cap'n Jin." Little Billy perched atop a coil of rope, cleaning his teeth with a stick the size of his skinny arm. "S'always got us after someone or other what's lost and has got to be brought home."

"Has he?" It explained a great deal, his determination and

unshakable focus—even, she thought, when he had been kissing her.

It had not escaped her that he might have kissed her to encourage her to do as he bid. Most men considered women half-witted. However much he teased her, though, Viola didn't believe Jin Seton thought of her like that. Irresponsible and mad, yes. But not a fool. The Pharaoh would not voluntarily serve under a master he believed to be a fool, not even in order to secure his goal.

"Don't matter where they is either," Billy chirped. "Or if they wants to come. Cap'n Jin don't stop till he gets his man." He clamped the stick between his teeth and it poked out of his mouth. "Or woman, ma'am. Cap'n ma'am, I means to say."

She smiled. Billy seemed simple on the surface, but his mind was quick. He knew Seton had come for her. Big Mattie and Matouba too. Her own crewmen were still ignorant of it, though.

Interesting discretion for former pirates.

"What sort of people has he hunted?" Other than her. *He had hunted her.* The notion still made her heady, in a sort of nauseous manner. The legendary former pirate had hunted her for money. For payment from her brother-in-law, the earl.

But he had not kissed her like he was being paid for it. He kissed her like he wanted to. Like he needed to.

"All sorts," Billy replied blithely, settling his bony behind into the coil with a grin. The wind was fresh and the men were glad to be nearing the end of the journey, while Viola's belly tickled with nerves. She ought to be thinking of Aidan. She ought to be thrilled with the prospect of seeing him for the first time in eons. She was. Certainly.

But another man filled her thoughts.

"Oh, really?" she pressed.

Billy nodded. "Sometimes they's ladies. Sometimes they's gents."

"Ladies and gentlemen?" Did he do this regularly now that he had ceased pirating? Did he seek out and drag home people who had been abducted like her? *Ridiculous*. How many people like her could there be?

"Some," Mattie said gruffly, peering at her from beneath bushy chestnut brows. "Somes is no-good ruffians."

"Like them Scots what we gone chasing up north." Billy nodded, chewing on the stick.

"Ladies, gentlemen, and ruffians? And up north too. You boys have been busy, haven't you?"

They both nodded.

She was only one of the many. The tingles of nerves in her belly clumped together in a sticky mass.

"I'll bet you have favorite haunts in every port," she heard herself say. "And favorite girls too." She smiled the way she smiled at Crazy and Frenchie when they spoke of their wives.

Billy's cheeks flamed.

"No, of course not, Billy." She chuckled. "But do you have a special girl somewhere, Matthew?" She could not seem to halt herself.

His dusky cheeks darkened as well.

"Got himself a right pretty gal in Dover," Billy supplied.

"Then she is a very lucky lady, just like your captain's girl, I'm sure."

"Cap'n ain't got no girl, ma'am." Billy scrubbed at the crown of his head. "He don't never have no girl more'n a night."

Viola's tongue stuck to the roof of her mouth. Big Mattie's heavy brow dipped.

"Cap'n don't go in for holding fast with petticoats," the hulk mumbled, his gaze fixed on her with peculiar focus. "He ain't the sticking sort."

"Ah. Of course not," she made herself reply, forcing a knowing nod.

She turned her attention to the land, tracing the unfamiliar coast. She'd only visited Aidan once since he purchased the farm. At that time his fields had been cleared, the cane growing in long rows. But for living quarters he hadn't even a roof over the rough floors of his new house. Two years later now, he must have finished it. No more bedding her in a corner of the kitchen covered by leaky palm branches and infested with flies and mosquitoes.

Although, on that occasion he barely bedded her. He'd been tired, anxious over a squabble between the foreman and the free men who worked the fields. He had satisfied himself in her quickly, then went off to see to the trouble, leaving her aching for more. For something else.

In truth, she knew nothing else. She had first given herself to him at seventeen, when Fionn fell ill and she went to Aidan for comfort, then later a handful of times. He never pressed her for it. He was a gentleman.

Her gaze scanned the rolling coast. Before she left this island two years ago, he had kissed her, told her she was the most important person in his life and that he had always loved her, and vowed to write. Months later when a letter arrived, she read his renewed promises of their future together with mingled confusion and gratification. He still wished to marry her. She must only allow him to settle more firmly into his new life before asking her to join it. He had been a clerk, then a sailor, and now he must accustom himself to the duties of a landowner. Then he would send for her and they would be wed.

Five months passed before the next letter. It mentioned poor weather, fractious laborers, and bothersome taxes, and again the assurance of his love. Six months later the next arrived, much the same in content. Since then she'd had only the quick note indicating he had received the news she would be visiting soon and was eager for it.

Along the coast the island rose dramatically, emerald green beneath the summer's morning sun. She drew in the scent of verdant land and searched for the nerves in her belly that should be there, the anticipation of seeing him again after so long. But her insides felt empty.

Perhaps she merely required food.

"Matthew, do you know this port?"

The helmsman nodded. "Came in here twice a year, for a spell."

"Will you take us in?"

"Aye, Cap'n ma'am."

"Thank you." She smiled, handed over the wheel to him, and turned toward the stair.

"Always so appreciative." Seton leaned against the rail at the bottom of the steps, watching her descend. "You are spoiling my men. They will expect me to fawn over them and be crushed when I refuse to oblige." He grinned, the merest tilt of his breathtaking mouth.

Tingles erupted in Viola's midsection.

She gripped the rail. This was not supposed to happen. She loved Aidan. She would see him within hours. She should be thinking of nothing else. She could not tear her gaze from her quartermaster's handsome face.

His clear eyes sobered, the grin slipping away.

"What is it?" He pushed away from the rail and met her at the base of the stair. "Something is amiss. Tell me."

She swallowed over her tied tongue. "It's nothing. I'm a bit light-headed, I suppose. I forgot to eat lunch."

His brow creased. "Small wonder. It is not yet ten o'clock."

"Then I'd better go see to that." She turned toward the stairs to below.

"We are nearly in the harbor. You do not wish to remain atop?"

"Yes." She halted. "Yes, of course."

He peered at her oddly, a question in his eyes. But her heart galloped and nothing occurred to her that she could say out loud. She pivoted and headed for the bow.

She remained there until they rounded the cape and tacked into the harbor. Then the business of heaving to and announcing their presence to the port officers approaching in a boat engaged her entire crew and there was no time for foolish confusions. She was a respected privateer making anchor in an ally's friendly port. This she could do with perfect ease.

Seton made it even easier. While Crazy usually ran about directing the men's every last move, as always the Pharaoh seemed to have perfect control over her crew with an economy of words. The remainder of the time he stood silently at her shoulder, stance solid, hands clasped behind his back, awaiting her orders.

The harbor was not particularly busy, only a handful of ships docked or at anchor. A tattered old sloop and a schooner not worth the price of its rigging bobbed on the calm green water at anchor, both foreign vessels from the looks of it, a mass of fishing boats and a pleasure boat or two.

When the customs documents had been signed, the contents of the *April Storm*'s hold duly recorded in ledgers so that the appropriate fees could be levied, and barrels and crates unloaded onto carts to the men's rhythmic chanting, Viola finally went below and collected her traveling case. Few of her sailors were still aboard when she came atop again, a skeleton crew to watch the ship overnight until the morning when she would move the *April* from dock and drop anchor in the harbor.

Seton sat on a barrel by the gangway, his long legs stretched out before him, gaze on her as she climbed onto deck.

He stood and came toward her. "Are you always the last person off your ship when you make berth?"

"Yes."

He nodded thoughtfully, then reached to take up her bag. She snatched it away.

"Don't you dare." Her throat was tight.

His brows slid upward.

"You are not my servant," she said.

"No."

"Then what business do you have carrying my belongings?"

He settled back on his heels, quick awareness in his eyes. "This is a show of denying your sex, I take it."

"Not denying it. Making it irrelevant."

"I see."

"Do you?"

"I think I am beginning to." He took up his own pack and slung it over his shoulder. "I hope you will not consider it an unforgiveable impertinence on my part that I have arranged for a carriage?" he said easily. He understood that she must prove herself at every port, that she must be seen to behave and be treated like any other shipmaster, that this had been her life for two years since her father died. That he comprehended this with barely an explanation from her only made her heart race faster.

"Thank you. First I need to visit the inn across the street there." She pointed into the town, the main street quiet now in the midafternoon heat.

"As you wish." He gestured with a hand toward the gang-plank sloping down to the dock. "Madam."

"Do *not* bow."

"Do you think you might leave off with the hissed commands now that we are on land?"

She shot him a glance. Her stomach somersaulted. A dent creased his lean cheek. Viola's vision quivered—twinkled—as though she hadn't sufficient air.

Stars. In the middle of the day.

"If you don't like it," she managed to mutter, "feel free to take your leave."

"Mm hm. I know that trick." His smile did not fade.

They passed onto the street and across the light traffic of people and vehicles. The brilliant sun bathed the town in heat and stirred up clouds of dust, making everything seem to shimmer.

That must be it. The sun. Not his smile. The sun.

"You are unusually cheerful. For a man who has made the sea his life, you seem to enjoy making land a great deal."

A three-story structure, the inn boasted fresh paint and impressively tall windows. To either side elegant buildings lined the street, all likewise clean and tidy, carrying the unmistakable aura of prosperity. This modest English island colony was thriving.

He paused to allow her to precede him up the stair to the door.

"I think, rather, that I enjoy my captain," he said quietly.

She jerked her head around, eyes wide. "What are you doing?"

His brows bent. "At a guess, entering the inn you have said you wish to visit?"

"I mean, don't compliment me."

He shook his head, rolling his eyes away, and walked into the building.

In the foyer, she went to the desk and pulled out her purse, motioning Seton into the taproom adjacent. Without comment he went. He would not allow her to escape, she knew, but she had the most peculiar feeling that he trusted her not to try to run away.

Foolish imaginings. Of course she would not run away with her ship at the wharf and most of her crewmen spread about town and probably three sheets to the wind already.

She paid for a private chamber and the innkeeper led her through the public room to a stairway that rose along the wall, then showed her into a modest chamber. Viola unpacked and a maid arrived with a basin of water. She scrubbed her hands and face and drank the remaining contents of the pitcher, reveling in the flavor of fresh water. Then she and the girl set about combing the tangles from her hair and lacing her into the change of clothing. When they finished, she pressed a coin into the maid's palm and dismissed her.

She stood before the narrow oval mirror and studied their work. Her shoulders slumped. It was always the same. She looked ridiculous.

Her face was brown as a berry, her masses of curls would never be suitably tamed, and she despised the dress. But the dressmaker in Boston had said it was the latest style, with a tight bodice ruched up beneath her breasts and puff sleeves that barely managed to cover her shoulders. At least the color was acceptable, light brown with darker brown pinstripes. The dressmaker had not approved, offering instead an awful pale yellow fabric with tiny orange blossoms embroidered all over it that looked like underclothing. Viola had refused. If she must dress as a woman, she would do so without shaming herself. In any case, she had a shawl to cover it all up, serviceable gray wool Crazy's wife had knitted for her.

She poked her feet into the thin, uncomfortable slippers her father had given her six years earlier, and stuffed her breeches, shirt, and shoes into her traveling case. Leaving the chamber, she caught a glimpse of herself in the mirror again and halted.

Probably it was an effect of the heat, or of her hair all pulled away from her face in the arrangement the maid had effected. Her cheeks seemed to glow, and her eyes were peculiarly large and bright.

But she still looked ridiculous.

Seton would laugh. Or he would remain so obviously silent she would know he was comparing her to the real ladies to whom he intended to take her—ladies like her sister, Serena—and finding her coming up pathetically short.

It mattered nothing. She would not go to England with him and she would not be obliged to stand beside those ladies to be unfavorably compared. She would remain here and marry Aidan Castle. Aidan had known her since she was fifteen, on board ship and off, and he never cared whether she wore breeches or skirts. Why had she changed clothes before going to his house?

In a stew of disgruntlement she descended the stairs, searching the taproom and wishing she didn't care what Aidan Castle or Jinan Seton would think of her now. Wishing she could ignore the need inside her for *him* to notice that she had changed.

She found him easily. Where other men drank and ate and talked, he stood alone. Shoulders against the wall, arms crossed, eyes closed as though he dozed, he appeared perfectly at ease, as though the possibility of threat or danger never occurred to him. Why should it? From Lisbon to Port-au-Prince to New York, sailors feared the Pharaoh, and respected him. He had nothing to fear.

As though he sensed her regard his eyelids lifted, and

beneath a lock of dark hair his crystal gaze came to her. It flickered down her skirts, then up again. His lips parted. His shoulders came away from the wall and he unfolded his arms.

He stared.

At her.

He did not seem displeased.

Viola's nerves spiraled. Her belly went hot, hands cold. He might say he did not intend to kiss her again. She might insist she did not want it more than air.

But they were both lying.

Her eyes danced. Yet wariness shadowed them, wariness he had not seen there before, that perhaps he had put there.

It ill suited her. The brazen, impish sparkle should not be dimmed.

Yet still she was lovely. From the bird's nest of hair pinned atop her head and the scuffed toes peeking beneath her hem, to the gown, plain and of a hideous color, her garments were a shambles. But by their shape they revealed the woman, and the woman claimed his breath. Slender and perfectly curved, with the tilt of her chin confident and the column of her throat pale, she appeared the lady she had been born.

She drew notice. Across the taproom men fell silent to watch her descend and walk to him. But her gait was a sailor's; she trod upon her hem and stumbled. He grasped her elbow.

"Damn," she muttered, and tugged away.

He smiled.

A little puff of air seemed to escape her, but she said peevishly, "What? Don't look at me like that."

"Like what? Like a beautiful woman has chosen me amongst all the men in this room to approach and I am enjoying my good fortune?"

Her lashes fanned wide, the violets springing to warmth. Then she frowned, marring the lovely cast of her features.

"Save your flattery for giddy females, Seton. I won't be flummoxed."

"I did not intend flummoxing."

"Apparently you don't intend plenty that you do."

"You are talking around yourself. Are you flummoxed or not?"

"In your dreams." She twisted up her sweet, full lips that tasted like honey, and he sought steadiness. But it eluded him. In his dreams of late she gave him those lips to please. In his dreams she drew him between her thighs and gave him all of her.

"Where, I wonder, has gone the perfumed ingénue from aboard ship," he murmured.

Her eyes flashed wide again for an instant, perfectly candid. "Not far. Why? Was she having an effect?"

He laughed. "How many women do you have in that body, Viola Carlyle?"

Her brow pleated. "Only the one, as I've been trying to convince you."

"What is the occasion?" He gestured to her gown. He did not again allow himself to glance at her breasts barely concealed by a strip of fabric tucked into her bodice, or he would commence slavering like the rest of the fellows in the place.

She tugged an ugly gray shawl about her shoulders.

"I am a woman, Seton. A woman is permitted to wear a skirt without particular occasion."

He lifted a single brow. "What happened to making your sex irrelevant?"

"I still am."

He glanced about at the dozen men in the taproom who clearly would not agree.

"Hm." He returned his gaze to her, to her lips. He could

pass his tongue over the spot of beauty riding the curve of her lower lip, then elsewhere—the soft gully of her throat, the firm tips of her breasts. He could do only that for an entire night and be satisfied. Nearly. "That scowl is taking, you know, but it does not quite suit your current fashion. Perhaps you should change clothes again."

"Perhaps you should leap off a gangplank into a nest of hungry sharks." She brushed past him, the caress of her arm grounding him in sudden, complete heat. For a moment, Jin could not move, every muscle strained against his nature.

Perhaps she intended it. But if she intended it, she would be slipping him demure smiles as she had aboard ship. Perhaps, instead, she hadn't any idea that a lady did not touch a man even in such an accidental manner. Perhaps despite fifteen years living among sailors, she truly did not know what happened to a man when a beautiful woman touched him.

"Sharks are always hungry, Miss Carlyle," he uttered, and turned to follow, but she pivoted back to him.

"Don't call me that here," she whispered, "or when we arrive at the farm. Please." Her eyes were dark, unsettling vulnerability coloring them as before on her ship. "Please promise me you won't." Her gaze searched his, anxious.

"It is that important to you?"

"I have nothing to bind you to a promise, I realize. But I know that if you give me your word you won't break it."

"How can you be so certain of that?"

She blinked, a swift shuttering of her expressive eyes. "I simply am."

Jin nodded. "I give you my word."

Her lashes flickered again, then she turned and made her way from the inn.

Chapter 13

During the drive along the coastal road then into the island's interior, she hid her face behind the brim of a plain straw bonnet and said nothing. He studied her, the tight set of her shoulders beneath the thick shawl she wore like armor despite the midafternoon heat, her slender, callused fingers twisted about one another.

She was a woman transformed—not so much in clothing as in attitude. As the ocean disappeared behind hills and palms and the calls of tropical birds and scents of soil and green, growing things became stronger, she grew stiller and stiller. But this was not the stillness of her sunset vigils on the *April Storm*'s quarterdeck.

She wished silence, and he gave it to her, content to await an explanation.

The coachman turned the carriage along a narrow drive flanked by enormous yucca trees, and their destination appeared before them. It was no mere farm. The drive was not long but the house was sizable enough, two stories, elegantly English in style, gleaming and whitewashed with a veranda wrapping about three sides. Fields of sugarcane stretched out along slopes with the perfection of a painted landscape.

Viola's head came up and a gasp escaped her lips. She stared at the house, fingers gripping the carriage's dusty edge.

Finally he spoke. "Whose estate is this?"

"It belongs to Aidan Castle. He was once a clerk in Boston, then worked on my father's ship for several years before purchasing this land." Her gaze traveled with reluctant greed over the house and outbuildings, not in any obvious pleasure. "The last time I visited, he hadn't yet built the house. It's impressive," she added in a subdued voice.

The carriage pulled to a halt before the porch, and a servant emerged from the beveled front door. Jin climbed out, his boots scraping on the pebbled drive from which heat rose with humid dust. He turned to offer Viola his hand. She ignored it, fussing with her skirts and shawl at the steep step, then releasing an exasperated breath and accepting his assistance. On the drive she pulled her fingers from his quickly.

"Good day, mum. Sir." The servant drew the luggage from the carriage.

"Good day," she replied. "Will you please tell Mr. Castle that Violet Daly has arrived?"

The servant bowed and disappeared within the house.

Jin proffered his hand again to assist her up the porch steps, but she grasped the rail and ascended alone. He held back, watching her pass her palms over her skirts several times and adjust bonnet and shawl again. Then he followed.

The door opened. With a confident stride a man came onto the porch. Dressed in a neat linen jacket and trousers, buffed shoes and silk waistcoat, he appeared about Jin's age, broader framed though not quite his height, his face and hands darkly tanned. His attention went directly to the woman standing between them.

She moved to him, tucked her chin down, and extended her hand.

Castle grasped it, said, "Dear Violet," and drew her into his embrace. She put her arms about his waist and pressed her face into his coat.

Jin stood perfectly silent, the late-afternoon sun slanting across the veranda and the pair before him, the slightest breeze rustling through the cane stalks in the fields and fluttering through Viola's skirts.

She had not told him the truth, of course. The occasion for her change of clothing and demeanor, apparently, was Aidan Castle.

He felt the same, thick-chested and solid. And he smelled the same, like shaving soap and tobacco smoke, so familiar that Viola almost sensed her father nearby now, as though if she were to look up Fionn would be standing beside Aidan.

He released her and she allowed herself to study him clearly. He looked the same as well. Light brown hair curled over his brow, somewhat long as sometimes he wore it when he forgot to have it cut. His face had not altered, square and tan, with the same slightly heavy nose, wide, bowed lips, the shallow cleft in his chin, and warm hazel eyes that smiled at her now.

"Your journey passed smoothly, I assume?" His voice was so familiar, a voice she'd heard every day until four years earlier when he left her father's ship to become a planter.

"Without mishap."

"I expected as much. We imagined the season early enough now that you would avoid rough weather." He looked so glad to see her, his gaze fixed comfortably in hers.

"We?"

"You will remember my cousin Seamus. He paid a visit last spring and never left." He chuckled, the same assuring sound she had depended on when her father fell ill and she so badly needed assurance. "My aunt and uncle were keen for him to leave Ireland, of course, getting himself up to tricks as he's always done."

"So . . . he is here?" She had met Seamus Castle only once on a long visit he made years ago to Boston, a young man with too much cheek and too little imagination.

"He's been a great help with the management of the workers. But let us not stand out here in the heat. Come inside and take something cool to drink." He reached for her hand then paused, his gaze shifting behind her. "Ah. Forgive me. This is . . . ?"

"My quartermaster while Crazy is on furlough. Aidan, this is Jinan Seton."

"Glad to make your acquaintance, Mr. Seton." He extended a hand. Seton stepped forward and grasped it.

"The pleasure is mine."

Something in Viola's insides did a peculiar little turn about.

Aidan screwed up his brow. "Seems I recognize that name from somewhere."

He released Aidan's hand. "Do you?"

"But I suppose Seton is a common enough surname in these parts, isn't it?"

"I daresay."

"Ah." Aidan smiled. "You are an Englishman."

"Mr. Seton holds a privateer's commission from the Royal Navy." Viola's gaze darted between them. "He is only serving as my lieutenant because— Well . . . He is—"

"Between ships," the bounty hunter finished.

"Ah. Of course." Aidan's glance shifted over his guest. "Any sailor from Violet's ship is welcome in my home." He gestured to the door. "If you will. I wish to make you acquainted with my other guests."

Viola went before them into the high-ceilinged foyer, stealing a glance at the man with whom she had sailed to this island. He wore a crisp white shirt, neat trousers, and a coat she'd never seen, finely tailored that did justice to his broad shoulders and lean frame. He looked as perfectly at ease in these garments as he did in those he wore aboard ship. During the drive, concentrating on trying *not* to look at him, she had not noticed his clothes.

Mostly, as usual, she had noticed his eyes. And his hands. And his mouth. Always his mouth.

She cared nothing about what he wore. He was handsome in anything and nearly nothing. Her gaze slipped up from his waistcoat and, as on that first day, he was watching her stare at him.

Aidan poked his elbow in front of her. For a moment she looked blankly at his sleeve, unable to blink away the memory of the sailor's bared chest streaked with rain.

Neither man spoke.

"Violet?"

"Oh." Her cheeks heated and she set her fingertips awkwardly on Aidan's forearm.

He chuckled. "My dear, you are priceless." He drew her into a drawing room. It was a lovely chamber, decorated with modest taste and English detail, yet another piece of the house he had built and furnished without telling her anything about it though she was to someday share it.

Within were four people. Seamus Castle leaned against a chair back, swinging a thick gold watch chain around his forefinger.

"G'day, Miss Violet." He ducked her the slightest bow. He was an attractive man, with a high brow like Aidan's and the same curly hair, but his mouth seemed formed into a permanent smirk, his green eyes hooded. "Pleasure to see you again." The last time, five years earlier, he had trapped her in a shadowed alcove and tried to put his hands on her breasts. Her knee had smarted for days from impact with the pistol butt hanging at his groin. His groin had too, clearly. Viola learned several new cuss words in that moment.

"Mr. and Mrs. Hat, allow me to introduce to you Miss Daly and Mr. Seton, friends of mine whose ship has just arrived in port." Aidan turned her to face them.

In an instant Viola knew them to be prosperous merchants from some northern city. New Yorkers, Philadelphians, or Bostonians all had the same look about them—the men overfed, the women overly superior, and both of them overdressed.

Bulges strapped into high-starched collars and a wool coat with enormous lapels, Mr. Hat creaked to his feet and shook hands with Seton.

"Glad to know you," he rumbled.

"Sir." The sailor turned to Mrs. Hat and bowed. "Ma'am."

She wore a pinch-lipped smile and a taffeta gown embroidered with black pearls, vastly expensive and thoroughly unsuited to the climate. She assessed Viola from brow to toe, then Seton, and finally nodded, the black feather in her headdress jerking.

"And this," Aidan said with a gentle smile, "is Miss Hat."

The girl was angelic, not above seventeen and pretty as could stare. And Viola did stare, wondering how Miss Hat made her pale blond locks curl against her brow and cheeks so perfectly, and how she could bear to wear so little in front of all these people. She was tall like her mother, with a willow's figure and soft blue eyes over which golden lashes modestly dipped. She curtsied, the diaphanous skirt of her pristine white gown gliding against her legs. Her hands tucked in its folds were lily white.

"Sir. Miss," she whispered. "I am pleased to make your acquaintance."

Seton bowed, looking so English, so perfectly like an actual gentleman, for a moment Viola stared again at him too.

Aidan guided her to a chair.

"Mr. Hat owns a dry goods mercantile in Philadelphia, Violet. He is visiting on business, hoping to expand his horizons. We are fortunate that he was able to bring his family with him, aren't we, Seamus?"

The Irishman screwed up his mouth into a grin.

"Course, coz. Always a fine thing to have ladies about to brighten the place." He leered at Viola.

Mr. Hat grasped his daughter's hand and patted it. "Wanted my little Charlotte to see the sites, don't you know, before I settle her on a lucky fellow for life."

Miss Hat blushed to her pale roots, eyes downcast, but her smile remained sweet.

The servant who had met them at the door came to Viola with a tray. She accepted a glass and smiled.

"Thank you."

"Dear me, Mr. Castle." Mrs. Hat's gaze fixed on Viola's feet. "I fear I have been remiss these past two days. I had no idea that in the islands ladies spoke to servants amongst company. I shall make certain to rectify my behavior."

Aidan chuckled. "Commerce between the serving class and their betters is sometimes freer here than up north, ma'am, it's true. But you could never be remiss in any manner, I'm certain."

The woman's gaze slid upward, halting at Viola's lap. Viola peered down. Her skirt was hitched up under her knees, her calves encased in cheap stockings perfectly visible.

Heat flushed her cheeks. "Oh." Hands damp, she tugged under her behind to loosen the fabric. She was obliged to tug harder, but after a little hop of her behind off the chair and another tug, finally her hem fell to the floor.

"Castle, I understand you have not owned this property long." Seton's voice cut smoothly into the thick silence. "I enjoy an acquaintance with several planters on Barbados and Jamaica, but none on this island. How do you find the business here?"

"Quite good, in fact. My closest neighbor, Perrault, is less than forthcoming with the stream that runs through his lands before mine, but I haven't yet had irrigation troubles." He looked about with a smile. "If the laborers demanded fewer privileges, I would be a thoroughly contented man indeed."

"I've told you, cousin," Seamus drawled, "if men are given their freedom they will misuse it whenever they can. You should have slaves working your land, not wage laborers."

Aidan shook his head. "I cannot agree with you, Seamus."

"A fellow can barely find a young slave in Philadelphia these days." Mr. Hat nodded. "It's all for the best. None at my warehouse, of course, though that damned Frenchman, Henri, uses them to unload his boats and undercuts the rest of us."

"It's a bad business, I say," Aidan muttered.

"It gets business done. And business is what you are here to do." Seamus folded his arms over his paisley waistcoat. "What do you say on the matter, Seton? Should Parliament be rushing about to free the slaves like the abolitionists would have it, or should we maintain order like rational men?"

He set an easy look on Seamus. "A man must invariably follow his conscience," he replied. "The law, whatever it might be, will never alter that."

"Well said," Aidan murmured, but his brow pleated.

Viola's cheeks burned, her throat tight. Mrs. Hat's disapproving stare had not abated, nor her daughter's curious regard now subtly upon Viola too.

She cared nothing for either.

He had rescued her from embarrassment intentionally. He

could not have known the conversation would take this turn. But she didn't think he cared that it had. As he said, he was not a man to be swayed by the arguments of others. He was the only man Viola had ever met who lived entirely by his own purpose and with thorough confidence in it. That, more than anything she had known of him before, frightened her. Frightened, and excited.

With nightfall, the soft breeze that had filtered across the plantation at dusk disappeared. Stillness enveloped all, the stalks in the cane fields falling silent, even the birds quieting with dark. They took dinner in the dining room, the heat released from the earth gathering heavy within the walls, stealing Viola's appetite.

The Hats mostly ignored her. Mrs. Hat complimented their host on the impressive removes. Mr. Hat plied Seton with questions about activity at the Boston port that Viola could have answered better than the Englishman. Miss Hat nibbled daintily at her food and kept her lashes modestly lowered. Seamus drank glasses of sugared rum and watched Seton with narrowed eyes.

After tea in the drawing room, the Hats announced their intention of visiting town the following day.

"Mr. Castle, we hope you will escort us." Mrs. Hat smiled in graceful condescension.

Aidan nodded. "Of course, ma'am. I will be glad to take you to the finest shops." He turned to her husband. "The lumber seller is a particular friend of mine, though not so much seller as merchant. He is intimately known to the owner of that copse of rare wood I mentioned to you yesterday. I will be glad to introduce you."

"Fine, fine." Mr. Hat patted his ample girth, stays protesting as he propelled himself from his chair. "Tomorrow then, Castle."

Mrs. Hat took her daughter's arm, Miss Hat curtsied, and they departed. Seamus glanced at Viola, insolence in his grin.

"Well, now, Miss Violet," he drawled, "now that you're the sole female present, how will you entertain us? Play a little ditty on the piano, will you now?"

Aidan cleared his throat. "Violet does not play, of course." He came toward her and extended his arm. "May I escort you to your chamber?"

She nodded, laid her hand on his elbow, and glanced at Seton.

He bowed.

The air thickened as they ascended the stair. It was a beautiful house, but it seemed poorly constructed for the climate, rather more in a style suited to chill, English weather. But the door before which Aidan drew her to a halt was elegantly stenciled, the paint fresh despite the cloying humidity. He had worked hard to make such a home for himself, and she must be proud for him.

He took her hands. "It is good to see you again, Violet. I have missed you."

"It is good to see you too after so long."

His brow puckered, eyes serious. "My dear, I recall now why Seton's name rings familiar to me."

Her throat felt dry. "I supposed you would eventually."

"From your look I see that you knew this when you took him on. Why did you do so?" His tone lightly accused.

"Well, it's complicated." She didn't want to tell him that she'd sunk the *Cavalier*. He had nothing to do with her ship and work any longer. Why should he know the details of it? And she found it difficult to speak aloud of Jin Seton; it made her feel unsteady inside.

Aidan gripped her hands tighter. "I cannot like this."

She tried to laugh it off. "The British government has forgiven him, Aidan. Is that not sufficient encouragement for you to put your trust in him too?"

"No." He shook his head. "You know how I care about you, and I do not approve of this man aboard your ship. Fionn would agree. A leopard might be collared, but captivity will not change his spots."

She stared into his hazel eyes and was inclined to agree with the notion of the constancy of a man's spots. Since she was fifteen, this man had courted her with his words, accepting her adoration as though it were natural to him. But again and again he never saw through on his promises. Upon her father's ship he had insisted he could not take a wife until he settled down on land and made a home for a family. For four years, he'd had that land.

Entitlement shone in his eyes now. After months of no letters and two years with no visit, he believed he could tell her how to arrange her life, that he could give her advice she had not sought and she must abide by it. She saw this now quite clearly.

Jin Seton expected much the same—that she would do as he wished. But when he was not looking at her like she was a madwoman, she saw in his eyes an awareness of her as a leader, and a woman, intriguing and desirable. She saw admiration. And heat. No matter how many times Aidan had teased and told her how much she meant to him, he had never once looked at her like that.

"I think you are wrong about him," she replied quietly.

"Pirates are thieves and liars, Violet. You are imprudent to trust him."

"I must be the judge of that." She slipped her hands from his. "Thank you for dinner. Good night."

Still frowning, he leaned forward and kissed her on the cheek. "I am glad you are here, my dear."

She nodded. For a moment he paused, then he descended the stairs.

Viola tapped her fingertips to the spot his lips had touched. She loved him. She had loved him for ten years. He knew so much of her, of her father and her life on the sea. Now, of course, he took no part in that any longer. But he was part of her past, and for so long she had known he would be part of her future. That he would *be* her future. But strangely, now, his familiarity seemed . . . unfamiliar. Even that insubstantial kiss felt alien.

Perhaps a few days in each other's company would correct that. Friends, even so well-known, required time to reaccustom themselves to one another. Didn't they?

She stood by the window and the heat seemed to envelop her. The bed was heavy with linens, entirely uninviting. As soon as she'd seen the other guests she knew Aidan would not ask her to share his bed. He never did when others were present. But it didn't bother her now. It was too hot for that sort of thing, anyway, and her stomach rumbled with hunger, her skin prickling with discomfort. Sleep seemed distant.

A modestly carved shelf offered some reading material, books of sermons and trade journals. She selected the least noxious and sat by the lamp. But the journal failed to distract and perspiration beaded on her nose that she was obliged to wipe away until her sleeve became positively soggy. She went to the window, pushed open the sash, and a cloud of night insects swarmed in.

"Oh!" She tugged the window shut with a clack.

No breeze. Perhaps that was why Aidan had been able to purchase such a large piece of land. With this stillness and humidity, inland property would not be at a premium. If it were this warm in June, it would be unendurable later in the summer. But she had weathered all sorts of deprivations in her decade afloat. If she were truly to be his wife, heat and mosquitoes must be borne.

It needn't be borne quite so oppressively at this moment,

however. If any air could be found moving, it would be in a garden, or even the drive if she must. And she felt restless. She missed the constant movement of her deck beneath her feet, and the swish of the sea in her ears. Here, tucked amid fields and copses and inside the house, she couldn't breathe.

Reluctant to touch wool, nevertheless she took up her shawl in the event that she should encounter the modest Miss Hat and her pincushion mother, and went to the lower story. The front door was bolted, but from the drawing room another door let out onto the veranda at the side of the house. She opened it and stepped into the moonlight.

She shrank back into the doorway's shadow.

Beyond the veranda a garden stretched toward the cane fields, dotted with old trees and exotic shrubbery, a neat white picket fence scrolled with vines defining its boundaries. Tropical flowers bloomed beneath the moon's silvery light, the strident songs of insects saturating the darkness.

Beneath the feathery shadow of a Mapou tree, a man and a woman walked close beside each other. Miss Hat's white gown seemed to shimmer, drawing the moonlight. The gentleman picked a flower and proffered it to her. He spoke quietly, and in the stillness the familiar timber of Aidan's voice carried to Viola. He took up Miss Hat's hand as though it were porcelain, lifted it to his mouth, and kissed it.

Then he kissed her lips.

Viola choked, cold nausea sweeping through her. She whirled around and slammed into Jin.

"Whoa." He caught her waist, his eyes snapping across her face then, swiftly, to the garden. His brow drew down. But tears welled in her eyes, and her palms pressing to his chest, feeling him so abruptly, only confused her further. Because she understood now abruptly that *he* did not truly make her feel weak.

Aidan did. With Aidan she always felt as though she were

not quite enough. But Charlotte Hat obviously was enough—beautiful, refined, well dowered, from a prosperous family of good quality. He could stroll in a midnight garden with her and kiss her hand while he made promises to Viola he never kept.

She lifted her eyes to Jin's and saw awareness in the crystal blue, and a flicker of anger.

Her insides twisted. He never pretended with her. He made her feel uncertain, yes—as though she might at moments allow herself to relinquish the iron grip she held over her feelings. But he also made her feel alive and full of possibility.

"Violet?" His hands tightened on her waist, strong and steady. He did not look again into the garden, his gaze instead focused entirely on her.

A tear tumbled onto her cheek.

"No," she whispered. She had demanded, but now she did not want him to call her that. She wanted him to call her by her real name.

She broke from his hold, dashed a hand across her face, and fled inside.

Chapter 14

S leep would not come. She lay on her bed in her ugly brown dress, staring into the sweltering darkness and holding back tears. Weeping would not help. It would only prove that she was as foolish as any other woman.

But she was not like any other woman. She was Violet *la Vile*, captain of her own ship and fifty men wholly devoted to her, privateer for the state of Massachusetts, and strong and clever enough to manage this as she had managed any number of scrapes, mishaps, and setbacks in her years on the sea. The woman who had sunk the legendary *Cavalier* would not crumple into a ball and cry herself silly simply because the man she had loved for a decade and intended to marry had kissed another woman—a modestly eligible maiden—in full view of anybody, including her. She would rather die.

But it hurt, and she hated that it hurt. In one instant, her future had changed, but her past had changed as well. All those times he promised her marriage, had he never intended to honor those promises? Had she been the greatest fool alive after so many years to believe he ever would? Worse yet, had her father known this all along? Had he given Aidan the money that allowed him to leave the ship so that Viola would not continue to hope on girlhood dreams?

She stared dry-eyed into the darkness, chest and throat tight, containing the sobs. When she heard the shouts, she thought they were in her imagination. But they came closer, more strident.

She darted from the bed to the window. In the distance, not more than a league away, a cane field was lit up bright red, smoke billowing into the midnight sky.

Throwing her sash across her shoulder and shoving her feet into her slippers, she bolted out the door and down to the veranda.

Pandemonium reigned. Men ran in every direction, dragging a pair of oxen, a mule, yelling to one another, Seamus and Aidan's voices shouting orders above it all. A donkey brayed, the air thick with a sweet smokey odor.

Aidan came toward her and grasped her hands.

"Violet, you must go inside and tell Mr. and Mrs.— Ah." His gaze shifted over her shoulder. "There they are. Thank you, Seton."

Viola turned and met Jin's gaze. Miss Hat's ghostlike hands clutched his arm as he drew her onto the drive, her parents before them garbed in nightclothes like their daughter.

"What is happening, Mr. Castle?" Mrs. Hat demanded. "Are we in danger of being overtaken by fire here?"

Aidan shook his head. "Not at all, ma'am. I assure you, my men are doing all that is required to contain the flames. Often we burn the stalk tops in the field in order to expedite the harvest. We are accustomed to this."

"The entire stalks are burning, Castle, and your men's alarm is clear," Seton said evenly, releasing the girl into her mother's keeping and moving toward Aidan. "Who would have reason to have set this fire?"

"Those damned laborers, trying to threaten you into further privileges." Seamus swung over to them. "That's who's done it. My cousin's fool notions have gone and burned down all we've accomplished here."

"It is only one field." Aidan raked his hand through his hair. "The men are watering the ditches. It will not spread."

"Every word that trips from your tongue may be gold to our family in England, Aidan, but here you're wrong." Seamus spat the words, his cheeks crimson. "If you used slaves like everyone else, this would not have happened."

"I will not use forced labor when there are men willing to do the work for wages. I *will* not." He spoke as though something were trapped in his throat.

Seamus swept his hand toward the burning field, the brays of the animals and shouts of men all about in the sweltering night air, sticky, acrid smoke clouding all. "You can see they are willing, can't you?"

Jin's attention shifted behind Viola and he moved past her. She turned. Little Billy ran toward them from the direction of the outbuildings, Matouba's barrel shape trotting in his wake.

"We seen them, Cap'n." Billy's eyes on Jin were eager. "We seen them light it, then run."

"Where have they gone?"

"Headed up the road," Matouba intoned.

"North? Toward the port?"

"Yessir, Cap'n."

"What are those men saying?" Aidan was stripping off his coat, his gaze shifting from the flames licking closer to the yucca trees between the field and the garden.

Viola touched Matouba's sleeve. "Why would Mr. Castle's hired laborers have run to the port? If they set the fire, why wouldn't they remain here and pretend innocence?"

"'Cause they ain't the hired laborers, ma'am."

"What do you mean they aren't the laborers?" Seamus spat.

"Them's sailors, sir," Billy said. "Talking Dutch, they was, just like them boys loading that sloop earlier today at the dock."

"Good God." Aidan's face blanched. "Perrault."

Viola shook her head. "Isn't that your neighbor?"

"Goddamn, Aidan!" Seamus swore. "See what I've told you? You there!" he shouted to a pair of men running toward the burning field. "Soak the heap rows. Those sparks mustn't reach the house." He ran off.

Jin moved toward the house. "Have you the horses?"

"Yessir," Billy piped. "At the road."

Viola called after him. "Where are you going? Why does Billy have horses? If we have a horse we might be able to—" Smoke clogged her throat. "What are you *doing*?"

"Collecting my effects," he threw over his shoulder.

"Good God, we've got to get this under control." Aidan's voice shook. He turned to her. "Violet, I must ask you to look after Miss Hat and her parents. They are unfamiliar with this sort of trouble and I do not wish them to panic. That would only make matters more difficult for me."

"Aidan, why do you believe your neighbor has a hand in this?"

"Violet—"

"Tell me."

"The native Curaçaons of these islands speak Dutch. Perrault is the only planter in this region who uses their services, trade sometimes. If these men say that Dutch speakers set the blaze, they could be Curaçaons in his pay."

"Why would he want to do that? Does he dislike you?"

"My dear, this is not important now. I must ask you to take the Hats inside and calm them. Do this for me, please."

Viola looked into his pleading hazel eyes and her heart thudded dully.

"I am going to the port. Matouba and Billy believe these men headed there. The sloop we saw earlier anchored in the harbor could be theirs. If the *April Storm* can stop them from escaping and I can bring you proof of your neighbor's crime, you will be glad for it."

"No, Violet. That is no business of yours. Leave it to those men and help me here instead. Miss Hat is a fragile thing, innocent and so young. She needs your comfort."

She pulled free, sobs gathering in her throat that she swallowed back.

"I'm sorry, Aidan. They must get along without me." She pivoted and strode toward the house. As she reached the veranda, Jin came out, buckling a belt slung with pistol and cutlass about his hips. His gaze flashed over her gown.

"Aren't you coming?"

Her battered heart climbed into her throat. "I'm coming."

"There is no time for you to change." He passed her and headed for the drive. "Can you ride astride in that?"

She sucked in acrid air. "Of course." She ran down the drive after him.

The arsonists had not counted on being followed. As Viola flung herself from the horse she shared with Billy, her skirt in tatters she'd torn in order to ride effectively, voices came to her across the docks. They were laughing, their movements relaxed and unhurried, as though satisfied with work well done. And they were speaking Dutch. She moved forward.

Jin grabbed her wrist, staying her in the shadows of the building.

"But—"

"Billy," he whispered, releasing her. "Run to the tavern. Get the men. Then get to the *April* as quickly and quietly as you can."

"Yessir." The boy ran off.

"Good thing we ain't at anchor." Matouba barely stirred air with his deep tone. "But there ain't a lick o' wind tonight."

"We'll prime the guns," Viola whispered, "then we will threaten them. If they don't surrender, we will fire upon them from the dock if we must."

"Get ourselves thrown in jail, shootin' from the wharf," Matouba muttered dolefully.

"It wouldn't be the first time for you boys." Her blood ran with nerves and pure energy. She glanced up at Jin and her insides tangled. A half smile quirked his mouth. His gaze remained on the sailors at the small vessel getting ready to make way in the middle of the night like thieves. Or like arsonists not worried about being discovered.

But the Curaçaons readied for putting to sea more quickly than they expected. Lit by several lanterns, the little vessel's deck was perfectly visible to them across the docks. By the time she, Jin, and Matouba had made their way through the shadows to her ship, then silently aboard, the Curaçaons were already pushing away from the opposite dock.

"No," she whispered, running down the stairs to the powder magazine, her shredded skirts flapping around her thighs. "They won't get away. I won't allow it."

Becoua rushed down behind her. "Evening, Cap'n," he whispered, then another dozen of her crew, scurrying across the decks in the light of the half moon, working swiftly to prepare the cannons. But they stank of rum and swayed as they slid the iron balls into the guns' muzzles and fixed the fuses. Drunk. On furlough, drunk, yet they had come.

She scaled the companionway to the main deck again. Below her, a gunwale creaked as a sailor slid it open too swiftly. The sound ricocheted across the harbor.

All went perfectly still atop the sloop thirty yards away. A shout in Dutch carried over the black water. Then movement, and more shouting.

"Orders, Captain?" Jin said at her shoulder.

Viola's pulse raced. She *must* do this. She must show Aidan what she was capable of. She might not be a fine lady whose hand he would kiss, but she possessed her own talents. She could not fail in this. "Do you speak Dutch?"

"I believe we have already passed the moment for that."

The crack of cannon fire, the fast hiss of shot, and a yardarm on the *April*'s mainmast erupted in sparks and smoke.

Her ship came alive. Jin shouted orders, the men ran to stations. Cannon blasts split the thick night with smoke and more heat. Flames leaped and were swiftly doused on both ships, sailors cussed, and the *April Storm*'s guns blazed again and again, the sloop's smaller battery echoing.

But within minutes Viola knew it was already too late. The sloop's sweeps cut the black water fast as dolphin fins, getting her under way swiftly as only a small vessel could without the wind to assist. She headed straight toward sea. Cannon shot flew, canvas on the *April*'s deck caught fire and plummeted, tumbling down the stairs to the gun deck in a flurry of sparks.

Alarm bells across the main street split through the pounding blasts. The port officials were awake.

Soon enough, Viola could do nothing. Moving out of range of even her long nines, the sloop sent off a final round of shot into the water between them.

"The men are ready at the oars," Jin said calmly beside her. "Insufficient numbers to make any speed and man the guns at once. But do you wish us to make pursuit?"

Viola clutched the rail, the sloop's lanterns fading into the dark. "Damn it."

"Is that a yes or a no?"

"No!" She swung around to him, heartbeat pounding. "Of course not. We could never catch them. What do you think I am, an imbecile?" She pivoted to scan the deck strewn with debris, pocked in places by shot and burn marks. "*Damn it.*"

"She is not badly hit. The men will clean her up within a day."

She knew this. The sloop had not tried to do damage, only to distract while they rowed away. At the mouth of the harbor the faintest flicker of white told her the Curaçaons had found wind and were hoisting sail. The arsonists had escaped.

Commotion sounded at the gangplank. A man wearing a hastily donned coat and a gray wig askew, his shoes unbuckled, clambered onto deck flanked by two soldiers uniformed in red with muskets at their shoulders.

"Where is the master of this vessel?" the bewigged man clipped with the persnickety officiousness only an English port official could manage under present circumstances.

Viola went forward, stomach tight, schooling her voice.

"I am her master. What can I do for you, sir?"

"You?" He took in her tattered skirts, then looked over her shoulder. "Is this the truth?"

"This is Violet Daly, sir, master of the *April Storm* out of Boston," Jin said smoothly, his English accent particularly pronounced.

"Does she know she has won herself a fine of one hundred and fifty pounds firing within the limits of the harbor?"

"I would not be surprised if she suspected as much."

"Bloody hell, man. Does she think she can blast away in the middle of the night without attracting anyone's notice?" He swept his arm toward the clusters of people gathered across the street. "She's woken up the entire town! Frightened my wife clear out of her nightcap."

"Miss Daly had reason to fire."

The port master finally turned his attention on her. "It had better be a dashed good reason, young lady."

Viola's belly twisted. No man spoke to her as though she

were a little girl, especially not in the wake of the second greatest heartbreak of her life. *No* man.

"A sloop full of Curaçaon arsonists has escaped your port." She controlled her tone with effort. "Not two hours ago they set fire to Aidan Castle's fields. We chased them here and attempted to waylay them despite the dead wind."

His eyes were wide. "Arsonists? And after all that firing you failed to catch them?"

She pinched her lips. "No doubt if we'd had you aboard to man the guns we would not have, sir. I am terribly sorry you arrived late."

The port officer blustered. "Now see here, young la—"

Jin stepped forward. "I suspect you are eager to return to bed, sir. Perhaps we could postpone this discussion until morning. I am certain Miss Daly will be happy to oblige."

"Stay out of this, Seton."

"At least someone aboard this ship is speaking sense," the port official clipped. He poked a forefinger toward her. "I will expect you at my office by nine o'clock, miss. And if I hear you have absconded during the night, I will not hesitate to send out a vessel after you to collect that fine and have you imprisoned."

She clamped down on the retort that rose to her lips and nodded. With another skeptical pass of his gaze over her garments and a shake of his head, the port officer turned and strode from the deck, the soldiers in his wake.

She rounded on Jin. "What do you think you're doing, speaking for me?"

"Assisting you."

"I didn't need your assistance."

The half moon glittered in his eyes. "Humbly, I beg to differ."

"There's nothing humble about you, you arrogant—"

"Perhaps you would rather continue this discussion in the morning as well."

"Damn it. One hundred and fifty *pounds."* She hadn't fifty pounds aboard ship let alone thrice that. She headed for the stairs to the gun deck, to refuge in her cabin, the one place that belonged to her, where no man could insist she do as he bid.

The fallen sail blocked the steps.

"Get this out of my way," she shouted to the nearest sailors. They bent to it, but slowly, weary from the battle or too much drink. Her gaze traveled around. The lot of them stood glassy-eyed and slump-shouldered. Somewhere in the back of her mind she knew they were as disappointed in the failure as she. But it was more than that. Becoua's dark eyes looked so soft gazing upon her, almost . . .

It could not be pity. She would not stand for it to be pity.

"No." She swept her hand across her vision. "No! Just go. Get out of here, off this ship until I tell you to return." Her hands shook. She was exhausted from the ride on the horse, the emotions, the entire day filled with far too many feelings. Her lungs ached and she wanted to be alone. She must be alone. "All of you, go!" She pivoted to Seton. "Except you."

She could not throw him off the ship. She still had one day. She might yet win the wager. She had no idea how. He was immovable. He would not be won over by her seduction or frustrated by her incivility. He would not be moved by her at all.

He was watching her now with his unreadable blue eyes, standing perfectly still while her men filed from the ship in cowed silence. Little Billy came last and she stopped him.

"Why did you bring horses to Mr. Castle's farm, Billy? Why were you and Matouba there tonight at all?"

He shrugged. "Cap'n bade us, ma'am." His footsteps descended down the gangplank. She sucked in the night air, trying to breathe, the sensations streaming inside her alien, like panic but deeper and cold.

This was wrong. She should be *hot* with anger and betrayal, she knew, filled with the heat of fury. This was worse. She had felt it only once before, months after Fionn stole her away from England, the day she finally understood that he would not take her back home, no matter how she pleaded.

She moved again to the companionway. The main topsail had fallen, twisted in its lines and far too heavy for a lone soul to move. She grabbed at its bulk anyway, pulling and tripping over the scalded ropes and her ripped hem.

"Viola, let it be. Or allow me to call some of the men back to move it before you injure yourself." His voice cajoled. More pity, from the most unlikely source.

The cold dug deeper.

"Damn and damn!" She cut her arm through the air as though she held a cutlass and could slash at the ruined canvas. "*Damn!* Give me your sword." She flattened out her palm.

"You don't need a sword, and you don't want to cuss like that."

She whirled on him. "You have no idea what I want."

"I do." His eyes said a great deal more. He had seen them in the garden. He had seen her cry. He understood. His face cast in moonlight was a portrait of sheer male beauty and unwavering certainty.

Viola's heart thudded in her constricted chest. She wanted the hurt to go away and she wanted him. *Him.* Not Aidan. She wanted Jin Seton so much she could taste it.

"You don't know anything. You can't." She hadn't even known until now.

He regarded her so steadily. "She is an infant," he said quietly. "Why would you want a man who wants a woman like that?"

Her breath failed. She turned and stepped down onto the sail. It sagged, her shoe slipped, she grabbed the rail and propelled herself to the lower deck. He came after her easily, as though he climbed over fallen sails draped across companionways every day. Which possibly he did, or had done at one time in his life, a life about which she had heard more from others than from him.

"Viola—"

"Look who knows all about what I want, the man who pretends he has no interest in kissing a woman after he has clearly demonstrated that he does."

In the new dimness of the cabin deck, his eyes darkened. "Now you are acting like the infant. Castle might set up an entire nursery." His jaw was taut. Was she affecting him? Nicking his pride, no doubt.

She wanted to hurt that pride. Because she hurt more than she could bear.

"Arrogant bastard." She barely whispered it. But in the stillness of the low-ceilinged deck, the word was crystal clear.

His eyes sparked, fire igniting in them. Her stomach sickened. She couldn't believe what she had uttered.

"Forgive me, Jin. Please." She pressed the back of her shaking hand over her mouth.

"For what, acting like a child?" His voice was low. And in response, finally, the heat rose within her.

"A *child*? Is that the best I can do?" The sensation of defeat tangling with desire overwhelmed. Her palm covered her eyes. "Oh, this is not at all what I—"

"This is idiocy." He grabbed her wrist, slung her against his chest, and kissed her. He kissed her not tenderly but as he had in her cabin, claiming her mouth entirely. Fierce and hungry and with perfect possession, he demanded that she not resist.

She couldn't resist. It was all she wanted. But this time she did not want it to end so swiftly. *Ever.* She kissed him back no less urgently, allowing him to mold her lips to his. She felt his strength, tasted his hunger, drank him in like a drug, hot and damp with smoke and pure need.

He broke the kiss, lifted his head. Her hand trapped in his grasp between them knew the hurtling of her heartbeat, or his. His gaze glittered like shattered glass traveling over her features, desire heavy in it. But uncertainty too, or perhaps a question. In the stillness, only their uneven breaths met the creaking of planking.

She could not bear the paralysis. She reached up, ran her fingers through his hair, and indulged in the simple ecstasy of touching him. A sigh quavered in her throat.

He gripped her hand tighter.

She went onto her toes, pulled him down, and he kissed her again, beyond pleasure, beyond sense, without hesitation and with one apparent object, to make her submit. She did, willingly, happily. His hand came around her face, his fingers on her jaw, the pad of his thumb pressing at her chin, and Viola found her mouth opening. Then his heat, his tongue, and her tender flesh that he claimed, fast, deep and urgent.

He dragged her against his body, his hands moving now, touching her neck, shoulders, the curve of her waist, then over her behind. She moaned, warmth bursting inside her as his big hand cupped her, then slipped behind her thigh. Heat wrapped around them, sinking into her body, beneath her skin, burning into their kisses. He pulled her knee alongside his hip and tugged her to him, his arousal coming against her. She moaned. Holding his face between her palms, wanting his tongue in her mouth, she drew him in. How could it feel this good yet she still wanted *more*?

She struggled against him, needing to be closer. "You said you had no intention of kissing me again."

"This is not kissing." He pushed her against the rail and

moved hard against her soft inner thigh. His hand sought her breast.

"*Oh, God.*" She had wanted him to touch her like this for weeks, his hands and arousal feeding hers. She ached with it. But it was almost too much, too sublime to have his hands on her so intimately, to be pressed to his body so thoroughly and insane with need. She tore at his coat and he shoved it over his shoulders, his shirt damp and clinging to his muscles. She wanted to climb up him, to climb right inside him. She twisted her foot around his ankle and her skirts snagged. She teetered. He caught her and bore her down to the canvas-covered steps beneath him.

He took her mouth again and his hand moved fast along her thigh, yanking up her skirts. His haste and purpose did not surprise her. She wanted it too. She arched into him, gasping in breath, and he pulled her against him. His tongue stroked hers then thrust inside her, his fingers clamping around her knee.

He separated their mouths. "Viola." An utterance, hard and taut. "I will not force you. Open up, or I leave."

Her knees were welded together. *What was she doing?*

"Off the ship?" Her voice shook.

"You wish." He caught her mouth and she sank into his kiss, into the fear and certainty that kept her knees locked, the alarm that everything was changing in this moment.

"I don't wish." She fought to meet his kiss closer, biting at his lips with little nips and sucking. She could consume him. She wanted to be consumed by him. She was frantic for it. "Not at this moment, that is." An inelegantly hasty amendment. But he seemed to approve of it. His hand stroked along the crease of her thighs. And so she gave to him her body, because it was what he expected and what she wished, an aching for union. Simply, she could no longer bear to remain apart from him.

She parted her thighs and took him between and, trembling fiercely, felt him at her entrance. He came into her in one thrust, hard and thick, with a groan of pure masculine pleasure. She fought for air. Her fingertips dug into his shoulders. She was stretched too hard, too tight, and it hurt. But it hurt to perfection. He moved inside her, pulling out, then stroking in again.

"*No.*" She clutched at him. "Oh, God, no." It hurt dreadfully, but not her body. Her body tumbled, overflowing with pleasure that shut out the momentary discomfort.

This pain within was worse.

He went still, breaths rough and fast, his hands tight around her hips holding her to him. "Viola." He spoke against her cheek. "It is too late for 'no.'"

"No. Yes. *Yes.*" She thrust to him, gasping at the mingled pleasure and pain. Unmoving, he kissed her, fusing them again in this manner as though he would be inside her as she longed to be inside him. Then, releasing her mouth, he took her.

She had thought she understood. She had done this before. But not *this.* With every thrust into her he forced her pleasure, moving in her so that she must take her pleasure on him. Hips low, he guided her on him with his hands, again and again making them one, harder, deeper with each joining until she whimpered with her rising need. It came so swiftly, the quickening, the tight building of sweet tension she had only ever felt alone, that she never knew she could feel with a man. Fast and overwhelming it took her. She gulped in air, arching desperately against his thrusts, crying out sounds. He bore her into the canvas, palms flat to either side, and she shook with her release as it came, as his muscles hardened. He dipped his cheek to hers, forcing himself inside her, and she couldn't get enough, the power of his body, the stumbling pleasure in hers. When it came again, she gasped, shouted at the beautiful, rippling contractions. He caught her hand—*her hand*—held it tight, and came inside her.

His chest moved hard against hers. She sucked in air, gulping from the delectable shock of his release within her. Nothing had prepared her for this, for him. The laughter of sheer euphoria bubbled up in her. And song, but her throat was parched and she cradled a pirate between her thighs, so singing seemed not quite right. She had never known it could be like this. Or that reclining on a canvas sail on a companionway could prove so uncomfortable after a time.

He pulled away. She drew her knees together and opened her eyes, and made herself drunker yet on the sight of him. Rivulets of moisture ran along his jaw, another droplet clinging to his taut collarbone, then sliding down his chest to be lost beneath his shirt. The linen clung, revealing every contour, every perfect detail of man.

He fastened his trousers and extended his hand. She stared up at him.

"Come." He curled his fingers in a gesture of encouragement, not insisting, but his gaze scanned her, peculiarly bright.

Viola's throat was like parchment, possibly from all the moaning.

"Where? What do you want?" she croaked.

He leaned down to her and curved his hand around her face. He passed the pad of his thumb over her tender lower lip and spoke close, his breath a whisper across her flesh.

"What do you think I want?"

She swallowed hard. Holy Magdalene, she wanted it too. Again. Immediately. She felt wonderfully satisfied, yet hunger still ground deep in her simply from looking at him.

His fingers curled around hers and he grasped her hand. "Come now." He backed off and her knees shook like canvas letting fly. Now, after all her gyrations beneath him, she could not move.

A crease formed between his brows. "Are you all right?"

"Yes. No, perhaps."

His jaw tensed, a flash of alarm darting across his handsome features.

"You—" He took a hard breath. "You have done this before? That is to say, I did not—?"

"*No*." Her face flooded with heat. "You did not. And yes, I have." She wished she were wearing breeches, pistol, and knife. She felt utterly exposed, utterly foolish, and utterly at a disadvantage. "Only not for some time now. And not quite like that." Not by far. How could she have made love several times with the man she had adored for years, and yet doing it once on stairs with this man drove the memory of everything that had come before clear out of her head?

A slow grin curved his perfect lips. "No?"

She frowned. That he might very well have done this plenty of times before did not sit well with her.

"A little unsteady, are we?"

"Don't laugh at me, Seton."

"I'm not laughing."

"Because if you do, I'll stick you through with my—"

"I am flattered."

"Don't be. I meant I have never done it on stairs. My legs have gone all pins and needles."

"Of course they have." He didn't believe her. With good reason. "Still flattered."

"You are beyond arrogant."

His smile flashed quick, utterly disarming, and of course stars sparkled across her vision. She was an idiot.

"Can't help but be. Now come." He drew her up until he held her waist. "I am of a mind to merit more flattery before the night is out."

Her body hummed in his hold. He really intended to do it again. She gripped his arms to remain standing. Her legs felt more like jam than pins.

"Need some assistance getting there?" he murmured.

"Yes, in fact."

His mouth quirked up at one side. "You absolutely do not want me to carry you."

"Absolutely not." She would rather die. "We could remain here?"

He laughed outright. Then he drew her arms around his neck, turned, and reached to the backs of her thighs. "Up you go, then."

Viola jumped onto his back and laughter spilled from her throat as she clenched her knees to his sides and hooked her arms around his shoulders.

"I am offering you perfect opportunity to strangle me now, of course," he said, moving toward her cabin.

"Perhaps later. I have need of your services at the present."

It was not a long walk, a mere ten yards. But in the corridor leading to her cabin, where he had first looked at her as though he would kiss her, then had not, Viola's patience disintegrated. She nuzzled his neck, then reached for his face, his jaw. The flavor of his skin, the rough texture of the day's whiskers, sent pleasure rushing about her midsection again. She turned his face to her and nearly climbed over his shoulder to meet his lips, perfect lips she wanted attached to hers again without delay. He gave her what she wanted for far too short a time. Then he pulled her around off his back and set her on her feet before her cabin.

She went inside and sat to remove her shoes. Peeling off her stockings, she glanced up. He stood in the doorway, his gaze fixed on her writing table. On it sat one item: the spyglass he had borrowed that day that seemed ages ago, that she taunted him about, teasing that he had stolen it. And he had replied that he did not take that which was not his by right.

Finally he lifted his gaze to her. The heated look of the lover was gone. Now the cool crystals were pensive, sober. And oddly assessing.

Chill skittered down Viola's spine. So many times during their journey he had looked at her so from across the deck. Never when they spoke, though, and never when he stood so close. Because it was a gaze of distance—not of feet or yards, but of a much more profound distance. When he looked at her like this, the loneliness within her blew like the wind off a Maine whaler.

"Tomorrow's interview with the harbormaster is bound to be uncomfortable," she said to break the silence and chase that distance from his light eyes. "I don't have one hundred and fifty pounds."

He moved into the cabin. "Here, or at all?"

"Here and at all."

"I have assets on Tobago. I will lend the sum to you."

"You have one hundred and fifty *pounds*? On Tobago? Whatever for?"

"Moments such as this."

Which recalled them quite abruptly to this actual moment in which their intent had nothing to do with pounds and port officers, only with each other.

Viola tried to speak. Her throat clogged. She made a second somewhat more successful attempt.

"Jin, I cannot accept—"

He pulled her off the chair into his arms and bent his head. "It is nothing."

"But one hundred and fifty—"

"It is nothing." And then their lips met again, despite the distance and the money and her astonishment, or perhaps because of them. They kissed as though they had not before, and then as though they could not cease, hands and mouths lost in a need both sublime and violent. Clothes were swiftly discarded—her gown, his shirt, her petticoat. But the removal of her stays proved too much for them both. He put his hands on her unconfined breasts, she moaned as he caressed her through her shift, and quite abruptly there seemed no more leisure for dithering with garments. He dragged her to the bed beneath him, hungry on her mouth as though he had not already satisfied himself in her tonight. But this need pressed inside her as well, and she did not wonder at it.

She ran her palms up his back, smooth, damp skin and muscle, and flattened her body to his—breasts, belly, hips—to feel him everywhere on her. He wanted her, clearly, as she had never known a man could want a woman in a single night.

But she had wept in front of him, because of Aidan.

She broke her lips free, sweeping her fingers through his hair and holding him away. Dear Lord, he was beautiful, his eyes liquid with desire, his perfect mouth hers if she wished it.

"Are you doing this from pity? Because of my tears earlier on the veranda?"

He covered her mouth, parting her lips and making her want him inside again so fiercely. He was hot and unbelievably skilled, and tasted like danger and deliverance at once.

She pushed him away. "Are you?"

"What do you think?" His hand came around her breast, his fingers sure.

She moved into him. "I don't *know* what to think."

"Then, yes." He bent and through the thin fabric of her shift took the peak of her breast into his mouth.

"O-oh, God." Her whole body shuddered. "Yes, *what*?"

"Yes, I did not want you like this before tonight." He pushed her shift to her waist, dragged her thigh around his

hip, and came intimately against her. "This is about pity."
He pressed her into the mattress. His thumb stroked across
her nipple, then around it, driving her mad and desperate for
more of him. "I pity you, Viola Carlyle, and wish only to
give you comfort."

She clutched his waist and arched against him, fed by the
hard heat of his arousal. A sound of pleasure came from his
chest, deep and powerful. Her power over him.

"I think you are lying," she barely managed to utter, her
flesh caught between his and heaven. He captured her hand.

"Of course I am lying." He guided her between their
stretched bellies to his shaft and wrapped her fingers around
him. It was satin and rock and more heat than she had ever
dreamed. He moved her hand on him, his eyes closed, his
jaw taut, and she quivered in every corridor of her being.
Then, with the greatest reluctance it seemed, he released her
hand and sank his fingers into her hair.

"Viola?" He sounded hoarse.

"What?" she whispered, alone now to caress him as she
wished, frightened and dizzy with it.

"Make this happen."

A breath shot out of her. "I—"

"On your terms. When you will." His brow strained, the
muscles in his arms and shoulders stripped with tension.
"But I pray you, do not be long about it."

She trembled in a mingling of anticipation and bliss. "My
terms? Entirely my terms?"

"*Yes.*"

She released him. "Onto your back, sailor."

Eyes cracking open, he rolled to his shoulder, and his perfect lips curved into a perfectly breathtaking half smile.

"Aye aye, Captain." Then he did as he was bid.

She had him then—again—this time on her terms.

Her terms seemed to suit him quite well. But she was his

captain, after all, and he owed her obedience. Like the excellent lieutenant he had been in matters pertaining to the ship, he proved his exceptional capabilities in this as well; at some point amid the heated touches and kisses, her terms clearly became his. Or perhaps they had been all along.

When eventually she arose from the daze of pleasure to once more find herself straddling a scoundrel, her body limp with satisfaction, the slight smile again slipped over his mouth, and the stars were no less bright though perhaps a bit hazier.

She snuggled into the crook of his arm, her cheek pressed to his ribs, the scents of cane smoke and salt and man filling her senses and holding at bay the sleep behind her eyes. His breathing seemed to slow, his chest rising evenly. But his hand was splayed against the small of her back and his arm holding her did not relax.

Aidan had never held her. He always left right after.

"You are holding me. You are not leaving."

His voice came forth as a low rumble. "Too exhausted to move."

He had not shown any exhaustion minutes earlier when he threw her onto the companionway, then the bed. But men could rouse themselves from the tomb for sex, and the pull of their bodies for each other was extraordinary. Which explained why since meeting Jin Seton she had forgotten to think of Aidan every hour. Whatever lies polite society fed a girl, at least men knew the truth of it: the rutting urge proved more powerful than reason or civility. Thus her mother and father.

She told herself this in no uncertain terms. But within her, mistrust of her own thoughts wound its way about her heart. She smoothed her palm across his flat, hard belly damp with sweat. He seemed to hold his breath, then release it gradually. Viola felt life beneath his skin, the thrum of fiber and flesh, and her heart fluttered.

She swallowed around the prickly sensation in her throat, steeling her voice. "You should leave, you know."

"I should." A pause. "Are you ordering me out of this cabin or off the ship?"

The shutter creaked in a finger of hot, tropical air, the nighttime calls of Kabrit bwa thick in the trees reaching out into the harbor, mingling with the gentle lap of water.

"I am winning," she whispered. "You are falling in love with me."

"Don't count on it."

"But I am winning. And when I do, I will have your new boat and you will go back to wherever you came from and leave me alone."

He pulled from under her and reversed their positions so swiftly she stared wide-eyed up at him, no time to mask her surprise from the moonlight. His hands surrounded her face; big hands, strong. He spoke looking into her eyes.

"Get this through your hard head now, Viola Carlyle. I will not leave without you."

Her heart lodged in her throat. "You will be obliged to."

"I will take you home whether you wish it or not."

"You will lose, Seton. You are losing already."

He regarded her for a long moment. Then he did the entirely unexpected. He bent and kissed her, a warm, wonderful kiss intended to please, as though the wager were reversed and he was trying to make her fall in love with him. And it did please.

He drew away, gazed at her for another moment, then released her and lay back.

"Now go to sleep, harpy."

"Don't give me orders."

He chuckled quietly.

He did not hold her now. But he did not leave.

Chapter 15

Blast!"

The drawing-knife clattered to the dock. Jin snatched his hand from the small boat's gudgeon and slid off its overturned hull. Blood welled from his palm, a long, thin line corner to corner. "*Blast.*" But it served him right for allowing a sleepless night.

Allowing.

Little Billy sent him a curious glance from the yawl's bow. "Take care, Cap'n. She's a sharp 'un."

Jin passed his good hand over his face, then gripped his neck, staring at the crimson on the other as it gathered in the indent, barely feeling the pain. Late-morning sun shone sultry upon the wharf and water slapping at the sides of the vessel before them. Weeks earlier, just as now, he had looked up at the *April Storm* and made a terrible mistake imagining he could easily corral a woman like Viola Carlyle. She was not a female to go placidly. Even her lovemaking shouted defiance.

The night's heavy heat had dissipated upon a northerly

wind. Caps of white tipped the swells far beyond the docks and the breeze grabbed at furled sails, jingling lines. If this wind held through the week, they would set a good pace toward England.

One more day. He believed her honest if not entirely sane. However reluctantly, she would leave this when he told her she must—when he told her what he must to secure his goal of returning a lady home. A lady he'd had no business making love to.

A carroty head appeared at his elbow.

"Best patch that up, sir." The cabin boy glanced down at the droplets of blood staining the dock.

"Thank you, Gui. I shall."

The lad's face lacked its typical animation. Sailors had straggled back to the ship all morning, tails between their legs. Chastened dogs that had displeased their master.

The back of Jin's neck was hot. Men should not be reduced to this. Damn it, they were on furlough, yet each had apologized to him for allowing the arsonists to escape. The spell she held over them was bewitchment. Now they all worked at minor tasks as though they were priming the *April Storm* for sea rather than simply moving her to anchor in the harbor. While Jin stood with his feet braced wide on the planking of the dock, and bled.

He swiped off his neck cloth and bound it about his hand.

"Sure's a nasty scrape," Gui piped.

"Cap'n ain't normally clumsy," Billy supplied with his usual good humor. "Reckon he didn't get no sleep last night, what with the excitement and all." He broke a toothy grin. "Never catch a wink myself after a battle."

Jin gripped his fist around the linen. He should not have succumbed to her. Not to a strong-willed armful of heat and determination. But also a woman with a wounded heart, and he had taken advantage of that.

Not his finest hour.

She had imagined he pitied her. He tugged the cloth tight, giving himself pain now and gritting his teeth against it. No pity involved, not toward that hellion harpy. Only the need to erase the hurt and confusion from her wide violet eyes. And lust. Barrels of it, not slaked even now. Her mouth, her hands, her strong shapely legs . . . The very thought of her primed his body. And her voice, her rich, soft cries of pleasure . . .

He swallowed and blinked hard.

"Cap'n? You all right there?"

"Fix that rudder into the gudgeon," he barked.

He wished he were merely bewitched. But this was something more, much more that he did not wish to consider—*could not* consider. A man whose wrists bore scars from iron shackles was no match for a lady who by her blood and birth belonged in London ballrooms, however far she had fallen from that state. He would see her restored to that life, and see his debt repaid. Nothing—not her stubbornness nor his desire—would stand in the way of that.

He bent to their task anew, but blood saturated the cravat and his hand slipped again. "Damn and blast."

"You don't want to cuss like that." The voice behind him was smooth as satin.

She wore sailor's clothing again, her usual heavy coat and broad hat, not the tattered gown he had hastily removed to touch the skin beneath. Yet in his impatience to be inside her again he had never removed her undergarment, and now his imagination beset him like a callow lad. His hands knew that she would be beautiful to the eye.

Her lips curved into the barest smile.

"Billy, Gui," he said, "go now."

The boys obeyed.

He rewrapped the linen about his palm. "How did your appointment pass?"

"That's a great deal of blood. You should see to that."

"What did the harbormaster say?"

"I have oil and bandages in my—"

"Blast it, woman, answer me."

"I don't take orders. And I'll do nothing until you allow me to dress that properly." She glanced at the drawing-knife. "Did you cut it on that old thing? It could fester in an instant. You will lose your hand." His hand that even now wished to trace the slope of her cheek lit by the sun, to explore again the body that had been his to touch in the dark.

He returned to his work. "Then I shall have a hook installed in its place to frighten off pestering females."

She set her fists on her sweet hips, the breeze catching up her tresses and fluttering them about her face and shoulders.

"You're in a wretched mood." She chuckled. "Didn't you sleep?"

"Your snoring wakened me." He sounded waspish. Not his finest self by far, but she brought out the worst in him. And the lust-driven Bedlamite. Her eyes bespoke tangled bedclothes and limbs, and her lips . . . Jin's vision fogged again imagining those lips wrapped around his—

"I don't snore."

"You do," he snapped, unraveled. "What? Has no other man ever mustered the courage to tell Violet *la Vile* that she snores like a drunken dockworker?" He released the line and moved toward the gangway.

"No other man has ever been present while I'm sleeping."

He halted. "I don't believe it."

"Cur."

"Ever?"

Her nostrils flared.

Jin's pulse skittered, cold and metallic like the panic he'd felt the night before when for a moment he believed he had taken her maidenhead. He tamped it down.

"Of course not." He forced a derisive laugh. "That would be like a lord allowing his valet to watch him sleep, wouldn't it? Mustn't allow the minions to see you vulnerable. Or rather, acolytes." Or a former slave whose first master had called him an animal because of the violence he'd seen in him—the nature that could not be tamed.

"You are a prize boor," she grumbled.

He strode up the gangplank, away from her, his head spinning. But the insane desire pressed at him to return to her and tell her the truth—that he had never felt a woman's touch like hers—that it had never proven difficult to leave a woman's bed until hers.

She had allowed him to see her sleep.

When he'd awoken before dawn he watched her shallow breathing, her full lips and the tilt of her chin, her lovely features peaceful, soft in slumber. But she was not his to hold, and without taking again that which he wished from her, he had torn himself away.

Now her footsteps followed him.

"You must come with me to the harbormaster's office. I told him I could be trusted to provide the money in time, but he didn't believe me. Only your name got his attention. It seems your reputation precedes you. Not a poor reputation in English ports, apparently."

He pivoted. "Why is it that I once more find myself obliged to remind you that I hold a commission from the Royal Navy?"

She stepped close, nearly as close as that first day when he was a prisoner aboard her ship, nearly as close as the night before. She swept her dark gaze over him.

"I'll admit it's difficult to believe. That a man like you would agree so easily to be bound seems improbable." A question lit her eyes; its meaning seemed more than the words she spoke. Jin's heart pounded. This could not be. He was not intended for her, not even to satisfy a temporary desire. She was intended for more.

"Do not mistake me, Viola," he forced across his tongue. "I do only that which serves my interests."

The grin slipped from her lips.

"Then you'd better accompany me to the harbormaster's office shortly or you'll be tossed into jail with the rest of us. That, I'll wager, would not serve your interests in the least." She moved across the deck away from him. "But first I will doctor that wound. That is an order, Lieutenant."

Chest tight, he stared at her disappearing down the companionway. Around him the ship rested peculiarly quiet. Sailors were motionless at their work, watching him.

"Hands at the lines!" he shouted. "Ready to make way." He swung up the stairs to the helm. At the wheel Mattie met him with a scowl and a shake of his head.

"What'd you say to put her back up, so short on last night and the loss o' them low-dunnits?"

"Nothing of your concern. Make for those mangroves, fifty yards to portside. We will drop anchor there."

"Saying something she don't like? Or *doing* something? Something you shouldn't be doing. Teasing her?"

"You are a besotted fool like the rest of them."

Mattie's thick brow lowered. "Don't like to see a lady treated poor." His gruff tone warned. "And this one, she don't deserve it."

Jin fixed his helmsman with a hard stare. "Decide now if you wish to aid or hinder me in this, Matt. But at this late date, if you choose to make trouble for me, take care to wear your knife close when you sleep at night."

The hulk's weathered face paled. "Got us fifteen years between us, you and me. You'd never."

"Watch me."

Jin descended to the main deck, then to the companionway, black anger boiling beneath his skin. Threats now, to a man he had known since he was a lad. But Mattie knew better than anyone of what Jin was truly capable. Mattie had seen it with his own eyes. Such images did not fade from a man's memory. Ever. Nor were such acts ever erased from a man's soul.

The ship rocked in the rough harbor like an old nag in the traces, reluctantly getting under way. Jin passed through the short corridor to the shipmaster's open cabin door. The chamber was empty, its accoutrements tidy, the bed in which he had taken his pleasure in a woman of aristocratic blood now neatly made. The sextant no longer graced the writing table, in its place a wooden medicine chest, its drawers carefully labeled, with folded squares of cotton beside it.

He took up a bottle of wine from beside the chest, uncorked it, and doused the cravat, then unwrapped the stained linen and flexed his hand. Blood oozed from the wound anew. He closed his fist, and his eyes, and breathed in her scent, all about him now—the scent of spiced roses and damnable woman.

"Afraid it'll sting?" Like water rippling over a rocky beach, her laughter came from the doorway. Her hat dangled in her hand.

He pressed the cravat to his palm. "Afraid you will swoon at the sight of blood?"

She moved to him. "I've been a woman for thirteen years, Seton. I've seen more blood than probably even you."

"Charming." He worked the alcohol into the slash, the pain nothing to him. "You may wish to curtail some of this delightful frankness when you again reside in your father's house in Devonshire."

She hesitated only a moment. "My father's house now belongs to me and it is in Massachusetts."

With each pass of the cravat the blood flowed afresh.

"Incompetent man." She grabbed up a scrap of cotton and trapped his palm between hers, lifting it and pressing down hard. "You've been master of your own ship for years and you don't even know how to treat a wound?"

He did. Perfectly well, of course. He had tended more sailors' injuries than he cared to count. But he had no desire to stanch this wound yet. Today he wished to bleed.

Brow taut, she took up a vial of root powder and dusted the cotton then replaced it against his palm, her movements deft and competent and her slender fingers strong upon him, as when she had clasped him to her in the moonlight.

"Do you truly care nothing for it? For them?" He watched her face as she concentrated on her task. "Does it not affect you that those who call you sister and daughter still hope for your return? That they yet consider you one of theirs?"

She opened another drawer in the chest and withdrew a small pot corked with wax. "You know nothing of it."

"I do."

She worked quickly, adept at this as she was at twining her crewmen about her will. With gentle application she spread the oily salve across his palm, then pressed a layer of cloth to it and bound it with a strip of linen. She tied it off and released him, then wiped her hands and closed the medicines in the chest. She slipped the key into her pocket and set her hands on her hips.

"Don't make a fist if you mustn't. And don't use it for anything but the most innocuous tasks." Her lashes flickered, as though a not-so innocuous task his hand might perform occurred to her. "If you mustn't," she repeated somewhat airily.

Beauty, bravado, and maidenlike confusion all wrapped into one. For the first time all day, Jin found himself smiling and he said unwisely, "And if I must?"

Her gaze snapped away. "Then I know a superb black-smith who could have a hook ready for you in less than a sennight." She hefted the medicine chest and set it on the floor at the foot of the bunk. Despite the shapeless coat that concealed her curves, he could not draw his gaze from her. He could watch her move, watch her grin or swagger or sit in perfect stillness upon the bow of her ship with her hair tangling in the wind . . . endlessly.

Heat washed through him—this heat entirely foreign, insistent, *not desire*. His heart raced, a reckless pulse he'd only ever felt once, twenty years earlier. That time he had run, evaded his keepers, and escaped through the dusty cane fields. As they gained on him, his limbs weak from starvation and bare feet bloodied by the dry stalks, his heart had raced thus. And when they had caught him, he'd fought.

He made himself speak.

"Why do you resist returning home, Viola? You cannot wish to live the remainder of your days in this manner." He did not need to gesture about him at the worn walls and narrow window of her tiny cabin, the shabby furnishings she maintained so neatly without the help of a steward, only a seven-year-old cabin boy. "You could have so much more. You were born to have more."

"Did Mr. Castle come here while I was at the harbormaster's office?" Her lovely face was immobile.

He had his answer, then, the answer he suspected despite the previous night.

"No."

She moved to the door, tugging on her hat. "I heard news of the fire in town. Apparently it spread to a second field, but no one knows if it reached the house. I hope they are all well." She went ahead onto the gun deck. Her sailors tipped their caps and she cast them smiles as ever, but distracted. Her mind was elsewhere. And, apparently, still her heart. With Aidan Castle.

"I sent Matouba on horseback," he said. "He should return shortly with news."

She darted him a glance, then climbed the stairs to the main deck. Round the capstan sailors pulled at long poles, chanting an old rhythm as they released the anchor one yard of massive chain at a time. Jin called for a boat to be lowered and passed orders to Becoua to have the sails furled and other chores completed. Ignoring Mattie's glare, he followed the master of the *April Storm* off her ship and across the harbor to town.

The harbormaster came around his desk and extended a hand.

"If I had known who you were last night, Mr. Seton, I should have insisted on your company for lunch today. But it shall have to be dinner tonight instead, and of course Miss Daly as well. Pity you've just missed Captain Eccles. He has gone on to Havana but will be sorry to have passed you by so narrowly."

"I don't believe I am acquainted with Captain Eccles, sir."

"Of course you are." The port master pulled a chair forward for Viola and gestured for her to sit. She did so gingerly, her violet eyes wide.

The harbormaster settled into his. "According to Eccles, when last you encountered one another he was not yet master of his own ship, but under the command of Captain Halloway."

"Ah. Halloway's lieutenant aboard the *Command*."

"That nasty business with that pirate Redstone and the earl, whatever his name was. Poole?" The port official waved it away, rummaging in his desk drawer. "An excellent story, though. My wife and I found it enormously diverting. Eccles gave me this to pass on to you if you should happen through port. Remarkable that you should do so not a sennight since his sojourn here." He extended a sealed envelope across the desk. Jin tucked it into his waistcoat.

"I thank you for the invitation to dine with you tonight, sir. But what of this fine on the *April Storm*? Will you give me leave to collect the sum from Miss Daly's banker on Tobago and return it to you within the sennight?"

"Of course, of course. We ain't savages here." He chortled comfortably, and stood. "But not until tomorrow, after you have supped on my wife's pork pie and jelly. A man hasn't lived until he's had a mouthful of that pork pie." He patted his belly, then ushered them affably to the door.

"By the by, Seton, I must thank you belatedly for apprehending the *Estella* last winter. Those Cuban pirates absconded with at least two loaded merchant vessels out of this port and I suspect a third that went missing and we never heard of again. Brutal fellows. Brutal, I tell you, from the stories I got from the few men who survived. Though there weren't many of those, of course." He shook his head, then clapped Jin on the shoulder. "It is a fine thing to have a ship like the *Cavalier* in these waters. Where is that quick little schooner now?"

"She is indisposed currently, sir."

"Cleaning time, I daresay. Well, best get her back in the water where she'll do honest men some good. Now don't you be late to dinner or the missus will scold me. Seven o'clock direct." He closed the door.

On the street again, amid shoppers passing by and carts laden with the commerce of a port town, Viola turned to him.

"Englishmen are the most peculiar people I have ever met. They do *know* what you were, don't they?"

Beneath the brilliant blue equatorial sky, Jin's blood ran cool now, anger gone for the moment. This was what he had come to know, what he had trained himself to for a decade. This game of pretending his past did not exist, the past in which the only identities he owned were slave, murderer, and thief.

"Indeed they do," he replied.

From the shadow of her hat brim, she studied him. "I suppose they prefer you as an ally rather than an enemy."

He saw no reason to reply.

Finally she spoke again. "I need to go to the shop. My dress was ruined riding that horse last night a-and . . . I . . ." She stuttered to a halt. "Perhaps you could wait for me at the inn."

"As you wish."

He watched her along the street because it seemed he could not do otherwise, no matter how he wished it. A pair of women carrying lace-edged parasols stepped hastily to the side as she passed. They looked after her, heads tilted close and lips moving.

Jin headed toward the inn, drawing the letter from his pocket as he went into the public room. He settled at a table with his back to a corner and slid the blade of his knife along the edge of the envelope.

It was not from the commissioners of the Admiralty. Not even from Viscount Colin Gray, his erstwhile colleague in the Falcon Club. The hand was delicate, that of another member of the slowly shrinking Club, the single lady agent, a lady with sufficient funds and connections in the Admiralty to send dozens of letters into the Atlantic Ocean searching for him. A lady who would not have done so without good reason.

Apparently, Constance Read needed him.

April 12, 1818
London

Dear Jin,

I hope this missive finds you well. But I will not waste time in pleasantries for which you care nothing; I will come to my point swiftly.

Our friend Wyn is unwell. He will not admit to it, but he speaks in riddles as ever, evasive, and I cannot penetrate him. But I fear for him. I have no doubt that Colin has written to you; he has a project for you in the East. I write to beg you to take Wyn with you, provide him with purpose and distraction to cure him. I do believe at this time, Jinan, that you are the only one amongst our small band of friends who can help him erase the past and begin anew.

Wishing for your quick return to England,

Fondly,
Constance

Wyn Yale, born in Wales yet more comfortable in London or Paris or even Calcutta than in his homeland. He was not even Jin's age, yet now, according to Constance, the Welshman was comfortable nowhere.

Among the five members of the Falcon Club, Wyn was the most suited to the work, stealthily ferreting out missing persons of distinction and returning them home. Colin, Viscount Gray and secretary of the Club, was a leader, a man meant for a position of power, not skulking about in shadows. Leam Blackwood had gotten into it reluctantly, avoiding for a time the responsibilities that weighed on him as a Scottish peer, and now he was fully quit of the work. But before Leam left the Club he had invited his young cousin, Constance Read, to join them. She had taken to their mission with alacrity, flitting from one society event to another, charming all with her wit and beauty, and carrying away secrets as they slipped off the tongues of unwitting informants. As for himself, Jin's search for atonement had made the Club a comfortable fit for him. For a time.

But Wyn was a spy through and through. He was made for better than the Club, much as Viola Carlyle was made for better than a former pirate.

He scanned Constance's missive again. She wrote to him now because he was the person she believed could best help their Welsh friend. Because he was the only other among them who had taken another human's life in cold blood.

He would help Wyn and ease Constance's anxiety. Today he would write to the Welshman in London and send the letter off in advance of his own departure with Viola. He would offer Wyn a task that the young, chivalrous fool would be unable to refuse. Jin knew the measure of his fellow agent well. When he arrived with Viola in England, Wyn would be waiting and ready to assist.

He went to the hearth and cast Constance's letter forth.

"A love letter from an unwanted girl, Seton?" Aidan Castle stood behind him, a riding crop gripped tightly in his gloved fingers. "Perhaps you already have your hands full at the present." He looked like precisely what he had become, a modestly prosperous planter, a man of comfortable distinction dressed neatly if not in the highest fashion. But his face was drawn. He had not slept either.

"Join me for a drink, Castle." He gestured him to a chair. "You must need one after the night you passed."

"One, or half a dozen. Don't mind if I do."

A serving girl brought them a bottle.

"Thank you for your assistance last night." Castle wrapped his hand about the glass. "I met your man Matouba when he arrived this morning. He told me of the sloop." He glanced about the taproom. "News travels swiftly on an island. Now of course the whole town knows."

"What occurred after we departed?"

"The fire didn't reach the house. But it took the storage barn and stable and two fields before we could halt it." He shook his head and took a full swallow. "The stain of smoke and ash is on every surface. The house will not be habitable until it is thoroughly cleaned."

Jin poured him a second dram. Castle drank it, then leaned back in his chair, finally releasing the riding crop.

"It must have been Perrault," he uttered, his tongue loosened by the spirits or simply because he had not rested until now. A man would reveal much at such moments.

"Your neighbor?"

"He is of the same opinion as my cousin. He believes that if planters like me continue using the labor of free men, and are successful, the island will press to abolish slavery. He does business with the Curaçaons occasionally. No other planter in this region does. Most consider them little more than mercenaries."

Jin knew this well. He had at one time worked for the Dutch-speaking islanders. "It could be coincidence."

Castle shook his head. "Perrault has threatened me on occasion."

"A man is bound to do so when he believes his interests are in danger."

Castle's gaze sharpened. Then, with an exaggerated shift of attitude that almost made Jin pity him, he took up the bottle and poured another glass. "How is Violet today? I cannot imagine how this has affected her, to arrive and immediately be thrown into chaos."

Jin studied his face, the tension in Castle's jaw and eyes as he sought to appear natural.

"Given Miss Daly's profession," he replied, "I suspect she is accustomed to such upsets." The pity clung, and another less comfortable emotion. Despite his foolishness with Miss Hat, this man cared for Viola. "She was concerned over the safety of you and your guests."

"Does she tell you such things, then? Are you in her confidence?"

Jin regarded the reason she had sailed south for a month to this island without him being the wiser for it. "Only in certain matters."

Then he saw again the suspicion and jealousy that had shadowed Castle's eyes the previous night. Abruptly, his next tack became clear. This man would serve as his ally—unwittingly.

He chose his words carefully.

"It seemed that you were displeased with her for pursuing the arsonists. With your long acquaintance, you must have known that would be her choice."

Castle shook his head.

"In truth, Seton, I don't know what to do about her. I never have." He chuckled, affectedly man-to-man, but behind his eyes Jin discerned the care he was also taking with each word. "Working for her, you must have seen it. But she has always been this way, willful and stubborn and misunderstanding all she sees and hears."

The first and second, yes. But not the last. Viola understood what she wished to understand.

But in seeking to paint her in a poor light, Castle offered him the perfect opening.

"Perhaps it is in her nature," he said. "And in her breeding as well."

"Her breeding?" Castle flashed him a curious glance.

"Fionn was a stubborn man, it's true, but a thinking man, all the same, with a fine understanding. Did you know him?"

"I know only her foster father," Jin replied easily, "the man who raised her as his own until she left England."

Castle stared. "Foster father? I don't understand. Her mother was English, of course. But after her death Fionn and his sister raised Violet entirely."

A metallic frisson of satisfaction ran through Jin. Castle had no idea of her true identity. He could not and appear so perplexed.

Now he would know. Jin would use him in this manner, as he had used men for his own purposes for years. Castle was courting the Hats for their connections and wealth. But he would turn his attentions swiftly once he knew of her true family. He would not hesitate to urge her to return to them.

And, in casting her into this man's arms, Jin would free himself of the need to have her in his own. He would have what he wished, his debt repaid, and she would have what she wished as well. From the English gentry, stalwart, steady Aidan Castle had labored to acquire modest wealth and status. He had never killed a man to secure his admirable goals, or thieved, or lied. And he cared for her.

"Until her eleventh year when Fionn Daly took her to America against her will," Jin said, "she lived on an estate on the coast of Devonshire. Her mother, the daughter of a gentleman of considerable means, had practiced infidelity upon her husband. Miss Daly was the product of that union."

Castle's face opened in astonishment. Then he said one word, a word that tightened Jin's gut in triumph and also something much less satisfying.

"Estate?"

"Her mother's husband was a baron. A nobleman." He paused. "Carlyle. The name he gave her is Viola, and although he has always known of her paternity, he has never ceased considering her his true daughter."

Castle's mouth worked. Then he blew out a muted whistle.

"A nobleman's daughter. Good Lord, I never would have guessed it."

"Wouldn't you have?"

He frowned. "How should I? She has been a sailor since I've known her." The crease in his brow smoothed. "The prettiest little sailor on the Atlantic, it's true. But . . . a noblewoman?" He shook his head. Then the spark of jealousy flared again. "How did you come to learn this? Did she tell you?"

"I became acquainted with her family before leaving England. I have come here, in fact, to convey her home. To Lord Carlyle," he added. But he needn't. Castle's eyes had brightened, their bewilderment no less apparent, but relief and excitement there as well. He assessed Jin with less intensity now, as though he understood.

He understood nothing. Nothing of what Jin began to fear he was at this moment giving up in order to give her what she should have.

"Am I interrupting?" She appeared beside them, a thick package under her arm.

He stood, Castle following to his feet. She glanced curiously at Jin, then her gaze went to Castle and softened.

"Are you well, Aidan? And your cousin, and the Hats? How do you all get along today? I heard at the shop that the fire was contained before dawn."

With a quick glance at Jin first, Castle grasped her hand.

"We are all well, myself, Seamus, and Mr. and Mrs. Hat and their daughter, who have moved here to the inn to lodge. And you, Vi—" He cleared his throat. "Violet?"

"Fine. I am sorry we did not manage to catch the arsonists, Aidan. The damage to your farm must be tremendous."

"We have lost a quarter of this crop and the house is un-inhabitable." He chuckled uncomfortably. "Now of course I have no place in which to offer you my hospitality."

"That seems inconsequential given all," she mumbled.

Jin withdrew a coin from his pocket and set it on the table.

"I have work to accomplish. I must take my leave of you, Castle." He picked up his hat. "Miss Daly, I will send the boat back for you." He bowed.

"My thanks for the drink, Seton. And conversation."

Jin departed. Viola stared after him. She did not wish him to leave. But he had been contrary today, confusing in his speech and actions, and yet simply looking at him made her ache in all the places he had touched her. Sweet, agitated aching that made her wretchedly peevish.

She turned reluctantly to the other confusing man in her life—or perhaps not so much in her life any longer. He stared at her intently.

"Why are you looking at me like that?" she asked.

"Like what?"

"Like you're seeing me for the first time, when we spent the entire evening together yesterday." Before she saw him embrace Miss Hat.

"I don't know what you mean, Violet. You are being absurd." He chucked her under the chin. She drew her face away.

"What will you do now?"

"Do?"

"With your farm, of course."

He glanced about them, then at her clothing. He seemed to assess, then decide silently. "Will you walk with me? I am so exhausted that I believe if I sit I might drop off to sleep." He chuckled.

"You weren't asleep sitting here with Mr. Seton. The two of you looked quite intent in your conversation." She allowed him to guide her lightly from the taproom, his fingers barely brushing her elbow. "What did you find to converse about?"

"You, of course."

Her belly twisted. She frowned.

"Is that so difficult to believe?" he said pleasantly. "We have little else in common than that we have both shared time aboard a ship with you."

They had a great deal more in common than he knew. Viola's cheeks warmed and she was glad for her concealing hat. They went out onto the street and he led her toward a pathway leading along the docks. She peered beneath her brim toward the wharf, but the place was busy with people and she did not see Jin or the boat.

"Allow me to carry your parcel for you." Aidan drew the package with her new gown and underclothes from her arms. "What did you purchase?"

"Nothing of interest. Aidan, tell me please about the farm."

"There is little to tell. It will be some time before the house is in comfortable condition again." They moved onto a path lined with palms and yucca, and insects buzzed about in the heat. Gulls wheeled overhead, playing in the breeze that tugged at her hat, fresh as a sailor liked to feel it. "You came here anticipating hospitality, so I hope you will allow me to offer you a chamber at the inn tonight." He smiled down at her.

"I anticipated nothing but your company, which I hope I may have with or without a sojourn at a hotel. And I have my quarters aboard the *April* to bunk in, of course."

He drew her to a halt beneath a young palm. "I did not intend to insult your honor, my dear, or to demand any familiarity with you that you are not happy to give." His voice was somewhat low, with an abrupt intimacy that made Viola's stomach feel peculiar.

"I did not suggest that you had. And since when have you been concerned with my honor? Since when have you ever thought I even had any?"

His wide lips curved into a smile.

"Please stay at the inn at my expense tonight. I will be at the farm, of course, supervising the laborers until late. But it will relieve me to know you are comfortable here." He squeezed her hand. "I recognize this packaging." He gestured with her parcel. "You have shopped at the dressmaker's."

She nodded.

"Will you wear it this evening for dinner?"

"Yes, but for dinner with the harbormaster. He has invited Mr. Seton and me to join him and his wife." Nerves jittered in her belly.

"What a great honor."

"Well, he says we will have excellent pork pie, at least." She screwed up her brow. "Aidan—"

"Then tomorrow. Will you wear your new gown for me tomorrow? I will drive you along the coast a bit and buy you lunch at the finest teahouse you could ever imagine. Better than in Boston, even London, I daresay."

"What do I care about London teahouses? I have work to do tomorrow, of course. But more importantly, you must have a great deal to do as well. And your guests—"

He grasped her hand to him tighter. "None of that matters now that you are with me and we can again begin planning our future together." His hazel gaze held warm entreaty. Viola's heart thudded.

"Oh, Aidan, cease this." She pulled her hand away. "I saw you kiss Miss Hat in the garden last night."

His face went blank. "You saw that?"

"Yes, I saw that. I was on the veranda."

"It was nothing, Violet."

"It looked like something to me."

His brow lowered and his shoulders seemed to tense.

"Well, if I did kiss her, it was because you had driven me to it."

"I *what*? I have only just sailed hundreds of miles to see you!"

"I thought you had a cargo to deliver."

"*April Storm* is a privateer, not a pack mule. I took on the cargo to make even on this trip. I must pay my crewmen, or have you forgotten those mundane details of my life?"

"Perhaps I have. But, Violet, have you forgotten mine? I have lived here for months alone. I had hoped when you arrived—" He broke off, ran his hand through his curls, then set a direct look on her. "When I bade you good night last night you were . . . distant."

Her eyes widened. But all she could see was herself again standing at the base of a companionway, foundering beneath a man's crystal gaze filled with heat.

"I did not know you expected that of me last night," she managed to utter. "I supposed with your guests you would wish to be discreet. We are not wed."

He shook his head. "I did not expect it of you, precisely, of course. Forgive me, I have misspoken. But Violet—"

"You should have been honest with me about your feelings for Miss Hat. To be met with such a sight on my arrival, well, I will tell you, it hurt."

He grasped her hands.

"Violet, please. I am out of my head and behaving irrationally. Though her parents wish for our match and have come here to engineer it, I have no feelings for her. But I saw how it was with Seton, and it made me—"

She tugged away again, stepping back. "How what was with him?"

He looked hesitant. "When I spoke caution to you of him, you defended him."

"I merely suggested that you might stay your judgment until you came to know him."

"Have you come to know him?" His hazel eyes bored into her. "How well, Violet?"

She could not halt the flush that rose to her cheeks. She was not proficient at lying, but she did not know if she must now. Aidan had not been faithful to her. Last night she truly believed he no longer wanted her as his wife. But she did not wish to hurt the man she had loved for so long, her friend for years before he was her lover. He seemed to understand so little of the truths of her life now. He did not need to know this one.

"He is a good man." She believed this, despite her confusion and Jin's past. His life now showed it, and his behavior with her crewmen—never cruel, always respectful and just. Even with her, now that she knew his purpose in seeking her out, he was honest. He made her no false promises. He told her only the truth, and very clearly he told her his intentions. "I trust him."

"Trust." The corners of Aidan's mouth were pinched. "You look at him as though . . ."

"As though?"

"When you look at him, I don't recognize you."

"How can you recognize anything about me? You know me very little now. A handful of letters and one visit over the course of four years amounts to little familiarity."

He grasped her hands so tightly this time she could not free herself without a struggle.

"Then perhaps you are correct and we haven't sufficient knowledge of one another any longer. But allow us to regain that familiarity we once shared. Remain here for a time with me. You will want for nothing."

"You've just said yourself that your house is barely habitable."

He smiled warmly. "We will fix it up together, just as we spoke of years ago."

"And what of Miss Hat and her parents?"

He bent his head. "They are to leave the island shortly. But even if they were not, it would not matter. Dear Violet, I beg your pardon for that minor infidelity. Please forgive me. It will not occur again, I promise."

His infidelity had not felt minor to her. In an instant that single kiss had cracked her world open. Or perhaps it had only widened the fissure that already existed. And Jin Seton had filled the void. For a time, in his arms, the loneliness that was her constant companion had abated.

Yet here was the man with whom she had dreamed of spending her life insisting that she could now live that dream.

She shook her head. "I don't trust you."

"But can you learn to trust me again?"

"Do you still wish to marry me, Aidan?"

"Of course, dear Violet. You are the best thing in my life. You always have been." The same words he had spoken before, numerous times. She could not look at his face now, but stared at his thick hands circled around hers. Still so familiar, in truth, and yet this familiarity seemed wrong now.

"Please release me."

He did so immediately.

"I've work to do, a new cargo to negotiate so that I can pay the *April*'s journey home. We may encounter unfriendly craft along the way and take a prize, but I cannot count on it, of course."

"But this will be your home now, Violet."

"I must have time to think." She had not considered returning to Boston so soon. Not until the words formed on her tongue. "I know it was only a kiss. I assume it was only a kiss—"

"It was."

"But it has changed much for me." She was not the same naïve girl she had been. And now she was withholding the entire truth from him too. "Perhaps you could return here tomorrow, or the day after, and I will be able to speak of this with you then. But not yet."

He nodded. His hand reached for hers again, but then drew back.

"Tomorrow, then." He leaned forward and pressed a kiss onto her cheek beneath the brim of her hat. She did not lift her head, and after a moment he walked away.

Chapter 16

As the sun dipped low over the mouth of the harbor, the harbormaster's wife sent Viola a written invitation. She was drawing her new gown from the packaging, its fabric stiff from pressing, when the note arrived with another. By the light of a lamp she perused it, her palms damp against the paper. Joining them to dine that evening would be six other guests, including two naval officers and their wives.

She unfolded the other message, from Aidan.

A knock came on her cabin door. She opened it, and felt like a perfect fool. How could it be that she could simply look at Jin Seton and her knees weakened?

He wore a coat of simple, elegant cut that fit him as though tailored for him. His shirt, cravat, and waistcoat were white and neat, and his handsome face clean-shaven.

His gaze flicked over her. "You are not yet dressed for dinner?"

"I am not going," she blurted out, clutching her hands behind her, the letters crunching together. "I—I . . ."

He lifted his brows.

"I have another appointment this evening," she said. "With—"

He held up his palm to halt her speech, the wounded palm she had insisted on doctoring so she could touch him again. In her hurt and indignation after he made his intentions clear to her that morning, she had not realized why she insisted. But she understood herself somewhat better now. And she knew that she could not accompany this man to a dinner engagement with strangers and acquit herself properly. She did not remember how to. In point of fact, she had never learned it. But she knew, simply by looking at the easy set of his shoulders and his stance, that somehow this former pirate did know. He would have no trouble making himself an equal of the harbormaster's other guests, if not indeed their superior in dress and manners.

"You needn't explain," he said. "Your business is your own. I will make your apologies for you."

"Thank you." She chewed on her lip. "I think."

The corner of his mouth lifted slightly and Viola's whole heart turned over, colliding with her stomach and making her a little nauseous.

"I don't know what 'make your apologies' means," she admitted.

"I will invent a plausible story so as not to insult my host and hostess with the announcement of your untimely absence. I suspect you wish to remain in his good graces."

"I am sorry. I had a prior dinner engagement with . . . with Mr. Castle, at the hotel. I hadn't the opportunity to tell you earlier."

He nodded. "I wish you a good evening, then."

"He has arranged rooms at the inn for us all, you know." She gestured with the wadded up letters. "For the Hats and me. And you. He hopes that you will accept his invitation for a comfortable chamber, since he cannot offer us hospitality at his house as we—as *I* expected."

He tilted his head. "Am I to understand that if I refuse and remain aboard, you will consider it mutiny on the wager?"

She couldn't resist a grin. "Most certainly."

"Then rest assured, I will be at the inn tonight." He turned, then paused. "But not as Mr. Castle's guest. I will hire my own room."

Her pulse skittered. "You carry a great deal of pride along with that arrogance, don't you?"

He regarded her for a steady moment. "Pride has little to do with it. Good night, Viola."

She stood for a silent minute in her doorway, listening to the creaking sounds of her ship, largely quiet in the absence of most of her crew. Then she packed a small bag. She had no plans to dine with Aidan. His missive only begged her to take up his offer to rest in comfort tonight at the inn while he tried to clean the house sufficient for her return to the farm shortly. She suspected the Hats would be at the hotel too, and probably dining there as well. But she doubted Aidan would call upon them, not after his promises this afternoon. He had seemed so sincerely sorry for his mistake and so ready to make a fresh start of it with her.

She would go to the inn, indulge in a bath, and wash her hair with soap. Then she would sleep in clean linens on a dry mattress and in the morning wake refreshed. For with the morning came the end of the wager, and she must be fully prepared to argue again with Seton when he demanded she return to England.

This time, she intended to win.

At the dress shop she had also purchased a new shift, one that cinched around the waist with a thin cord and laced up the front with ribbons. In her small, simply appointed bedchamber at the inn, she bathed, then donned the new garment. She combed her wet hair and it sprang into loose curls, but refused to dry completely in the humidity that rose at nightfall on the tropical island. Tendrils stuck to her brow and clung to her neck.

She went to the window and opened the shutter. Breeze stirred in her hair and against her shift, brushing the crisp linen over her breasts. The sensation of Jin's mouth on her, sending heat through the fabric of her shift, came to her with a sudden weakening of her limbs, then warmth between her legs. She was still tender there, but abruptly the tenderness throbbed. With only the slightest suggestion, her body was eager for him again.

It was unnerving. And . . . delicious.

Her fingers gripped the windowsill and she gazed out at the sparkling black water of the bay. The *April Storm*'s masts towered the tallest; no other vessels in the port tonight to match her in size, though there were plenty of other newer ships and boats.

She stared at her father's old brig across the moonlit water, the familiar pain of fading grief hovering like a shadow inside her. The ship should be scrapped, in truth, but she hadn't the funds for a new vessel. Without the *April*, she would be without employment except on another captain's vessel. That was not an option, of course. Women aboard ships served one role—whore.

She would have to take at least four or five hefty prizes to even begin to imagine purchasing another ship of the *April*'s size. But prizes were scarce these days now that the wars were well and truly over up north. If she remained in these islands she might take a Mexican or Cuban pirate or two. But against that sort of enemy she was just as likely to get herself killed—or worse—especially in unfamiliar waters.

She needed that ship sitting in dry dock in Boston. Jin Seton's new ship. She needed him to lose the wager.

He had been irritated with her earlier in the day because he desired her. Clearly. This she was not fool enough to mistake. But he did not want to desire her. Because perhaps he desired her too much? More than he wished? To the point of falling in love with her and losing the wager?

It seemed unlikely. He could have been peevish because of exhaustion, like her. But perhaps not. Perhaps she could still win. Perhaps, if she gave him one more taste of her, he would finally fall in love.

She could at least try.

Her fingers around the edge of the shutter quivered. She drew out her father's old watch, the gold chain long since traded for some necessary ship supply. Ten o'clock. He must have come to the inn by now. But she'd no idea which room he'd taken.

Her pulse raced. She couldn't simply go to his room and seduce him. Could she?

She could. If she knew which room. But she couldn't very well ask the innkeeper.

She went to her bed and curled up on the mattress, her whole exhausted body jittering with nerves. A solution would come to her. She closed her eyes to think. Instead, she pictured his mouth, then for good measure his hands and jaw and eyes. Then she thought of how he had looked at her and touched her like he couldn't get enough of her. And how she never wanted him to release her. Never wanted it to end. Never . . .

She awoke with a start to voices in the corridor. The lamp still flickered on her bedside table, but the candle on the mantel had burned to a stub. She shook herself awake and listened.

Her insides melted, then tensed. It was he. And Mr. Hat?

She stole off the bed on silent feet and pressed her ear to the door. A giggle welled up and she stifled it. For pity's sake, they had attacked each other on a canvas-draped stairway the night before; she needn't really skulk around at this point.

But tonight was different. Tonight if she went to him and he accepted her, neither of them could claim it was a lustful inspiration of the moment.

No female voices met her strained hearing, only the two men. But she must be certain of what she would be walking into, and she could not delay; it sounded as though they were bidding each other good night. She flicked open the bolt on her door and with trembling fingers turned the knob and peeked into the corridor.

From ten feet away his gaze came directly to her. Then he returned his attention to Mr. Hat.

"Good night, then, Seton. Pleasure making your acquaintance."

"I wish you and your family a safe journey, sir." He turned and walked down the corridor to the door at the end, drew out a key, and went within. Mr. Hat disappeared up the stair. Viola closed her door, returned to her bed, and sat on the edge of it. Her hands shook. Her entire body shook.

It was *nothing* like the night before. She couldn't do it.

But if she did it, and she won the wager . . .

Her lips even quivered now, and her lungs seemed to be doing odd, unsteady things. She lowered her toes to the floor, the soles of her feet, her heels. She unbent her knees and went to the door.

Down the corridor lit only by a single sconce in the stair below, his chamber seemed miles away. But she was Violet *la Vile*. She'd been the one to give herself that name, of course, but it stuck because she'd taken several fat prizes right away. And before that she'd helped her father take any number of enemy ships as well. She had sunk the infamous *Cavalier*, for pity's sake! She could conquer its master.

She strode to his door. The knob turned in her hand. Without knocking, she went in.

He sat in a chair by a small table, his sharp gaze fixed on her, his injured hand holding a book, his other wrapped about the hilt of a dagger in the process of drawing it from his boot.

"Don't throw it!" she gasped. "Though I suppose you might wish to."

Slowly he withdrew the weapon and laid it on the table. "Not at the present. Although there have been moments." He set down the book and rose to his feet. He had removed his coat and waistcoat, and a pair of suspenders hung from his trousers. He wore no neck cloth now, the button on his shirt unfastened. Golden candlelight revealed every perfect sinew of beautiful man. She found it difficult to breathe.

"Why did you leave your door unlocked?"

"I did not realize that I had."

"You didn't?"

"I am tired. And distracted by thoughts of the evening I have spent. The day." He seemed perfectly sincere. As always. Except that morning when he'd sounded strange, panicked almost, entirely unlike himself.

"It wasn't because you thought I would come?"

A glint of wariness entered his eyes. "Why are you awake? You look as though you have been sleeping."

"I do?"

He gestured. "Your hair."

She patted a hand to her head. Curls jutted out at an angle and she could feel a bald spot, dried like that during her doze, no doubt. Oh, God. She had no idea how to lure a man in this manner. She'd never had a mother to teach her, or anyone.

But she had her instincts, and from living with sailors for years, she did know what men liked most about women. Her hand slipped to her throat and she untied the bow, then drew the ribbon through the holes and parted the linen.

"Then don't look at my hair." Her voice quavered. She shrugged her shoulders out of the fabric and allowed the sleeves to sag at her elbows. She stood bare-breasted before him, her heartbeats fast. But now she was no longer shaking. Instead, she was certain.

He didn't move. Nor did he so much as glance at her breasts. But in his ice eyes, illumined with firelight, heat flickered.

"Viola." His voice was low. "No."

She gulped. "No?"

"You will not achieve what you wish with this."

He understood that she still hoped to win the wager, and he was refusing. But the desire in his eyes like blue flames did not dim, and the taut line of his jaw and the tensed muscles in his neck and forearms suggested he was not averse to temptation.

She took in a breath of courage. Another. Then, lifting her hand, she trailed a single fingertip down the gully between her breasts. Aidan had once asked her to touch herself. She had not been able to do it, too ashamed of the request and her inability to please him simply by being naked before him. But now, beneath Jin's gaze, it seemed the most natural thing in the world to slide her fingers around the curve of her skin and circle the nipple. She must please him. She *wanted* to please him. And it felt surprisingly good, slightly wicked yet honest.

He came to her.

Standing close, he drew her hand away and said in a beautifully husky voice, "Allow me."

Then Viola began trembling again, but softly, a waiting

anticipation of pure, delirious desire. Barely touching her, he drew one sleeve from her wrist, then the other. The heat of his body caressed her skin but her nipples were firm, as though she were quite cold. His attention moved to the cord at her waist. With careful movements he untied the bow and loosened the gathered fabric. He bent his head and seemed to inhale deeply, his chest rising, then slowly falling. Her eyelids fluttered. She wanted him to touch her so much. Her nipples inches from his shirtfront felt tight and tingling.

Finally, gently, he urged the shift over her hips. It crumpled on the floor. She wore nothing else; she'd been ready for bed.

She reached for his waist to tug his shirt free and he pulled it over his head. Viola got dizzy. Quite dizzy and quite weak in the knees again. She'd barely seen him the night before in the darkness. Now the golden light on his skin and glimmering across his wide shoulders washed her with need. She reached for the bulge of his arousal beneath his trousers. He grasped her hand.

"No."

"No, again?"

"Not yet." He spoke quietly. "Slow down."

But she wanted to touch him. She ached for it. "What happened to 'on my terms'?"

"That was last night. Tonight you have come to me. You have put yourself in my hands voluntarily. Tonight is on my terms." He stroked the backs of his fingers across her cheek, then the spot beneath her mouth where she was marked. "Do you know how beautiful you are? With all your clothing on." His voice seemed to smile. Then it dipped low again. "You needn't remove it to entice."

"Men look at me with lust in their eyes." And they believed themselves in love, because they did not know any better than to confuse one with the other. She was counting on that now. She tilted her face into his touch, her eyes drifting closed. "But men are in general lustful creatures."

"Indeed they are." His fingers trailed along her throat, down her neck, sending shivering tangles inside her.

She whispered, "The way you look at me is different."

"Is it?" His knuckles skimmed the curve of her breast.

"*Ye-es.*"

He bent his head and with his fingertips stroked her breast slowly from the swell and around the peak, then his palm encircled her. But still he did not touch the hungry crest. "How do I look at you?"

"I don't know." Her breaths stuttered. "I don't—" She arched into his touch. "Oh, Jin, I—" He passed the pad of his thumb across the peak, only once. "*Ohh.*" Her whole body shuddered. She grabbed his arms to stay upright. "Do that again."

"If I do," he said, soft amusement in his voice, "do you think you can remain standing?"

"If you do," she replied, "I will try."

He did so again, and again, the rasp of male callus against female tenderness sublime perfection, so simple, sending pleasure through her whole body. With such a slight caress he made her into liquid longing for him.

"I don't know that I can continue standing after all," she said on a rush.

He lifted her like a child and took her to the bed. No teasing, no laughter, no shame that she could not manage the journey of five feet's distance by herself. Nothing to prove. He removed his boots and as he did so his gaze traveled over her body, his breaths obviously fast. She reached for him, and he for her, and their mouths came together.

It was as before, the closeness and completeness, like their first kiss, beautifully familiar in its newness. His hands scooped around her head, holding her to him, and she gripped his shoulders and opened and allowed him entrance. He did not tease her, but gave, the pleasure of his tongue meeting hers, his teeth coaxing on her lips. His fingers curved around her jaw, touching her face, exploring as though he would feel their kiss in this manner too. The heat of his palm slipped to her throat, then her shoulder, and he followed with his mouth. She clutched his arms and with each caress she trembled and wanted more urgently for him to press her back onto the mattress and come inside her. She inched her knees apart, hoping she would not be required to tell him she could not wait, to beg. Then his tongue stole around her nipple, and quite swiftly begging seemed like a perfectly reasonable option.

She moaned, his tongue stroked, and she surrendered all hesitation, all concern for what she should or should not do. She slid her fingers into his hair and nothing mattered but this. Nothing but his perfect mouth seducing her, the hot, singing readiness of her body, and a desire beyond anything she had ever felt to make love to a man.

She slipped her fingers over the hard ridge beneath his trousers. He grabbed her hand and pulled it to his lips. His eyes were aflame.

"Don't," he said harshly against her palm.

"Don't? But—"

He captured her mouth with his and she feasted on him, the taste of him and heat and his hard body beneath her hands. He grasped her shoulders and lifted her onto her knees and kissed her again, and again. His hands swept down her arms to her waist, encompassing and spreading heat. Then he touched her. He touched her and her world ended and began at once.

He had not touched her there the night before. Their coming together so swift both times, like summer storms breaking, had not truly allowed for it. Now to have him touch her so intimately, she was changed.

She had never thought much about the womanly parts of her body. They were to be used as any other parts for their proper purpose—for pleasure with a man, certainly. But she had never known what it felt like to be worshipped.

Gently at first he caressed her, and she trembled, and their mouths stilled upon each other's. His breaths came unevenly like hers. Her face tilted upward, eyes closing, and he stroked deeper. She whimpered from the pleasure that made her need more with each stroke, from the certainty of his touch. In that touch he must know he could control her, command her in this manner, know that at this moment she would do anything he asked. She pressed into him, lost to his caress, and did not care that she had lost.

"Viola, open your eyes." He spoke at her brow, his deep voice taut. "Look at me."

Her eyelids fluttered, heavy like the aching pleasure mingled with desperation in her body. "Yes," she sighed, working her hips against his hand. She whimpered, with each caress needing him inside her, seeking for him. "Why?"

He impaled her upon his fingers.

"*Oh!* God."

He thrust again, a hard, sublime possession. "I want you to see that it is I giving you pleasure."

She moaned and rode his fingers, pushing him deeper, wanting him deeper, everywhere inside her. She sank her hands into his hair. "Of course it is you." She kissed him, but the need was too much, too painfully good in its intensity. She jerked her hips to him, his fingers a sweet agony in her. "Jin, take me now. Now. I cannot bear it any longer."

"You will bear it."

"*No.*" Would he deny her?

"You will not only bear it," he said huskily, then finally—
dear God, finally—pressed her back to the mattress. "You
will ask for more." Meeting her desperate thrusts with his
hand, he parted her knees and took her with his mouth.

She did not ask for more.

She begged.

She pleaded.

Upon an astounded, needing sob she cried for more. For
she had never known this. She had never known any of that
which he so beautifully gave her body. Yet each time he
brought her to the edge, each time she thought he would
give her what she craved, he did deny her. With his tongue
hot and soft and devastatingly good he made her wild, with
his fingers plunging inside her he made her helpless, until
the pleasure was so great and continuous that only one wish
tumbled to her lips.

"*Please*." She gripped the bedclothes. "Let me give to you
too."

That seemed to decide the matter.

She reached for him and he came to her, then inside her
in one smooth thrust, surrounding her with his body and
filling her with his hard heat. She choked back the joy of the
pleasure, wrapping her arms about his shoulders. They were
joined, finally, fully, and completely motionless save their
breaths pressing her breasts against his chest.

He threaded his fingers through her hair, kissed her brow,
her cheek, her throat. His hand trailed along her waist, circled a taut nipple, making her gasp and murmur his name
and shift against him to feel him more, to revel in his presence in her.

Then, slowly, he moved in her, and he took what gift of
pleasure she was able to give him, which as it happened was
a great deal of pleasure. For, perhaps predictably (if either of
them had paused to waste time predicting), their lovemak-

ing did not remain languorous more than a moment. She drew him in, he sank into her, and they proceeded to prove quite definitively that it did not require a burning cane field, a frantic horseback ride, cannon fire, or even a staircase to inspire them to mate with the urgency of animals and the ecstasy of gods. The bed creaked furiously, she made sounds she had never before heard, he caused her previous gyrations beneath him to seem tame, and when it was over she felt fantastically sated and thoroughly battered. Additionally, four neat pink stripes were rising in welts across each of his shoulders.

"I have wounded you," she gasped, struggling to fill her lungs.

"You have. Witch." He seemed to be unsatisfied with the quantity of kissing that had already gone on, and now leaned down to press his mouth to hers again. But the caress of his perfect lips was nearly too much, the sweetly dissipating pleasure within her tender and unstable. Perhaps his excessive sensual teasing had overstimulated her exhausted flesh. But now with the leisure to feel his entire body against hers, again she trembled. Quite fearsomely.

"Your hand is bleeding again." She stroked her fingers along his arm sleek with muscle. "You will wear a hook after all."

"It will have been worth it." He pulled off her and fell onto his back, taking her hand in his. Then for a moment he went very still. He released her hand, leaned over her, and drew a coverlet over her body. Without a word, he settled onto his back again.

She turned onto her side to face him, and curled her knees and arms tight to her. "I am not actually chilled."

"You are shaking."

"I'm exhausted."

"Then sleep." Lit only by the fading lamplight, his face

and body were beautiful, his dark hair tumbled across his brow, black lashes low over ice eyes that could glisten with heat. A spot of crimson spread from the center of the single scrap of cloth on his body.

"I would like to tend to your wounds first."

"They will keep until later." His voice sounded quiet and deep, as though he were already descending into slumber.

"Don't you want me to leave now?"

He did not look at her or even open his eyes. "No."

She sat up, the covers falling to her lap. "I must dress that wound again."

With an indolent, thoroughly uncharacteristic motion, he swept his forearm in an arc and laid his bandaged hand beside her, palm up.

"As you wish, harpy."

Tingling warmth scurried around her belly. He seemed . . . *happy*. Simply happy.

Carnal pleasures made men happy. Viola knew this as any woman would who had lived among men her entire adult life. Men were simple creatures, most of them, and when they were satisfied carnally—be it on food or a woman's body—they were content. Still, as little as she understood Jinan Seton, she knew he was not a simple man. Happiness did not, she thought, come easily to him.

She slid off the bed and went to his luggage, where she found what she expected, fresh bandages and salve. Although earlier when she needed an excuse to touch him she'd taunted him about tending his wound, she knew no shipmaster would actually be that negligent. Certainly not this man. She returned to the bed and unwrapped his hand.

He seemed to sleep through her ministrations, although the wound must pain him; it was deep across, though a clean slice. It would heal well. She rebound it, then laid his hand on the counterpane. Next she dipped all four fingertips into the tiny pot of salve, leaned to his shoulder, and painted a path along the tracks she'd dug with her nails. His skin was taut and damp over firm muscle, and she wanted to linger and breathe in his scent, to continue touching him. Instead she repeated the salve on his other shoulder, then drew away.

The caress of linen bandage and warm skin on her naked behind arrested her.

She swallowed through her constricted throat. "You mustn't use that hand now."

"Kiss me."

"I don't take or—"

"Kiss me, I pray you, Miss Carlyle?"

She bent and did as requested as his fingers skirted the crease between her legs, then smoothed along her thigh to trail away. When she pulled back, his eyes were still closed, his mouth ever so slightly curved upward.

"Thank you," he murmured.

"For the nursing or the kiss?"

He smiled fully.

She pulled the coverlet over them, closed her eyes, and allowed the stars to lull her to sleep.

Chapter 17

Viola grinned, stretched, flinched from the wonderful soreness all over her body, and finally opened her eyes. Sunlight peeked through the draperies, casting the bedchamber in a hazy morning glow.

She sat bolt upright.

Except for her shift draped across a chair and herself in the bed, the place was empty of everything but furniture. The man with whom she had made passionate love mere hours earlier, who had hired this chamber for himself, might never have been there at all.

Viola sat for a moment quite immobile, considering how among the various foolish things she had done in her life, to have practiced this lack of forethought was perhaps the most foolish of all. Unwisely, she had not assumed that the moment the wager ended he would leave her side, no matter the circumstances.

Now the discomforts in her body did not feel so wonderful. Instead she felt rather ill, her stomach tight and all her limbs soggy.

She swiveled, climbed from the bed, and took up her shift. It got stuck going over her hair, knotted strands tangled in the laces. She shoved it down and tied it over her breasts. Her sailor's blood accustomed to rising with the sun told her it was still early morning, so she might not encounter others in the corridor. But her blood had also told her that Jin Seton would be present when she awoke. So it looked like her blood wasn't as clever as she'd always thought.

Hand on the doorknob, she paused.

The wager was over. He had left. But that did not necessarily mean she had lost. It could, in fact, mean she'd won. If he fell in love with her, he was to admit to it, then to deed his new ship over to her and leave her alone forever. Even now he could be sailing to Tobago to collect his assets, which would allow him to complete the purchase of the sleek little schooner in Boston. Perhaps he had simply gone to fulfill the terms of the wager.

Or perhaps not.

She went to her chamber, dressed in breeches, shirt, and vest; slung her coat over her shoulder; and took up her bag. Depositing the key with the proprietor, she pressed a coin into the housemaid's palm, then went out into the sunny morning.

The walk to the wharf was only fifty yards. Sam sat on the dock beside the yawl bobbing in the water, dangling a piece of straw from between his teeth. He sprang up and tugged his cap.

"Morning, Cap'n. How was that hotel? I ain't never stayed in no hotel before."

"Good morning, Sam. It was fine, thank you."

She boarded the little boat and Sam rowed her to her ship, tentative nerves of triumph twisting about her belly now. Jin must be aboard or Sam wouldn't be waiting for her at the dock.

She climbed the ladder and set her feet on her deck's solid planking. Her home.

She called down to Sam, "You may have the day now. Take the yawl, but return by midday to bring me ashore." To negotiate a cargo for her return trip to Boston, as she had told Aidan.

She started across the empty deck. Only old Frenchie dozed on guard duty atop the quarterdeck, another two sailors below on rotation. Otherwise her ship was deserted.

Except for Jin Seton.

He ascended the stairs from the main hatch, and Viola's heart climbed into her throat. He looked nothing out of the ordinary—simply dressed, sober, handsome. Perfect.

He saw her and paused at the head of the stair. They stared at each other, the deck between them crisscrossed with shadows of spars and lines cutting through morning sunshine. Heart galloping, she went forward and he did as well, and they halted at a distance. Viola's insides twisted. With what words could she possibly begin this day?

Instead, he began it.

"When can you be ready to leave?"

She could not breathe. His gaze was quite serious.

"I suppose this is your way of telling me you've won the wager?" She forced through her closed throat.

His gaze remained steady upon her.

He had made love to her and she had given him some pleasure, but at the wager's commencement he had promised to tell her the truth of it. So this was the truth: she had not succeeded in making him fall in love with her. And she, her insides howling strangely like a hurricane, must abide by the terms upon which they had agreed.

"I can be ready in a sennight. Less than a fortnight, certainly," she heard herself say without knowing how the words came. "I will need to conclude negotiations regarding the cargo my ship will carry to Boston. And arrange matters with the men, of course. Becoua will captain the *April* back to Boston and put it into Crazy's care."

"I regret that I must return you home against your will," he finally said. "I wish it were otherwise." He spoke with a gentle sincerity that actually hurt in the pit of Viola's gut like someone was driving a pole into her. "Viola, I am . . ." He paused. "I am sorry."

He was sorry for her. Sorry that she had lost the wager. Sorry that she had not succeeded in making him love her.

In this, however, she trumped him. Because she was a great deal sorrier than he. A very great deal. For now the truth slammed into her like a jib boom swinging in a crosswind. It had been many days since she wished to win for the reason she had given him—that she did not want to return to England. In truth, she had wished to win because it would have meant that he loved her, and she wanted that. She wanted him. He filled her longing, stretching the loneliness that made her ache at sunset through her like a storm that only he could calm. She was in love with him. She knew now that she had given herself to him the night of the fire not because she needed comfort, but because she was in love. She had been in love with him long before her ship docked at Port of Spain.

She had played a very foolish game, and lost.

"I won't back down on my part of the wager, if that's your concern."

"I know you will not." It might be pity he felt, but the distance in his crystal gaze struck her even more forcefully now.

And quite swiftly, her anger rose. Perhaps so swiftly because she had anticipated this outcome. In her heart she had known even last night when she went to seduce him that she would lose. Yet she had gone anyway.

"I have hired a sloop," he said. "I will sail for Tobago this morning to visit my bank to pay the fine on the *April*, and I will purchase a ship to take us east. I've been told there is a suitable vessel for sale at port in Scarborough."

"I suspected you wouldn't want to wait to collect your schooner in Boston first." She didn't truly care whether they sailed in a yawl or a hundred-gun frigate across the Atlantic. She didn't care about anything except berating herself for the fool she'd always been.

She was tired of loving men who could not love her back. Aidan never had. He spoke the words and even made the gestures. But he did not treat her with love. She saw this now more clearly than she had seen anything before. She saw it perhaps because the man standing before her had never spoken the words or made the gestures, and she wanted him more than she had ever wanted Aidan.

It infuriated her—her weakness. Her hardheadedness. Her blind foolishness. Beginning now, she would never again love a man until he loved her first. Never. To not be loved in return hurt far too much. Her insides felt as though someone had scooped them out with a galley ladle.

"We should depart before the storm season commences," he replied. "It is best we not delay."

"Of course." She would write to Mrs. Digby and her renters and Crazy and let them know she would be gone for an extended absence. She would negotiate a cargo so her crew would be able to carry back home at least some gold in their pockets. She had much to do and no practical reason to stand around mourning a misguided attachment except that her body seemed to want to remain near his as though he were a pole and she a pathetic little compass needle. She wiped her damp palms on her breeches. "I should get to business if all is to be ready by the time you return from Tobago," she said briskly. "You'll be gone a sennight or so?"

"Yes." His eyes were quite cool now.

"All right." She nodded. "Until then, Seton." She passed him and strode aft toward the companionway on which he had made love to her. She knew he watched her as she went below, and hoped he felt buckets of guilt for forcing her to do what she didn't wish to do. But he was not stupid and they both knew the truth of it. He had always known this would be the outcome. As he said from the beginning, her wager had been a child's game.

And she had lost.

She had lost him before she ever had him. No amount of anger would ease the pain of that.

"Mr. Julius Smythe?"

Jin swung his gaze up from the glass of rum gripped in his fist.

"The very one." His voice sounded dull. But most everything did in this palm-frond-and-plywood excuse for a rum house along Tobago's least traveled byway. The pub was so close to the breakers crashing against the rocks twenty feet below, little else could be heard. Occasionally a gull's cry. More frequently the protests of his own conscience.

He studied the man as though seeing him for the first time. Spare of frame and height, with curly brown hair, skin the color of oakwood and quick eyes—English, African, East Indian, Spanish—he appeared an unremarkable specimen of humanity. A mestizo. Not a man of distinction. No one of note. Which made him particularly good at the living he pursued. And particularly useful to Jin since they'd first met years ago.

Joshua Bose extended his hand, a charade they enacted on each encounter in the event that any interested party might be watching.

"I am Gisel Gupta," Joshua said, East Indian this time, apparently. "I am pleased to make your acquaintance, sir."

Jin gestured him to the chair across the table.

"You will have a glass with me, Gupta?"

"Thank you, sir." Joshua sat almost daintily, straight-

backed on the edge of his seat. He placed a thin leather
satchel on the table, then his palms flat on the satchel. "I
hope your journey to Tobago was a smooth one."

"It was fine." Brief, the sloop he had hired at Port of Spain
a fair enough vessel.

"Mr. Smythe, at the time of our previous meeting I had
been misinformed as to the whereabouts of the object which
you seek."

Jin revealed none of his surprise, or disappointment. He
had hoped that this time Joshua would bring him the box.
He had, in fact, prayed. But prayer from a man like him did
not take God's attention, only right actions. Of late, Jin's actions had nothing of rightness about them. But perhaps God
simply did not exist, which would explain a great deal.

"Ah," he only said.

"The information I received from my contact in Rio did
not satisfy me, you see. He indicated that the object had
changed hands in Caracas in October of 1812, when in fact
from the itinerary with which I supplied you last August, it
seemed impossible that its courier *at that time* would have
been anywhere in that region. He was, in fact, in Bombay."

"Bombay, hm?" Jin nodded thoughtfully. He cared nothing for this minutia. But Joshua would insist on relating it;
he relished the details of his work, and he could not share
it with any other. Jin only wanted the contents of that box,
if after sixteen years its contents yet remained within. He
was fairly certain of that impossibility. Nevertheless, he
played this game. He had become quite adept at playing such
games, like the game he had played with Viola Carlyle three
days earlier on the deck of the *April Storm* before he left
Trinidad.

The barkeep dropped a smudged tumbler on the table and
glanced at Jin's full measure of rum. He wrinkled his nose,
then thumped the bottle down and moved off.

Joshua reached into the pocket of his paisley waistcoat and withdrew a kerchief. With precise care he wiped the glass clean, refolded the linen and returned it to his pocket, and set his glass forward for Jin to fill. He took one sip, then placed the glass on the table.

"As I said, I was unsatisfied with this information. So I went to Rio to pursue that avenue personally." His smile flashed. "I am happy to report that in Rio I discovered that which we have all along sought."

Jin's heart tripped. His fingers slipped across the glass in his palm ever so slightly.

"Did you?"

Joshua's narrow nostrils flared, his mouth curving into a smile now.

"I did. And may I say, sir, how happy I am to now offer you the information which you hired me to find three years ago?"

"You may."

A wave hurled itself against shore, sending white vapor into the pristine blue sky. Wind whipped at the heavy palm fronds about the pub's roof, the heat of the sun bearing down all around the shaded canopy. Because of this moment, whatever the outcome of his quest, he would remember this place clearly. His curse was remembering that which would be best forgotten—like the woman he had called mother, and the last thing she said to him before she allowed her husband to take him to be sold at the slave market.

"Where is it, Gupta?"

"It is in the possession of His Excellency Bishop Frederick Baldwin of the Church of England." He fairly wiggled on the chair, growing taller as his spine stretched in pride. "In his house in London, sir. It has been there for several years as part of a collection of treasures from the East."

London. Not in a distant land. Not gone forever, destroyed

as it should have been with the rest of his mother's belongings when she died five years after her husband sent her bastard son away.

In London. And so Jin would be in London by late summer, after he returned Viola to her family in Devonshire.

"Thank you for this, Gupta." He stood. "Where would you like your fee delivered?"

Joshua blinked, his eyes widening. Jin supposed he ought to reward the man with more, with some display of satisfaction or anticipation. But at present he hadn't the will for it.

Shaking his head once, Joshua stood and tucked his satchel beneath his arm neatly. "To the usual place, Mr. Smythe."

Jin held out his hand. "It has been a pleasure doing business with you, Mr. Gupta."

"Likewise, sir. I hope you will not forget Gisel Gupta the next time you have need."

"I will contact you."

Joshua stepped away from the table.

"Gupta. Wait. I do have need of you at this time. In Boston."

"Yes, sir. Boston is a fine city."

"I need you to find a sailor and interview him for me. The sailor's name is Crazy."

Two minutes later, he watched Joshua weave through the tables and chairs and walk across the pebbly yard to his horse, then mount and ride away.

He glanced down at his untouched glass of rum. He might indulge in a moment of celebration. For three years he had paid Joshua Bose to search out the box. For twenty he had thought about it, imagining that box held his salvation—the key to his identity. Now, finally, he knew it to be within his reach. But he had no taste for rum, or any of the other spirits he'd had before him over the past three days.

Three days, and the sweet, rich flavor of her still lingered on his tongue. Three days and he could not yet erase her scent from his senses. Three days that already felt like a millennium.

He still wanted her. He wanted her hands on him and her soft lips caressing his skin and her dark eyes hot with desire and pleasure as he had her. He wanted her again. Goddamn it, he wanted her every day for a month. A year. He told himself to cease thinking of her. He failed at it.

Castle would follow her home; he was certain of it. He had passed the planter heading toward the *April Storm* as he left Port of Spain.

He had engineered it, but he did not like it. Castle might be an unexceptional sort, but he didn't like the opportunist bastard.

But, no. That was unjust. Castle was not a bastard. Jin had spent the evening with the harbormaster and naval officers and their wives learning about Aidan Castle, and he was unsurprised. Castle was the favored son of a modestly situated family in Dorset, a solid member of the respectable English gentry, a man who might as well try his hand at marrying into a noble family through an illegitimate daughter.

Jin was the bastard. The man without family or home. The mercenary. The thief. The murderer who would never fully atone for the evils he had done. Not when he was still committing deeds that went against his conscience.

She did not wish to return to England, to leave her life on the sea, and yet he was forcing her to do so. Perhaps his guilt was mitigated by what he was giving her in return. She deserved better than Aidan Castle, but she loved him. Jin might take comfort in his good deed if he weren't so damned distracted by his own desire.

The journey would take a month or six weeks if the wind stayed with them. The neat little thirty-gun brig he'd purchased the previous day would make it a comfortable trip. But it was going to be a hellishly long month trying to remain aloof from her. If he touched her again, he would be playing them both false. He was not the man for Miss Viola Carlyle.

When she had come into his room at the hotel seeking to seduce, he told himself it would not harm either of them to enjoy another night together. But when she asked if he wished her to leave, he'd had the insane urge to grasp her hand again and insist that she never leave. The panic that had sloshed through him then lingered even now.

"Captain Seton?"

Slipping his palm over his cuff, the slim weight of the dagger tucked within his sleeve at ready use, he turned.

"Aha! I knew not that I would be so fortunate so swiftly! They told me at the wharf that you had gone in this direction not two hours ago." The naval officer rode toward the canopy on a fine dappled gray, in blue and white uniform with gold encrustations of rank and honor on his shoulders and chest. Behind him two other officers drew their mounts to a halt at a distance, the wind blowing about their hat plumes.

Jin released the dagger hilt and moved to the edge of the lean-to, into the sun.

"How may I help you?"

The officer removed his hat and bowed smartly from the saddle. "Captain Daniel Eccles, at your service, sir."

Eccles, Halloway's lieutenant when the Royal Navy finally caught up with the pirate Redstone.

"As I am at yours, Captain." He bowed.

Eccles smiled broadly. "May I join you for a drink?"

"Of course."

Eccles motioned his officers to dismount and introduced them. They were sober-browed and neatly disposed in their crisp uniforms, so different from the ragtag collection of sailors aboard the *April Storm*. But men of the sea were largely the same at heart. With few words they made themselves agreeable and showed their intelligence, and both were gentlemen, as was Eccles.

"That must be your ship anchored at Scarborough," Jin said, watching them drink. "She is impressive."

"I was fortunate to get her. But I did not see the wily *Cavalier* at dock. Where is she berthed, at Crown Point?"

"She has been sunk."

Eccles's eyes widened. His officers glanced at one another.

"Sunk? The *Cavalier*?" His brow wrinkled. "I hadn't thought it possible, not with you at the helm."

"It was, I admit, unexpected." As was this tightness in his chest that would not abate. "Where are you bound? I understand from the port official at Port of Spain that you have been cruising this sea for some months."

"Ah, then my next question is answered. I hope he gave you the letter I left with him for you."

"He did. Thank you."

Eccles smiled. "When my admiral commands a task of me, I obey, of course. You have influential friends at Whitehall, Seton. I think I am nearly jealous."

"A man with a ship like yours needn't be jealous of anyone, Eccles."

The naval officer laughed. "You are quite right. But we are bound for England shortly, in fact. Our cruise is at an end and we've only to take on provisions, then will be heading home."

Slowly Jin leaned forward, finally taking up his glass of rum. Here was a solution.

"Captain Eccles, I myself have been given a challenging task for which I am in need of assistance. I wonder if you could help me."

"If it is within my power, of course. Any favor for the man who turned the crafty *Cavalier*'s purpose from thieving to good work. Redstone would not have done it, no matter how we hounded him." He regarded Jin quite seriously. Eccles knew Redstone's true identity, as only those who had been there on the sea off the coast of Devonshire that day. The pirate Redstone who had preyed on the vessels of wealthy peers had not been forgotten—or entirely forgiven. It was ironic, given that Jin had actually captained the *Cavalier* most of the time Alex Savege—in his other persona—had been its master. Yet now Jin was the hero and Alex ever after the mistrusted villain despite his noble lineage.

Not irony. Rather, a mockery of decency.

"Thank you," he replied. "I have the honor of conveying a lady from Trinidad to Devonshire, the daughter of Lord Carlyle. I have no doubt she would be infinitely more comfortable aboard a ship of the line in the company of naval officers, than otherwise."

Eccles nodded. "We have accommodation for ladies aboard. Modest, but suitable. My wife is with us and will be glad for feminine company. Will you join us aboard then?"

"I will accompany you in my vessel."

Eccles nodded. "The more guns the better should we meet with threats."

Jin swallowed the last of the rum, and felt the heat slide down his throat into his gut.

"Eccles, might you have room aboard your ship for yet another passenger? I have an acquaintance, also on Trinidad now, who may be looking for passage to England shortly as well."

"We can make space for him if you wish." Eccles lifted his glass. "Any friend of yours is welcome aboard my ship. Who is he?"

"A planter. English-born but now quite American. And he is a friend of the lady. His name is Castle." The man who would spend the month with her instead of him, as she would have if he had not found her and altered her life.

He glanced at Joshua's half-filled glass still on the table. After three years, his search for his father would soon come to an end. And after two years, he would finally cease living with Viola Carlyle as the purpose for his actions. His quest would be over, his debt paid.

Eccles raised his rum. "To England, then," he toasted.

Jin shifted his gaze to the querulous sea. "To England."

Chapter 18

Fellow Subjects of Britain,

The arrogance of the aristocracy never ceases to amaze. Consider the following, which I received yesterday from the Head Bird Man:

My lady,

It is with great pleasure that I alert you to the news that Sea Hawk has returned to England and is forthwith available for you to run to ground. I fear that once you become acquainted with him you will have no use for the remaining members of our inconsequential little club; as many sea captains, he tends to turn ladies' heads. If this comes to pass, my heart will suffer for loss of your attention. But I cannot regret that finally you may discover the identity of one of us. Therefore, if you should in fact learn his true name, pray do me

the honor of conveying to me your meeting place and
time so that I might hide in the bushes and sigh over
the loss I am myself now bringing about. A lady must
be given that which she wishes, however, and if I am
able to fulfill your desires even in this manner I will
eagerly do so, even though it is to my disadvantage.

Yours devotedly, &c,
Peregrine
Secretary, The Falcon Club

*He teases as though I were some demirep he could
charm with childish flattery. He imagines women
bereft of the capacity to reason, susceptible to empty
foolishness instead.*

*Note this, Peregrine: I am unmoved by your flirta-
tion. I will discover Sea Hawk's true identity and will
reveal him and all of you to the poor citizens of Britain whose wealth you squander playing games like
little boys at Pick-Up Sticks.*

—*Lady Justice*

Chapter 19

"It is . . . bigger than I remember." Viola stared through the carriage window at the house rising before her.

Not house. Mountain.

Savege Park was a rambling mass of stone, mortar, parapets, and about a hundred chimneys, with dozens of windows to the west reflecting the ocean, and windows to the east mirrors of emerald green hills dotted with sheep and striped with late-summer crops.

The country home of her sister, the Countess of Savege.

Not five miles away, Glenhaven Hall, the manor house of the Baron of Carlyle where Viola had lived her first ten years, was tucked behind a high bluff. But when they had disembarked in Exmouth and Jin offered her the choice, Viola decided to come here first, to meet Serena before again encountering the man who was not truly her father.

Possibly she had made a mistake.

"But I only saw it once or twice, I think," she mumbled. She was weary from the swift journey, her bones and muscles rattled from the carriage's constant bumping, but her nerves jittered like a cabin boy in his first squall.

"It's a pity your friend, Mr. Castle, is not here to enjoy the sight," the gentleman sitting beside her said pleasantly. Mr. Yale was always pleasant, although slightly satirical, and certainly inebriated. But the latter did not seem to affect his gentlemanly address or the clever glint in his silver eyes. During the long drive he had provided agreeable company. Distracting company.

Jane, the dust-colored-beanpole maid Jin insisted she accept in Trinidad, barely said a word.

Jin had ridden.

For a man who six weeks earlier said that he would not allow her out of his sight until he delivered her to her sister's home, he'd been conspicuously absent lately. In Trinidad before departing they had a single conversation in which he introduced her to Jane and told her she would be traveling to England with the navy. It seemed he had many influential friends. Like the Admiralty.

During the voyage she'd seen only glimpses of him across the sea. They were two ships strong, and encountered no unfriendly vessels. Captain Eccles's frigate boasted one hundred twenty guns, and the ship Jin had acquired in Tobago was remarkably fine—not as beautiful as the *Cavalier* but considerably better than the *April*. Viola had not been worried, merely perpetually out of sorts.

Aidan's company aboard hadn't helped. His announcement at Port of Spain that he must travel back to England to visit his family astounded her. He insisted he could leave the repairs to his farm in the hands of his steward. But his solicitous, appreciative attention on board had swiftly begun to chafe, and Seamus's company was predictably awful. The naval officers as well as Captain Eccles's wife provided some relief. But mostly she'd kept to herself reading in her cabin. She didn't like being a passenger aboard another master's ship. She wondered how Jin had borne it.

And now he was fulfilling his promise to deliver her home. He had been a shadow for a month. Shortly, he would disappear altogether.

It must be for the best. She could not forget him if he remained constantly in her life.

"Yes, I suppose Mr. Castle would like it," she replied, shifting her gaze from the sprawling mansion to Mr. Yale. At the dock in Exmouth, Aidan had taken one look at the darkly attractive Welshman who was to accompany her and Jin to Savage Park, and his face went stony. Viola didn't know why he should bother being jealous. The elegant Londonite was certainly handsome, his black hair, coat, waistcoat, and breeches giving him a decidedly mysterious air. But he couldn't hold a candle to the former pirate. Still, Aidan had been fidgety about leaving her to see his parents in any case, constantly repeating during the final days of their voyage how sorry he was not to be able to be there for her reunion with her family.

"He's no doubt accustomed to this sort of thing," she murmured, "being English, of course."

"As are you, of course." Mr. Yale slanted her a sidelong glance.

He hopped gracefully out of the coach, then proffered his hand. She maneuvered her skirts over the steps without tripping. Despite the gentle admonishments of Mrs. Eccles, she'd worn trousers and coat during the voyage. But when Captain Eccles informed her they were to dock, she changed into the dress. She hated herself for it. She hated her weakness.

The cause of that weakness dismounted, gave his horse into the care of a waiting servant—a servant wearing, *good Lord*, black and gold *livery*—and moved toward them. His gentleman's clothes suited him, his garments simple although their quality seemed finer even than Mr. Yale's.

But she didn't care about that. Just as that morning in the gray of dawn at Exmouth, she met his dispassionate gaze and the nerves in her belly clumped together in a sticky mass.

The door of the mansion swung open and a woman came to the top of the stair. She was beautifully gowned, elegantly coiffed, and—despite fifteen years—perfectly, achingly familiar. The same thoughtful, smiling eyes sparkled with tears now. The same lovely long fingers spread upon her cheeks. The same wide mouth opened in an O of wonder.

"Vi-Viola?" she uttered. "*Viola?*" she whispered.

Viola nodded, a few times, tiny quick jerks of her head.

Serena flew down the steps, skirts fluttering, and enveloped her in an embrace. She was half a head taller, and fragrant of cinnamon, and Viola buried her nose in Serena's square shoulder, cinched her arms about her sister's waist, and squeezed her eyes shut. She had not known what to expect. But somehow, *this* had not occurred to her. This homecoming. This love. She thought, perhaps, that she was a very poor prophet of her own life.

Serena loosened her hold only enough to draw back and curve her hand around Viola's cheek.

"I do not know where to begin." Serena's eyes, wonderfully mismatched blue and violet and bright with tears, seemed to drink her in. "I would exclaim what a beauty you have become, but you always were a beauty. I would barrage you with a hundred-score questions, but you must be weary from your long journey." Her arms tightened. "But mostly I will stare in utter bemusement. I cannot believe it is you."

"It is I." Viola spoke in barely a whisper. Now, here, beneath the adoring gaze of her sister, her insides jumbled entirely. Only three further words came to her. "I am sorry."

Serena's winged brows tilted. "Whatever *for*?"

"For not coming home before this."

The smile slipped from her sister's lips, but her eyes remained soft.

"Oh, Vi, we have a great deal to talk about, you and I." She laughed a sweet laugh between sorrow and joy, and hugged her again. "Fifteen years of a great deal," she whispered. She grasped Viola's hand tightly. "But first, I must give thanks." She turned to the men standing back somewhat.

"Mr. Yale, it is a pleasure to see you. I hope you will make a lengthy visit." She spoke with regal grace and curtsied with perfect poise, her elegant gown and honey hair shimmering in the light of the lamp a servant held to dispel the falling dusk. "Thank you for assisting in bringing my sister home today."

Mr. Yale bowed. "My greatest pleasure, Lady Savege."

Serena's fingers slipped from Viola's. She walked to Jin, extended her hands, and grasped his. She said very softly and somewhat thickly, "How shall I ever begin to thank you?"

Jin's eyes glittered as Viola had never seen, with a light powerful and entirely at peace. "You need not."

"In fact, I *cannot*. There is nothing I could say or give you to compare."

The corner of his perfect mouth tilted up ever so slightly. "I am justly compensated." His gaze shifted to Viola.

She could not breathe. His words and gaze always caused the same state inside her rebellious body—thorough lack of functionality. Only this time, it was worse, because shortly, when the earl paid him, he would leave.

"Miss Carlyle, may I escort you in?" Mr. Yale offered his arm.

Serena swirled around. "Oh, no, sir! I will not allow her one moment in another's company until I have had at least a sennight to myself." She circled Viola's waist and drew her toward the stair, bending her head. "My husband is briefly from home but will return within the week, I hope. When I received Jinan's note from the courier earlier today I sent off a missive to Alex entreating him to speed his journey. He will be so glad to know you. But I beg of you, do not allow anything Mr. Seton told you about him to predispose you one way or the other. You must fashion your own opinion."

"Mr. Seton told me nothing of Lord Savege, in fact."

Serena chuckled. "That is very much like Jinan, of course." She looked over her shoulder. "Gentlemen, do come in and allow Mr. Button to provide you with refreshment in the drawing room while the servants see to everything."

Servants were seeing to everything indeed, a veritable army of footmen in black with gold piping carrying luggage or simply standing at duty as Serena led Viola across the three-story entry hall to a sweeping staircase. The floor was tiled with gray and white marble, the stairs carpeted in Oriental luxury, the banister gleaming wood, all lit with dozens of candles. On the wall of the balconied landing above, a portrait hung of Viola's sister. With an infant.

She stared. In the picture Serena wore an opulent gown of gold, diamonds hanging on her neck and ears and in her hair. She cradled in her arms a tiny child garbed in white. The mother's gaze rested on her sleeping babe with quiet tenderness.

"Oh, don't look at that silly thing. Alex insisted. He is an overly proud papa. But I loathed every moment of the sitting, and Maria did as well. She fussed throughout."

"You have a daughter," Viola whispered.

Serena squeezed her waist. "Your niece."

"You named her Maria."

"After Mama." She took Viola's hand. "Now come. Mrs. Tubbs has made up for you the very best chamber, and tea and a hot hip bath both await. Then dinner once you are dressed, if you are able. I cannot complain, but I haven't a notion as to why Jinan insisted you make that entire journey in a single day. It is sixty miles to Exmouth, if only that, and over hills. You must be exhausted."

"Not very," she barely managed. Her eyes were wide as a child's. The corridor went on and on, turning corners and going up and down stairs before Serena finally halted before a beautifully fashioned oaken door.

The chamber within was not quite as large as the *April Storm*'s quarterdeck, but nearly if one counted the adjacent dressing room. Partially paneled in warm wood, the walls painted a delicate shade of rose, and appointed in soft gold and ivory fabrics with a sumptuous curtained bed and a delicate gilt-edged dressing table and sparkling mirror, it seemed a fairyland. Like the fairylands Serena had so loved to dream about as a girl.

"Is this your bedchamber?" Viola uttered.

"No, silly. It is yours. There is your bath, and a maid will be here momentarily to assist, although I would like to remain while you settle in, if you will allow me."

Viola turned back toward the corridor. "I think Jane is—"

Serena took her arm and drew her again into the room, closing the door behind them.

"Mrs. Tubbs—that is my housekeeper, a very excellent person—will see that your maid has dinner and ample rest before she returns to your service tomorrow. For tonight my own maid will be yours." Her brow puckered. "Will that suit you? I am terribly sorry. I should have asked first, but I assumed that after your long journey . . ." She bit her lower lip, an action so thoroughly familiar, as though from a dream, but in fact from memory. "Viola?"

"Hm?"

"You are unwell, of course." Serena's voice wobbled. "Exhausted, no doubt." She crossed to the dressing table where a silver tray with a delicate porcelain pot and cups were arranged about a plate of sugar-coated biscuits. "You must have a spot of tea. It will put you to rights, I am certain. Oh, dear." The china clinked in her hands. "My nerves are a disaster. You would think I have never before reunited with my sister whom all except me presumed dead for a decade and a half." She turned her face away, the cup and pot suspended. Her shoulders shook.

"Oh, Ser." Viola's eyes overflowed.

Serena turned her head, her cheeks streaked with tears. She set down the dishes, and they walked to each other and enfolded each other in their arms. They remained like that for a very long time.

Serena sent their apologies to the gentlemen, and ordered a light supper to be delivered to Viola's chamber instead. Viola bathed, changed into her usual shirt and drawers, and saw quite clearly Serena's thoughts on her lovely face. That she had always been able to read her elder sister's thoughts even when they were children did not dissipate the twisting in her stomach.

"You don't like my nightclothes."

"Nightclothes? Oh, I *am* relieved." Serena's mouth tipped up. "I thought perhaps you intended to go about the house like that. It would scandalize the servants, you know." She giggled.

Viola cracked a laugh. Then she remembered her state of undress when Jin had visited her cabin seeking the sextant, and her amusement disintegrated.

"Forgive me, sister." Serena came to her and touched her on the cheek, a gesture of feminine intimacy their mother used to make that Viola had never forgotten. "I haven't any notion of how you have been living. I fear I will be very stupid about it all." Little creases appeared between her brows, her gaze traveling over Viola's face. "Jinan says you have been at sea for some time."

Viola put her palm up to her face. "I am very brown, I know."

"No. I mean to say, you are not brown. But your skin always glowed so beautifully like this when we were girls."

"So did yours."

"Not like yours. You were so full of life. Are you still full of life after all these years?"

Viola blinked. "I—I expect so."

Serena grasped her hands, but Viola could not withhold it any longer.

"Ser, why didn't you reply to my letters?"

Her sister's eyes went wide. "What letters?"

"The letters I wrote in those first years."

She shook her golden head. "There were no letters. I received nothing."

Viola's stomach lurched. "No letters?"

Serena gripped her fingers tighter. "You wrote to me?" she whispered.

Viola's throat seemed filled with pitch. "She must not have mailed them."

"She?"

"My aunt. I lived with her and her children. I took care of them." She fought for breath, but Serena cradled her hands to her cheek.

"Vi," she whispered, "tell me everything. From the beginning."

She began with Fionn, comparing her story to Serena's. Her father had learned the truth of it; everyone thought her dead except Serena, the dreaming girl prone to invent stories of fairies and knights in shining armor and to whom no one listened. But their mother waited on the cliff side all night in the rain. A fortnight later, without ever mentioning Fionn, she died of fever taken that night.

Serena told her of the baron's second wife, now gone, and the daughters she had left behind—sixteen-year-old Diantha and little Faith—who still lived at Glenhaven Hall. Charity, the eldest of Serena's stepsisters, had married, and Serena's stepbrother, Sir Tracy Lucas, held an estate in Essex. Clearly Serena cherished her three stepsiblings and her half sister Faith, but as she related her tale she grasped Viola's hands even tighter.

In turn, Viola narrated her story, including Aidan's part in it. In the safety of her sister's affectionate interest she again felt the comfort of his affection that had borne her through the worst times when Fionn fell ill and slowly slipped away.

"You care very much for Mr. Castle, don't you?" Serena asked softly.

"I do." For she did. It was silly to cast away their past together in blame or disappointment when she had never really pressed him to wed. Instead she had pursued her life aboard ship single-mindedly.

"Where is he now?"

"Didn't Mr. Seton tell you?"

"I have barely seen him to tell me anything."

"Mr. Castle traveled with us from the West Indies to Exmouth. He has gone to Dorset to be reunited with his family after many years. He said he wished to make a visit here, if you wouldn't mind it."

Serena set down her teacup and grasped Viola's hand. "Of course I won't." She squeezed her fingers. "Vi, what do you say to delaying meeting our father and stepsisters for several days while you and I have a holiday here together? Before Alex returns. Only the two of us."

"What of Mr. Yale and Mr. Seton?"

"Mr. Yale will be perfectly happy entertaining himself, and Jinan will likely be leaving tomorrow anyway. He never remains long here, or anywhere I daresay." She smiled conspiratorially. "We shall have the house nearly to ourselves."

Viola's belly felt hollow. But the warmth in her sister's gaze filled some of the emptiness.

"That sounds wonderful."

She slept that night on the divan. There was nothing to be done about it; the bed was simply too large, too soft, and too motionless, and she could not get comfortable. To spare her sister's feelings, in the morning she mussed up the bed linens, and while her maid fussed with her hair she sat on the laced-scalloped pillow to make it appear used. Jane's lips remained pursed throughout.

"I have a sore . . . back," Viola mumbled.

"Of course, miss." Jane twitched a few more strands of hair into place.

"Ouch!"

"You don't think Her Ladyship fidgets about while her maid is fixing her hair, do you?"

Viola glared into the mirror. "Aren't you supposed to be a servant? *My* servant? Did you speak like this to Mr. Seton when he hired you? Did he get references?"

"No and yes, miss." Her lips looked as small and wrinkly as a raisin.

When Jane completed her ministrations Viola peered at her reflection and nearly laughed. Or wept.

Scrunching up her nose, she snatched out every pin from the tidy coiffure, took up the brush, and tore through her hair. When the mass of waves was once more thoroughly distressed, she bound it in a queue, poked her nose in the air, and passed Jane by to march from her chamber and descend to the breakfast parlor.

She got lost. Along the way three different footmen had to give her directions. She finally arrived a bit dizzy and without any idea of how she had gotten there. But it was a very pretty chamber. Two footmen flanked it and glimmers of sunlight twinkled in through the tall windows.

"Good morning, Miss Carlyle." Mr. Yale set down his newspaper and rose from the table to bow.

Standing by the window, Jin turned to her and nodded in greeting.

A cloud took up residence in Viola's head. He did not bow *now* when they were in an earl's house, but he had *aboard ship*? He was a detestable tease, and simply seeing him again after weeks of his absence was like being marooned upon an island, then slaking her thirst on fresh water.

His gaze flickered along her shirt, waistcoat, and breeches, and a ghost of a smile lifted the corner of his mouth. She got weak all over. On the outside, except for the weapons sash she'd packed away, she still looked like a sailor. But inside she felt like one of those French cream puffs Serena had pressed on her after dinner the night before. And, oh, God, it felt *good* to be a cream puff. For so long she had toughened her insides to iron, but she had never truly liked it. It was not in her nature.

It was in her nature, however unfortunately, to fall in love with men who did not love her. He must go away. He simply must. Then she might enjoy this sojourn among the lives of the rich and powerful much better.

"I thought you would have left by now."

He lifted a brow. "I intend to shortly. I hoped I might take breakfast first."

She felt shaky. Foolish foolish foolish. "Where are you going?"

Mr. Yale chuckled. "That is rather like asking a shark what he plans to eat for dinner. Mr. Seton ever goes where he will, Miss Carlyle, and none of us is ever the wiser for it. Isn't that right, my friend?"

Jin moved to the sideboard and took up a cup. "Hoping to

track my movements, Yale?" He poured a cup of coffee. "I imagined you finished with that sort of thing."

"Old habit." Mr. Yale waved it off. He drew out a chair for her. "May I command one of these fine fellows to make you a selection of delicacies, Miss Carlyle?" He gestured to the footmen.

Viola's stomach was in knots and a little queasy from all the cream puffs the night before. Rich, sticky cream puffs that could not possibly be good for a stomach accustomed to hardtack and weevil-infested biscuits.

"Tea." She sat, aware that all four men were watching her. She cleared her throat. "How do you come to know one another, then?"

"An old friend introduced us," Mr. Yale replied.

"Who?" She stood up to take the teacup and saucer from the footman. Their hands collided, tea sloshed, and her cuff and his white glove turned brown. "Oh! I'm sorry!" She snatched up a napkin and dabbed at his hand.

"It's nothing, miss," he mumbled, his cheeks fiery red.

"Oh. I should not have— But I'm so sorry."

The servant bowed and retired from the room. Mr. Yale moved to the sideboard and poured from the teapot. "Viscount Gray made us known to one another. A serious, responsible fellow, but a good sort nevertheless. And as he allowed me the acquaintance of our seafaring friend here, he has indirectly given me yours, for which I can only be grateful." He placed a steaming cup beside her, smiling kindly.

"I can't imagine your flattery is sincere, Mr. Yale," she mumbled.

"Perfectly sincere, Miss Carlyle," he rejoined. "It is not every day a man has the good fortune to admire a lovely lady who has done something useful with her life. Your delightful conversation about your ship yesterday positively sped the journey along."

"Thank you." She flickered a glance at Jin. He seemed to be staring into his cup. "I must admit I am not even certain of what we conversed, although I liked that story you told about how Lord Savege's sister met her husband while trapped at an inn in a snowstorm. But . . . I was tired, I suppose." Rather distracted, thinking of the man riding behind the carriage and how she might purge her heart of him.

"Ah, yes. We did take the journey at an unusually speedy clip. Our mutual friend here is a punishing fellow, with very little regard for the wishes of anybody else, let alone a lady." Mr. Yale spoke in his perpetually amused tone. "Beastly, s'truth."

She met his gaze and something other than sardonic teasing colored it. Then, with clear intention, he slipped it across the chamber to Jin.

"There you are!" Serena swept into the parlor wearing a wide smile and a gown of sea blue muslin trimmed in lace. She grasped Viola's hand and peered at her damp sleeve. "What have you been doing, Mr. Yale? Throwing tea at my sister? You knave."

"I like the medieval ring of that." He grinned, narrowing his gray eyes. "Miss Carlyle, if I claim the role of knave, would you consider playing the part of the damsel in distress? You might reform me, you know, and then your sister will look upon me with greater mercy."

She wished she could smile, but it would not come. "Mr. Yale did not spill the tea, Ser. I did, of course."

"It doesn't matter in the least who did it, but you mustn't be made to wear it for a moment longer. Come, darling." She drew Viola from her chair. "You will change, then we will take our breakfast on the terrace. It has the view of the sea and the breeze is lovely this morning so we shan't be overly warm." She tucked Viola's damp arm against her side. "Jinan, Mr. Button tells me you have ordered your horse brought around already. Must you leave so soon? At least remain until Alex returns from London."

Jin bowed. "I regret, my lady, that I have business to attend to in town."

Viola's heart clenched. He sounded so *English*. And so strangely formal.

"Always business," Mr. Yale murmured, "despite vows and pronouncements."

"I beg your pardon, Yale. I do not recall making any pronouncements."

"You noticeably fail to include 'vows' in that denial."

"That I do. But you are no doubt boring the ladies with this line of speech. Lady Savege, if you please, convey to your husband that I shall return when I am able, and look forward to it."

"Excellent." Serena squeezed Viola's hand. "Shall we go then?"

Viola nodded. He was looking directly at her. That he said he would return meant little; he could intend a sennight's absence or a year's.

This was good-bye.

She made her tongue form words. "Have a safe journey," she only managed.

He bowed now, but said nothing, his bearing quite still. Tears gathered thick at the back of her throat. She dragged her gaze away and went with Serena.

"Ser," she said when they were ascending the steps to the upper story. "I would like a new gown. Perhaps a few gowns. Is there a shop nearby at which I might purchase some?"

"But of course. Whatever you wish. But I won't hear of you going to a shop. We will have the modiste in from Avesbury. She makes the loveliest frocks in Devonshire. It will be great fun dressing you up as I used to do when we were children. You never did care much what clothing you wore so long as you could run about comfortably in it."

Viola took a deep breath. "And I should like you to teach me how to be a proper lady."

Serena's brow knotted. "But, Vi, you already are a—"

"No, I am obviously not. If I ever even learned the things a lady must know I have forgotten all of it." She set her shoulders. "But I should like to learn how to be one and try it out before I decide whether it will suit me."

"Whether it will suit you?" Serena's voice hitched. "Are you planning to return to America then? Soon?"

Viola grabbed both her hands. "No. No. I don't know for certain. Really. Though I do *wish* to remain here with you. But, you see I have left my entire life behind, my ship and crewmen and— But never mind that. Ser, you must teach me to be a lady. I promise I will be an apt pupil." As she had learned to hoist a sail and rig a boat, she would learn this. Fifteen years ago throwing herself into mastering sea craft had been the only way she'd borne the loss of her family and life at Glenhaven Hall and the knowledge of her mother's death.

Now she would throw herself into becoming a lady that Serena could be proud of, not one who slept on a couch, dressed like a man, and doused servants with tea. And in busying herself with this monumental task, she might occasionally forget the crystal blue gaze and devastating embrace of the beastly man to whom she had very foolishly given her whole heart.

"She is astoundingly pretty." Yale spoke beneath his breath, staring at the empty doorway through which Lady Savege and Viola had disappeared. "Quite."

Jin caught the footman's eye and gestured him from the room.

The Welshman sighed affectedly. "Ah, we are not to chat about pretty girls, are we, but get right down to business. More's the pity." He settled back in his chair, a lean, dark portrait of elegant indolence. Jin knew better than to be fooled by this posture.

"You will have ample opportunity to flirt with Miss Carlyle once I am gone."

"But it would be much more fun to flirt with her while you are still here. I like to see wealthy men suffer."

Jin didn't bother denying it. Yale's perception of others remained acute as always. It was one of the reasons he trusted the Welshman, and one of the pair of reasons he was leaving Savage Park so quickly. The other was less comfortable and had everything to do with his inability to be in the same room without wishing to touch her. But he could not touch her again, and he did not like his every thought spied upon.

He had elsewhere to be. His other goal to achieve now that this one was settled.

"Still in the suds, Wyn?"

"Why else do you think I responded to your summons from across the ocean so swiftly? Hoping you'll lend me a pony, don't you know."

"I don't, in fact. You have never before asked me for a pound." He leaned back against the sideboard. "Constance wrote to me. She is concerned about you."

"Of course she is. She must be concerned about someone, and she hasn't got Leam to worry over any longer. Colin, Lord Commander and Chief of All, doesn't give a fretful woman anything to work with, and is in any case so busy teasing Lady Justice that he is perpetually cheerful. And you, of course, have been absent for so long the rest of us barely recall what you look like. So I suppose it must be me."

"Quite a speech." Jin took up his coffee cup. The brew was cold now, but outside the day was already turning sultry and he would be warm enough on the road. The road that would take him away from Viola Carlyle, finally and permanently. "Constance is hardly a fretful woman. Does she have reason for her concern?"

Yale swiveled to him, his eyes slightly narrowed and his usual half smile thin. "Can't you determine that yourself, old friend?"

"I haven't got anyone following you, if that is what you are suggesting."

"Ah." Yale nodded. "That must be a first."

"It was, of course, only that once that I set a trail upon you."

"And I suppose you will claim it was Leam who most concerned you on that occasion."

"I will. And it would be the truth."

Yale assessed him thoughtfully. "You never lie, do you, Jinan?"

"Can I help you with anything, Wyn? Do you need money?"

The Welshman tapped his fingertips on the gleaming tabletop. "Rather, I need a drink."

"Thus Constance's letter to me."

The Welshman's gaze flashed up. "Do you know, I have just had the most marvelous idea, Jinan. Constance needs a man to worry about, and you are a fellow who truly lives his life dangerously. Why don't you marry her and get her off my back?"

Jin lifted a brow.

"No. Listen," Yale persisted, the light of deviltry in his silver eyes. "An heiress wed to an adventuring Midas. The perfect pair. Then she could worry over you from now until kingdom come instead of me. Why not?"

"Why not, indeed."

"What? Extraordinary beauty and an enormous dowry are

insufficient enticements?" He crossed his arms in a pensive attitude. "I suppose a lady must also know how to captain a ship to be truly appealing to the Hawk of the Sea."

Jin pushed away from the sideboard and moved toward the door.

Yale chuckled, then said more soberly, "Colin wants you and your ship in the Mediterranean. Malta, apparently."

He paused at the door. "Malta?"

"I believe so, yes. Something about a plot to oust we Brits and some heiress or other who eloped and her parents disowned her but now she must be unearthed before she is caught in the crossfire. He's asked me to go and wishes you to do the driving, as it were."

"I will let you know." He went to the foyer, then onto the drive where his horse awaited him, his traveling pack strapped to its haunches. Without another glance at the house or the terrace where she might now be taking breakfast, Jin mounted and set off.

He had not lied. In London he had a bishop to meet and a small casket to purchase. He would put up in the rooms he kept in Piccadilly, pay a call on Colin Gray and an admiral or two, and pursue his goal of retrieving his mother's box.

But the pressure in his chest insisted otherwise. It said that now he rode nowhere, to no purpose, and with no aim. As the distance stretched between him and the woman from whom he must remove himself, for the first time in twenty years Jin felt like a man truly at sea.

Chapter 20

At first, recreating herself into a lady did prove quite a lot of fun. The modiste arrived, tossed about fashion plates, fabrics, and laces, and oohed and ahhed over Viola's figure while clucking over the indelicate hue of her skin. Viola was then draped with tissue-thin silks, crisp taffetas, and light muslins, strapped with measuring tapes, poked with pins, and generally treated like a mannequin. Petticoats and shifts of the lightest fabrics were produced in abundance. Silly little coats called pelisses, punishing stays, fringed shawls, gloves in every color, and a panoply of bonnets followed.

Viola found a paper and pen and scribbled the names of each garment so as to be able to recall them later. The activity of making the list, however, reminded her of those first months aboard ship when she had done the same, noting spars, lines, sails, and armaments until she had memorized the name of every single piece of wood, iron, hemp, and canvas aboard. And simply writing made her miss her ship's diary, jotting down the day's monotonous events each evening before turning in. With the memories swimming about, she could not fully enjoy the dressmaker's antics. But Serena's pleasure in the activity was patent, and Viola could not begrudge her happiness.

When Mr. Yale peeked his head in the door to query about their progress, the dressmaker shooed him away. A lady's boudoir was no place for a man, apparently. Viola wondered what Mrs. Hamper or Serena would think if she told them she had shared her "boudoir" with a man, eagerly.

Viola slept again on the couch, vowing to make a try at the bed the following night. The sound of the sea swishing and cracking on the beach below comforted.

A second day of fitting followed the first. Mrs. Hamper adjusted one of Serena's muslin wraps on the spot, and Jane strapped the stays around Viola's ribs with obvious relish and tied her into the confining garments. Viola submitted to having her hair yanked again, which her maid performed with gusto. By the morning of the third day she was able to descend to the breakfast parlor looking something like a lady who belonged at a house like Savege Park, if not feeling like one.

Clothes, however, did not make the lady.

"Which one do I use for the eggs?" she whispered to the man sitting beside her.

Mr. Yale leaned over and replied in an equally hushed tone, "The egg spoon."

The room was empty save for Serena across the table and a footman standing to either side. Viola flickered a glance at the servants. They wore poker faces.

She murmured, "Which one is the egg spoon?"

"The diminutive one," Mr. Yale supplied.

"The two of you sound like perfect nincompoops," Serena said. "What must George and Albert be thinking of you?"

Mr. Yale pointed his forefinger at the smallest spoon, then

settled back in his chair. "Why don't we ask them? George, Albert, do you think Miss Carlyle and I are nincompoops? Now be honest. It is your mistress that you will offend by replying in the negative."

George furrowed his brow beneath a white wig. "Well, I don't rightly know, sir."

"Noncommittal. Wise man. And you, Albert?"

"Wyn, you must cease quizzing the servants."

"Albert?" Mr. Yale pressed.

"It does seem odd, sir," the younger footman replied earnestly, "that there be a spoon only for the likes of soft-boiled eggs, I always thought."

"Ah, do you see, my lady? Albert agrees with your sister and me. We in society use far too many spoons at breakfast."

"I would like to know which ones to use for what purposes," Viola said firmly. "Last night at dinner I was completely confused. I think I may have used my soup spoon for the jelly, or perhaps the other way around." She looked up as Serena lowered the paper.

"We don't care what spoon you use, Vi. Do we, Mr. Yale?"

"Of course not."

"But I do. And when Lord Savage returns I'll wager he will too. Could this be lesson number one?"

Her sister smiled gently. "Viola—"

"You said you would teach me how to be a lady, Ser. I am holding you to that."

"All right. If you wish."

"I wish."

"May I join in the project?" Mr. Yale speared a piece of bacon on his fork and peered at it curiously. "I am in desperate need of a refresher on the finer points of noble dining."

"Mr. Yale, I am quite serious about this." Viola turned to him. "I don't want to embarrass my sister or Lord Savage when we go into company."

He met her with a sincere regard. "And I, Miss Carlyle, am quite serious about assisting you. If it is a lady you wish to appear to society, then a lady you must and shall."

"Thank you," she replied for the hundredth time in four days. Except to Jinan Seton. To the man who had insisted her family still wanted her and made her return to England to reunite with them. To the man who had suffered her silly wager and made love to her as she had never known it could be. Who had, simply by being himself, shown her that she would have made a great mistake in marrying Aidan.

The man who had left her without even a word of good-bye.

He deserved no thanks. He was a thorough blackguard. He'd said he did not take that which was not his by right, but he had stolen her heart. Just like a pirate. She owed him nothing. Not even a fond memory.

Once Viola was suitably garbed (and remarkably uncomfortable), Serena and Mr. Yale set about instructing her in a young lady's accomplishments: drawing, painting, singing, playing, and achieving a smattering of French and Italian. It swiftly became apparent that she must first learn more fundamental tasks.

"I know how to walk. One puts one foot in front of the other."

"Ah, yes," Mr. Yale said, drawing her from a chair before the tea table to the center of the terrace. "But when one is a lady, one puts them in front of the other rather less resolutely than one has been accustomed to doing aboard ship. That is, if one wishes to glide across the floor like an angel."

"Ha!" Viola cracked a laugh. "An angel?"

"Quite. As all will believe you are until they see you trip on your hem or hear you guffaw like that."

"I didn't guffaw. Don't ladies laugh?"

"Of course they do," Serena offered. "Only they are not supposed to do so with any gusto. A very silly rule if you ask me."

"It is indeed, but I did not invent it," Mr. Yale commented. "I am merely acting as a conduit of the foolishness that is English high society." He grasped Viola's hand in his quite comfortably strong fingers and stepped away. "Now, Miss Carlyle, if you will walk four paces allowing only two small inches between your forward heel and following toe, I will be gratified."

"*Two* inches?"

"To commence." His silvery eyes twinkled.

"I must learn to walk heel to toe as though I were a girl in some Oriental king's harem?"

Serena cracked a laugh as loud as Viola's guffaw.

"Certainly not," Mr. Yale assured. "We will commence with exaggeration and when that is achieved, relax our standards to suitability."

"I see." She took a step.

He shook his head. "That was at least six inches. And ladies do not mention Oriental harems."

"Or any harems at all, really." Serena plied needle to embroidery board.

"Two is ridiculous." Viola stepped again.

"That was five."

"Changing Maria's nappies is a great deal more fun than this."

"Five again."

"Then *here*." She hiked up her mass of frothy skirts and took the daintiest step imaginable.

"Ah. Much better. And of course a lady must never lift her skirts above the instep."

"Is that true, Ser?"

"I'm afraid so."

Viola ground her molars and stepped forward again.

"She is a quick learner," Mr. Yale murmured.

"She always was," Serena replied.

"It is impressive."

"Truly."

Viola whistled. "I'm still here."

"And young ladies must never press themselves into a conversation into which they have not been invited. Or whistle."

"Young ladies sound like no fun at all."

"Most of them aren't."

Viola made her way back to her chair in mincing steps. With a great sigh she threw herself down into it, scooped up a pastry from the tea tray, and popped it into her mouth, then chewed contentedly. At least the rewards for her hard work were delicious.

After a bit, it seemed very quiet in the parlor. She looked up. Mr. Yale and Serena were both looking at the spray of sugar across the lap of her pretty green gown.

"Oh, bother."

The next lesson had to do with cutlery, the lesson following that with taking a gentleman's arm, and the lesson after that with her speech.

"I know I've got an American accent. A little. But I don't see what's so bad about that," Viola said, clutching her bonnet to her head as the sea breeze whipped across the coastal road. The sight of two horses' rear ends so close in front of her was still a little unnerving, but Mr. Yale handled the ribbons with ease and Serena seemed comfortable. Both had said she must become accustomed to riding in this sort of vehicle.

"Your accent is charming, Miss Carlyle."

"Then what's wrong with the way I speak?"

"You must curtail your use of contractions." He always gave instruction like this, with masculine grace, whether he was sober or inebriated. He had not yet been drinking today but would probably as soon as they returned from their drive.

It never seemed to affect his manner with her, though, which remained openly admiring and entirely unthreatening. Why she imagined he *should* feel threatening, she hadn't a very clear idea, except that he was an actual gentleman and she had not known one since she was a girl. And he was quite attractive.

"What's wrong with contractions?"

"Not a thing," he replied readily. "If you wish to appear very fashionable and somewhat fast, you may employ them."

"Fast?"

He lifted a single brow.

"Oh. I don't suppose I do. Do I?"

"Definitely not," Serena stated.

Lessons in comportment were interspersed with visits to the nursery to coo and tickle her niece's tiny fingers and toes, as well as periods of torture visited upon her by Jane and her sister's haughty maid, whom Serena insisted was quite nice once one got to know her. But since on one occasion she plucked viciously at Viola's eyebrows until her head ached, on another she commanded the maids to scrub the soles of her feet and elbows and palms with pumice until raw, and on a third submitted her to the sheer boredom of having her nails cut, cleaned, and buffed as though she weren't capable of grooming herself, Viola had no very high opinion of the woman. When the maid suggested to her mistress that her hair be cut short to suit present fashion, Viola finally balked.

"My hair stays. When the wind is high, it must be long enough to tie back in a queue."

Serena stroked her fingertips through Viola's thick waves. "It is perfect as is."

When Viola mastered the proper use of forks, spoons, and knives, and the task of pouring out tea, she felt ready to move on to more challenging tasks. Her optimism proved overly ambitious.

"My hands aren't made for this." Her fingers, raw from the scrubbing, slipped on the paintbrush. A smear of blue watercolor decorated the paper on the easel before her.

"Are not suited," Mr. Yale corrected. "Your hands are not suited to this. But in any case ladies must never speak of their hands."

"Why not?"

"Because it gives gentlemen ideas they ought not to entertain in company."

Serena's eyes popped wide. Viola grinned.

Mr. Yale looked between them, his brows innocently raised. "I understood we were being frank in the service of Miss Carlyle's education."

"We are. But Wyn, *really*."

"My lady, given that your husband was once one of the greatest libertines to grace London drawing rooms, I wonder at your squeamishness."

"He is reformed. Of course." Her mismatched eyes danced.

Viola dashed more paint onto the canvas and tilted her head sideways. Her ship looked a lot like an armadillo. She sighed. "He has a good point, Ser. It isn't as if—"

"It is not as though."

"It is not as though I don't know what men are thinking half the time. I lived with fifty-four men aboard ship—"

"You have been marginally acquainted with fifty-four— Good God, *fifty-four*?"

"I have been *well* acquainted with fifty-four men for a decade. Men are interested in one thing above all else." Like the man she had imbecilically fallen in love with who wanted her only for that one thing . . . other than bringing her home.

"Not all men." Serena dabbed at her own canvas with a cloth, her lip caught between her teeth. "Mr. Yale has spent a sennight helping us school you without any thought of that sort of thing, haven't you, Wyn?"

She and Viola both looked at him for confirmation.

"Quite so," he said without inflection.

"See?" Serena returned her attention to her painting.

The gentleman's mouth lifted at the corner and he winked at Viola.

She laughed. "Don't fret, Mr. Yale. I know you haven't that sort of interest in me."

His eyes widened. "I beg your pardon. I am as susceptible to a pretty face and form as the next fellow."

"You don't have to— That is, you needn't pretend indignation with me, sir." She flapped the paintbrush back and forth.

"I shall endeavor not to consider that an insult."

"Oh, you shouldn't. Mustn't. Although I'm— I am still uncertain as to why you remain here helping when you are not interested in me in that manner."

Serena chuckled. "You are as refreshingly honest and confident of your charms as ever, Vi. I adore you for it."

"Was I confident when we were children?"

"Entirely, to the very moment those sailors walked up that cliff and strode toward us. You flicked your black lashes and gave them a saucy grin, demanding in the sweetest tones imaginable that they state their names and business on your father's land. They were so bemused that I believe if we had thought to run we would have had plenty of head start on them."

"But we did not think to run. And now I am here learning how to paint watercolors instead of having already mastered it ten years ago."

"You never would have mastered it." Mr. Yale peered over her shoulder. "You haven't a jot of natural talent for it. Piano, anyone?"

Serena set down her brush. "What a relief. I don't care for painting in the least."

"Then why on earth have—"

"You said you wished to learn a lady's every accomplishment." Serena moved toward the door. "The piano is in the drawing room, as well as the harp, of course, and so shall tea be in a quarter hour."

Viola watched her sister disappear and chewed on the end of her paintbrush. She glanced back at her mishmash of a painting. Her shoulders sagged. Merely seven days of this and already she'd had enough. She would master it, but she wished painting and eating and walking were as easy as tying an anchor bend or rigging a jib sail.

Mr. Yale stood and offered his arm.

She expelled a frustrated breath. "I don't really need to take your arm to walk to the drawing room two doors away, do I?"

"Practice, practice."

She eyed him. "You are as disinterested as you insist, aren't you, Mr. Yale?"

"Not disinterested, Miss Carlyle," he said quite soberly. "Merely loyal to a man who has saved my life more than once."

She stared.

"Ladies do not gape."

She snapped her mouth shut and stood. She looked down at their feet, his shining shoes, her delicate slippers peeking out from beneath her hem that did not look like her feet or hem at all.

"Tell me again how you and he know one another."

"I am not at liberty to divulge that." He drew her hand to his forearm. "But perhaps if you ask him, he might be inclined to tell you. I suspect indeed he would."

"You have mistaken matters, you know."

"I am quite certain I haven't."

A sick sensation lodged in her stomach. "What did he tell you?"

Mr. Yale regarded her for an extended moment then said, "He did not tell me anything. He did not need to."

"Well, you are wrong. But I don't believe I will ever see him again to ask him anything, anyway."

"I fear I must churlishly insist, madam, that you are quite likely to be disproven in that."

"Do you know, Mr. Yale, I think the greatest challenge to becoming a lady is accepting that gentlemen seem to think they know better than me. In fact, I have quite a strong suspicion that I won't ever manage that. So perhaps I will never be a lady after all." She flashed him a smile. "Oh, what a relief. I was beginning to worry."

She turned and left the room without any assistance from him or anyone.

"His Excellency refuses to sell." Viscount Gray sat across the rough wooden table from Jin, the late-summer morning spreading the pub with murky light. The establishment tucked in a quiet corner of London was empty of all but the pair of them. Like Jin, the viscount had dressed simply for their rendezvous, but the confident set of his jaw and his direct gaze marked him unmistakably as an aristocrat.

"The bishop's secretary assured me that no offer could tempt him to relinquish any part of his collection of Eastern art. Especially not that piece." Gray lifted his tankard of ale. He glanced over the rim. "What is in the box, Jin?"

"Nothing of note." Only his identity.

"Then why ask me to assist you? You have never asked for my help with anything before." His voice remained mild, his posture relaxed. But Colin Gray was no fool. The Admiralty and the king did not trust the head agent of their secret little club without good reason.

"It seemed the most likely route to acquiring it."

Gray nodded. "Of course."

Neither needed to speak the truth: Jin held the respect of several commissioners of the Board of the Admiralty. But Gray had social connections that made making an inquiry into the sale of an antiquity in a lord's private collection unremarkable.

"Given that I have assisted you without question, however," the viscount added, "I might be granted an explanation."

"Your assistance has garnered me nothing. And if you had not wished to render it, you need not have." Jin moved to stand up.

The viscount's hand wrapped about his wrist like an iron band.

"You asked me because you wish anonymity in this." An edge sharpened Gray's voice. "I expect to know why."

"Take your hand off of me, Colin, or I will cut it off."

Dark blue eyes locked with Jin's. "You are unarmed."

"Are you quite certain of that?"

Gray released him but his gaze remained unyielding. "Seven years ago when we began this I did not understand why Blackwood trusted you so thoroughly."

"Didn't you? Then what game have you been playing all this time to include me in your Club? Hold your friends close but your enemies closer?"

"Perhaps at first. You were a remarkable asset, with your connections at ports and through every layer of London, it seemed. And your ship."

Jin leaned back and crossed his arms loosely. "I have my uses, then?"

"But I soon came to see what Leam knew long ago," Gray said as though he had not spoken. "You and I have never seen eye to eye. You are unpredictable and your every move appears designed to further only your own goals. But appearances are deceiving. Beside Leam, Jinan, you are the one man with whom I would entrust my life." He held his gaze. "Tell me. I may be able to help."

Jin studied the nobleman. Gray pursued his mission not because he must; his wealth and title were secure. He served king and country because honor and duty meant more to him than his life. Gray considered each one of his fellow agents in the Club—Leam, Wyn, Constance, even him—part of that duty. Indeed, his first duty.

"This is not entirely about me, is it, Colin?"

"Blackwood. And Yale. I know better than anyone what you have done for them. I know you shielded Leam from me when he wished to escape the Club. You took your ship to the North Sea to hound those Scottish rebels when you wished to be already sailing west. You did it because you hoped it would deter me from involving Leam."

Jin did not deny it. Gray was wise for a man only a few years his senior.

"And although Yale has never said a word about it, I know you were there the night he shot that girl. I know Constance has asked for your help with him, and suspect that you have just seen him not because he sought you out upon your return but rather the opposite."

"Do you know all that? And what did you learn from it, I wonder?"

Gray ran his hand behind his neck. "Good Lord, it's like speaking with Socrates. An improvement over speaking to thin air, though, after sending you letters for a year and a half that you did not answer." He stood up. "Jin, if you find you should need my help, you shall have it. Until then, the director must know whether you can be counted on to see to the trouble in Malta. Yale told you of that matter, I hope."

"He mentioned it."

"Are you with us still, or have you gone the way Blackwood has after all? Constance insists you are yet part of the Club, but I will have it from you now, finally."

Why not? He might as well sail across the Mediterranean on another errand for the king and the Falcon Club's secret director. For the first time in two years he had nothing better to do, and distance from this island would suit him well. The box he wanted was not within his reach, nor the woman. Both were now part of a society that, like this man, tolerated him for his skills but would always mistrust him because of those same skills. He had forged his reputation on violence and he was not, despite all, one of them.

"I will contact you."

Gray nodded. "I expect to hear from you soon." He extended his hand. Jin grasped it.

"Colin." He paused, uncertain. The words came then without thought, from a place within him he did not wish to acknowledge. "Thank you."

The viscount's dark eyes glinted. "You are welcome."

Jin sat in the pub alone for only minutes before Mattie and Billy arrived.

"Matouba says as he's tried out this place afore and they don't like his sort, he's waiting at the ship." Billy grinned, sliding into a chair.

Mattie grunted at the barkeep and lowered his mass. "We seen His Lordship leaving. Looked black as Matouba. Put his knickers in a knot, did you?"

Jin leveled an even look at him. "Have you learned anything of value?"

"Junior footman. Not many of them in the house, though. Bishop's got a load of goodies he don't want servants messing with." Mattie's thick brow furrowed. "Don't know if this'll be an easy one to nab."

"When's that ever stopped us afore?" Billy showed all his teeth.

Mattie shrugged and took up his glass.

"What is this junior footman's name?" Jin asked.

"Hole Pecker."

He lifted a brow.

Billy smiled even broader. "Mattie and I didn't believe it neither, Cap'n. But that's the name his mum gave him."

"His schedule is regular?"

"Leaves the house 'bout ten o'clock, when the bishop turns in." Mattie swallowed the last of his brew and laid his palms on the table. "See here. Billy and me and Matouba, we want to do this 'stead of you."

"I have no intention of doing anything at this time. Merely an innocent interest in the bishop's household staff."

Billy's eyes went wide. Mattie's narrowed. But Jin had intended the warning in his tone.

"Listen here." Mattie's hand fisted. "You can't be doing this sort of thing no more."

"He's right, Cap'n," Billy piped, his smile momentarily dimmed. "Ain't right no more."

"I am doing nothing, as I have just said. We are no longer in that line of business, gentlemen. At least not as long as you work for m—"

"He's gonna say we got to keep out of his business now, Bill," Mattie broke in. "Reckon Miss Carlyle weren't wrong when she said we got us the most stubborn arrogant ass of a captain this side of the world."

"She sure did say that." Billy's head bounced thoughtfully.

Jin's mouth crept into a grin.

"I sure do miss the lady." Billy's downy cheeks shaded to pink. "How's she doin' in that big ole house, Cap'n?"

"Well, when last I saw her."

"Were she well, then?" Mattie leveled him a penetrating stare beneath bushy brows.

Billy grinned. "Bet Lady Redstone's got her tricked out in skirts and ribbons and all them lady things."

As it should be. And it still astounded him after these weeks that the only place he wished to be was there with her. Wherever with her, wearing whatever she chose. Or nothing. "Gentlemen, is the ship fitted out?"

"Right ready to haul away. We going somewheres?"

"Perhaps."

Mattie pursed his fleshy lips. "You ain't going to bribe Pecker into stealing that box for you, then, or p'raps unlocking the back door so you can go on in and steal it yourself? 'Cause I thought maybe that's what you'd been planning."

"No plans, Matt." He stood. "Idle curiosity."

He left them then, walking through the streets busy with the traffic of carriages and pedestrians, hawkers and flower girls and all the whirl of London he had come to know years earlier when he had first made his way to England in search of atonement in the land of half his ancestors. The unknown half.

Gray was right. All of London's strata were known to him, from the lords who sat in Parliament to the boys who filched those lords' billfolds to feed hungry families. He had known it all, and the life he led had satisfied him to some extent.

No longer. Restlessness spun through him now, and he could find no peace. But neither did he have a goal any longer, and the one avenue of hope he had retained after leaving Viola in Devonshire was closed to him now. Perhaps his father had been a gentleman of name and means. Perhaps. Without that box he would never know.

He paused to slip a guinea into the pocket of a blind beggar woman. Fast as a whip she gripped his fingers.

"Bless you, son," she rasped, opaque eyes restive in a face

weathered by day after day of hopeless labor on her street corner.

"I have never been a son, grandmother," he said quietly. "But I will take your blessing, nevertheless." He returned the pressure on her bony fingers, released her, and continued on his way through the bustle and life that no longer held the sharp fascination it always had for him. He did not wish to ponder the change or how it had come upon him. He did not wish to walk down that road. He knew better than to even consider it.

Malta looked more attractive every minute.

Chapter 21

"Your sister, Lady Savege," the curate's wife said in pale tones, "will never be a great proficient, I fear."

"Won't she, Mrs. Appleby?" Serena's voice sympathized.

"She does have the necessary calluses to pluck, you see . . ."

From behind the doorpost in the corridor, Viola could not see the shadow of a woman, but she knew Mrs. Appleby must be wringing her hands. She had done so through each of her harp lessons. She was an accounted virtuoso on the instrument, but she was a sad shade of a person. Viola thanked God she hadn't had to contend with women aboard her ship. She would have gone stark raving mad.

Although, of course, Jin already thought she was mad.

" . . . but she hasn't the delicacy for it."

"The delicacy?"

"The grace of poise a harpist must bring to her art."

"I haven't got grace of poise," Viola whispered to the gentleman leaning over her shoulder.

"I would never say so," he rejoined in a hush.

"But you believe so."

"I should rather be horsewhipped than admit to it."

"You are very peculiar, Mr. Yale."

"A lady has never called me quite that. Dashing. Handsome. Debonair, yes. Peculiar, no."

"Well, according to Mrs. Appleby I am not a lady, so you are still safe."

Serena and the curate's wife turned toward the door. Mr. Yale snatched her arm, then moved forward decorously across the threshold.

"Ah, Mrs. Appleby, we will be so unhappy to suffer your absence but it seems that Miss Carlyle has injured her pinky finger on a . . . a . . ." He squeezed her hand.

"Block! That is to say . . . a pulley!"

"Ah, yes, a pulley"—he shot her a speaking glance—"and thus cannot continue her lessons with you." He released her and took Mrs. Appleby's arm upon his. "Allow me to escort you to Lord Savege's carriage. Albert will see you home himself." They moved off. "Oh, Albert? Capital fellow, you know. Hasn't any use for egg spoons, of course, and I cannot blame him a bit for it . . ."

"He is positively absurd." Serena drew her arm in to link with her own. "And I think he admires you very much. He would be long gone back to London by now if not for you."

"He is very nice. I hadn't remembered gentlemen being so very . . . so very . . ."

"Young and handsome?"

"I was going to say silly, but then I recalled that the baron used to play ridiculous games with us. Didn't he?"

Serena's face sobered. "He did. I remember those games well."

A servant appeared at the door and bowed. "My lady, a gentleman awaits you in the blue parlor. He asked to be unannounced, and for you to attend him alone, if you would."

"How odd." Then her eyes widened slightly. "Vi, I shall see what this is about and return in an instant. The gardener has cut dozens of flowers and I thought we might make some arrangements."

"As long as it does not entail sewing or playing a musical instrument."

Viola wandered to the window and stared out at the ocean stretching to the horizon. The day was blustery, suggesting a summer storm to come. If she were aboard her ship she would have the men batten the hatches and furl the sails, leaving a few aloft to guide her through the wind. She would send three quarters of them below and set a watch in shifts if the tempest raged long. Afterward, she would break out the rum or Madeira, Becoua would play a tune on his mandolin while Sam and Frenchie sang, and they would celebrate making it through yet another danger of life upon the sea.

She sighed, her exhalation condensing on the glass and disappearing just as swiftly. Two months now away from her ship and crew, and . . . She did not miss it.

She did not miss it.

She missed Crazy, her oldest friend, of course. She missed Becoua's steadiness, Sam and Frenchie's good humor, and little Gui who had cried hearty tears when she departed from Port of Spain. She missed her cozy, shabby cabin, and wondered how the men were getting along in Boston now. But she did not miss her life at sea, and it sat on her poorly that she did not.

She should. She had loved captaining her own ship, trawling the Massachusetts coast for ne'er-do-wells, remaining hundreds of miles away from Aidan because she could not bear to give it up. Now she had, and she did not miss it.

She missed Jin. Quite a great deal.

The project of becoming a lady was not proving sufficient to erase him from her thoughts. Or her insides. Inside, in her chest and belly, a dull ache reminded her daily that he had turned her life upside-down, but whether it was for the best was yet to be seen.

She toyed with the ribbons dangling beneath her breasts, trying to pull in a full breath against her stays. Her feet were pinched in the silly little slippers, and she was tired of sitting before her mirror every morning for an hour while Jane played with her hair.

"Starting tomorrow," she murmured to the window, making mist again, "I will tie my hair in a queue and Serena will smile and Jane will glower and I will be much"—she poked her finger into the mist—"much"—another poke—"more comfortable."

"Vi?" Her sister stood at the door.

"Yes?" She turned. "Who was it that called?"

"You will be cross with me, I am afraid." Her hands folded together. "He heard that you were here through the servants, of course, and he wrote to me straight off. But I told him he mustn't come until you were ready. You haven't spoken of him, though, and I did not wish to rush you . . ."

"It is the baron, isn't it? He is here."

Serena nodded. "He wishes very much to see you."

Viola crossed the chamber, drawing in as much air as the wretched corset would allow and taking her sister's hand. "Then we must not keep him waiting."

She walked the corridor to the blue parlor quite as steadily as Serena and Mr. Yale had taught her, but her palms pressed against her skirts were like clams. Serena gestured to the footman and the door opened.

The gentleman standing in the middle of the room did not suit it in the least. Amid the rich gold and sapphire of the parlor he was a sand-and-hay scarecrow, thin of hair and frame, and garbed somewhat shabbily. But his kind eyes were the same, and filled with tears.

Her throat thickened.

"Viola?" he uttered.

She attempted a curtsy. "Good day, sir."

His papery brow crinkled. "Will you stand on ceremony with me, then? Has my little girl grown into such a great woman of the world that she will not come to me now and take my hand?"

She moved forward. He stretched out his hands, she put hers in them, and a tear overflowed onto his sunken cheek. Then onto both of hers.

"Your hands are the same," she whispered—warm, encompassing, and safe as they always had been. As she had remembered every night aboard ship that first month and for so many nights after, dreaming of home and wondering if her papa would come after her. Then Fionn told her they all thought her dead, and she ceased dreaming. Dreams might suit Serena, but not an adventuresome girl like her. Not the girl her papa believed her to be. He would wish her to be brave.

And so she had been brave. But now she trembled like a ten-year-old again.

"You are a beauty, so much like your mother." His face, careworn and aged as she had never imagined it, creased into a gentle smile. "My little girl. My Viola. How I grieved for loss of you."

Perhaps she saw in his eyes the extent of that grief. Perhaps she only felt it in her heart. But she could not withstand his affection, even were she to again lose it, Serena's, and the affections of all whom she had striven so hard to forget.

"I missed you too," she said on a catch in her throat. "Papa."

His hands tightened around her hands and Serena choked on a laughing sob.

After that there was much conversation and many, many reassurances.

* * *

"Vi, they are here!" Serena stood in the kitchen doorway on the balls of her feet.

"They?" Viola laid down a sprig of rosemary and drew off her apron.

"Alex. And friends. There are four carriages coming along the drive."

Her heart did a strange little jig. *Four* carriages. With four carriages—even *one*—it was possible that . . .

She should not be so eager. She cast a quick glance at the herbs spread over drying pans. It was the most innocuous ladylike task she had accomplished yet, and her favorite so far. But it could wait.

She hated herself for hoping. But she could hate herself and still dash after her sister toward the front of the house where servants already were hauling in portmanteaus and traveling cases. They reached the foyer lined with maids and footmen as a gentleman came through the door. Tall, strapping, and remarkably attractive, with walnut-colored hair, an elegant air, and the smile of a man who knew his worth, he announced in a bold voice, "Where is my lady wife?"

"I am here, my lord."

Viola had never heard Serena's voice thus, low and touchingly sweet. Lord Savege's regard alighted upon her, and his face relaxed into a raffish grin.

"She is there, indeed." He came to her, took up her hand, and pressed quite a lengthy kiss onto the back of it. Then onto the palm. Viola's toes curled watching it. Her gaze darted toward the door.

"How are you, my lady," the earl said, "and how is our daughter?"

"Quite well, both of us. She is napping now." Serena slipped her arm through his. "Alex, allow me to present to you my sister, Viola."

"Miss Carlyle." He bowed. "Welcome home."

Three ladies and a gentleman entered the foyer then, none of them known to Viola. The footman closed the door behind them and her heart fell. Silently she berated herself.

In the next minutes she found it entirely believable that her sister had fallen in love with the Earl of Savege. He was not what she imagined an earl should be, stuffy and proper. He tended rather toward an open manner and enormous charm.

"My sister, Kitty, Lady Blackwood, wishes to meet you," he said, "but remains in town with her little one in the hopes that we will all return there shortly. She has however sent her bosom companions with me as temporary replacements."

A willow of a girl with tumbling silken brown locks and dark eyes curtsied. "I am Fiona Blackwood," she said upon a gentle Scottish lilt. "Lord Savege's sister, Kitty, is married to my brother and she is my very great friend. And you are ever so pretty."

"But does she have two sticks to rub together in her head, is more to the point." Behind gold wire spectacles framed by short flaxen locks, green eyes studied her. "How do you do, Miss Carlyle? I am Emily Vale but I would prefer you call me Lysistrata."

"You have changed it again, my lady?" Mr. Yale drawled as he entered the foyer. "You must have wearied of Boadicea."

"Boadicea was Emily's chosen name before Lysistrata," Lady Fiona whispered into Viola's ear.

"I did not weary of it," Lady Emily replied to Mr. Yale. "But I am already weary of you and I have only seen you for ten seconds." She paused. "Now it is fifteen and I am still weary."

Mr. Yale chuckled.

"Pay no attention to *ma petite Emilie, chère mademoiselle*." An elegant lady of black, white, and red contrasts pecked Viola on either cheek in a waft of Parisian perfume. "She does not like the long carriages, you see."

"This is Madame Roche, Miss Carlyle," Lady Fiona said, dimples denting her alabaster cheeks. "She is Lady Emily's companion and positively diverting." Her gaze followed Mr. Yale. "But I see you are already enjoying diverting company."

Serena drew forward a lean, fair-haired man with bright blue eyes. "Viola, meet our stepbrother, Sir Tracy Lucas."

"You must call me only Tracy, I hope." He bowed and gave her an attractive smile. "And I will be honored to call you sister."

"This is a lovely party, isn't it, Miss Carlyle?" Lady Fiona's smile lit up her face. She was taller even than Serena, lithe maidenly perfection in white muslin. "It will be quite splendid coming to know you, and I know Lady Emily—rather Lysistrata—will like it too once she has thrown off the discomforts of travel." She darted another glance at Mr. Yale, this time sly and not in the least bit innocent. "Do you think we may have dancing?"

Viola lifted her brows. "I do not know how to dance, actually."

The girl's face brightened. "How perfectly splendid! We shall give you lessons."

The house abruptly became quite merry. Accustomed to living among many people in close quarters, Viola did not mind the activity. These people from London, however, were not like her sister and the baron, rather a bit more like Mr. Yale—clever, fashionable, and very gracious to her. Still, Viola found herself stealing away to the coastal path over the bluff where far below waves bathed the narrow beach in froth and gulls' cries could be heard more stridently. She sucked in the briny air, the sun warmed her cheeks, and she was nearly happy, except for the empty, twisted space in her middle that would not seem to go away.

Mr. Yale remained kindly attentive. But his pleasure in his visit to Savege Park seemed to have paled.

"Lady Fiona admires you." She slid her gaze to the pretty girl perched at the pianoforte playing a lilting tune, her voice sweet as nothing at sea ever was, rather more like the songbirds in Serena's terraced gardens on the inland side of the house.

"Yes, well." He swallowed a mouthful of port. "If I were to pursue that admiration her brother would have my neck in a noose."

"I thought you and Lord Blackwood were quite good friends."

"Precisely."

She studied his silvery eyes, not a bit misty with drink although she had watched him consume at least three glasses of wine with dinner.

"You have no interest in her, do you?"

"She is all that is lovely." He sipped again.

"But—"

"Miss Carlyle, I find that I am unable to pursue this particular avenue of conversation. Pray, forgive me."

"Mr. Yale, after three weeks in my company, you have not yet come to understand the measure of me?"

His mouth slipped into a grin. "Ah. I have mistaken myself." He looked at her directly. "I shall put it differently: I haven't any interest in girls barely out of the schoolroom."

"And yet you tease Lady Emily nearly every occasion offered to you. She cannot be more than twenty."

His silvery eyes sparkled. "She is quite another sort."

"She thinks you are an indolent fop. Are you?"

"Naturally you must make your own judgment."

"I have very little upon which to base a comparative judgment. Only Lord Savege, Sir Tracy, and Lord Carlyle, really."

"You omit our mutual friend from that short list. Is he not a gentleman, Miss Carlyle?"

Her cheeks warmed. "I don't know what you can mean."

A grin split across his face. "Why, you have done it! You have truly become the lady you sought a month ago."

She did not know whether to laugh with him or to cry. Had the world she had inhabited for fifteen years truly disappeared in a matter of weeks? If she donned again breeches and sash, would the calluses on her palms renew themselves swiftly, or slowly as when she had first trained her hands to labor?

The skirts of a white dress flittered into her sight like the wings of gulls about a topsail.

"Mr. Yale," Lady Fiona said, her long lashes dipping over pretty brown eyes. "If I play tomorrow, will you teach Miss Carlyle how to dance? Lady Savege says we are to have a party at week's end, with the neighbors from all about. But Miss Carlyle insists she cannot dance and I will not have her sitting on the side while the rest of us enjoy ourselves. She is far too pretty for that." She grasped Viola's fingers and pressed them warmly. "Our host is an exceptional dancer as well. With your assistance, Mr. Yale, I am certain Miss Carlyle will be more than prepared to take the floor for the party. Will you, sir?"

"It would be my honor. Miss Carlyle?"

"Well, why not?" She could not possibly acquit herself worse at dancing than at painting and the harp.

She did. Considerably worse.

"Oh! I am sorry."

"No need for apologies, my dear. I am no doubt at fault." Lord Savege's grin glimmered.

Viola narrowed her eyes skeptically and tripped over the earl's feet again.

"This is hopeless."

"Ladies do not mutter on the dance floor." Mr. Yale winked as he took her hand from the earl's.

"Ladies do not wish for their cutlass to cut off the bottom six inches of their dress either, or to tear a space to breathe in their stays, I suspect."

"Oo, la!" Madame Roche laughed. "Miss Carlyle, she is *vraiment charmant*, no?"

"I daresay," Mr. Yale said with perfect equanimity. Serena chuckled. From Lady Fiona at the pianoforte came a delighted ripple of notes. Even Lady Emily sitting removed from the dancing with a book cracked a smile. Warm breeze drifted in through long windows open to the late-summer afternoon, billowing the draperies out like Viola's skirts, and she could not be unhappy. There was great joy to be had in her new friends' company, great challenge to overcome in mastering new skills, and great comfort in which to revel in her sister's beautiful home. To feel this persistent emptiness inside, despite all, seemed ridiculously contrary. She should have become accustomed to it by now.

Lady Fiona set her fingers to the keyboard again and Viola set to dancing with renewed application. Turning about, she came to face the drawing room door, and there he stood. Jin. Without warning. Perfectly handsome as always, and watching her.

Quite abruptly she knew that she would never become accustomed to the emptiness inside her, not even were she to try to distract herself from it by sailing all seven seas in a leaking ship. Nothing on earth existed that could distract sufficiently. For there was no more dangerous venture than loving Jin Seton and not being loved by him in return.

Chapter 22

He could not look away from her. He knew he ought. But as she stumbled through the set, tangling her feet in her hem and her partners' steps and generally making a hash out of the dance, the knot that had taken up residence in Jin's chest during the past month loosened. She was beautiful—as beautiful groomed like a lady as she had been garbed like a sailor. She moved about the floor smiling and laughing, her pleasure and occasional uncertainty unrehearsed and unrestrained. As she captained her ship and bewitched her crewmen, she danced with all her heart, if not with all her limbs in concert.

Finally her gaze came to him, her eyes widened, and the breath went out of him. She tripped again.

"Jinan, you have returned!" Lady Savege clapped. Her husband swiveled about, a smile crossing his face. He came forward in long strides. Hand outstretched, he took Jin's.

"I shall not embrace you here before these others," the earl said quietly, roughly, his grip hard. "I've no doubt you would knife me for the indignity. But know that could I, I would."

Jin allowed himself a slight grin, the mountain of purpose he had carried slipping finally from his heart. The debt of life that had bound him to this man, his friend, for twenty years was now paid.

Alex shook his head and laughed. "So that is where you were all those months when we heard nothing from you? Looking for a girl everyone believed dead?"

"It seemed as good a task to pursue as any." He released his friend's hand.

"And how is my ship? Your ship, that is."

"At the bottom of the sea, Alex."

"You *say*? How? By whom?"

"By a lady." His gaze flickered over Alex's shoulder to Viola once more. Alex followed, then came back to him, open eyed. "Yes." Jin smiled. "She is . . . remarkable."

The others waited for their host's cue, curious. But the lady whose dark eyes he saw in his dreams each night averted her face from him now.

Serena came to them. "Welcome back, Jinan. Allow me to introduce you to the others. Lady Emily—"

"We are already known to one another from a brief encounter at my parents' house nearly two years ago," Lady Emily said from her chair with a nod at him. "How do you do, Mr. Seton. I don't suppose you will take Mr. Yale away with you when you go this time, will you?"

"The lady is all charm, as always," the Welshman drawled. "How was town, Seton?"

"Well, thank you." Empty of the one person he wished to see, who still did not look at him. "Lady Emily, it is a pleasure to meet you again. I am afraid, though, that I haven't any plans to depart soon."

Then Viola glanced, a flicker of her violet eyes in his direction, her lips parted. He had not known his intentions until he spoke them, and he had spoken them entirely to draw her gaze.

Panic slid through him again. He should not have come. But he had been drawn and now it was too late. Willing himself steady, he turned to Lady Emily's companion and bowed.

"Madame Roche, *j'espère que vous allez bien*."

"*Je vais très bien, monsieur. Merçi.*" She curtsied, then gestured to the girl standing by the piano. "But you know Mademoiselle Fione, the sister of your good friend, the Lord Blackwood, I think?"

He bowed. She curtsied, a flutter of lashes over dark brown eyes.

"Of course, I needn't introduce you to my sister." Serena beamed as she took Viola's arm snugly. "Now, shall we have tea? All that dancing has given me a dreadful thirst."

"My dear," Alex said, "if you will excuse us, I will take the gentleman to seek out stronger refreshment. Seton, Yale, Lucas, shall we?"

"Superb suggestion," Yale murmured and, casting Jin a grinning glance, moved toward the door. Jin bowed to the ladies and followed willingly. It was one thing to dream of a woman's eyes and lips and touch from hundreds of miles away, and to regret the distance from her. It was another entirely to remain in the same room with her, his blood spinning with need and that hot thread of alarm, and to remain any saner than she.

He had returned. Just like that. Viola had no warning of it, no announcement even of his name by the servants who seemed to otherwise declare it each time a member of the company of ladies and gentlemen at the Park yawned or blinked.

Not this time. In the midst of the minuet he had appeared,

standing at the threshold to the drawing room as though he had been watching the spirited group romping about the floor for ages and was perfectly content to remain there indefinitely. And now as the party gathered in the drawing room before dinner, he again enjoyed a comfortable position, this time by the piano. Lady Fiona flashed her pretty dark lashes at him, showing him her sheet music. Madame Roche stood nearby, but the thrice-widowed Frenchwoman of indeterminate age and a remarkable froth of black organza did not bother Viola, despite her sharp eyes and elegant looks. Only the lovely, highly maidenly Fiona mattered, the girl she had come to like very much and felt absolutely wretched envying now. Lady Fiona had his attention, and it made her sick to her stomach.

He wore a dark coat, buff trousers, and white linen, as though he had not come from the road only that afternoon. But so he had always appeared aboard ship, in command of himself and of everyone else he encountered. Including his very foolish captain.

She found it difficult to breathe properly and she felt like a ninny. Violet la Vile was most certainly not a ninny.

She would best this. This time, she would not allow him to affect her. Now she had her family around her—the affection of her sister and the baron, and new friends, however grand they all seemed at times. Moreover, she had the strength to resist him. In Trinidad, her feelings had blindsided her. But now she knew the danger in which she stood. Even without her pistol and dirk, she would fight it. And if that didn't work, she was not averse to digging her weapons out of her traveling trunk and threatening him to depart at dagger's point.

Beside her, Serena and Mr. Yale discussed potted plants or piquet or something equally mysterious, she hadn't an idea. But the baron's stepdaughter, Diantha Lucas, apparently did.

"Lord Abernathy and Lord Drake played for prize orchids, but it ended in a draw." Her wild chestnut curls bobbed, obscuring a pair of blue eyes shaded with curling lashes. "I read it in the gossip column in *The Times*."

"How eccentric of them." Serena chuckled.

Mr. Yale's mouth slipped into a grin Viola had come to recognize. That grin said, *I have consumed a bottle of brandy this afternoon and cannot be moved by anything, even foolish lords playing cards for hundreds of pounds over exotic plants.* But he only said, "How admirable that you read the paper, Miss Lucas."

Beneath a liberal sprinkling of spots no young lady could like, Diantha's cheeks and chin clung firmly to the roundness of childhood, and then some. But her regard remained bright. "Papa does not like the paper, but I learned to enjoy it at the Bailey Academy, of course."

"Of course." His silvery eyes glistened.

"Mr. Yale, you should drink less and read the paper more often."

"Diantha!"

"I am only saying, Serena, that handsome young men ought not to ruin their lives in this manner. There are ever so many alternatives to depravity, you know."

"For a lady of—" He broke off, his brow creasing. "What is your age, if I may be so brash as to inquire, Miss Lucas?"

"Sixteen and nearly three quarters."

"For a lady of sixteen and nearly three quarters, Miss Lucas, you have a remarkable quantity of opinion."

Her face opened in innocent surprise. "Why shouldn't I?"

His brows quirked up. "Why shouldn't you, indeed? It is admirable."

"A moment ago you thought it impertinent."

"Never. Or if I did I must have forgotten myself for an instant. I beg your forgiveness."

Her lips screwed up into a skeptical frown. "You are not sincere."

"Nearly always. But I do indeed find an informed mind admirable, Miss Lucas, even when paired with impertinence." With a slight grin, he unfolded from his chair and stood, bowed to each of them, and moved off.

Serena patted her stepsister on the arm. "Don't pay him any attention, Diantha."

"Miss Yarley at the Bailey Academy says gentlemen always drink to excess. I told her Papa does not, but my real father did, so perhaps Miss Yarley is correct in the case of *some* gentlemen." She stared after Mr. Yale, her eyes bright with curiosity and something warmer. Lady Fiona played a trill of notes and Viola's gaze crept back toward the pianoforte.

Jin was looking at her.

She snapped her eyes away, the hollow ache inside her never greater. Beyond the propped terrace doors, thunderclouds gathered to the ocean, bands of fiery gold striped across their bottom swells from the setting sun. She stood and went through the glass doors onto the terrace. The air glowed pink all about, and she forced herself to appreciate the beauty as she always had from her helm.

"Missing your quarterdeck?" His voice came at her shoulder, quiet and deep.

She sucked in breath and turned to him. "Thanks to you."

He bowed. "It is a pleasure to see you again too, Viola."

"I suppose you expect me to curtsy now."

"That is the usual custom, I believe." His eyes glimmered. Her belly felt quivery.

"I have learned how, you know. And countless other ladylike accomplishments."

"I have no doubt of it."

"Why did you come out here? To bother me?"

"Merely to say hello. But I will certainly congratulate myself if I achieve more with so little effort."

"Oh. I am laughing uncontrollably. Can you see?"

"I can see." It seemed from the appreciation in his regard as it flickered along her hair and shoulders that he meant something other than his words. She could not bear it, not wanting it as she did.

"Don't look at me like that."

"Like what? Like a beautiful woman is standing before me and . . ." He paused. "I seem to recall once already having a conversation quite like this."

At the inn when they arrived at Port of Spain, before her whole world changed.

"You are only looking at me like that because I have been plucked and powdered and am now essentially unrecognizable."

"Rather, recognizable and irrational."

"*Je vous en prie.*" She curtsied, flicked open her fan, and smacked herself in the nose. She rubbed her palm over it.

His perfect mouth crept up at one corner. "You have learned French in a month?"

"*Où peut-on danser?*"

His grin broadened. "You do know what that means?"

"Yes, but the only other phrases I have memorized are 'The prawns are delicious' and 'Will there be cards tonight?' And were we to dance, I would almost certainly tread upon your toes, which would be satisfying. Why did you call me irrational? This time."

"You know that I thought you beautiful before this. I told you."

And there she stood, on the terrace of an earl's house, warm and aching in places she knew no proper lady should be warm and aching under such circumstances, and wishing to throw herself upon his chest quite urgently.

She must say something to press away the desperation inside her, to push him away before she cast polite society and every ounce of her pride to the wind and adhered herself to him like a mollusk to a rock.

"Mr. Yale flirts a great deal more subtly than you."

"I am not flirting with you, Viola."

Oh, God. Why had he returned? It hurt and she didn't know how to make it stop hurting.

"He calls me Miss Carlyle."

Something glimmered in his eyes now. Something not perfectly settled. "Do you wish me to call you Miss Carlyle again, then?"

"No," she answered too quickly.

"Viola."

Something in his tone—a question, perhaps—made her heart trip, which made her snap, *"What?"* because the tumult of these emotions was not welcome.

His brow lifted and he made a sharp sound as though to retort. But he halted, his mouth becoming a line. "No."

She did not wish to know what he meant by no—why he had stopped himself from responding. It could not be good, and every mote of blood in her was shivering now.

"No . . . what?"

"No, I will not match your foolishness with foolishness of my own. I came out here only to say hello and that I have missed you."

Her stomach dropped to her toes. "H-have you?"

"Yes."

The horizon overtook the sun and the pink fell away from the sky, draping the sloping lawn and austere walls of Savege Park in pearly gray. But, tinted pink or blue or any color, his eyes were still beautiful, his jaw still resolute, and Viola did not like the sensation of sinking onto the slate terrace like a puddle of melting jelly.

She attempted a smirk. "You had your chance, Seton."

The single brow rose again. "I did not miss this, though."

"Oh, well." She struggled to maintain a light tone. "I am certain you can find more conciliating company inside."

"I have no doubt of that." His mouth crept up at the edge again, scattering stars across her vision.

"My sister, for instance." She spoke to smother her distress. "She seems to like you very much, God knows why. And of course, there is Lady Fiona."

"I am being dismissed, it seems, as though I am still a lieutenant aboard your ship."

"You are being dismissed as though you are a man that a lady does not wish to speak with."

"Hm." Finally he smiled. It hit her midsection full force.

"Why are you grinning?"

"You told the truth that day when you said you were only one woman. One . . ." He paused. "One woman." He turned and went toward the terrace doors. Her fingers itched to grab his arm and stay him, to keep him with her in the waning light. Simply, to touch him. She wanted to touch him more than she'd wanted anything for weeks. Or perhaps forever.

"What did you do in London?" she blurted out.

He looked over his shoulder. "Nothing of note."

"I thought you had business to attend to there. Why did you return here?"

His eyes sobered once more. "To settle a debt."

"With Lord Savage, concerning me, of course. But he was in London. Didn't you see him there?"

"No." He came back to her until he stood very close. She tilted her chin to look up at him and the evening breeze stirred the dark lock dipping over his eyes. She saw him draw a slow, deep breath, her own breaths short and quick. "Are you happy here, Viola?"

"This is a surprise. I cannot imagine that you actually care."

"I do."

"If you did, you would not have forced me to come here."

"The wager," he said, his voice low, "was your idea, of course."

Her cheeks were hot. Every part of her was hot. He was standing too close, but she could not move away. She wanted to be even closer. His body radiated a waiting tension, his gaze scanning her features, and it was as though he was touching her with his fingertips, on her cheeks and brow and lips. She could not stop staring at his mouth. She wanted to kiss him quite a lot. She wanted to make love with him again. She had never wanted to make love like this with a man before. And she wanted him to hold her, to not wish to let her go.

"Are you happy?" he repeated quietly.

The intimacy of it tangled her insides unbearably. She stepped back and crossed her arms over her chest.

"Wouldn't you like to know?"

A muscle flickered in his jaw, his gaze hardening. "Yes, or I would not ask. But apparently the child has returned and I shan't have my answer." He moved away.

She wanted to shout that she was not a child but a woman, and the woman hurt. But she only swallowed back the thickness in her throat and wondered if real ladies allowed gentlemen to make them feel like they were dying. If she were on her ship—

If she were on her ship she would not allow him to chastise her, then walk away.

She went after him. Perhaps he knew she pursued him. At the threshold with beveled glass doors the like she'd never seen before, which were simply another part of this house that had nothing familiar about it—except *him* now—he waited for her.

"I am . . ." She sought any words. "Too *stationary*." It was true, after all. And she could not tell him what was really in her heart. Let him think she resented him for her changed life, but nothing else. Nothing for which he could imagine he had bested her. "I am unaccustomed to being stationary."

"That is to be expected."

"You aren't going to say that I will soon become comfortable with it? That I will forget all about my life before?"

"Why should I say that? I never wished you to be unhappy, only reunited with your family. If you wish to resume your life in America, I will not hold you from it, nor will Lady Savege or anyone else, I suspect. They care for you and want only your happiness." He said this not to her eyes, but to her cheeks and brow and mouth. Quite a lot to her mouth, where his gaze lingered on the spot beneath her lower lip. She could feel the memory of his tongue there. It made her knees watery. It made her lashes dip.

"Jin, I am sorry to be so contrary," she said on a little rush.

"Viola, I misspoke earlier." His voice seemed hoarse. "I cannot remain here long. My ship . . . You see . . ."

Her nerves shimmered. "Is it berthed in London?"

"Yes." His chest rose on a breath.

She gripped the doorjamb behind with trembling fingers. "Are Matthew and Billy and Matouba there as well?"

"Yes. I am expected shortly in Malta."

"*Malta?*" No. *No.* How could he look at her like this now and speak of going so far away? Without *her*? She shook her head.

"Viola, I—"

"I hope I am not interrupting?"

Jin turned to the baron, but she could not tear her attention from him. His eyes did not look normal, and her heart did not feel normal, and *she wanted to know what he'd been about to say.* On her ship this interruption would not happen. But she couldn't very well flash the baron a sparkling smile and order him to hare off deck.

"My lord." Jin bowed.

"I am glad to find opportunity to speak with you in private, Mr. Seton." The baron's soft brown eyes were not so soft now. He took her hand and clamped it beneath his arm. "You brought my daughter home to us. I thank you for it most sincerely."

"It was my honor, sir."

"I understand that you are a sailor." He said the word like it tasted a bit sour.

"Yes, sir."

"And that you have known my son-in-law many years, since you were both quite young."

"I have."

Viola's gaze snapped to Jin's face, but his attention was fixed on the baron. He hadn't told her this.

"Now that you've settled my daughter back in the bosom of her family, the Admiralty must have need of you again." A chary glint lit the baron's eyes.

"I sail shortly for the Eastern Mediterranean. Your daughter was gracious to my crewmen on the journey to England," he said so smoothly she nearly believed it herself. "I was just now conveying to her their best wishes."

"Then you will be leaving Savege Park soon, before the winter weather becomes troublesome on the sea. A brief visit only." His head bobbed in satisfaction. "But I am glad to have had the opportunity to convey to you my gratitude."

Jin bowed again.

"There is the butler," the baron said in a lighter tone. "Dinner is served, and thanks to you, Mr. Seton, I have the pleasure of taking in *my* daughter on my arm." He smiled warmly at her and drew her away. She cast Jin a backward glance, but he had turned his attention onto the terrace again.

Not the terrace, in fact. He was staring beyond, at the sea.

Chapter 23

Lady Justice
In Care of Brittle & Sons, Printers
London

Dearest lady,

Enclosed in this modest package find not a kettle of
edibles nor another portrait of yourself (with a tail).
I see how those trinkets of my affection may have
missed the tide. I give to you now only that which
any gentleman admirer might give to a lady: poetry.
Samuel Taylor Coleridge, to be precise. I offer it because having received back all the gifts I have sent
you, I need guidance as to what you may accept from
me as gift. Quoth the Ancient Mariner:

If he may know which way to go;
For she guides him smooth or grim.
See, brother, see! how graciously
She looketh down on him.

*My lady, looketh down on me with gracious mercy
and return not this humble gift.*

> *Yours &c,*
> *Peregrine*

> *Secretary, The Falcon Club*

To Peregrine, at large:

*You preen. You strut. You will be plucked. Then I
will have only this to say to you, "The game is done!
I've won! I've won!"*

> *Lady Justice*

Chapter 24

M r. Yale departed the following day. Viola went with him into the foyer, where he took her hand and lifted it close to his lips but did not kiss it.

"It has been a remarkable pleasure, Miss Carlyle. I hope to see you in town anon."

"Thank you. You have been very kind."

"Kindness has little to do with it."

"I don't think you know what it has to do with." She twisted her lips. "That was inelegantly said. Or at least grammatically unclear, I think. And after all your coaching."

"You are charming, Miss Carlyle."

"I still have not mastered which glass is meant for which beverage or how to fasten my garters."

"Or apparently which matters are inappropriate to discuss with a gentleman." His gray eyes twinkled. "But, no worry. A footman will always see to the former, and another man altogether is no doubt quite happy about the latter."

Her cheeks warmed.

He grinned. "Do you know, I believe I will kiss your hand after all. I mayn't be allowed in the future."

She snatched her fingers away. He chuckled, donned his hat, and left.

Lady Emily stood in the doorway to the foyer and came forth now. She wore spectacles the color of her short silvery-gold hair, and carried a book.

"Has he gone for good?" Her voice was unusually bright.

"Yes. He likes to tease you. Why is that?"

"Because he hasn't a thought in his head. I prefer Mr. Seton. He does not plague a woman with idiotic banter trying to pass it off as conversation."

Since their frustrating conversation on the terrace, Mr. Seton had not plagued Viola with any conversation at all. She had not seen him to be plagued or to plague in return.

"Mr. Seton is taciturn," she mumbled.

"No. He is a thinking man, Miss Carlyle. Such men are not to be dismissed as merely taciturn."

"A thinking man?"

"He reads." She opened her book as though searching for something in it. " 'Words frighten not him who blanches not at deeds.' Sophocles. I encountered him in the library this morning settled comfortably with Herodotus. An inestimable companion."

Herodotus? It could be coincidence. Then why did her heart beat now as it had that evening when he stood at her cabin door and she touched him for the first time?

She adopted her most innocent posture. "Herodotus? Did another gentleman arrive at Savege Park that I have yet to meet?"

"Herodotus perished in Greece over two thousand years ago. I should hope he is not present at this gathering." She looked so sincere. Viola laughed.

Lady Emily's emerald eyes narrowed. "You quiz nearly as well as Mr. Yale, Miss Carlyle." But she grinned.

"You do not hate him, do you?"

"Unfortunately I cannot. He helped me in a difficult situation with my parents and I cannot forget that, although I certainly wish to. He is like a bothersome elder brother."

"I am glad. I like him. He has been very good to me."

Lady Emily bent her fair head over her volume anew. "I should not account that a particular accomplishment on his part, Miss Carlyle." She turned another page. "You are quite easy to like. If all ladies were more like you I shouldn't mind going about in society half so much." With that, she wandered through the opposite door, head in her book.

After lunch from which the gentlemen were absent, Viola went to the library seeking out something or another to read. More than once.

She was the greatest idiot alive. He was not there, of course. Back in the parlor, Lady Fiona said the gentlemen had gone out riding. Viola considered going to the stable and saddling up a horse, but she didn't know how.

The gentlemen returned just before dinner. In the drawing room Sir Tracy said many pretty things to her, but she didn't mind his foolishness. At least he spoke to her.

At dinner and afterward during tea conversation was lively and general and Jin did not come near her. She had learned enough of polite manners to know that she could not very well abandon her seat and put herself near him. But she would if he showed any interest in her doing so, which he did not. He seemed distracted, his attention little on the group and occasionally directed toward the terrace again.

She slept poorly, listening to Madame Roche's snoring through the wall from the bedchamber beside hers and wondering where his bedchamber might be. The idea that he might be in one of the more accessible rooms now, perhaps in the parlor having a drink or playing billiards with Alex and Sir Tracy, nearly inspired her to dress and go searching.

But the wound to her pride would not allow it. He did not want her; she would not chase after him.

The following day, Serena enjoined the ladies to take tea with her at the teahouse in Avesbury, a quaint establishment beside the modiste's shop. After the repast, Serena took Viola alone next door.

"What are we doing, Ser?" She looked about the tiny place stacked with bins of ribbons and laces and skeins of fabric. "I am certain Mrs. Hamper delivered all my dresses directly to—" Her hand flew to her mouth. "Holy Mary Magdalene. For *me*?"

Serena's delight shone so clearly, the shimmering gown in the dressmaker's arms must be for her.

"Do you like it?"

Viola reached out to stroke the butter-soft silk in the perfect shade of sunset, sewn with tiny pearls and sequins across the bodice and dripping down the filmy skirt like rain falling through sunshine.

"How could I not? But—"

"It is for the party tomorrow night. The gowns we made for you are all so lovely yet none of them suited a truly grand celebration."

Viola's eyes widened. "Do not tell me this party is for me."

"It *is*. Everyone for miles around has heard you are here. They are all mad to meet you again after so many years." Serena's face crinkled. "But . . . you do not want this?"

"Of course I do." Not at all. The mere idea of being the center of this sort of attention turned her hands cold. She was certain to do something atrociously wrong and shame Serena, Alex, and the baron. "Thank you, Ser. You are so generous and I will be happy to meet everyone again. I wonder if I will remember them?" She didn't much care. She wanted only the company of one man whose company she would soon be denied forever.

Malta. *Malta*. Halfway across the world . . . Wasn't it?

When they returned home she went to the library. He was not there, but a gold-embossed atlas of the world was. She flipped open the huge volume, found England, and traced a path all the way to the boot of Italy with her fingertip. She blew out a giant breath. Good Lord, she was acting like a child, just as he had said. But the tear upon her cheek came from a woman's sorrow.

She scrubbed it off, slammed the book shut, and shoved it back in its place on the shelf.

She didn't give a fig where he went or what he did. She would be perfectly fine without him. And perhaps when the project of becoming a lady finally wearied her beyond endurance she would go back to Boston where she belonged. If Alex floated her a loan, she could purchase a new ship and, better equipped, take on new projects. The trip to Port of Spain with that cargo might have been lucrative if she had gone about it with the intention of making money. She would hire out her ship to one of those outrageously wealthy merchants like Mr. Hat, and pay back her brother-in-law within a year or so. Hopefully. With a truly sturdy vessel she would also be able to return to England every so often to visit her family. That would be lovely. Activity suited her so much better than this ladylike sitting around waiting for something to happen, or waiting for other people to make decisions for her such as throwing a big party at which everyone for miles about would attend, or waiting for a man to look at her again like he wanted her and wished to tell her something significant.

Oh, God.

She pressed the heels of her palms into her eyes and drew a long, shuddering breath. She did not wish to return to Boston or the sea. She only wanted Jin. But she was not to have him. She *must* get a hold of herself. Straightening her shoulders, she marched to the door, pulled it open, and slammed into a hard body.

Jin grasped her shoulders. And just like that, she was lost, drowning in the pleasure of touching him again, heat filling her. She dragged lashes that seemed remarkably heavy up to see his beautiful mouth hovering above hers, a muscle working in his jaw. In silence she begged, *Kiss me. Kiss me.*

He put her away from him, turned, and disappeared down the corridor.

Shaking, confused, and furious that for the first time in her life she could not manage to tell a man exactly what she was thinking, Viola went to find Serena to help prepare for the party the following day—the grand event that would introduce her into polite society, when all she wished was to be back sitting on the forecastle of her old ship in the sunset with an Egyptian pirate.

Her sister reclined on the chaise in her dressing chamber draped in a blue dressing gown, a tiny bundle of infant in the crook of her arm.

"You are very relaxed for a woman about to have a party," Viola commented.

"I am savoring a moment of peace. I have spent the day greeting all our guests who will remain the night here and seeing to everything that needed seeing to. Now my husband is managing the rest. He is quite good at throwing parties." She smiled a sweet, private sort of smile. Viola's chest ached a little.

"Did Papa hate Mama after she died, or only Fionn?"

Serena's eyes popped open. "I don't believe he hated either of them."

"No. I am quite certain he hated my father." Viola toyed with the string of her delicate gold and white fan painted with exotic birds. Serena had just given it to her, after Jane strapped her into her pretty gown and fussed with her hair. "He was remarkably uncivil to Mr. Seton when they spoke the other night. Especially when he said the word 'sailor.' He nearly choked on it."

"He did?" Serena chewed on her lower lip. "That doesn't sound like Papa at all. But I guess it should come as no surprise given Mama and Fionn's attachment to one another."

"I suppose devotion that lasts ages despite them never seeing one another is impressive." Again she had not seen Jin all day, yet her nerves tangled merely thinking of spending the evening with him. That she would be spending the evening with about seventy other people really mattered very little.

"They never should have met, let alone spoken." Serena sighed. "But they did, and he could not give her up, nor she him entirely."

"No wonder Papa dislikes sailors."

"You are a sailor and he loves you very much."

"May I enter?" Dressed formally, the earl radiated the sort of elegant, confident masculinity a woman could not fail to notice. Viola had heard enough from Madame Roche to suggest that in the past many women in fact had *noticed* Alex Savage. How her kind, dreamy sister had ever seriously considered the suit of such a man, Viola marveled. But there could be no doubt of his fidelity to Serena now; his devotion was patently clear.

"Do come in." Serena stroked her fingertip along the crown of Maria's wooly head. "Your daughter has just fallen asleep, so shh." Her glance flickered over him. "You are quite handsome tonight, my lord."

"I must make a vain attempt to meet your splendor, my lady." He bowed. "I do not wish to shame you."

"But I might." Viola wrinkled her nose.

"Of course you won't," Serena said firmly. "You look

beautiful, and you have excelled in nearly every lesson Mr. Yale gave you." Her eyes danced.

"*Nearly* being the operative word. I stepped all over Alex's toes while we danced—don't deny it."

"If you do not wish to dance tonight," he assured, "you needn't."

"I suppose it would be all right if I danced only with you and Papa. But to step on a stranger's toes, that I should rather not do."

"Jinan is not a stranger," Serena said. "You can step on his toes and he won't mind it at all. Tracy won't either."

The earl leaned his broad shoulders against the door frame. "Jin at a party like this is a marvel in itself. When Yale made the announcement the other day that he was departing I half expected Jin to take to the road with him. That he has remained here longer than a day astounds me."

"It has been nearly two years since you have seen one another."

"That wouldn't matter to him. His loyalties and affections don't operate on those terms. But I have never seen him so restless. He is not himself."

"Perhaps he is merely at a loss for suitable activity. He must miss his ship." Serena's gaze slipped to her. "As perhaps you do, too, Vi?"

Viola's mouth was dry. "Only a little."

"Serena," Alex continued, "do not be surprised when he departs as abruptly as he arrived. Tomorrow is as likely as next week."

"I will expect it. I am not all that ignorant of the ways of sailors, my lord." Her eyes twinkled. Alex smiled. Viola's heart felt as though it might implode.

She stood. "I will go finish preparing now." She hurried to the door.

"But you are already pre—"

She fled. She could not bear to imagine him gone. Not again. Not so soon. Because then it truly would be good-bye. He would leave and she would never see him again and she would be much better off for it.

Damn him. Damn him for returning and oversetting her so thoroughly. *Oversetting?* She was not *overset* like some maidenly ninny. She was confused and thought perhaps that any moment, the moment he chose to leave abruptly as Alex prophesied, her heart would finally break.

Guests had been arriving all day. By the time the sun set, dipping over the ocean in a froth of gold and pink stripes, the house was brimming. It was not too large a gathering, Madame Roche assured her.

"*Jusque le petit fête.* No more than one hundred of the peoples."

One hundred seemed like quite a lot of the peoples to Viola. All richly garbed and talking of town and when they would return for the fall session, they seemed enormously elegant and sophisticated. Servants wandered about with trays of champagne as ladies gossiped in little clusters and gentlemen partook of wine and stronger drink. In the drawing room, Lady Fiona played beautifully on the pianoforte, followed by another young lady who also sang. There was much animated conversation, more music by a hired quartet, and a buffet supper, and finally dancing. Candles glimmered on every surface. Laughter spilled onto the terrace lit with paper lamps and dancers followed into the warm, blustery night. All indulged in the evening's pleasures, smiles and gaiety abounding.

Viola tried to hide.

At first, she enjoyed it a little. But she remembered few people. The older ladies cooed and exclaimed over her, insisting that she had been a remarkably pretty girl.

"And so . . . *spirited*," one lady proclaimed with an overly wide smile. "Why, do you remember, Amelia, that Sunday in church when she bathed her kitten in the baptismal font?"

"She said it needed holy water to heal its tiny wounded paw." The lady bobbed her head. "And you mustn't forget the toad pie she brought to tea at Mrs. Creadle's, Hester. I always told dear Maria that her little Viola was a wild thing. A *wild* thing." She said this last as though Viola were not sitting right beside her.

"Yet she has lived such a retiring life with her aunt in Boston, none of us even knew she was there. What a lovely demure young lady she has become, hasn't she, Amelia?"

"Remarkably lovely, Hester. I commend her American aunt."

They had to be lying through their teeth. Or ignorant. Or simply very foolish. She hadn't any idea where these rumors had come from, but she doubted Serena and Alex spread them.

Swiftly, she grew weary of pretending fifteen years of her life at sea had simply not occurred. The only person in the place who knew the full truth of the life she had lived was a former pirate, but he didn't look anything like what he had once been either. Tonight he was arrayed gorgeously in dark coat and waistcoat, a single blood-red gemstone glinting in the fall of his neck cloth. He was perfect, and he did not come within a league of her.

To save herself from complete misery, she pretended he was not present. She remained on the opposite side of the room, did not look in his direction, and in general tried to not think of him.

Lady Fiona had clearly decided on the opposite tack. With the departure of Mr. Yale, her attentions were now all for Jin. With actually demure smiles she engaged him in conversation that did not seem to tax him in the least; talking with her he did not roll his eyes or frown even once.

"She is not the girl for him, *ma chère*." Madame Roche wagged a red-tipped finger before Viola's face.

She blinked. "Pardon me? Oh, I mean, *pardonnez-moi*?"

Crimson lips split into a charming smile in a face tinted with white powder. "Mademoiselle Fione is not the girl for him. *Non*." She waved a scented black kerchief about, lacy shawls floating. "She is *très jolie*. But he is not taken with her."

"How do you know that?"

"Because all the night he has been looking at you." Her shawls floated off, taking her with them.

Viola's heart beat quite swiftly. She glanced up. He was, in fact, looking at her.

Then why hadn't he kissed her at the library? Why had he walked away? Rather, fled. And why did he not come speak to her now?

She turned away, went into another room, and found a trio of old gentlemen to entertain with outrageous stories. She made up most of them. If they were married to the old ladies who made up all those stories about her, they would be accustomed enough to it anyway.

She danced a little, first with the baron, then with Sir Tracy, and once with one of the old men. She almost did not tread on any of their feet. Several young gentlemen asked her to dance. She declined, smiling. "Your shoes are far too shiny. I would not wish to scuff them with my heel." Indeed, she smiled incessantly, laughed in delight at every witticism, invented story after story, each more implausible than the next, and generally attempted to prove to herself and probably to him that she didn't care the least little bit about him or the lovely girls with whom he enjoyed his evening.

Sometime in the very late hours, or perhaps the very early,

when Viola had begun to believe her feet would fall off if she could not rid them of her punishing slippers, guests began to depart. Those who lived close by went to their carriages, and those who had come from a distance staggered to bedchambers in the labyrinthine corridors of the Park.

"Everyone adored you." Serena curled her arm about her waist and kissed her on the cheek. "And you looked as though you were enjoying yourself. I am so glad."

"Thank you for the wonderful party, Ser. It was splendid." And finally over, so that now she could go to her room and spend the remainder of the night crying over a man she had been quite, quite foolish to fall in love with. The last she had seen of him, Lady Fiona had been wrapping her hand about his arm while two other young ladies stood by looking on with patent jealousy. So at least Viola was not alone in her envy, which made her feel absolutely ill.

"Come," Serena said, "I will tuck you in."

"Oh, no. You will wish to visit Maria before going to bed, and you must be exhausted."

"We will walk up together. And there is my lord to escort us. Will you see us up, Alex?"

He came toward them and took Serena's hand to kiss. "I am charged with playing cards. Cards, as though I haven't a lovely wife waiting for me. Some fellows will never learn."

"But you must act the gracious host," his lovely wife replied, and drew Viola toward the stair.

On the landing to the third story, Viola released her. "Thank you. Now go see Maria."

Serena's tired eyes smiled, and she went.

Dragging sore feet, Viola moved along the darkened corridor, wishing she'd brought a lamp or candle, then happy she hadn't. She was so weary and wretched, she must look like she'd been through a squall. And to be so wretched after her sister had thrown her a fabulous party made her more wretched yet. Halfway along the corridor she met a pair of matrons, gray head to gray head, still gossiping madly. She bade them good night, they waved, never ceasing their whispered chatter, and she slogged along on blistered toes and heels.

Five minutes of slogging later it occurred to her that she was once again lost. This time quite literally. Amber circles from sconces lit the corridor at long intervals. She recognized nothing, not the side table nor the painting on the wall; she had never been in this corridor. Voices came from a distance. The ubiquitous footmen seemed to have eschewed their ubiquity.

She halted and turned around. Jin was walking toward her. Her heart did an awful leap against her rib cage.

"What is the chance that I get myself lost and you appear out of nowhere to take me back where I belong?" she whispered very unsteadily.

"No chance." He came right to her, as close as he had on the terrace the last time he spoke to her, and at the library door when he did not. "I was looking for you."

"*Me?*" She could not bridle her tongue; it was apparently firmly attached to her heart. "Are you certain you weren't looking for Lady Fiona, rather?"

"Quite certain." His eyes covered her all at once, it seemed, her face and hair, shoulders, and the place where her quick breaths pressed her breasts against her bodice. She wanted him to look at her like this, but he had looked at her this way before and then rejected her.

"She wants you," she uttered, trying to push him away with words.

"I don't want her." He grasped her arms, not gently, and bent over her mouth. "I want you." Then, finally, he kissed her again.

Chapter 25

After what seemed a lifetime without him, he was kissing her. It was no tender, tentative caress, instead complete and perfectly confident that she would kiss him back. She did, meeting his seeking mouth eagerly, drinking him in like a drowning woman struggling for air and filling her lungs with yet more water. For surely this would kill her. But she simply could not deny him. His hand encompassed the back of her head, holding her to him as he had that first time, and quite swiftly it all got quite hot, and deep. Astoundingly deep. And not at all silent. His teeth grazed her lower lip, and she gasped and let him taste her tongue next. He groaned and broke away.

"I want you, Viola," he repeated over her lips.

She fought it. "But I don't want you."

His fingers hooked in the edge of her bodice and tugged open gown, corset cups, and shift, exposing her breasts. "You will have to produce more convincing evidence."

Viola looked down. Her nipples stood at aroused peaks.

She met his gaze again, sinking inside at her body's betrayal. "That is only lust."

His clear irises seemed to melt with heat. "Do you need more?"

More? She needed *everything* more from him. Everything he would not give her. He was not the sticking sort, Mattie had said. His behavior with her proved it, and Alex's words that he would leave soon frightened her beyond reason.

"You are an arrogant ass," she uttered to save her pride, and perhaps even to try to convince her heart. But it had no effect upon him, or upon her heart; his gaze of sheer need did not alter, nor did the gripping pain beneath her ribs abate. "Why have you not spoken with me? Why didn't you kiss me yesterday at the library?"

"I was trying to be strong." His hands tangled in her hair, his gaze consuming her so that even her blood sought him.

"And now?"

"Now I have had to endure an entire night of watching Viola Carlyle command a house full of people like she commands a ship of sailors, charming every one of them." His voice was very rough. "Strong can go to the devil."

She wrapped her arms around his neck and let him kiss her and touch her breasts, encouraging him with soft sounds of want she could not prevent. She should not do this. On her ship she'd been a sailor and free to do as she pleased. But Fiona Blackwood would never stand in the dark corridor of an earl's house with a man's hands on her breasts. A real lady would not allow it.

But she was not a real lady. They both knew that.

His tongue drifting across her lower lip melded with his caressing thumb, darting pleasure low in quick, aching bursts. She gripped his neck and flattened herself against his body. He kissed her harder, his hands sweeping around her rear and dragging her against his arousal. It felt good. Too good. And a little desperate. Because he only wanted her for this. But this was better than nothing, and he truly wanted her, with the same urgency as that first time on her ship. It felt like heaven. Or at least the path leading up toward heaven, never mind the gates remaining fully closed and locked against her.

"Come to my bedchamber now," he whispered against her mouth as though he did not wish to separate enough to speak.

"I don't take—"

"Orders. I know." He kissed her, over and over now, a delectable repetition that despite its simplicity made her cling to him tighter. "Then your bedchamber."

She pressed to him, aching to be closer than clothing would allow. "It shares a wall with Madame Roche. I cannot—"

He grabbed her hand and dragged her along the corridor. He opened the first door they came to.

"A linen cabinet?" But they had managed perfectly well on a staircase once. *Perfectly.*

She almost giggled, but he pulled her in, closed the door, and covered her mouth again. His fingers sank into her hair and she returned his urgent kisses; fierce, hungry kisses that filled the famine in her. He wrenched her around and pressed her back against the door panel, bringing his entire hard, perfect body against hers.

"You are yanking me about a lot." She was breathless.

"I am. Feel free to reciprocate." His mouth on her neck was delirium, his hands tugging her skirts to her hips sure and focused.

She pulled at shirt buttons and linen and found smooth, hot skin beneath. "Any parts in particular you would like yanked?"

"Whatever you wish." He kissed her throat, fast hot caresses, to her smiling mouth. "Just don't stop touching me."

His palms cupped her behind and fused her to him. "My God, you feel so good. I have wanted you in my hands again for weeks."

Viola suspected she ought to be able to respond, to taunt and laugh. But she could only touch him as he wished, her fingers pulling fine linen up and palms adoring the texture of his hot skin over breathtaking muscle. She let him have as much of her as he wished, his mouth and hands moving intimately over her making her desperate for more. And when he touched her until she could no longer bear the pleasure, she opened her thighs and let him inside. Let him— She *loved* him inside her, his hard need stretching her and making her wild. With her skirts hiked to her hips and her body yearning, she rode the demand of his thrusts until her breaths fled and she had none left even to cry out the pleasure he gave her.

"Viola." He whispered her name. His body crushed hers, palm flat on the panel behind her as he bored up into her. Then again, "*Viola*," and it moved her inside, the tenor of his voice, urgent and deep and unbound. Because it was different. She felt it in her sinews, her blood, her soul. It rocked through her as she came, moaning and clutching him. He followed, making her his again.

Their frantic pace fell to stillness. For a moment they remained like that, brow to brow, breathing heavily. Then, carefully and with strong hands, he pulled away and set her feet on the ground. She unwound her arms from his neck and smoothed her wrinkled skirts back in place, and her hair. He buttoned his trousers. Without a word, he took her into his arms again.

She had not expected that.

She pressed her face into his shoulder, breathing in his scent shakily.

"Stay with me tonight," she whispered, already dreading

the next moment when he would release her again and she would be obliged to reaccustom herself to distance from him. "Stay with me."

His hands fell away.

"Viola—"

"Tonight, the party was not— Though I managed it, it was not easy for me. I think you are the only person who can understand that," she hastened to explain, in truth to pretend. "This one night. Only for comfort. You needn't make love to me again." She was begging, and frankly lying. She wanted him for more than comfort and rather forever. "I want your arms around me."

He regarded her for a long moment, his eyes shining like crystal in the darkness, again distant, and it swept the life from her.

"Were I to hold you in my arms tonight," he finally replied softly, "I could not prevent myself from making love to you again."

She blinked back prickling heat, swallowing over her hope. "We could be very quiet?"

"I do not believe that is possible for you. Under any circumstances."

Her throat caught. "Ass."

"Harpy. Where is your bedchamber?"

"I am not quite certain. I was actually lost."

He threaded his fingers through hers. "That is apparently what I am here for." He opened the door a crack. "All clear." He drew her into the corridor and released her and she started back the way she had come, bemused, shaken. She wanted him to make love to her again, yes—but even more keenly for him to again hold her hand. She reached back and found his. He curled his strong fingers snugly around hers and her heart thudded madly.

But after only moments of that unmitigated pleasure, his

hand slipped from hers. Then voices came to her. Good Lord, he had acute hearing. No wonder he had been such a successful criminal.

A gentleman appeared, then another.

"There he is." Sir Tracy gestured. "Seton, our host has sent me to find you to make up even numbers at our table." He turned a bleary smile upon Viola. "Evening, Miss Carlyle. How do you do?" He flashed a grin at his friend. "Hope you're jealous of me, Hopkins. Isn't every day a fellow inherits a stepsister pretty as can be. Though I suppose it happens to me more often than most. Least once a decade."

They laughed.

Jin smiled slightly.

Viola wished them at the bottom of the ocean, which was not very sisterly of her, to be sure, but she saw how this would go.

"What do you say, Seton? Care to lose a few guineas to a good cause?" Mr. Hopkins smacked his waistcoat pocket meaningfully, tilting like a schooner at full sail.

Sir Tracy leaned forward confidentially and said sotto voce, "He's got his eye on Michaels's matched pair coming up for auction week next. But he can't afford 'em yet. I told him you're a sure steal at the card table, Seton. Want the pair myself, don't you know." He winked. "Give a friend a hand and fleece him, will you, old chap?"

"Pollywog," Mr. Hopkins exclaimed at large.

"Miss Carlyle has mislaid her quarters." Jin's smooth voice at her shoulder nearly sent her to the floor. She needn't even look at him to become jelly at his feet. "Allow me to escort her there and I will join you shortly, gentlemen."

"Actually." She flicked a glance at him, heart sinking; there was no getting around it. "There is my door." She pointed. "Thank you, Mr. Seton." That was it. No being

held in his arms and making love to him now. He would not
return. He had already gotten what he wanted.

He bowed. "Good night, Miss Carlyle."

She nodded to Sir Tracy and his friend, and went into her
room. She closed the door, pressed her brow against it, and
tried to breathe. Probably just the tight stays. Or *not*. She
climbed onto her bed and stared at the canopy, blinking in
time with Madame Roche's snores in the next room.

It was better this way. Jin always caused her to make all
sorts of inappropriately intimate noises when he made love
to her. There could be no privacy here.

She stared at the canopy a little longer, then wiggled back
and forth a bit. The bed knocked against the wall. Madame
Roche's snores halted. Silence reigned. Suddenly a great
huffing snort cut through the wall and the snoring took up
its regular cadence again.

Viola sighed and closed her eyes. Even if he were to come,
they could not make love. The bed would not allow it. But
he would not come anyway. She must rest content with the
lingering warmth in her from their adventure in the linen
cabinet.

She cracked her eyes open and peeked at the rug before
the hearth. She'd sat on it quite comfortably picking kitten
hairs out of her shawl the other day after she visited a new
litter in the barn. She supposed the gossiping ladies had
gotten one thing right; she always liked barn kittens. She
always loved barns, so full of adventure and messiness. The
April Storm reminded her a little of a barn. A floating barn.
Perhaps that was one reason she hadn't yet scrapped it.

She slid off the bed, dragging the top coverlet with her.
A servant had made up the fire; the rug was warm and soft.
She knelt, then curled up on her side and pulled the coverlet
over her. As she drifted off she allowed herself to imagine a
handsome pirate making love to her all night long.

* * *

She slept like a sailor, hard and motionless. But she looked like a lady, slender hands tucked beneath her cheek and hair sparkling with bejeweled pins. She still wore the glowing gown that caressed her curves and had every man between the ages of eighteen and eighty staring at her all night. Now her breasts pushed against the low neckline, soft rose-colored aureoles peeking out.

Jin's mouth went dry even as he told himself he had seen her body already, had enjoyed it, and should not be so affected by a mere glimpse of it now. But he could stand about all day and night trying to convince himself that she was just another woman. He would never succeed.

He crouched and touched her cheek. Her breaths hitched, black lashes flickering. He slipped his fingertips through the tangle of dark curls straying across her brow, imprinting upon them the texture of perfection.

Her eyes opened. "You came back."

"You did not wait long for me. I think I am disappointed by your lack of eagerness." He smiled and stroked the graceful column of her neck.

She blinked, sleep clinging. "Not long? I am eager." She stifled a yawn. "How long?"

"Perhaps thirty minutes."

"That was a quick game."

"I threw it."

"Mr. Hopkins will have his matched pair, then."

"I couldn't give a damn. Viola, I will leave you to your sleep."

Her fingers clamped about his wrist. "Don't!" She pushed up to sit, her thick hair tumbling across a shoulder and half-exposed breast. "Don't leave."

Never, if it could be. "I shan't now."

The tip of her tongue stole over her bottom lip, moistening it, then flicked upward. Jin could not look away. Remaining aloof from her had been the most difficult challenge he had ever met. He didn't need Carlyle's disapproval to remind him that he was not a suitable suitor for this lady; he had known that since the first. But she wanted him, and he would not deny her what little he could give her, tonight.

"Have you come back to make love to me again?"

"Indeed I have." He brushed his fingertips across her cheek again, the silken skin he could not seem to take his fill of, then trailed the backs of his fingers along her throat to the cleft between her breasts. Her lashes dipped, her breath pressing her soft flesh against him.

"But . . ." She sighed, her eyes closing. "I must have something to drink first. Wine."

He smiled. "You must?"

"My mouth is all wooly. I don't want you to kiss me until I have washed it out."

He laughed and her eyes snapped open. "What?"

He shook his head. She claimed confidence, but she had no idea of her true allure. It made her more beautiful yet.

"Viola, I don't care about that."

Her full lips tweaked into a frown. "Well, I do. There is cordial on the nightstand."

He stood and retrieved the cordial. When he turned again she was standing facing the fire, hair cascading down her back, gown crumpled but the curve of her behind still discernable, the profile of her features delicate. He nearly dropped the cordial. She was the most beautiful thing he had ever known, and even now it was nearly impossible to believe his good fortune.

She looked over her shoulder at him, her sleepy eyes reflecting the flickering golden light. She accepted the cordial and sipped, took some time with it in her mouth, then swallowed, the sweetness of her throat's movement working like a drug on him. Finally she set down the glass.

The entire operation had taken far too long. His pulse pounded. Curving his hands around her shoulders, he drew her back against his chest, bent to her neck, and breathed her in. No heavy perfume now, only her scent—sweet, stubborn, intoxicating Viola.

"Tell me where you wish to be touched." He stroked back her hair and set his lips to the nape of her neck where she was perfect woman. Everywhere she was perfect woman. But he would begin here.

Her breaths came fast. With such a slight touch, he could do this to her. He could almost pretend that she had been made for his hands. Hands that had made men suffer in the most brutal fashion.

"What do you mean, where do I wish to be touched?" she whispered.

He kissed her shoulder, the curve of feminine beauty. "A lady deserves to be touched where she wishes it," he murmured against her skin, watching the peaks of her breasts barely hidden at the edge of her garments grow taut. He wanted his tongue there. He needed to taste her everywhere. "Only where she wishes it."

"Where, on *me*?"

He smiled. "Where, on you."

"Don't laugh at me."

"Where, Viola?"

"Everywhere," she whispered.

He knelt. "Put your hand on my shoulder."

"What are you doing?" But she obeyed. He lifted her foot and removed first one shoe, then the other. "Oh, *yes*. I hate those slippers. *Hate* them."

"We will burn them when we are through here." He

stroked his hand up the inside of her calf, then her thigh.

She leaned into his touch. "I don't ever want to be through here." Her palm flew to her mouth. "What I mean to say is— *Ohh*."

He had intended only to unfasten her garters. That touching her body made him insane with need and prone to behave contrary to his intentions could not, however, be regretted. She was beauty incarnate, and already slick for him. She moved her hips against his fingers.

"*There*," she whispered, eyes closed, head back. "I want to be touched there."

Softly he caressed her, then not so softly as her breaths came faster and her knees parted. Then she was pushing herself onto his hand, begging with her body, and whimpering. It happened quickly, and the ecstasy upon her face awed him and made him hard beyond endurance. She cried out, thrust against him, and her mouth opened in a sweet, rich moan.

She collapsed into his embrace.

"I—I—" She caught her breath, twining her arms about his neck. "I do *not* want to do it standing up wearing clothes again."

"I was actually trying to remove yours just then."

"Well, you didn't do a very good job of it." Her eyes were alight. She began unfastening the buttons of his waistcoat. "Ladies and gentlemen wear far too many garments." She pushed it over his shoulders.

"Perhaps to discourage this very activity." He shrugged out of the waistcoat and she tugged his shirt up and off. Her hands spread on his chest and she stared at them. At him.

He had never, even with her before, been so ready for a woman.

"Oh, Jin," she murmured, "if all gentlemen were fashioned like you, ladies would need quite a lot more garments to discourage them from stripping naked on the street every day."

He laughed, but it came forth a bit strangled. "Thank you, I think."

"Thank you, most certainly," she breathed, making an exploration of his chest with her fingertips that left him needing her hands on him entirely. But something was different.

He grasped her wrist and brought her palm up to the firelight.

"Your skin—"

She grabbed his hand, covered her breast with it, and exhaled audibly.

"My skin has been filed raw." She reached behind her back. "Ladies do not have calluses. But it doesn't matter, because callused or smooth I still cannot get out of this damned gown by myself. At this moment I absolutely despise being a lady. Jin, undress me now. *Please* undress me."

"So gracious in your demands." He slid his hands around to her back and started on the tiny hooks.

"Of course. I don't like how all these people who came into this house today for the party never said please or thank you to anyone. Don't they know you can catch more bees with— *Ahh.*" She leaned back into his palms. "Thank you. You are much quicker than Jane with the stays."

"I have good reason to be." He kissed her neck, silk and lace and sparkling fabric sliding through his fingers until she came into his hands wearing only the thinnest shift. She pulled it off and threw it aside.

"Thank God. Now you needn't serve me any longer . . . in that capacity." A maidenly flush stole across the cheeks of the beautiful woman straddling his lap, naked of all but stockings and garters. Jin stared and he thought perhaps he was trembling. For the first time he could recall. Trembling.

"Viola?" His voice barely sounded above his thundering heart.

"Y-yes?" she whispered. She stroked a single fingertip down his waist, pausing at the front fall of his trousers. "What?"

"If you were to ask—whatever you asked of me—I would serve you."

She blinked a number of times, swiftly, her throat doing a little dance. Then she closed her eyes and, ever so deliberately, touched him.

For the first time in his life, serving came quite easily.

First she traced the contours of each muscle in his chest and arms, which was wonderfully satisfying although it did make her want to eat him with her teeth. And tongue. So she did so, a little. Since he seemed to enjoy that, and she enjoyed it quite a lot, she pushed him back onto his elbows so she could have greater access. He was made like a god. Rather, like her pharaoh statue, although a great deal larger, of course. And hot. And touching him, tasting him with her mouth like this, made her quite hot as well.

"Viola." His voice sounded taut. She jerked her head up. He was staring at the ceiling and breathing hard.

"Is something wrong?" She spread her hands on his chest and moved up his body to kiss him on his jaw, the day's shade of whiskers wonderfully rough to her lips.

"On the contrary." His eyes were liquid sapphires, like the sea. "But at the risk of sounding impatient, I am—"

"Impatient?"

"Eager to consummate the moment."

"That is the same thing."

"Not entirely." He wrapped his hand around the back of her neck, drew her to him and kissed her, then murmured against her lips, "And might you consider not arguing now?" He released her to remove his trousers. Viola got all quivery inside.

"Y-yes." She snapped her gaze back to his face. His eyes glimmered with amusement. "No. I mean to say, *no*, I *will* argue if I wish to, or if there is suitable cause to—"

He pulled her onto his lap and quite abruptly she had nothing whatsoever to argue about with him.

They made love. She did not argue. He did not tease or make her suffer, not in the usual manner, at least. But he did serve her as he said he would, although she did not need to ask him to do so.

Perhaps it was this serving that altered the rhythm of their desire for each other. Or perhaps it was the wonder that trembled in her from the beauty and sobriety in his eyes as he touched her. For shortly there was heard no laughter, no clever ripostes, no demands or even reasonable expressions of gratitude. There were instead the soft sounds of pleasure freely given and fervently taken, and the thunder of hearts poised on the brink of that greatest and most thrilling abyss.

Viola fell into the abyss quite willingly. In truth, she had fallen months ago and would not, she realized now, ever climb out of it no matter how she tried. Jin held her tight, his strong arms banded around her, face buried in her shoulder. Every nerve strained toward the completion he would give her, she trailed her fingertips down his back.

"Jin?"

He looked into her eyes, and the intensity of his gaze knocked the air from her lungs. There was distance there, and pain.

Alarm sluiced through her. "*Jin?*"

He dragged her off him, took her down onto her back on the soft rug, and thrust inside her. He groaned and pulled out entirely, then thrust again.

"*Ohh.*" It felt so good. Better than good. She clung to his shoulders, meeting him with each powerful thrust he drove into her. Then more, and more. She grabbed the edge of the rug, steadying herself and arching beneath him to make it come faster, the need twining frantically. She fought for breath, fought against his punishing thrusts that pleased— *such pleasure*. Then, clutching his waist, she forced him to her. Again and again.

When it came, it was deeper, harder, tearing her apart and bursting out her fingertips and toes. "*Oh, my God.*"

"Christ, *Viola*." He shuddered, his muscles like rock as he shook beneath her hands.

She gulped in air, circled her arms about his shoulders, and welcomed his weight atop her.

He did not remain long.

"I am crushing you." Every muscle in her body had gone lax, but his voice was strangely tight.

"I don't mind it much." *At all*.

"Nevertheless." He drew away from her, onto his heels. But his gaze did not leave her. Simply, quietly, looking only into her eyes, he said, "Miss Carlyle, you are beautiful."

Through her exhaustion and thorough satisfaction, she attempted a saucy smile. "I am familiar now with the wicked flattery of gentlemen, sir. You are only saying that because you hope I will take you to my bed."

The edge of his mouth curved up the slightest bit. He scooped her into his arms. "Better late than never." He laid her down on the thick coverings and she burrowed beneath, her damp skin cold in the night and the fading coal fire. Now he would dress and say something perfectly reasonable or perhaps infuriating, and he would leave. Then she would spend the next forty years sewing the pieces of her heart back together again.

But he did not leave. Instead he lay down beside her and, as he had done at the inn, closed his eyes. It seemed to him the most natural thing in the world to do. Yet it turned her world upside down.

Nerves ragged, she remained awake, staring at him for a long time. The handsome planes of his face did not soften in sleep but were enhanced into severity by the light of the dying embers. And slowly she saw what she had not seen before, a man wary and troubled, as though in sleep he could not conceal what he would never reveal when waking.

It pulled at her heart. She wanted to know what worried him. She wanted more than anything to touch that delectable mouth and smooth the tension from his jaw, to wrap her arms around him and tell him that whatever he faced, he needn't face it alone.

But he would not take *that* well. He was a man who needed no one. She was coming to understand this, and it made her heart ache more than she had imagined possible.

Still, she leaned toward him, her fingertips hungry for the grave line of his cheek.

"Do you always have difficulty settling down to sleep?" His voice rumbled.

She jerked back. "I thought *you* were asleep."

"As you might be as well."

Her heart thumped as it had when he first appeared in the corridor, but with a yearning so much more powerful.

"I am afraid that if I sleep," she whispered, "when I wake up you will be gone."

His eyes opened and the warmth in them seized not her breaths this time but her very soul. So, she supposed he owned that too now, not merely her heart.

He turned onto his shoulder and cupped her face in his big palm, and passed his thumb gently across her lower lip.

"I will not go."

"You did upon each of the other occasions." She didn't care that she was revealing herself. She loved him so thoroughly.

"If you do not wish it, Viola, I will not go."

She wanted to ask if he meant only tonight or this week or

forever. But the courage that had seen her through kidnapping and tempests and grief and loneliness deserted her. She could not bear to hear his reply now because she knew what it would be. Tonight she wanted, for one precious moment, to be only with him and imagine it would last forever.

She leaned forward and placed her lips on his. His hand moved to the back of her head and he kissed her softly, tenderly, making her imagine that he cared for her. He had a truly black heart to string her along like this. If she were a typical flimsy sort of female she might be devastated when he did leave. Fortunately she was made of sterner stuff.

She drew away, pulled the covers to her chin and, feet and heart both quite sore, finally she slept.

Chapter 26

He woke her before dawn with kisses. First on her mouth, then her cheeks and neck, rousing her gradually, then not so gradually when his hand cupped her breast. With his fingertips he caressed the peak, then with his tongue. She murmured her consent and pleasure. Eyes closed, she slid her arms about his waist and welcomed him to her.

This time it was different. They knew each other's bodies, the familiarity of skin and heat, and they moved slowly, luxuriously savoring their joining. There was no urgency or haste, only the perfection of form and feeling uniting into one.

At first.

Soon enough they might as well have been standing up in a closet again for all the luxurious savoring they did. Still, they enjoyed it, athletically and considerably, despite the early hour and paucity of sleep.

"I—" He exhaled hard into her hair. "I did not intend that."

"Truly?" She ran her palms over his broad shoulders

and along his back, wishing he never had to leave the place between her thighs and suspecting that in terms of feminine modesty, in this she was a complete failure. "The bed did not knock against the wall as I expected it to. Did you notice?"

"Nothing." His voice was quite rough. "I noticed nothing but you."

Her heartbeats halted, which was quite silly of them because *of course* he had noticed nothing but her. What man wouldn't under the circumstances?

A lock of dark hair fell across his eyes and his mouth curved into a tilt. "I intended only to kiss you."

"Admit it." Bravado might save her. "You have no control over your actions with me." But looking into his sparkling eyes, she doubted it. Nothing could save her now.

"Little," he agreed. "Enough, however, to leave here before a servant appears." He pulled away, drew on his trousers and took up his shirt, then returned to the mattress and sat beside her. "Are you satisfied?"

Her eyes widened.

A roguish grin crossed his mouth. "Satisfied with not being left alone while you are sleeping."

No. "Yes." Not in the least. "Thank you." If she dared, she would reach out, drag him back to her, and lock her fingers together so that he might never leave, so that the coal maid would find them together and Serena and Alex would demand he marry her. That was what gentlemen did when they compromised ladies. Those were the rules.

But Viola had long ago compromised herself without his assistance, and Jin knew she was not really a lady. He needn't play by all the rules, only those that suited him best.

He pulled his shirt on and leaned down to her.

"No, Miss Carlyle." He touched his lips to one side of her mouth softly, then the other. "Thank you."

She grabbed his wrist. Impulsive. Foolish. Reckless. She could not help but be herself, no matter how she tried.

"Tell me you are leaving Savege Park this morning, Jin Seton, and I will walk over to my dressing table, retrieve my pistol, and put a bullet through your heart."

It seemed to her then that many thoughts passed behind those blue eyes, many emotions. Surprise. Satisfaction. Hope. *Assent.* But those that remained dashed ice over the rest: caution and—once more—wariness.

She released him, her frayed heart in her throat. He glanced down to where her fingers lay spread atop the counterpane beside his hand, not touching.

"I told you I would not go," he said.

"That you did." She tried to control the quaver in her voice. "And a sailor is only as good as his word, isn't he?"

He stood and went to the door, then paused there. "And his deeds."

"Like returning a lost daughter to her family?"

He glanced back at her, his brow sober. Without replying, he left.

Viola dressed in her prettiest morning gown, whistled through Jane's ministrations on her hair, and could not eat a bite of the breakfast brought to her at the shockingly late hour of ten o'clock. She had no idea if Jin would still be at Savege Park, little faith in the possibility, and all the hope in the world.

When she finally descended on blistered feet to the ground floor, she discovered the front of the house in a bustle. Party guests with haggard faces and bloodshot eyes dragged their own weary feet through the foyer to their carriages on the drive. Footmen and maids scurried through the open front door, laden with bags and cases. But three gentlemen and two ladies entered.

The back of her neck prickling, she paused on the stair

and watched the gentlemen remove their hats. Her stomach went flat. Followed by a panicky tickle. Her joints locked and she could not take another step down.

As though drawn by her stillness amid the bustle, Aidan turned his attention up to her. His countenance opened in a smile of pure pleasure. He walked to the base of the stairs, and she met him there.

"Hello, Aidan."

"Violet. Oh—" He shook his head. "I told myself I would not do that, and now already I have. Miss Carlyle, how do you do?" He bowed.

"Violet will do. It is what you have called me our entire acquaintance."

"But you are a grand lady now." His gaze passed over her. "I should not be so bold."

She frowned. "That is ridiculous. But . . ." She glanced past him to the others. Seamus sketched her a smirking bow. The others, an older man and lady and a girl just out of the schoolroom, looked about with wide eyes. "Aidan, what are you doing here?"

"We invited him, of course." Serena swept past her down the stair. "Mr. Castle? And this must be your family." She drew them out of the flow of servants and departing party guests. "Mr. and Mrs. Castle, what a pleasure to make your acquaintance."

"Lady Savege, it is our pleasure indeed." His mother spoke in a soft voice with a pleasant tone. Aidan had gotten his wide, well-shaped mouth from her, and his hazel eyes. His brawn and nose had clearly come from his father.

Mr. Castle bowed. "My lady, we are honored to be guests in your home. Our son told us much of his friendship with Miss Carlyle and her father over the years. We are glad to finally have the opportunity to know her. Miss Carlyle." He nodded to Viola. "How do you do?"

"This is my sister, Caitria." Aidan drew the girl forward. She curtsied modestly. "And my cousin Seamus."

"You can see we are all at sixes and sevens here." Serena gestured. "Will you come to the drawing room for refreshment while my housekeeper prepares your private chambers?" She ushered them forward. "Caitria, what a lovely name. My husband's sister is Katherine too, you know, though she goes by Kitty."

Aidan and Seamus hung back.

"Pretty house you've got here, Vi." The Irishman winked at a maid hurrying past.

"It is not my house. It is my sister's and the earl's. I am visiting."

"How has your visit been?" Now Aidan took her hand. "Have you enjoyed your reunion with your family? I had no letter from you, though I anticipated one. When Lady Savege's invitation came, I admit I leaped at the opportunity to come here. I wished to earlier." His eyes showed a mixture of hope and mild chastisement.

"You could have written to me." She tugged her hand away, resisting the urge to dart a glance about the foyer.

"I was eager to, but I didn't know if you would like it."

"Why wouldn't I have liked that? We have written to one another for years. You are my oldest friend." But he was no longer her lover, and he no longer held her heart. He never had. Not the way Jin held it. Not completely and irretrievably.

Finally he grasped her hand. "You are so changed, Violet. Viola." He chuckled uncomfortably. "So changed I don't even know what to call you. I feared this would happen if I remained away for even so few weeks, and so it has. You look like a lady."

"Well, I am the same inside."

"No." He shook his head, his brow creasing. "I am indeed your oldest friend, and something is different about you."

She drew her hands away. "Nonsense. Now come to the parlor for tea. I would like to finally speak with Caitria and your parents. It seems I already know them."

"And they are anxious to speak with you. I'll admit my real delay in coming sooner was that my mother had planned a dinner party and we could not leave until after. Or I would have been here a fortnight ago at least." He smiled and turned to his cousin. "Seamus?"

"I'm off to the stable, cousin. So busy around here, I'd best make certain the cattle are attended to." The Irishman lifted a brow and sauntered toward the door. He passed a maid going through it and his hand disappeared. The maid gasped, then ducked her head and hurried on.

Viola frowned. "Why did he come?"

"We are returning to the Indies. We will be sailing from Bristol a week Monday, driving there straight from here."

"So soon?"

"By the time I return it will have been nearly four months since I departed. Plenty of time for the repairs on the house and outbuildings to have been completed and the new crops sown. I must get back before my steward and his wife grow too comfortable sleeping in the master bedroom." He smiled.

She could not meet his eyes. Instead she allowed him to tuck her hand into his elbow and went with him to find his family.

Jin reined in his horse at the edge of the bluff. The leathers lay damp against its glistening neck and it blew mist into the sea air. But only one of them had gotten satisfaction from the hard ride.

Breakers beat the beach below, gray and white. Heat thickened the salty breeze, and thunderclouds gathered, rendering the sun's rays unsteady. Unsteady, just as he felt. Unsteady and thoroughly out of control. Viola had turned him inside out and he did not want it—not the desperate need to be with her, the attachment that was almost violent in its strength. Such attachment could come to nothing. It *would* come to nothing, as another attachment he'd long ago felt with this strength had come to nothing.

His mother had kept him close, not allowing him beyond the quarters of her personal servants for fear of discovery. But he knew he was hers and that he was loved. A private child by nature, he never shared their secret with the others, and her husband's anger was commonly known. Even at that young age Jin understood what could happen were the truth discovered.

Then it was discovered, revealed by a fellow servant who saw too much and wished to curry favor with his master. And in an instant she gave him up. Her love had not proved strong enough. In her clear eyes he'd seen pain and grief but had not believed it. Ripped from his world, bound in shackles, and beaten for his defiance, he had readily believed that she did not suffer to see him go.

After that, at any chance he was able, he took out his anger on the world—anger born of a blood-deep panic that there would be nothing else for him no matter how hard he fought. That goodness and peace were not for a soul like his.

Now the panic rolled in him anew. Viola was mistaken in her wishes. Strong-willed, hardheaded, and passionate, with her every word and touch now she offered him that which he could not fathom. Could not trust. Could not accept. Not for her sake. She deserved better. A great deal better than him. And she could have better. She must.

But the truth battered at him that—simply—he feared. He knew every path from this world to hell and back again. He had paved those paths with his deeds and made himself master of them. But he knew nothing of that which now glimmered tantalizingly before him, that other realm. That perfection. And it frightened him.

He had not felt fear in so many years, he had forgotten he could.

Blindly he walked his horse along the cliff, the blustery gray above presaging the storm that would come when the heat rose later in the day, like the heat he found in her. He wanted her sharp tongue and foolish arguments and courageous defiance and sheer lunacy. For years he had been searching for forgiveness from a higher power, imagining that was his single desire: to atone. But now he only wanted her, and he was terrified.

Riding until his horse dropped, however, wouldn't solve anything. He stroked the animal's neck, then turned it inland. The outbuildings of Savege Park sprawled amid scrubby trees and hedges set back from the coast, the stable a massive complex of paddocks, stalls, and carriage buildings. Jin entered through the rear of the wing farthest from the comings and goings of guests, dismounted, and pulled off his hat and gloves.

There wasn't a stable hand in sight. He dragged the saddle and blanket off his horse's back, then slid the bridle over its ears. The bit jingled as it came from between the animal's teeth. When it quieted, he heard the sound.

Prickling heat spread in his belly.

Muffled sound. Not the muffled scuff of hooves in straw or an animal's whinny.

Muffled screams. A woman's cries beneath a heavy hand. In a stall not far away. Seven—eight stalls along the row.

He snapped the halter to the door latch and broke into a run. Horses turned their heads. At the seventh doorway he reached for his knife, but his palm flattened on his empty waistcoat.

He'd come out unarmed. But his fists had never failed him before. He pushed the door of the eighth stall open.

The man's white shirt was stained with blood at the hem, like the insides of her white thighs. His hand over the lower half of her tearstained face held her head to the straw while his other buttoned his breeches.

"Shut up, or I'll do it again tomorrow." He pushed her face away. "And if you squeal like a pig, I'll tell your master you begged me for it."

"Her master would be unlikely to believe you. He is a just man."

Seamus Castle swung around.

Jin advanced into the stall. "But I am not." He looked at the girl. "Go find Mrs. Tubbs and tell her what has occurred."

She didn't move. He held out his hand.

"It will be all right. Come now." With a sob she grasped his hand, and he pulled her to her feet. "Now hurry and find Mrs. Tubbs. Tell her I sent you."

She fled.

"Touching, Seton." Seamus sneered. "I knew you had a soft spot for slaves, but I didn't take you for a nursemaid to serving wenches."

Jin's fist collided with the Irishman's jaw so hard the crack reverberated through the stable. Seamus slammed to the straw. He clutched his face with both hands, slurring a curse. Jin came toward him. The Irishman's eyes shot wide. He scrabbled back like a crab, blood—his own now—staining his chin and shirtfront. But he still managed to sneer.

"What's got you ruffled, Seton? Not satisfied getting into Violet's drawers, after all? Want that little maid all for yourself, too, do you?"

Jin's gorge rose, his fists tightening. The Irishman laughed and started to push to his feet. So Jin hit him again.

And then he beat him.

Chapter 27

Jin paced the floor of Alex's study, but the sound of his footsteps did not drown out the memory of Seamus Castle's shattering bones. He could not be still. He had washed the Irishman's blood from his hands and changed clothing, but it mattered little. The animal inside him could wear a diadem and ermine and he would still be nothing more than an animal.

Alex entered and closed the door behind him. His brow was sober.

"He will live. Barely."

Jin turned his face to the window beyond which the sea stretched beneath a curtain of rain.

Alex crossed the room. "The doctor has nearly finished. He stitched the wounds and set what bones could be—"

"I don't want to hear it."

Behind him, glass clinked against glass. "I told you to have a brandy."

"Damn you and your brandy. How is the girl?"

"Frightened. The doctor says she will heal. Mrs. Tubbs

and Serena are caring for her now." Alex came to his side and pressed the glass into his hand. "Drink it. Then I will pour you another and you can drink that as well. Drink the whole bottle."

"Don't patronize me, Alex, or you will find yourself the doctor's third patient today."

"I'd like to see you try." The earl settled back against his desk, a massive mahogany piece topped with marble, fit for a lord, like everything in this house. A house in which Jin did not belong.

He set down his glass. "I nearly killed him. I might have killed him."

"That you could have, yet did not, is telling." Alex folded his arms loosely across his chest. "I know why you did it."

"You do not."

"I suspect I am the only one that could know. I met Frakes, if you recall."

Jin locked his jaw. "You don't know the half of it."

"I know what he did to those girls aboard ship while he had them chained up." Alex spoke simply of the gruesome memory. "You told me. I was only twelve years old and I'd never heard such a thing. But at nine you had seen it, and chained as you were too, could do nothing to stop him. I understand what that must have done to you."

"More to the point, however, is what I did to him."

"To Frakes?" Alex's gaze shot to him. "When?"

"Four years later."

A lengthy pause.

"You hunted him down, didn't you?"

Jin's jaw hardened.

Alex knew him. Perhaps not as well as Mattie did. But well enough.

"I hunted him down. I found him."

"You killed him in cold blood."

"Him? No." Rain speckled the windowpanes. "Him, I castrated." He looked beyond the rain. "I thought it fitting."

"Good God, Jin." Alex hissed in a breath. "You were only thirteen."

"A strong, clever thirteen. And indeed the animal Frakes said I was. I merely proved him right."

"You were young and angry. You could not have fully understood what you were doing."

"I would have done the same to Seamus Castle today if I'd had a knife on me at the time."

"You wouldn't have."

"*Goddamn it.*" He covered his eyes with his hand and dragged in breath, fighting the wave of nausea that came upon the fury and despair. "Indeed I would have." But he could not hide from himself. He had never been able to, no matter how many seas he crossed or how many slaves he set free. No matter the perfection of the woman in whom he lost himself. He pulled his palm away. "It is the man I am."

"You are a good man, Jin."

"And you, my friend, are living in a fantasy world." He moved away, to the window. "Will Castle bring charges?"

"I doubt it. His uncle and cousin are furious, and ashamed, as well they should be. And since Carlyle is the magistrate—"

"Not you?"

"No. But Carlyle will take your word and the girl's over Castle's. No concern there."

"I am not so certain of that."

"You can be. Carlyle is a reasonable man."

"I mustn't remain here." Jin spoke the words to make himself enact them, though nothing in him wished to go. Nothing but the fear. "I should not remain, and I have business elsewhere."

"In London?"

"Elsewhere." He went to the door.

"Frankly, I've been surprised you remained this long. I don't remember a time when you have before."

Hand on the doorknob, Jin paused. He met his friend's gaze.

"Alex, I am in love with Viola."

Slowly the earl leaned back. "Ah. That would explain it." He frowned. "Carlyle is protective of her now, of course. Have you given him reason to—"

"No."

He nodded. "All right. It's your business. But I don't see how leaving here will suit your purpose."

Rapid knocks sounded on the door, then it opened. Jin stepped back and Viola came flying through.

"Where—?" She halted before him. "There." She glanced aside. "Hello, Alex. Serena is looking for you."

The earl pushed away from the desk and came forward. "Then I'd better not keep her waiting. Do bid my wife adieu before you depart, Jin. She will be sorry to see you go."

The door clicked shut.

"Go?" Viola's cheeks paled. "Go, as in go over to Avesbury to buy yourself a new waistcoat that is not soaked in blood? Or go, as in *go*?"

"It is time I leave here, Viola."

Her dark eyes swam with distress. "Setting aside for the moment that you said mere hours ago that you would not leave if I did not wish you to, tell me that you can beat a man to a bloody pulp, then feel comfortable saddling up your horse and riding off the very same day? You cannot be serious."

"He took a serving girl by force."

"I know that! I just heard the story from Jane, who heard it from the third upstairs maid, who heard it from the scullery maid, who heard it from Cook, who heard it from Mrs. Tubbs, who heard it from the poor girl herself. And do you know why it had to pass through so many people before I could hear it? Because everybody in this house except you believes I am a bloody *virgin* because that is all unmarried ladies in this society are." Abruptly the hysteria seemed to slide from her, her shoulders sagging. "I'm sorry. I am upset. Everyone is upset. Aidan and his parents, and Serena of course, because she invited them thinking that I—"

"You have a right to be upset. You have known Seamus many years."

She screwed up her brow. "When Aidan wasn't looking, Seamus used to push me into corners and fondle my breasts—*uninvited*. Someone should take him out to a barn and give him more than a beating. For what he did to that girl he deserves to be castra—"

"*Don't*, Viola."

"Don't what?" She stepped forward. "I regret that it was you who came upon them. I regret it for your sake. But Seamus Castle is a very bad man. I could never tell Aidan what I thought because they were always so close. But that family would be far better off washing their hands of him. Or better yet, sending him off to the navy where he could get a real education in misery."

"You know nothing of such misery."

Her eyes flickered. "What?"

"You know nothing of it. Nothing." He spoke quietly, a burning in his gut urging him on. "And you do not wish to. You never have. You kept your hands clean while Fionn and your crewmen ensured your safety."

"*What?*" She blinked. "What are you talking about? You have no idea what my father and crewmen have done."

"I spent a month aboard ship with men who have known you for years. Do you think I did not learn a thing or two about Violet Daly and her father?"

Her eyes darted over him, twin red blotches staining her lovely cheeks. "What are you saying?"

"Do you know that Fionn wanted you to return here? He did everything in his power to protect you from the harsh realities of his life and to return you to this life from which he had stolen you. Where you belong. But you—goddamned stubborn, quarrelsome woman—would not oblige him. Every time he threw opportunity before you, you refused it."

"You cannot know this. Who told you these lies?"

"Not lies. Truth from men who were loyal to their captain to the moment of his death. He wanted what was best for you. They all did."

"If you stand here and try to tell me that I took so few prizes the past two years because my crew was bamboozling me, I swear if I can't find my dirk I will find a prawn fork and stick you with it somewhere it will hurt you quite a lot."

"Your father made Castle promise that after he died he would wed you and bring you back to England. He believed that were you finally here again, you would voluntarily return to your family."

Her mouth dropped open. "He did not. That is positively ridiculous."

"I have a letter in my possession from your former quartermaster. Your father left him with instructions to tell Aidan the truth about your family once you were married, with the request that he encourage you to come back here. Is Mr. Crazy typically a liar, Viola?"

"A *letter*? Why on earth would you have a letter from Crazy? What have you been doing, spying on me?"

"It is one of my many talents," he said, but it passed her by.

"Crazy must have misunderstood. My father liked to invent stories. He was a sailor." But she looked like she was struggling not to believe it. Behind her rich violet eyes he could nearly see her recalling the moments Fionn had encouraged her to return to England, and her willful choice to defy that. It sufficed for Jin. But driving her away was even more painful than he had anticipated. He could not have her, but he did not want to throw her into Aidan Castle's arms either.

"Did you know Aidan planned to return to England at this time?"

Her brow drew down. "I thought he would stay in the Indies for a few more years. His decision to return here so soon after the fire surprised me."

"As much as it surprised him, I suspect."

"What are you saying?" Her eyes narrowed. "Did he tell you something? That day at the inn, after the fire, you both looked so peculiar when I came upon you. He told you something, didn't he? And he kept it from me."

He could tell her the truth, but then he would not be able to leave her. He could barely leave her now. Carefully he fashioned the words to seal his fate.

"Viola, I have lied to you since the moment we met. Yet still you trust me."

"I do not understand. You have not lied to me."

Her heart racketed and she was shaking, but he only met her gaze with that cool, steady glimmer of distance. Then he went through the door and was gone.

For a moment, she stood absolutely still, stunned.

She bolted from the room and grabbed a footman. "Which way did Mr. Seton go?"

He pointed.

She caught up with him as he descended the stairs to the drive empty of carriages now, the expanse of the Park's sloping lawn mottled with trees and sheep. She ran through the puddles.

"Don't you dare imagine you can make cryptic statements, then turn around and walk away."

He halted. "I said nothing cryptic. But if it will help for

me to repeat it, I have lied to you. A number of times. Is that plain enough?"

She gripped her hands together so she would not grab him instead, rain falling between them.

"It is plain. Now." She bit down on her uncertainty. "But I don't know that it matters." .

"You don't know," he repeated. He passed his hand over his face and released a hard breath. "Viola, go back inside where you belong."

She shook from the cold rain on her arms and the certainty that this quarrel was not about Aidan or Fionn or her crew and ship. It was about this man and the life he had led and still wished to lead. A life that *was* truly unlike anything she had known, that frightened her a little bit. But *he* did not frighten her. He felt like a part of her.

"This is because of Seamus, isn't it? If I had seen him do that, Jin, I would have beaten him to a pulp too. That is, if I possessed the strength for it."

He came to her in a stride and stood so close she could trace each drop of rain on his jaw and lips with her hungry gaze.

"Why did you challenge me with that wager on your ship, Viola? After fifteen years on the sea did you understand nothing of men like me? Did you not?"

A fist clenched her heart. There were no other men like him. None.

"I challenged you because—because I *wanted* to come home." Her voice quavered. "Is that what you wish to hear? I missed it more than I could bear, even after so many years, though I tried to pretend I did not, and I longed for it." As she had longed for him. She had believed she could not lose.

But now she was losing again. The hunted light in his eyes told her that more clearly than anything had yet, and the violence he had done against Seamus earlier. This life was killing him. He could be a gentleman if he wished. His manner and education allowed it. But he would not choose this. And, even if she cast all this aside and went back to the sea, clearly he was not choosing her either.

She backed away. "Why did you even return here if you knew you would only leave again? And don't tell me it was to settle that debt with Alex, because you could have seen him in London."

"I returned here, Viola, because I could not stay away from you. Even now when I wish to be gone from here, when I have matters I must attend to elsewhere, you hold me here. You alone." The manner in which he spoke these words was the least loverlike she had ever heard him. Instead, anger seemed to color them, attuned to the sharply glittering crystals of his eyes. Yet still her joints turned liquid.

"At this particular moment you do not seem as though you wish to be where I am," she managed to utter.

He came to her, wrapped his hands around her arms, and bent his head.

"I once believed you were insane. I was quite certain of it. But now I know, rather, that I am." His voice was rough by her brow. "You are merely willfully naïve."

"I cannot imagine how you think that, when I know a great deal more of the world than any lady I have encountered in England."

"You do not understand why I am not the man for you. That makes you naïve. And impossible."

He wanted her, yet he did not want to want her. This was quite clear. Raw panic enveloped her, colder than the rain. This was truly the end.

"So you are really leaving? At this moment? Now?"

He released her and nodded.

No. God, *no.* "From London? Is that where you have your ship berthed?"

"Yes."

"London? *All* this time since we returned? That must be costing you a fortune. How on earth can you—?"

"Viola." He looked away, it seemed with impatience.

"Where will you go?" She had lost. She had lost again. But this loss was beyond the greatest pain she had endured, beyond the cruelty of heartbreak during those first months in America, beyond the endless ache of loneliness. "To Boston, to your new ship? Or I suppose Malta."

"East."

"After you conclude your business there, you could return here." Her tongue ran on its own, driven by desperation. "Or you could simply delay your journey a bit." She was laying her heart open for him to stomp on again. She didn't care. *She could not let him go.* "Serena and Alex were talking about having an open house at the Park soon, which from all I have heard seems to be a lark, although—"

"Viola, stop."

Her lips snapped shut. He watched her distantly, like that day on her ship when her hope had been new and untested, when she had indeed been naïve enough to believe this man could love her.

"Just say it." She steadied her voice with the greatest effort. "You may as well. You look exactly as you did that day when you won the wager." She needed to hear him say he did not love her. Of all things, she knew he would not lie to her about that.

"My sentiments have not altered since then." Just as on that day, it seemed difficult for him to tell her. He cared for her enough to pity her.

Viola's insides quivered, then simply melted into misery.

"Well, I suppose you are entitled to your sentiments, whatever they are." She squared her shoulders, but the gown pulled and the stays poked and she felt trapped and quite like she might begin to cry shortly, which would be categorically disastrous if she were still standing before him.

"Well then, good-bye, Seton. I hope you have a nice life." She thrust out her hand for him to shake. He did not move to take it.

"Aidan Castle does not deserve you."

Viola swallowed over the foremast stuck in her throat. "As astounding as it may seem to you, Master Arrogance, I do not particularly care for your opinion on the matter." This hurt beyond bearing. She pivoted, blinking back rising tears. *"Bon voy—"*

He grasped her wrist and pulled her to a halt and lifted her fingers to his mouth.

"Someday a man who deserves you will come around, Viola Carlyle." His voice was low. "Do not settle for less." He kissed her knuckles, then her brow. She gulped in the scent of him, his nearness and everything she dreamed of. He released her, then turned and strode toward the stable.

Viola went inside the house, locked herself in her bed-chamber, and wept tears enough to fill the Atlantic basin.

Chapter 28

With Jane's starchy assistance Viola managed to make her puffy eyes and pale face look presentable enough to join her sister and the others the following morning for breakfast.

"Is your megrim improved, Miss Carlyle?" Caitria asked kindly. "Lady Fiona and Lady Savege have worried about you. Mama and I too. And my brother, of course."

Viola glanced at Aidan across the dining room. He looked tired, but he offered her a tentative smile.

Later, he found her alone in the library.

"I suppose a rainy day calls for a good book and a pot of tea," he said as he came toward her.

She closed the volume she hadn't read a word of in an hour and watched him take a seat on the chair beside hers. He was comfortable, decent, and she understood now finally why she had believed she loved him all those years; she'd needed a friend and hadn't known what love truly was.

"What are you reading?" He drew the book from her hands and flipped open the cover. "Virgil? Isn't this Latin?"

"Oh, is it?" She untucked her feet from beneath her and smoothed out her skirt. It was wrinkled, but she didn't care.

He set down the book and reached for her hand.

"Viola, this is a terrible time for us all, with what Seamus did and how he is paying for it. I have asked Lady Savege's pardon for bringing my cousin into her home, and she has been forgiving. But . . ."

"But?" She didn't care what he had come to say. Mostly she wished he would leave her to solitude. Somewhere about the house Lady Fiona and Madame Roche were teaching Caitria how to braid rushes in the French style, Lady Emily no doubt sitting nearby with a book making clever comments. Her sister would be in the nursery with the baby. But she only wanted to be alone to lick her wound that would never heal.

His fingers tightened around hers. "Viola, Seamus will not be returning to the Indies with me. Nevertheless I must be on that boat when it leaves Bristol in six days. I want you to be with me. As my wife."

"You are asking me to marry you now? To *be* married now, finally, that is to say?"

"I know it has been a long wait for us. But I have always known you would be my wife, Viola. Always."

She drew her hand away. "Aidan, why did you leave Trinidad two and a half months ago? I imagine it was difficult leaving the repairs and new building in another man's hands. Honestly, it surprised me that so abruptly you decided to visit your family."

His eyes crinkled in a tender look. "You must know that I came here because I did not wish to be apart from you."

"After all those years of being apart, suddenly you could not tolerate it?" She frowned. "Did my father lend you the money for your farm on the condition that you would marry me and bring me back to England to live?"

His face slackened.

She stood, feet sore, heart sore, uncertain that any man could be trusted not to lie to her. They would all use her for their own purposes. Her father had used her for bait to win back his lover. The baron was now trying to use her to enliven the memory of that same woman. And Jin had used her for gain, and for pleasure. That she had wanted him to did not exonerate him. It only made her a tragic fool.

"That day at the inn in Port of Spain before you apologized to me about kissing Miss Hat and assured me of your lasting devotion, Jin told you the truth about my family. My whole family. Didn't he?"

He came to his feet. "Violet, I have loved you since you were a girl, and yes, I promised Fionn to bring you to live in England, but I had no idea of your family then and I would have wed you still. What does it matter?" He gestured impatiently. "Marry me and let us put the past behind us now and make a new future together."

Her throat was thick but her eyes dry.

"No, Aidan. I do not wish to marry you. I am sorry to disappoint you, but I am not the same girl who followed you about deck ten years ago. I have changed."

"I see," he finally said, brow pleated. "Then I have lost my opportunity. I acted too late."

She needn't respond.

"If you wish to be rid of me," he said stiffly, "I can be on my way this afternoon. My parents and Caitria must remain until Seamus is well enough to travel. But I will go if you wish it."

"You needn't." In truth, she didn't care where he was. He nodded reluctantly and left the library.

But his stiffness persisted and she didn't care about that either. After two days, she greeted with relief Serena's suggestion that they all remove to town.

"You will not miss Papa too much?"

"A little. But, Ser, he is . . . clingy."

"Clingy? Is that another delightful Americanism?"

"Aren't you impressed with my accent lately? I sound fabulously English." She attempted a smile, but Serena's clever gaze studied her a bit too intently.

She turned away. "When will we leave?"

"Tuesday. Fiona and Emily and Madame Roche are no doubt eager to return to town as well. Tracy will come with us and we will make a party of it."

"It sounds delightful."

She watched Aidan ride off down the drive alone. He had gone sanguinely, in the end accepting her refusal with resignation. Despite his broken bones and raw wounds, Seamus refused to remain after his cousin left, and the Castle family departed.

The following day five carriages laden with servants, gentlemen, ladies, and Viola started on their way to London. She had seen a little of the countryside during the rushed drive from Exmouth to Savege Park. Now they took the journey in slow stages, pausing at charming inns along the route and dining merrily each evening, all as if it were some sort of holiday. After the first day Viola managed to claim the carriage with Lady Emily each time, whose nose in her book and lack of conversation made the trip bearable.

London was to Boston what Savege Park had been to Aidan's plantation. Sprawling, with endless streets and countless people and every sound imaginable—from animals' snorts and neighs to the clatter of carriages and the shouts of vendors. Thick with coal-scented air, it teemed with motion and life. She stared out the window, pulling off her shawl and peeling away her gloves from sticky palms.

"The air in town is remarkably insalubrious this early in the autumn, Miss Carlyle," Lady Emily said, finally closing her book, her green eyes bright. "But there are a great many places a lady may enjoy the finer pleasures of life."

"Lady Fiona told me about Gunter's confectioner's shop," she said distractedly. Far to the right the unmistakable points of ship masts clustered beyond the roof of a building. A trickle of relief went through her. London was not all alien.

"I meant museums and scientific exhibits and lectures, of course."

"Are we near the river? I see ships."

"Several blocks to the north. Are you fond of sailing, Miss Carlyle?"

"A little."

A grand, elegant, and astoundingly large abode, Alex and Serena's house sat on a corner of a square and seemed a veritable mansion. It boasted two parlors, a receiving room, a drawing room, dining room, broad foyer, a modest ballroom at the rear, a garden behind, and innumerable bedchambers above. Serena had furnished it with an eye toward comfort but also with simple beauty. Viola supposed she must become accustomed to the splendor. Despite being titled nobility, Serena was still Serena, after all, and Alex was as kind and solicitous as ever, and baby Maria had made the journey well. She told herself she was more fortunate than most anyone she had ever met.

But without the constant company of friends, and without a bluff overlooking the sea to wander along, she swiftly grew restless. *Stationary.* When Sir Tracy called to drive her in the park in his new curricle, she gladly accepted. When Lady Emily invited her to an afternoon lecture by a noted female essayist, she agreed with a bit less alacrity but enjoyed it even better. The famous essayist employed any number of cuss words that Serena and Mr. Yale had strictly enjoined Viola never to utter, and her lecture was all about how women should be allowed to explore the professions as any man. Several ladies left the lecture hall pale and whispering behind their fans, but Viola felt positively buoyed up.

It took very little to batten her down again, however. Against her inclination she accepted an invitation from Lady Fiona and Madame Roche for an evening of cards.

"But, *ma chère mademoiselle*, you play less well *ce soir* than at the country house of your sister." This said in a French whisper.

"In point of fact, I am playing wretchedly." This said in a grumble.

"How are the pins doing to hold up your hem?" Lady Fiona looked hopeful.

"They are sticking me in the ankles. But that is the least I deserve for stepping all over them when dismounting from the carriage."

"The tears, they will occur!" Madame Roche laid down the King and Queen of hearts.

"Tears?" Prickles erupted at the backs of Viola's eyes.

"Tears as in rips, Miss Carlyle." Lady Emily peered at her cards with a furrowed brow. "Clarice's accent is quaint but occasionally inconvenient." She flickered Viola a focused glance.

Indeed, Viola feared her friends and sister mistook none of her melancholy. They were solicitous to the point of annoyance. London's sights and marvels could not be fully enjoyed in such a state of irritation, and in any case Viola disliked feeling irritated. She required activity to scare away her fidgets.

With that in mind, four days into their London residence she accompanied Serena and Alex to an evening supper party with dancing. She danced. She trod on gentlemen's toes. None of them teased, or laughed, and perhaps most devastatingly of all, when the music halted there was no perfect man striding down the corridor to take her into his arms and make love to her.

He was gone. She was living like a lady although she most certainly was not one, with no connection to what she had known for so many years. And that was the mess she had made of her life.

The following evening, beyond the parlor windows the sunset layered gold and gray, terraces of shimmering bronze stacked upon billowing smoke. But Viola could not enjoy it. She sat in a beautifully upholstered chair, an embroidery frame on her lap, a book on the table beside her, and could do nothing but stare out through the glass and wish she were back at sea on the quarterdeck of the *April*. For then she could revel in the loneliness that gripped her so powerfully still, here in London, surrounded by those she loved. All but one.

Serena touched her on the shoulder. She jumped, knocking the embroidery frame to the floor.

"I am sorry." Her sister sat on the ottoman before her, a vision in aqua silk and pearls.

"Are you going out tonight?"

"Yes. At breakfast I told you of this evening's musicale fete. I came looking for you to tell you the carriage will be about shortly. But I see you are not dressed." She tilted her head.

"I am sorry, Ser. I don't think my disposition is suited for company tonight."

She touched her on the back of her hand. "Vi, are you unwell? What I mean to say is, are you happy?"

He had asked her that, told her he could not stay away from her, then he left.

"I am so glad to be here with you, Ser. And Alex and Maria. And tomorrow we shall meet Kitty and Lord Blackwood. After all I have heard of Alex's sister, I do look forward to that."

Serena's fingers tightened around hers. "But are you *happy*?"

Viola's throat tightened.

"He brought me here," she whispered, allowing the words to finally come, "and you made me a lady, but I will never really be one. Not truly, no matter how hard I try. On the outside I might rub my face with lemon juice and pluck at the harp—albeit wretchedly—but on the inside I am still cussing like a sailor." She turned her gaze back to the sunset, now pale pink and gray, the gold entirely gone. "But I cannot go back to my old life. Oh, Ser, what am I fit for now?"

"Don't you want this, Vi?"

"Yes, I want this." She ducked her head and pressed the heels of her palms into her eyes. "But I want him more."

"Him, Mr. Castle?" Serena sounded skeptical.

"Him, Mr. Seton."

A moment's silence. Then, "Oh, Vi."

"I *know*," she groaned, leaped up and went to the window, as close to the sunset as she could. "I *do* know. I think I have known since the moment I met him." She gripped the brocade drapery and leaned her brow into its thick folds. "Yet to him I have been nothing but a bounty to line his pockets." And momentary pleasure. She had given him that, at least. Perhaps even some amusement. It felt good to make him smile, to see stars. But that joy was not to be hers again.

"A bounty?"

Viola sank onto the window seat. "The bounty Alex paid him for finding me and bringing me home."

Serena came to her. "Alex paid him no bounty, Vi."

"Of course he did."

"No, he did not. Even if Alex had offered him payment, Jinan would not have taken it. Why, he is rich as Croesus. Quite likely wealthier than my husband, given the many nights Alex spent at the card tables at one time. Didn't you know that?"

She swallowed through her thick throat. "No" came out like

a peep. "I did not." She shook her head. "But then, why did he spend so many months searching for me, and so much effort convincing me to return here, if not for Alex's money?"

Serena sat at her side. "It was rather the other way around. He felt he owed Alex a debt."

"*He* owed a debt?"

"It is not really my place to share this information, but now I think you must be told. As a boy, for two years Jinan was a slave. Alex, not much older than him at the time, had him freed."

Her breaths came fast. "But that was twenty years ago."

"Then you do know."

"I didn't know Alex's part in it."

"Jinan found you for me because he believed it was the only manner in which he could repay my husband. Of course Alex never expected or asked it. Jin needn't have ever done anything."

Viola stood and crossed the chamber, abruptly hot all over.

"All this time I believed—" She could not think. "I never—" Her return to England had meant more to him than she had ever imagined. He had understood his friend's love for his wife, and somehow also Serena and Viola's bond as children. He was a man as alone as any could be, both by life's tragedy and by choice, yet in this manner he had chosen to pay his debt. Because what Alex had given him meant everything to him.

She ached inside so profoundly, for the boy he had been and the man he had become. And she loved him beyond bearing.

"Viola, will you dress now for going out?" Serena's voice sounded strange.

She turned and swallowed back her grief. "Ser, I don't really wish to—"

"Please dress. I should like us to pay that call on Kitty

before the party tonight, actually. You needn't even dress for the evening. We will drop you off here again after we visit Lady Blackwood."

"Well, all right." She moved to the door, head heavy and not particularly caring where she went.

Jane buttoned her into a gown suitable for making calls, muttering all the while that Viola should use cucumber slices over her eyes at night to relieve the puffiness. Viola ignored her and met her sister and Alex in the foyer. Serena and the earl made superficial conversation as they drove the two blocks to Lord and Lady Blackwood's town house, a more modest establishment than their home but still remarkably elegant.

The lady that met them in the receiving room was as elegant as her surroundings, tall and slender, with dark hair and gray eyes much like her brother's, and exquisitely dressed in the richest shade of blue. She came forward, took both Viola's hands into her own, and kissed her softly on either cheek.

"How eager I have been to make your acquaintance." She spoke as beautifully as Viola had ever heard, her laughing eyes belying her superior mien and dress. "And how immeasurably glad I am that you are in our family now."

"Thank you, my lady."

"Kitty it shall be to you. And I shall call you Viola, the long-lost sister I never had." She cast a sparkling smile at Serena and winked. "My other long-lost sister." She glanced at her brother. "You will not find Leam at home. He has gone out for the evening. He is attempting to track down Wyn, who cannot be found lately and who, by the by, was so charmed by you, Viola, he vows he will never glance at another lady unless she possesses a thorough knowledge of the sea and no desire whatsoever to paint watercolors."

Viola wished she could smile. She managed a wobbly grin. "I hope he is well."

"He is playing least in sight these days, so we don't have any idea and it is a bit worrisome." Kitty released her hands. "But at least before he disappeared he told us all about his time at the Park and about you. Naturally, he was much more forthcoming than Jinan, who I suspect had many stories to share but was predictably reticent." Her lips twisted. "One never does know what Jin is thinking or doing, does one, Alex?"

The earl leaned against the mantel, arms crossed. "Rarely." He glanced at Viola.

She had the most peculiar sense they all expected her to speak next. And so, though it cost every ounce of her self-possession to hold her voice from trembling, she obliged.

"I suppose he was very busy preparing to depart. Perhaps now that he is on his way across the sea he will have leisure to write l-letters." Her voice stumbled. "I always kept a journal aboard ship, of course. And—sometimes—I wrote letters." The last came forth as a mumble. It was not pleasurable speaking of him. That he was apparently well known and liked by all her family and friends was a wretchedly unwelcome discovery.

The room had gone silent. She glanced about. Kitty was looking at Alex, her brow drawn. Alex nodded.

"Viola," Kitty said, "Jinan is not on his way across the sea. Not yet, at least. He is here in London."

"Here?" She stared at Kitty, then Alex. "In *London*?"

"Yes."

"He told me he was putting to sea, sailing to—" Her voice cracked. "He lied."

"Not necessarily. That may be in his plans, eventually."

"And until then?" But the truth didn't matter. He had left Devonshire almost certainly knowing how she felt. "What is he doing in London?"

Serena said softly, "He is looking for his family, Vi."

Viola's heart tripped. "What family? He said his mother died long ago."

Serena shook her head and shrugged. Viola found nothing useful on Alex and Kitty's faces either.

"I suppose I am relieved not to be the only person with whom he shares so little," she finally muttered, winning a grin from Alex and a tender smile from Serena. But Kitty remained sober.

"It is difficult not to understand him, I know, Viola. But Jinan is a good man. He is doing what he believes to be right. If you care for him—which I think perhaps you do?—you must trust him."

An hour later, as Viola paced her bedchamber, Kitty's words still racketed about her head. Perhaps he was doing what he believed to be right. But need he do so alone? He might not love her or need her. But she loved him and she wanted to help him. She *longed* to help him, as he had helped her.

She would.

Serena and Alex had no direction for him, nor did Kitty and Lord Blackwood. He lived like a shadow in London, apparently. But Viola knew her way around docks better than her aristocratic relatives. If his ship were still there, she would find him. She could not go about it, however, dressed as Viola Carlyle.

She darted to her garderobe, dug deep, and found her breeches, shirt, and waistcoat. The challenge of escaping the house and getting to the docks without being noticed by her sister's solicitous servants would be considerable. She was tugging on her left shoe, tucking in her shirt, and hopping on one foot while sticking her head out the window to study the trellis crawling down the side of the house, when Jane entered.

Jane gasped.

Viola dropped her shoe.

Jane's eyes narrowed. She backed toward the door.

"Don't. You. Dare."

Jane's lips pinched. "Where are you going?"

"To the docks."

"You won't get away with it."

"Of course I will." Viola stalked forward, limping on one stockinged foot. "And you will assist me."

"Oh, no, I will not."

"Oh, yes, you will. Because if you do not, I will tell Lady Savege how you stole one of Mr. Yale's neck cloths and are hiding it amongst your underclothes."

Jane's palm shot up to cover her open mouth. "You wouldn't," she hissed.

"I would." Viola cocked her head. "So what will it be? Assist me now, or never find another position amongst the Quality again?"

Jane glared. But she assisted.

Viola thought she was getting the hang of being a lady quite nicely.

She found Matouba first. It was remarkably easy. The footman that Jane bribed with intimate favors (possibly chosen for the task for his black hair and gray eyes that resembled a particular Welshman's) found a hackney coach for Viola. Once spirited out the back door while said footman and Jane distracted the other servants, it was a quick trip through evening traffic to the docks.

Pulling her hat down around her face, she went into the first pub she came to, and there he was. Ebony among chestnut and leather and walnut and rawhide, he stood by the crowded bar, his white globelike eyes trained directly on her. Her father's Irish luck was with her tonight. Or perhaps her father himself was watching over and guiding her actions. Fionn was wily enough to succeed in this plan. He had stolen a girl from a baron, after all. Stealing back a man's family ought to be a breeze.

She shoved her way through the crowd.

"I am glad to see you. Where are Mattie and Billy? But more to the point, where is he?"

To Matouba's credit, he tipped his hat respectfully before grasping her arm and trundling her out of the pub without a by-your-leave. She yanked out of his hold. Lamplight from the pub's door shone on the pavement and voices and laughter tumbled across thresholds all down the block. It was the sailors' district, and she was perfectly comfortable. But Matouba clearly was not happy with her presence. His eyes continually flickered about, and he stood close, his stance protective on the dark street.

"Where is he, Matouba?"

"Well, miss, I reckon I can't be tellin' you that now."

"Why? Because I am not supposed to know?"

"Because he don't know," came from behind her.

She swung around to face Mattie. Billy hovered at his beefy elbow wearing a toothy grin.

"It sure is good to see you again, Cap'n ma'am."

"Thank you, Billy." She turned her attention up to the hulking helmsman. "Do you know where he is?"

Mattie shook his head.

"We don't never know, Cap'n ma'am." Billy's head bobbed. "He don't never tell us."

"Then how do you communicate with him?" Her gaze flashed between them. "He tells you when and where, doesn't he?" She lodged her fists on her hips. "And he says *I'm* impossible."

"Begging your pardon, miss." Mattie's grin lacked several teeth. "But we know where he *ain't* tonight. Where we were thinking about going us'selves. Fact is, we could use a sailor that can talk good as a lady for the job." Bowls and jugs clinked from within the pub and a fiddler took up a tune, a cart clattered past, stirring up dust that smelled like sweat and fish, and the most glowering, harrumphing sailor Viola had ever known winked.

Her heart pattered fast. She thrust out her hand, palm down. "I'm in."

A skinny freckled hand slapped atop hers. "I'm in, Cap'n ma'am."

Fingers like pitch-coated sausages covered Billy's. "Me too, miss."

Mattie's came last, big and brown and as comforting as a whole ham on Easter Sunday. "Let's go."

Chapter 29

In the deep gray of London midnight Jin stared at the ceiling, his heart racing as he sat perfectly still in a chair in his flat. Though his body ached with need, no female companion awaited him in the bedchamber. Not with Viola Carlyle two hundred miles away. Never again, no matter how many miles distant she was. Thus his life of celibacy commenced.

But it was not a time that would linger long. She had taken his heart and after all he had done, all his voluntary damnation, he was quite certain he could not live without it. He could not live without her. So he may as well throw himself into certain danger. If unrest stirred in Malta, it would be as good a place as any to die. There he might finally be killed, after all, and end the torture of not having her, and of knowing another man would.

She deserved more than Aidan Castle. She deserved everything.

Unprofitable thoughts. She would have what she needed, whether it was Castle or some other man lucky enough to win her. And, as he had been for twenty years, he would be alone, as it should be. Or dead.

But it was all a lie. A blasted lie. Not to Viola this time. To himself.

He had come back to London and remained here, delaying his departure for the East on the Club's mission, because he wanted that damned box. He'd made a second and third attempt to purchase it, anonymously through his own man of business days ago, then through Blackwood's agent again today. The bishop was immovable, and suspicious now of the interest others were taking in the antiquity. He would not sell. He was adamant.

But Jin had to have it. He could think of nothing else—except Viola. He would never be a good man; his past would remain with him always. But he was damned if he would let her go forever without first knowing if he was a man with a real last name. He owed at least that to himself. And to her.

He stared into the darkness, night sounds coming to him through the open window, and waited for the Watch to call the hour. Then he waited longer. He had no master ordering him to his nightly prowl, no purpose to prowl in the first place. He would not steal the box from the bishop's house and he would not harm anyone to get it otherwise. He was through with that. Seamus Castle's bloody face and Viola's impassioned defense of the punishment had seen to that. He never wished to hear her excuse him again, for in doing so she sullied herself. If he were ever going to deserve her—if he had a chance of deserving her—he would do it by cleaning his soul first.

Finally, he rose from the chair and dressed in clothing suitable for such work. He had not yet spoken with the bishop's junior footman. He had studied him, though, every night for nearly a fortnight. Within the hour the man would be leaving his employer's house. As he did each night he would walk three blocks to his favorite gin house where he would drink two drams of Blue Ruin, then spend fifteen minutes in the back room with the red-haired whore before heading home. If the redhead was not working, he would go with the blonde rather than the brunette. Some men were misguided that way, Jin supposed.

He walked to the bishop's house. It was not far from his rooms in Piccadilly, and the muted rumbling activity of London at night kept him alert, his mind focused and off a beautiful little sailor with violet eyes.

The moment he arrived he felt the change in the night air. The windows of the house, usually black at this hour, were not all dark now. From a window on the ground floor, a sliver of gold light peeked out between drawn drapes. It flickered. Then receded.

Someone was moving through the house with a lamp; but it was not Pecker. From where he stood hidden in a shadow across the street, Jin watched the footman stroll up the narrow alley between the bishop's house and the house beside it. Pecker whistled cheerfully, tossing an object into the air as he went, up and down. It caught a glimmer of moonlight and Jin stilled.

Gold coin. Payment for allowing a stranger's entrance?

His anger simmered. That morning again they had tried to convince him to allow them to break into the house and steal the box. Matouba had been quiet but firm, and Billy typically enthusiastic. But Mattie had only stared at him above his cauliflower nose and said, "S'about damned time."

Now they had gone in, despite his forbidding them to. But they were sailors, trained to thieve in open waters on ship decks, not to skulk about a gentleman's drawing room. They would get themselves caught on his behalf, and he could not allow that.

It looked like his appointment with death might come sooner than anticipated.

Swiftly on silent boots he crossed the street and stole into the alley. The tradesman's door stood propped open. Cautiously, he entered the narrow basement corridor and ascended to the first floor, no servants in sight. Peculiar. But the hour was late and the elderly man kept an early schedule. Two doors let off the short corridor that ran to the foyer—a parlor and a dining room, most likely. Bishop Baldwin's house was stacked in every corner with objects—statuettes, compasses, clocks, books, jewels on pedestals, musical instruments, and a thousand other trinkets, but it was nevertheless a modest establishment for a retired man of the cloth.

Light flickered at the base of a door. Then from within— all in rapid succession—furniture scraping across floor, shattering glass, a muffled curse, and a thud.

There was nothing to be done for it; he opened the door. In the near perfect darkness, a lamp lay in pieces on the floor at the edge of a thick carpet. A slight figure stood over it, a small casket clutched in her arms.

Emotion rocked him like a gale force wind slamming him down and under. He remembered the gold and enamel mosaic box as if he'd seen it only yesterday sitting on his mother's dressing table in her chambers strewn with silks and cushions. And he would recognize Viola Carlyle no matter how dark it was or what she wore—even if he were blind, deaf, and bereft of all other senses—until the day he died.

Her gaze shot to him, then swiftly up at the ceiling. Footsteps sounded above.

"*Damn.*" Her hushed curse was as smooth and rich as every word of hers he carried in his soul.

He widened the door and stepped back from it, gesturing her through. They would not escape; pursuers, three men at least, were already on the landing above. But he must make the attempt, if he could force his thoughts to function properly. But his head swam and all he wanted in the world was moving toward him now.

She barely glanced at him as she darted into the corridor. He followed. Lamplight scorched the stairs above, bouncing closer, the footsteps quick, feet and legs appearing.

"You there! Halt!"

She shot down the narrow steps to the basement, he behind. Billy leaped from a doorway, tugged his cap, and ran for the rear entrance where Matouba stood in silhouette framed by two uniformed men.

They were caught. But he could assure she would not suffer for it. He reached forward and grabbed her shoulder.

Billy skidded to a halt at the other end of the corridor as Jin slammed her back against his chest.

"Do not speak unless I tell you to," he whispered harshly into her ear as the sheer relief and joy of being touched by him again flooded her. Then he released her and there was a great deal of commotion—men crowding into the basement corridor from either end with lamps and candles and at least one fireplace poker—in livery and uniform. An old man with a long hooked nose and nightcap askew atop his scraggly yellowish-gray hair stepped forward.

"Ha ha! I anticipated subterfuge." He shoved his candle in her face, wax spitting onto her coat. "Set a trap for you! I let that fool Pecker take your money, you thieving whelp. Ha! I have you now, by George." He thrust his candle into a servant's hand and gripped the box. "You won't have my casket now, but ten years in Newgate."

Viola held on tight. "Oh, just let me have it, you mean old man. I will pay you for it."

Gasps all around, except from Billy in the hands of two servants, and except from the silent man at her side.

The bishop's face opened in surprise, the candlelight making his wrinkles into a complex set of tracks across his skin.

"A girl!"

"I am not a *girl*. And you are a selfish, miserly fellow. Why won't you sell this box?"

"Because I found it fair and square and I don't sell my treasures, young missy." His eyes narrowed. "I suspect you think that because you are a female I won't turn you in. But you are wrong. God forgives penitent miscreants, but the law makes examples of them first." He yanked the box out of her grip, and her stomach plummeted to her shoes. "Officers, I shall want to visit her cell in Newgate tomorrow to hear her apology. Take her, and her thieving, good-for-nothing companions in crime." He flicked a disinterested gaze at Jin. "I am going back to bed. With *my* casket."

"She's not to blame, Your Grace."

Viola started. Jin's voice was not quite his own, deep and beautiful as always, but tinged with some other sound, like Billy's twang or like the footman Jane had bribed.

"Oh she isn't, young man? Then who is? You?"

"Well, you see, it's my sister who's the troublemaker, Your Excellency." He shifted his weight from one foot to the other as though uncomfortable. Viola gaped. His *sister*? What was he doing?

"This is your sister?"

"No, *sir*." He flickered her a glance she could have sworn seemed shy. But that was impossible. "My sister is this here lady's maid."

"Lady? This one?" The bishop grabbed a candle and pushed it up to her face again.

"Yessir. Sister of a lord, just like you, begging your pardon, Your Grace."

"Well I don't see it. She doesn't look like a doxy, it's true. But she's got the look of an urchin about her."

Jin nodded. "She's not your typical lady, that's for sure, Your Lordship. But, well, take a look at her hands."

The bishop frowned. "Show me your hands, missy."

She did so.

The bishop's brow terraced. He leaned to the servant beside him. "Do those look like the hands of a lady to you, Clement?"

"Yes, Your Grace. I believe they do."

The bishop's lips screwed up and he narrowed his eyes at Jin. "What is she doing in my house stealing my casket, then?"

"Well, sir, I want that casket. And my sister, well, she's a troublemaker. This lady here—" His whole demeanor spoke abashed. It was astounding. Viola would have stared wide-mouthed if her heart weren't aching so fiercely. "This lady likes a bit of fun and games, you see, Your Grace. So when my sister dared her to steal the thing, she thought it'd be something of a lark."

"And you came with her to steal it?"

"I couldn't very well leave her to it alone, sir, she being a lady and all."

Viola nearly fell to the floor. He was actually blushing. She had not thought it possible. It made her a little nauseated to realize that he could act so well. A lot nauseated.

The bishop nodded. "Then you are the one bound for New-gate tonight, young man, if not for aiding in a robbery then for not being man enough to take your sister in hand and teach her right and wrong. Eve is the weaker sex and prone to sin. Adam must subdue her wild spirit and with his strong hand demonstrate both his superior will and compassionate mercy."

Churchman or not, Viola could not be happy for this chastisement.

"But he did not—"

"Be still, missy, and give me your brother's name."

"The Earl of Savege, Your Grace," Jin replied.

"Savege, you say? The libertine." He scowled. "But he'll have her back tonight. A man should keep better rein on that which is his." He clutched the box tight to his chest.

"But—"

"Hush, missy, or I'll send you to Newgate with the rest of these thieves after all. Officers, I'll see you at the prison tomorrow. Clement, bring Lord Savege's sister up to the parlor, and call my carriage." He pushed away through the crowd.

Men's hands circled Jin's arms.

"Wait," Viola exclaimed. "No—"

"Woman," Jin said in his own perfect voice, "if you do not follow the bishop up those stairs and return home now, I vow I will never speak to you again."

Her lungs compressed. "Does that mean you were considering speaking to me ever again before this?"

"Go," he growled.

"But—"

"*Go.*"

They pulled him away, and Billy and Matouba. Where Mattie had gone she hadn't an idea. But she would get them all out of jail. Alex would. She turned from the sight of him being taken away in handcuffs, and hurried up after the bishop.

Not long before dawn, Mattie arrived at the mass of stones and mortar called Newgate Prison, which was grand and superior on the outside, thoroughly stinking and filthy within. With the contents of a sac the size of his fist, Mattie bribed the entry officer, the wing warden, and the cell guard.

The guard drooled over the two sparkling guineas in his palm as he picked his teeth with a rat's bone, then he unlocked the cell.

"Be seein' ye, Mr. Smythe. Do come again. And bring

yer friends too." He bowed with a smirk and spit in the dirt.

The sky was still dark, the autumn air chill when Jin walked out the front door of the prison as though he hadn't been brought up on charges of thievery by a lord of the church mere hours earlier. Wealth had its advantages.

His clothing clung to him, soaked with sweat from his brief tenure in the dank cage of men, his body's uncontrollable response as he'd sat motionless, swallowing back the dread. But she had not had to endure the filth or discomfort of a similar cell, or the real dangers a woman faced in such a place. The regular denizens of jailhouses knew no shame, modesty, or pity; they would have made a meal of Viola Carlyle. Unless, of course, she cozened them as she did everyone else—except unfortunately the bishop. With him she had been inconveniently petulant.

He crossed the yard and passed through the outer gate, sucking in air, the sour remnants of terror slipping away from his exhausted limbs.

"You ain't gonna talk to us?" Mattie grumbled. Matouba and Billy slogged silently behind. The boy was wily, but the hue of Matouba's skin had not been popular with several of their cellmates. Jin had allowed them to manage on their own. They deserved whatever discomfort they suffered for dragging her into it, as did he. But he would spend a thousand nights of hell in a prison cell if it meant Viola would be well.

"I have nothing to say which you do not already anticipate." He walked to the street. "Did you manage to set aside a coin for a hackney coach, or must I walk home?"

Mattie jingled the remains of the purse. Jin took it.

"Not even a thanks, a'course," his helmsman grunted.

He halted and turned to them. "Mattie, give me your knife."

Three pairs of eyes went round. Even Matouba's cheeks turned gray.

Jin rolled his eyes. "For later. As mine was taken from me by our hosts, I am now left without, and you have another on the ship." He accepted the blade and slipped it into his boot. "If I wanted to kill you," he added, turning back to the street, "I would have done it years ago."

"We're plumb sorry Miss Viola dropped that lamp, Cap'n," Billy peeped uncertainly. "She was doin' a right bang-up job o' the thing till then."

He had no doubt of it. "Amateurs. You should all be ashamed."

"Never meant for her to go into the house at all. Tried to stall, but she insisted," Mattie mumbled. "We thought you'd get there sooner. You got there every night earlier this whole past fortnight."

"You ain't never been late for nothin', Cap'n," Billy's tenor piped.

"Picked a fine night to dilly-dally." This in Matouba's bass.

Jin pivoted slowly, restraining the laughter building in his tight chest.

"You are a pack of imbeciles."

"We might be imbeciles." Mattie crossed his thick arms. "What we ain't is blind. Not nearly so blind as you, at least."

For a series of moments Jin stared at his crewmen. Then he hailed a hackney and went home to sleep.

Chapter 30

He awoke midafternoon, washed off the salt and stench of his prison sojourn, and sent a message across town by courier.

He waited.

Three quarters of an hour later a reply arrived. In illiterate phrases, Pecker explained how he had taken advantage of the bishop's absence that morning (when His Lordship went to Newgate to check on his prisoners) to remove the box from his employer's bedchamber and hide it. In the intervening hours, however, he had grown overly anxious to rid himself of his prize. Jin was to meet him at a specified location at the London Docks, where he would exchange the box for gold.

The location was Jin's hired berth.

Removing Mattie's knife from his boot, he set it on the table. He was not willing to harm another person again. Not gravely. Not since he had set eyes on Viola Carlyle standing in a dark parlor in the middle of the night dressed in breeches and a man's shirt.

He rode to the docks, stabled his horse, and made his way

down the quay. Looking toward his ship, he could not resist smiling. Amid her distress in those last moments at Savege Park, she had paused to marvel over the exorbitant amount he was spending to dock at the busy port for so many weeks. She had a quick, relentless spirit, and a madness that twined about his heart and made him thoroughly hers. Whatever happened with the box, and whatever treasure it held for him—or did not hold—he would not let her go. He would rather forgive himself and ask the rest of the world for forgiveness every day of his life than lose her.

The quay was settling down to quiet for the evening, lumpers hauling cargo onto ships that would depart in the morning and sailors busy with tasks on board vessels stacked two deep at each berth. The bishop's footman was nowhere in sight. But a sailor leaned against the base of the gangway on the vessel before Jin's. The angle of his hat brim revealed a face uncannily like Pecker's.

"Thought it was you," he greeted Jin. "Told my brother Hole it was. But he was suspicious. Thought I just wanted to take all the money and run." In the warm September breeze that clanked lines in blocks and fluttered banners atop masts through the failing sunlight, he wore a heavy overcoat, especially bulky at one side of his chest. "But I wouldn't do that to kin, you sees. And I was curious."

"Do you expect me to know you?"

"No. But I know you, Mr. Smythe. Or should I say, Pharaoh?" He grinned smugly. "You bought a girl off a bloke I was working for a few years back. Pretty little girl, that one. A real screamer, too. Have some fun with her, then, did you?"

"Have you brought the casket?"

The sailor straightened. "Well, now don't be getting all high and mighty with old Muskrat. Can't blame a fellow for trying to make a bit of friendly conversation afore transacting business, like."

"Your brother agreed to my price. Produce the casket now and I will give you the gold."

Muskrat rubbed his ragged whiskers and looked thoughtful a moment. "Now here's my problem, Mr. Smythe: Hole, he ain't no genius. I got me all the brains in the family, you see." He tapped a fingertip to his hat. "And I been needing a little task taken care of that I— Well, you see, Mr. Smythe, old Muskrat just don't have the heart for it." He shook his head sorrowfully.

"I haven't time for theatrics. What do you want?"

"You see, I got me a little problem I need out of the way." He wrinkled his brow. "As in dead out of the way. You see." The wind picked up for an instant, pressing the overcoat against the bulge beneath his arm. "I heard you was partic'arly good at getting little problems dead."

"I am no longer in that line of work. I have, in fact, come to this meeting unarmed." It felt remarkably good to admit that. Insanely imprudent, too. But perhaps she was having an even greater effect on him than he knew.

"You don't say?" Muskrat scratched his chin again. Then he pointed up the dock to the base of the gangway of Jin's ship where a boy sat with a lantern. "That's Mickey. Me and Hole's youngest brother. Now, Mr. Smythe, Mickey there is going to take you to the place I know that little problem is guzzling gin right now, you see. Then you're going to take care of my problem, and when you're finished, old Muskrat will be waiting right here for you with that box. What do you say to that?"

"I say you haven't any idea with whom you are dealing."

Muskrat's face pinched. "They said as you was a tough one."

"They said right."

"Also said you ain't hurt a fly in years. But I thought if you was properly motivated . . ."

"On that account, they were wrong. I may no longer be in that line of work, but a man may do anything for simple amusement." Merely suggesting it wouldn't damn him. "Properly motivated, of course. Give me the casket, Muskrat. Now."

"My soul," the sailor cooed. "The mighty Pharaoh's asking me favors, without even a pistol or knife on him, eh?"

"But I do have my bare hands. Give me the box and you needn't have concern over that soul quite yet."

Muskrat narrowed his eyes. Then his gaze flickered to the side, and widened. The boy leaped up, the lantern jiggling light across the dock's shadowed planks, his gaze fixed over Jin's shoulder as well.

"Well, I'll be. Looks like an angel coming my way." Muskrat wiggled his brows. "Guess it's old Muskrat's lucky day."

"Not today, I am afraid." Viola's satin voice came just behind Jin; then she appeared at his side. "Now, what have I missed?" She wore a gown of spring green, a delicate shawl and gloves, and her hair was swept up beneath a neat little hat. She lacked only a parasol to be fit for a stroll in the park. Jin had never seen anything so beautiful and his heart had never beaten so hard.

"You were not invited to this meeting, madam," he said as evenly as he could. "I suggest you retire from it now."

"Oh, phooey." Her dark gaze darted between them. "By the by, the bishop is hopping mad. You should have seen him storm into the house this morning demanding justice. It seems he went to Newgate and, discovering your absence there, decided to accuse Alex of disloyalty to both church and crown." Her lips curved into a grin of perfect pleasure. "Alex pretended he'd never seen the bishop before, when they had spoken mere hours earlier in the middle of the night! I had no idea my brother-in-law was such a proficient actor.

Or you, for that matter." She slanted him an acute look. "In any case, when Alex insisted that I had spent the entire night tending our dear old maiden aunt at her deathbed, the bishop turned six different shades of red. He left believing himself quite addled. It was all remarkably great fun."

"Do not tell me you came here alone."

"I must! For I did. I did not wish to involve Billy, Mattie, and Matouba, not after last night, so I didn't tell them I bribed Mr. Pecker to tell me everything. What good fortune that he actually had something of worth to tell me, all about your meeting right here with his brother, Muskrat. And Hole, can you imagine? I think their mother must have been a very peculiar person. But then I worried I would not arrive on time. Am I on time?"

"Violet, leave."

"No. I am here to help."

"Can you not stay out of anything, woman?"

"Probably not." She reached into a pocket and produced a dagger. "Here. Billy said they commandeered your weapons at the prison, so I brought this."

Muskrat drew back his coat to reveal the butt of a firearm stuffed into his trousers. "And I brought me my pistol. We can have us a nice party now."

She set her hand on her sweetly curved hip. "Pistol or no, give him the box or he will kill you for it."

"Got your fancy piece doing your work for you now, Pharaoh? P'raps you have turned over a new leaf." He winked at her.

"Miss Daly," Jin said in a low voice, "it is now high time that you depart."

"I am not his fancy piece, whatever that is. I am the daughter of a lord, the Baron of Carlyle, and I will get you in a lot of trouble if you do not give him that box this very instant."

Muskrat scoffed. "If you're a baron's daughter, then I'm Bonnie Prince Charlie."

"Well then, it is an honor to meet you, Your Highness." She curtsied prettily. "Now give him the box."

He looked skeptical. "If your da is Carlyle, why did the Pharaoh here call you Daly?"

"Anybody knows that a man's surname may not be the same as his title, you ignoramus. But mine does happen to be Carlyle. Mr. Seton called me Daly to protect my identity. But since I don't care about that anyway, it's all well and good."

"Viola, this is not helping," Jin muttered.

"Of course it is. Can't you see he is already starting to cave?"

"I admit to not yet having noticed that."

"Well, your powers of observation are clearly less keen than mine."

"Not concerning some matters."

Muskrat's gaze was flickering back and forth between them.

"You mean Aidan and his strong desire for impressive social connections? Which I figured out finally."

"I wondered if you would."

"He is not a bad man. Not as bad as you certainly. Rather, uncomplicated. Again, unlike you."

Muskrat shot a snickering leer at Jin.

"Must we do this here and now, Viola?"

"You introduced the topic into conversation."

"She got you there, Pharaoh."

Viola shrugged. "Sometimes he's not very bright, it's true."

Turning away with rolled eyes, Jin took an obviously frustrated breath, and—so swiftly Viola barely saw it happen—swung at Muskrat. The man went down hard to the boards. Jin didn't give him a moment to recover but fisted his neck cloth and twisted it tight. Muskrat struggled, swinging back and coughing, and the casket tumbled out from beneath his overcoat. Viola leaped for it, but his arms and legs flailed in her way. A boy darted in, grabbed the box, and bolted.

"Jin, the casket! That boy has it!"

The lad ran, his little arms barely able to hold the box and his lantern at once, down the dock and to the next gangway. He turned to look back, tripped on the gangplank, and casket and lantern flew—the casket into the Thames, the lantern onto the deck of the closest vessel, where it shattered. In a flash, fire licked across the deck, following the lamp oil.

Viola's hands slapped over her mouth. "Holy Mother Mary. Isn't that *your* ship, Jin?"

Muskrat's eyes were saucers. "You can have your box, Smythe." He bolted, the boy chasing after, pushing through men running toward the deck on fire.

Viola rushed forward, but by the time she reached the gangway the flames were already doused and black smoke curled from the steaming planking. Dockworkers and sailors carrying charred cloths disembarked. Several glanced at Jin and tugged their hats respectfully before moving off.

Viola gaped in a terribly unladylike fashion as he came to her side. "I think it is a very good thing I had no idea who you really were when you appeared on that dock in Boston demanding I give you work. As it was, I was enormously impressed with myself for gaining the attention of the notorious Pharaoh. But if I had known the entire truth I would have been terrified to even speak with such an exalted personage."

"Then I am very glad you did not know the entire truth."

Gathering courage, finally she looked up at him. His gaze shone in the failing light.

Her hands flew to her mouth again. "The casket! Oh, Jin, I am so sorry," she groaned. "It's gone."

"I don't want it. I don't need it any longer."

Her eyes went wide. "You don't? But I thought—"

He shook his head.

She fisted her hands. "Then what do you need?"

"You." His gaze consumed her. "I need you. Viola, I need you."

"You are repeating. You are trying to convince yourself, aren't you?"

"You are an impossible woman. I am declaring my love to you and still you quarrel with me."

"Well if you had mentioned the love part right away I might not have—"

He halted her speech with the most beautiful kiss any woman had ever gotten, she was certain. They both became quite breathless.

Abruptly, he thrust her to arm's length. Shabby treatment, as always, but she didn't care. And a lump had taken up residence in her throat so she could not quarrel even if she wished.

"I love you, Viola. I want you. I want you forever." His voice was thoroughly uneven. Heavenly. "Say you love me too."

"I don't take orders," she barely managed to choke out.

"It is not an order. It is a plea."

She swallowed thickly. Twice. For the first time in fifteen years since a band of scruffy sailors had gagged her mouth, she actually could not manage to speak.

Jin's gaze covered her face, at once warm and anxious. "Viola, I am perishing before you. *Perishing*." His tone was strained. "Say something."

She nodded.

"What does that mean?"

She nodded again, faster, her throat a clogged mess of joy.

His eyes seemed to sparkle. "You do love me."

She got dizzy nodding.

"Why aren't you speaking? What is—"

She clutched her neck. "C-an-not—" she rasped. "Fr-*frogh*."

He looked astounded. Then he pulled her hand away and bent to set his mouth atop her windpipe.

"Function, beautiful harridan's voice," he murmured, trailing soft, sweet kisses along her throat. His fingers tangled in her hair, tilting her head back. "Speak. I want to hear the words. I *need* to hear them."

"Of course I love you," she whispered, barely a sound through her thick throat. But it was enough for him, apparently. His arms wrapped around her and he pulled her tight to him. She buried her face against his chest and squeezed her eyes shut. "At Savage Park you said that your feelings had not altered," she said on a damp little hiccup of happiness.

"They had not." He kissed her brow. "Have not."

"But—"

He silenced her again with his mouth. Quite nice. Quite perfect. Quite as much like paradise as Viola had ever dared to hope or dream. Because this time he was hers.

Abruptly the import of his words struck her. She pushed him away.

"You were in love with me *then*? At the end of the fortnight?"

He kept hold of her wrists. His eyes were bright but he said nothing.

"You allowed me to believe—" She gaped. "You mean to say, *I* won the wager?"

"Yes."

"You lied to me so you could repay your debt?"

"I did. And because I believed you belonged here."

She understood. But not entirely. "You nearly broke my heart!"

His brow creased. "You were, Viola, in love with another man at the time."

"I—" She clamped her lips shut. He was already far too arrogant and some things were better left unsaid. Or perhaps not. "I may not have been . . . at *that* time."

For an instant, his eyes widened. Then his mouth curved into an unabashedly proprietary smile. "I promise to make it up to you."

"Make it up to me?" She plunked her fists onto her hips. "You have no honor whatsoever."

"I've never said I do." He slipped his arms around her waist, pulled her so she fit snugly against him, and bent to nuzzle her neck. "I am not a gentleman, Viola. I will never be one."

"No, I can see that."

His mouth was warm in the tender place beneath her ear. "Marry me anyway."

"I will consider it," she said shakily.

His hands slipped down her back, his cheek against hers. "I love you, precious woman. More than you can fathom."

"I have considered it. Yes."

He laughed and kissed her on the lips. She pulled out of his hold. He looked dazed, and she nearly plastered herself to him again. Instead she unpinned her bonnet, pulled her shawl and gloves off, and stepped out of her slippers.

"Hold these." Her heart pattered swiftly.

"Hold these?"

She kissed him on the cheek, turned, ran three strides, and dove into the river.

The water was quite a bit colder and darker than she liked. Fingers of early evening sunlight filtering through it only served to illuminate all sorts of flotsam and jetsam that she did not wish to study. But she hadn't time to do so anyway, and her skirts proved tricky to maneuver. The bottom was rather farther down than she had imagined, too, and thick with silt and muck, pulling at her arms and hands. It took her quite a while to locate the casket.

She broke through the surface gasping for air. Jin was there, holding her above the murky water and pressing kisses onto her filthy face, then hoisting her into the hands of a pair of lumpers dockside. She clutched the little box to her until he climbed from the river and his arms came around her again.

He brushed away her sopping hair and kissed the bridge of her nose. "You are insane."

"No, I am only very much in love with you and I want you to be happy."

His eyes shone. "I do not need that box to make me happy. Not any longer."

"Yes. But isn't it nice to have it anyway?" She dimpled. "By the by, Jin, what's in it?"

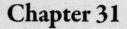

Chapter 31

Lady Justice
In Care of Brittle & Sons, Printers
London

My dearest lady,

I write with unhappy news: Sea Hawk has quit the Club. Thus our numbers are once more diminished. We are now a sorry small lot—only three. If you could see your way to resting your campaign against our poor little band of companions, I would nevertheless eternally count you the most worthy adversary and continue to sing your praises to all.

I admit, however, that should you do so, I shall regret the loss of you.

Yours &c.
Peregrine
Secretary, The Falcon Club

To Peregrine:

Your cajoling fails to touch me. I will not rest. Be you three, two, or only one, I will find you and reveal you to public scrutiny. Take care, Mr. Secretary. Your day of reckoning will soon be at hand.

—Lady Justice

P.S. Thank you for the salted herring. You ought to have commenced with that. I simply adore *salted herring. You cretin.*

Epilogue

The little casket of gold and enamel rested on the piecrust table, lid broken off, interior empty. The hands gripping the letters that had emerged from it were pale and quivering, skin translucent where it peeked from beneath lacy cuffs.

"They wed in secret." The elderly lady's voice was thin, unaccustomed to activity. "The vicar did not approve, but he saw young love and he was a kind soul." Her brow creased delicately. "But she was not as brave as she wished. Days later when her father took her to marry the man he had chosen—a powerful man and influential in that world of warlords—she did not refuse. She saw her punishment, and the danger to my brother in her land, and feared it greater than she feared God's disapproval."

Viola leaned toward her, mouth agape. "She married a *second* time?"

The lady nodded. "She did not believe it bound her in any sacred bond to her new husband. My brother wrote her these letters each month after he left Alexandria. From

Greece first, then Prussia. Then from here." She smoothed her fingers across the sheets of foolscap and her pale blue eyes were soft. "He had not wished to leave Egypt, but she insisted. She told him that she had lost the child, that she could no longer see him, that her husband would discover them and they would both be killed." She lifted her gaze to Jin. "But she lied. She did not lose the child."

He took a visible breath. Across from him in the parlor furnished with simple elegance, his aunt offered him a kind, wrinkled smile.

"She only wished to protect your father. My brother was still a young man, with his whole life ahead of him. She told him to return to England, to forget her, indeed to imagine her dead, to marry and have a family."

"But he never did," Viola said eagerly, "did he? Marry again."

"He never did. He was the fifth son. Of a baronet, yes. But our brothers already had many sons of their own, and our parents never pressed him for it. I had been married quite young, and widowed after few years, childless. So when my brother asked, I was glad to come here to live with him and run his household. It was a quiet life we led, and he never ceased writing to her, sending them to the priest and hoping she would receive them."

Her fingers curled around the letters Jin's father had written, stored in that sealed box for two decades. "Then, finally, she wrote to him."

Jin's lips parted.

Viola jerked forward on her seat. "She did? When?"

"When her husband had me sent away." He spoke with certainty, looking at his aunt. "Was it then?"

She nodded. "She told my brother of you, the truth she had withheld years earlier, begging him to find you, for she had no power to do so herself. Her life was more curtailed than she had even imagined in those first months. She was no more than a prisoner in her husband's home. She took a great chance even sending that single letter."

For a moment silence stretched through the room, motes of dust floating in the golden light that filtered in through the broad windows of the country manor house.

"Did he do as she asked?" Jin finally said, his voice uncharacteristically gruff.

"He did." Thin lines appeared between her eyes. "He finally told our brothers the truth, then he went searching for you, determined to find his son. He wrote to me for a time, telling me of his progress, always hopeful. And then nothing. Months later we heard news of the ship he had taken passage on. It was missing, presumed lost. He never came home."

She looked up again, set down the letters, and reached for Jin's hand, her frail fingers gripping his strong ones weathered by life on the sea. His steady, beautiful hands Viola loved.

"But now you have come." His aunt's eyes crinkled into a watery smile. "Welcome home, Jinan."

He closed the carriage door and took the seat beside Viola, his hand finding hers and fingers lacing together as the vehicle started away from the house. He did not look out the window but straight ahead, in his eyes the distance she had come to know so well. But that distance did not mean what she had once believed. Now she knew it to be hope only masked by certainty.

She curved her palm around his cheek. He turned his lips into it.

A smile tugged at her mouth. "She was not what I expected."

He drew her hand down but did not release it. He rarely did these days, as she rarely released him unless necessary. They were, she supposed, making up for the many days and hours spent in each other's company when they had not touched although they longed to. Or perhaps they simply liked it.

"How long will you wish to stay?" he asked, stroking her palm softly, the sensation riding straight through her body despite her gloves. They were very thin kid gloves, only the finest purchased by her very wealthy husband. Far too wealthy. She must find a charitable depository for some of his gold. If someday he once again felt the desire to take to the sea, he mustn't have enough money to purchase his own ship. For she knew well that he would never again agree to sail on another master's vessel.

On the other hand, if he must someday sail again, she would simply go with him.

"We can stay for as long as you wish, of course. Your aunt's invitation included Christmas. Quite a lengthy visit, probably so that you can meet all your uncles and aunts and cousins." She smiled. "She is very sweet, and seemed regretful even to see you leave for the afternoon." She smoothed her skirt. "And, Jin, why *did* we leave just now?"

"So that I could do this." He pulled her onto his lap.

"Oh! You are crushing my dress. And I have tried very hard today to keep it neat as a pin. I so wanted to impress her."

His fingers threaded through her hair, dislodging her bonnet.

"You did impress her." He nuzzled her cheek. "But more to the point, you are impressing me, wife. Too well."

"Again with the calling me wife as though I have no name." She tilted her face to give him leave to kiss her throat. He obliged, quite deliciously. "Why could you not have taken to captain as easily, I wonder?"

"I did take to my captain easily." His hand slipped beneath her cloak. "And she to me. Quite easily."

She sighed. "Will your arrogance never pale?"

He stroked beneath her bodice. "Viola, I am going to make love to you now."

Warmth shimmered through her, and the yearning only he satisfied. "What— Here in the carriage?"

"Yes, here in the carriage." Already he was gathering her skirts.

"You cannot wait?"

"I cannot wait." He tugged at fabric, pushing it to her hips.

She helped, a little breathless. "You must have me now?"

"I must have you five minutes ago, but now will do."

"This is highly irregular."

"How would you know that?"

"Lessons. Endless lessons." With eager hands she set to his trousers. "And books of etiquette specifying that a lady must never allow her husband to make love to her in a carriage in celebration for having just found his lost family."

His hands came around her hips and she wrapped her arms about his neck, the motion of the carriage rocking her against him.

"The books are wrong." He kissed her lips. "For you are a lady, Viola Seton." He kissed her again, his perfect mouth hungering and tender at once, and her heart filled to overflowing. "My lady," he whispered, his crystal eyes sparkling. "And my master."

Then he made her prove it.

Author's Note

Due to the long, hard struggles of abolitionists and notable Parliamentarians, England banned the slave trade from Africa in the year 1807. It wasn't until 1833, however, that Parliament passed an act abolishing slavery altogether. But Britain was ahead of its time compared to other colonial powers, and slaving vessels operated by subjects and citizens of other nations continued to trade humans for gold throughout the Americas.

By the end of the eighteenth century, a boy with light skin like Jin would have been an exception in Western slave markets, acceptable only insofar as his captors and subsequent owners considered him a mulatto—of mixed blood. Thus Frakes, my nasty slaver, lied about Jin's origins to the market officials on Barbados, most likely claiming Jin was the son of an African slave and a white master from another Caribbean island. Such misrepresentations of truth were common enough in the slave trade, with peoples from throughout the world sold or indentured whenever the price was right.

My sincere thanks go to Eleanor Mikucki, whose copyediting on this manuscript was positively superb. Ecstatic thanks also to Gail Dubov of the Avon Art Department, whose work on my covers is always spectacular, and who left me breathless with how perfectly she captured Viola and Jin for this book.

It is my great honor to enjoy the friendship of scholars and readers of remarkable kindness and generosity. The vast knowledge of Professors Vincent A. Brown and Laurent M. Dubois concerning the Caribbean islands, the slave trade, and a plethora of matters concerning Atlantic and imperial history in the eighteenth and nineteenth centuries enabled me to give Jin and Viola's story its powerful historical moorings. Likewise, Professor Michael Jarvis's astonishing command of shipping routes of that era set my hero and heroine's journey on its rightful course. Stephanie W. McCullough once again generously shared her nautical expertise with me, and Dr. Marie Claude-Dubois charmingly came to my aid with French yet again as well. Not least, Georgann Brophy and Marquita Valentine's keen appreciation for a truly worthy hero helped Jin become the best man he could. To these outstanding gentlemen and ladies, I offer most profound thanks.